## PRAISE FOR THE CHLOE ELLEFSON MYSTERY SERIES

### *OLD WORLD MURDER*

"A wonderfully-woven tale that winds in and out of modern and historical Wisconsin with plenty of mysteries—both past and present ... Enchanting!"—Sandi Ault, author of the WILD Mystery Series and recipient of the Mary Higgins Clark Award

"Character-driven, with mystery aplenty, *Old World Murder* is a sensational read. Think Sue Grafton meets Earlene Fowler, with a dash of Elizabeth Peters."—Julia Spencer-Fleming, Anthony and Agatha Award–winning author of *I Shall Not Want* and *One Was A Soldier*

"*Old World Murder* is strongest in its charming local color and genuine love for Wisconsin's rolling hills, pastures, and woodlands ... a delightful distraction for an evening or two."—*New York Journal of Books*

"Clever plot twists and credible characters make this a far from humdrum cozy."—*Publishers Weekly*

"This series debut by an author of children's mysteries rolls out nicely for readers who like a cozy with a dab of antique lore. Jeanne M. Dams fans will like the ethnic background."—*Library Journal*

"Information on how to conduct historical research, background on Norwegian culture, and details about running an outdoor museum frame the engaging story of a woman devastated by a failed romantic relationship whose sleuthing helps her heal."—*Booklist*

"Museum masterpiece."—*Rosebud Book Reviews*

"A real find ... 5 stars."—*Once Upon a Romance*

## THE HEIRLOOM MURDERS

"Interesting, well-drawn characters and a complicated plot make this a very satisfying read."—*The Mystery Reader*

"Engaging characters, a fascinating (real-life) setting, a gripping and believable plot—this is the traditional mystery at its best."—Jeanne M. Dams, Agatha Award–winning author of the Dorothy Martin and Hilda Johansson Mysteries

"Chloe is an appealing character, and Ernst's depiction of work at a living museum lends authenticity and a sense of place to the involving plot."—*St. Paul Pioneer Press*

## THE LIGHT KEEPER'S LEGACY

"Chloe's third combines a good mystery with some interesting historical information on a niche subject."—*Kirkus Reviews*

"Framed by the history of lighthouses and their keepers and the story of fishery disputes through time, the multiple plots move easily across the intertwined past and present."—*Booklist Online*

"Deftly flipping back and forth in time in alternating chapters, the author builds up two mystery cases and cleverly weaves them back together."—*Library Journal*

"While the mystery elements of this books are very good, what really elevates it are the historical tidbits of the real-life Pottawatomie Lighthouse and the surrounding fishing village."—*Mystery Scene Magazine*

"A rich and satisfying third novel that makes me ask what all avid readers will: When's the next one? Well done, Kathleen!"—Jane Kirkpatrick, *New York Times* bestselling author

### *HERITAGE OF DARKNESS*

"Chloe's fourth ... provides a little mystery, a little romance, and a little more information about Norwegian folk art and tales."—*Kirkus Reviews*

**ALSO BY KATHLEEN ERNST**

Nonfiction
*Too Afraid to Cry:*
*Maryland Civilians in the Antietam Campaign*

Fiction
*Old World Murder*
*The Heirloom Murders*
*The Light Keeper's Legacy*
*Heritage of Darkness*

American Girl Series
*Captain of the Ship: A Caroline Classic*
*Facing the Enemy: A Caroline Classic*
*Traitor in the Shipyard: A Caroline Mystery*
*Catch the Wind: My Journey with Caroline*

American Girl Mysteries
*Trouble at Fort La Pointe*
*Whistler in the Dark*
*Betrayal at Cross Creek*
*Danger at the Zoo: A Kit Mystery*
*Secrets in the Hills: A Josefina Mystery*
*Midnight in Lonesome Hollow: A Kit Mystery*
*The Runaway Friend: A Kirsten Mystery*
*Clues in the Shadows: A Molly Mystery*

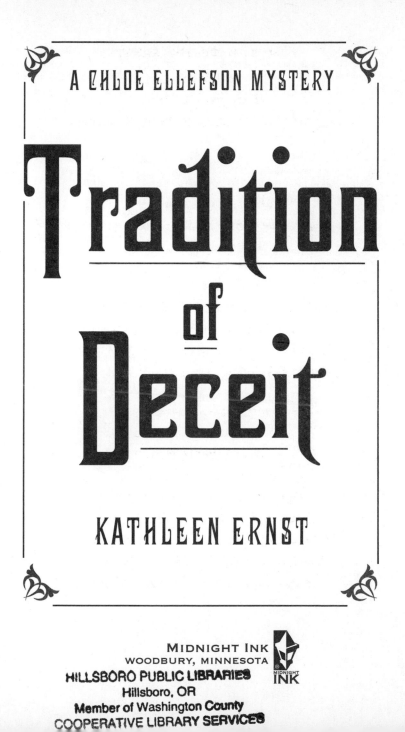

A CHLOE ELLEFSON MYSTERY

# Tradition of Deceit

KATHLEEN ERNST

MIDNIGHT INK
WOODBURY, MINNESOTA

FIRST EDITION
First Printing, 2014

Book format by Bob Gaul
Cover design by Kevin R. Brown
Cover illustration by Charlie Griak
Editing by Nicole Nugent
Interior photos: 1. Turn-Head Distributor © Scott Meeker
    2. Pillsbury-Washburn Mills © Minnesota Historical Society
    3. Bohemian Flats © F.M. Laraway. Minnesota Historical Society
    4. Kosciuszko Park © Roman Kwasnieweski. Archives
       Department, University of Wisconsin-Milwaukee Libraries
    5. Wycinanki sample © Wisconsin Historical Society

Midnight Ink, an imprint of Llewellyn Worldwide Ltd.

**Library of Congress Cataloging-in-Publication Data**
Ernst, Kathleen, 1959–
   Tradition of deceit: a Chloe Ellefson mystery/Kathleen Ernst.—First edition.
     pages cm
     ISBN 978-0-7387-4078-2     *5548 9511 12/14*
   1. Women museum curators—Fiction. 2. Murder—Investigation—Fiction. I. Title.
   PS3605.R77T73 2014
   813'.6—dc23
                  2014014596

Midnight Ink
Llewellyn Worldwide Ltd.
2143 Wooddale Drive
Woodbury, MN 55125-2989
www.midnightinkbooks.com

Printed in the United States of America

The Mill City Museum, operated by the Minnesota Historical Society, was created in the ruins of what was once the world's largest flour mill. The museum is a testament to the vision of many groups and individuals, who persevered in the face of enormous challenges—including a disastrous fire that took place after the events depicted in this novel. Today the museum is surrounded by a revitalized urban area. I have of necessity simplified the redevelopment process within the novel.

The Washburn A Mill was constructed in 1874 on the banks of the Mississippi River in Minneapolis. It was known for much of its history as the Washburn-Crosby Mill. Gold Medal Flour became a brand in 1880; in 1928, the Washburn-Crosby Company merged with others to form General Mills. I kept things simple by generally referring to the mill by its original name, but I've otherwise done my best to present an accurate glimpse of the mill's human history in the century or so spanned within the story. Much has also been written about Bohemian Flats, and I relied heavily on accounts and photographs when describing the colorful community.

In Milwaukee, Kosciuszko Park and the Basilica of St. Josaphat remain at the heart of the vibrant Lincoln Village neighborhood. It is impossible to visit this historic community without imagining the hardworking immigrants who not only created new homes, but monuments to their faith and cultural history as well. The district police station, the basilica, the park, and Forest Home Cemetery are all located along Lincoln Avenue in the Old South Side.

When appropriate, I made choices to help readers visualize places that may be familiar. For example, Lincoln Village wasn't named until later.

To learn more about the featured historic places and museums, visit:

*The Mill City Museum:*
http://www.millcitymuseum.org/

*Lincoln Village and Kosciuzko Park:*
http://en.wikipedia.org/wiki/Lincoln_Village,_Milwaukee

*The Basilica of St. Josaphat:*
http://thebasilica.org/

*Old South Side Settlement Museum:*
http://www.urban-anthropology.org/Museuminfo.html

*Milwaukee County Public Museum:*
http://www.mpm.edu/

You'll find photographs of some of the artifacts and places mentioned in the story on pages 343–345.

You can also find many more photographs, maps, and other resources on my website, http://www.kathleenernst.com.

## CAST OF CHARACTERS

*Contemporary Timeline (1983), Minneapolis*

Chloe Ellefson—curator of collections, Old World Wisconsin

Ariel Grzegorczyk—curatorial assistant, Minnesota Historical Society

Toby Grzegorczyk—Ariel's brother

Jay Rutledge—architectural historian, Minnesota Historical Society

Owen Brinkerhoff—graduate student, historic preservation

Dr. Everett Whyte—university professor, industrial history

Sister Mary Jude—advocate for the homeless people who shelter in the mill

Officer Crandall & Officer Ashton—Minneapolis Police Department

Star—runaway teen living in the mill ruin

Camo John—Vietnam veteran living in the mill ruin

Byron Cooke—curator of interpretation, Old World Wisconsin

Ralph Petty—director, Old World Wisconsin

*Contemporary Timeline (1983), Eagle, Wisconsin*

Libby—Roelke's cousin

Justin and Dierdre—Libby's children

Marge Bandacek—Deputy Sherrif, Waukesha County

Chief Naborski—head of Village of Eagle Police Department

*Contemporary Timeline (1983), Milwaukee*

Roelke McKenna—officer, Village of Eagle Police Department

Rick Almirez—officer, Milwaukee Police Department

Jody—Rick's girlfriend

Dobry Banik—officer, Milwaukee Police Department

Lucia Bliss—sergeant, Milwaukee Police Department

Chief Bliss—Lucia's father, head of Milwaukee Police Department

Sergeant Conrad Malloy—Field Training Officer, Milwaukee
   Police Department

Captain Heikinen—in charge of police district in Milwaukee's
   Old South Side

Olivette—dispatcher at the local police district

Sherman—homeless Vietnam veteran living in Old South Side

Kip—bar owner

Danielle and Joanie—Kip's employees

Fritz Klinefelter—officer and head of clerical department,
   Milwaukee Police Department

Erin Litkowski—domestic abuse survivor

Steve Litkowski—Erin's husband

Pauline—Erin's sister

Lobo/Alberto Marquez—felon

Patrick McKenna—Roelke's brother

Mrs. Dombrowicz and son Donny—residents, Old South Side

Helen—director of Eve's House, a shelter for survivors of
   domestic abuse

*Historical Timeline (1878–1923), Minneapolis*

Magdalena—Polish immigrant

Dariusz—Magdalena's brother, deceased

Frania (Franciszka)—Magdalena's daughter

Pawel—Polish immigrant at Magdalena's boarding house

Lidia—Frania's daughter

Tomasz/Thomas—Lidia's beau

# ONE

CHLOE ELLEFSON WAS NOT having a good time.

"So," Roelke said, sliding into his seat at the banquet table. "Are you enjoying yourself?"

Chloe smiled brightly. "I am!"

Roelke raised his eyebrows.

Drat the man. With sincerity, Chloe added, "After hearing so much about your band, it's fun to actually hear you play. You guys are great." She patted his thigh.

"You better keep Chloe around, McKenna," Rick Almirez said to Roelke. "You'll never find another woman who actually appreciates the band." He put his arm around the young woman sitting beside him. "After Jody sat through an entire practice session, I knew I'd found the one for me."

Jody's smile was half indulgent, half adoring. She was a small woman, with honey-colored hair swirled stylishly behind her head. She looked maybe twenty-five, which made Chloe, who was fast approaching her thirty-third birthday, feel a wee bit ancient. But Jody and Rick were clearly good together.

Chloe had only met Rick a few times, but she liked him a lot. He and Roelke had been best friends since their police academy days. Roelke had left Milwaukee, but he kept in touch with old buddies at practice sessions. The Blue Tones was an all-cop band.

"Keeping Chloe around is the plan," Roelke said. He looked happy, but he was also wired. Chloe could feel his knee bouncing like a piston. So, was this good-wired? Or was something making him tense? Since Chloe was completely out of her element, she had no idea. She was only here because two MPD officers had asked The Blue Tones to play alternate sets with an accordion player at their wedding reception. "Want to come with?" Roelke had asked, with an *Either way is fine with me* shrug that was, she knew, completely bogus.

The wedding ceremony had been traditional enough—glowing bride, nervous groom. With Roelke in the pew beside her, Chloe had been quite at ease. But once everyone adjourned to the private party room at a popular Milwaukee bar and he switched from guest to entertainer, she'd felt adrift. This was largely an urban crowd. Chatter was studded with casual crime talk. Cigarette smoke hazed the air. Until now, Chloe and Roelke had spent most of their couple-time either alone or with her family. The man on stage during the band's first set had seemed a stranger.

Rick gave Chloe a devilish grin. "Did Roelke ever tell you about the time he put a guy's driver's license down on the hood of a car and it blew into a storm drain?"

"It wasn't my fault that a semi blasted by," Roelke protested. "Jody, did Rick ever tell *you* about the first time he drew his gun on duty? It flew out of his hand, did a triple flip, and landed in the street."

Dobry and Tina Banik rejoined the group as Roelke spoke. "The PD frowns on throwing guns around," Dobry said, holding the chair for his wife. Dobry had sandy hair and a round, freckled face that was, probably to his professional dismay, remarkably boyish.

Chloe sipped her wine, watching the men trade barbs in practiced style. This is good for Roelke, she thought. He was completely committed to the small, rural village PD he worked for now, but he also felt a bit isolated. He'd spent six years with the Milwaukee PD and had a shared history with Rick and Dobry. Now, Chloe thought, I really am enjoying myself.

"Remember the time in training when Rick got surprised during a traffic stop? Oh, man." Roelke hooted with laughter.

"I didn't make sure the trunk was securely closed," Rick confessed. "An instructor jumped out and scared the crap out of me." He laughed, too. "You better believe I check now, every single time."

"He's got quite the obsessive routine for approaching cars now," Roelke began. "You should see how—"

"Excuse us!" Two young women presented themselves. The blonde wore a clingy red dress with plunging neckline and stiletto heels that made Chloe's feet ache in solidarity. "We need to identify a cop who *doesn't* work in Milwaukee." She waved a piece of paper. "For the scavenger hunt."

Roelke produced his badge. "I'm with the Eagle PD, out in Waukesha County."

"Ooh, *thank* you!" the brunette squealed. Her clingy dress with plunging neckline was black, as were her equally torturous heels. When Roelke spelled his name she leaned over to write on the table, displaying enough cleavage to hide a broadsword. "What an unusual name! How do you say it?"

"It's pronounced Rell-kee," Chloe said helpfully. "And I'm Clo-ee."

The young women made a big, big point of ignoring her. "It's good to meet you, Officer Roelke McKenna," the brunette said.

As the pair sashayed to the next table, Jody rolled her eyes. "Badge bunnies."

"Now, now," Rick said.

The accordion player launched into a cheerful rendition of "Beer Barrel Polka," and Chloe raised her voice to be heard. "So, guys. When are you going to play the chicken dance? And the hokey pokey?"

All three groaned. "Never," Roelke said. "We write that into our contract. Playing for the dollar dance is as kitschy as we get." Although some of the old neighborhoods were changing, Milwaukee still had a strong Polish-American community, and the dollar dance was expected at Polish weddings.

"I believe the word you're looking for is *traditional*," Chloe suggested.

He gave her a *Yeah, right* look.

Dobry drained his beer. "Come on, boys. We're up in five."

"Rick and Dobry have to work graveyard shift," Roelke told Chloe. "But we can get one more set in." He squeezed her hand and headed for the stage.

Rick kissed Jody before leaning close to Chloe. "Be patient with that guy," he whispered with a wink. "You're good for him."

He was gone before she could find a response. Touched, she watched the other cop saunter away. How very sweet.

Dobry's wife lit a cigarette and surveyed the crowded room. She wore a long-sleeved but slinky dress of her own, and makeup she'd evidently applied with a trowel. Chloe tried to think of something to say to Tina and came up blank.

Jody leaned close. "You doing okay? When I started dating Rick and hanging out in cop-world ... " She made a wry face. "It can be overwhelming."

"A bit," Chloe acknowledged. "Do the badge bunnies make regular appearances?" She generally didn't approve of denigrating any woman based on how she chose to present herself to the world, but ... in this case she was okay with it.

"Evidently a lot of women fantasize about dating a cop," Jody said. "I don't think you need to worry about it, though. Roelke adores you."

Chloe was okay with that, too.

"So, what do you do?" Jody asked.

"I'm curator of collections at Old World Wisconsin. It's a big historic site in Waukesha County."

"Maybe Rick and I can visit in the spring," Jody said. "And I know the guys are planning a double-date at Mader's." The German restaurant was a Milwaukee landmark. "Oh—and we're having a *M\*A\*S\*H* Bash on the twenty-eighth, when the final episode airs. I hope you and Roelke can come. All the martinis and grape Nehi you can drink."

"Sounds like fun!" Chloe smiled. Maybe she really could make friends within Roelke's circle.

"Tell Roelke he has to come as Klinger."

The mental image of Roelke McKenna wearing vintage drag was so surreal that Chloe almost snorted wine out her nose. "Not likely," she gasped. Jody laughed, too.

The Blue Tones blazed through a playlist largely comprised of jazz and blues. Roelke, who played electric bass, looked stoic through Foreigner's "Waiting for a Girl Like You" and a few other pop ballads grudgingly added at the bride's request. He perked up when they circled back to Bonnie Raitt.

Chloe thought the set was winding down when someone in the back of the room bellowed, "Bliss!" Other voices took up the call. "Bliss! Bliss! Bliss!"

Chloe leaned toward Jody. "Pardon me, but what the heck?" Like every other Wisconsinite blasted daily by media accounts of Lawrencia Bembenek's infamous murder trial last year, Chloe had seen photographs of a few cops partying with wild abandon. Cops needed to let off steam, she got that, but—geez Louise, there were grandparents and little kids present.

Jody cocked her head at a woman wearing black silk trousers and a silver top who was making her way to the stage. "Lucia Bliss. She's a cop."

"That's her name? Seriously?"

"Seriously."

Lucia Bliss huddled with the musicians before taking the microphone. The band swung into a Pointer Sisters song. Bliss smiled lazily and began to sing of the midnight moon.

The woman had a good voice, Chloe had to give her that. She wasn't beautiful in a traditional way—big-boned, oval face, plain features, shoulder-length brown hair pulled back into a simple ponytail. She didn't prance about, but she exuded a unexpected sultry grace.

Jody leaned closer. "She's a sergeant, actually."

"Really? There can't be many women sergeants in Milwaukee."

"Her dad's the chief of the MPD, so she grew up in a cop family. That couldn't have hurt."

Somebody turned on a disco ball—Chloe hadn't seen one of *those* for a while—and spots of light twirled over the room. She reached for her wine goblet, then decided she'd had enough. On the dance floor, young people clung to their partners like limpets.

The bride and groom looked ready to get down on the floor and go at it, right here, right now.

Chloe glanced back at the stage. Watching the man she'd made love with that morning, she felt disoriented. Roelke's bass was slung low on his hips. He moved to the beat, a lascivious grin on his face.

Bliss crooned about wanting a man's slow hands. She glanced over her shoulder. Had she grinned at Roelke? It really looked like she did. He definitely grinned back.

The smoke-filled room crackled with repressed electricity. Chloe squirmed as some of that tension tingled through her. She couldn't tell if she was ill at ease or turned on.

———

"So," Roelke said later, as they settled into his truck. "Are you glad you came?"

"Sure!" Chloe held her hands toward the heater vent with anticipation. The February night was clear and cold. A few glittering stars reminded Chloe of the disco ball.

"I couldn't tell. If you were enjoying yourself, I mean." He backed out of the parking space.

Chloe tugged her skirt down over her knees. She wasn't used to wearing nylons, and her best dress—a lacy Laura Ashley number that must have amused the young women in their tight minis—was not designed for a Wisconsin winter.

"Well?"

"I loved hearing the band," Chloe said again. "And watching you play. And it was good to meet more of your friends."

"But?"

Chloe frowned. "What's up with you?"

"You just didn't look like you were having a good time."

It wasn't like Roelke to be argumentative. She shifted on the seat, trying to figure out this unexpected mood. "Well...I felt a little out of my element. It's a very different crowd than I'm used to." Many of the guests at the last wedding she'd attended had worn historic attire. The musicians played waltzes and reels. The guests had received handmade boutonnieres and information about the Victorian era's "language of flowers." Quite a stretch from the chocolate handcuffs guests had received tonight, prettily gilded with the date stamped on the side: *February 4, 1983*.

"I've tried really hard to get to know your family and friends," Roelke reminded her.

"I know you have." He'd gone above and beyond on that one, actually, especially in the family arena. "And as I *said*, I enjoyed meeting your friends. I already liked Rick, and Jody's really nice."

Roelke turned onto the I-94 ramp. "They make a good pair."

"So...the woman who came up on stage and sang is a sergeant?"

"Bliss? Yeah. She was a year ahead of us at the academy, but we all worked the same district. She's sung with us a couple of times before."

"I could tell."

"What's *that* supposed to mean?"

"Nothing!" Chloe folded her arms, hoping that was true. The thought of becoming a jealous lady friend was repugnant.

Roelke didn't respond. Chloe lapsed into silence as well, watching lights go by, bummed that the evening was ending on a down note. Roelke had *loved* playing tonight, but something was bugging him. She knew that some of his buds still chided him for leaving Milwaukee. Maybe Roelke was entertaining regrets.

She also knew that he'd been reproaching himself for two months about a complicated murder case. Roelke was not a detective, but he'd become involved in the investigation—and failed, in his opinion, to identify the killer. Sometimes Chloe thought he'd put it behind him ... and then she'd spot him staring into the distance, jaw muscles tight, and knew he had not.

The drive to Palmyra took over an hour. Roelke pulled into the parking lot behind his walk-up apartment in the village. "I'm going back to my place," Chloe said.

"I thought you were staying over."

"I was," she said, "but this doesn't seem to be a good night for that. Besides, I'm driving to the Twin Cities in the morning, remember? I want to get an early start."

"Chloe, I ... " He stared out the windshield. "Never mind. Thanks for coming. Drive safe tomorrow."

"I will. And I'll call you from my friend's place." She leaned over, gave him a quick kiss, and got out of the truck.

———

I can be a real jerk, Roelke thought an hour later, lying lonely in his bed. Honestly, he didn't blame Chloe for leaving. The last thing Rick had said to him that night was, "We've both found good women. I'm hanging on to Jody. You better hang on to Chloe too, dumbass."

Roelke stared into the darkness, trying to figure out why he'd picked a fight with Chloe. Tonight at the reception he'd been conscious of every off-color joke, every crass comment about some recently-arrested asshole. Such talk had never bothered him before. Hell, he was part of it.

Chloe, however, was not. She'd once told him that they were too different to make a good couple. Other people had hinted at the same thing. Now they *were* a couple, and doing just fine all in all, thanks very much. But obviously, Roelke thought, the whole idea of our differences still bugs me.

Well, he'd apologize, first chance he got. He wished she wasn't going away for the rest of the weekend, visiting some friend.

Some *museum* friend. From her *grad school* days.

Roelke punched his pillow, ordered himself to quit stewing, and tried to get some sleep.

———

When the phone rang, Roelke jerked awake and grabbed it. "McKenna here." The clock read 5:10 a.m. Maybe Chloe was calling to say good-bye before she hit the road. No, probably not. Her definition of "hitting the road early" was still several hours away.

He realized that too many seconds had ticked by. "This is Roelke McKenna."

"R-Roelke? I'm sorry to—I—it's Jody."

Roelke felt every sensory detail sharpen: the smooth plastic against his palm, the illuminated clock's glow, the whisper of Jody's irregular breathing in his ear, the infinitesimal quiver of every hair standing erect from his skin.

"What's wrong? Where's Rick?"

"Rick … He … Somebody shot him."

Roelke grabbed the pencil on his nightstand. "Where'd they take him? How bad is he hurt?"

Jody's words squeezed out between sobs. "He's dead, Roelke. Rick is dead."

# TWO

CHLOE FELT RELIEF AS she drove west on US Highway 12. Other than worrying that her decrepit Pinto would crap out, and feeling guilty for burning gas instead of using public transportation (which wasn't available near her house anyway), she loved road trips. And the timing for this particular trip was, evidently, good. She was still confused about Roelke's mood when they'd left the wedding reception. Had the wedding itself put him on edge? Taking a date to a wedding was dicey. Had he worried that she might misinterpret the evening? Was he afraid that she might think he was getting more serious than he really was?

Lovely, she thought. Just when things had actually been going pretty well.

Six inches of snow blanketed the landscape, but the sun was out and the roads were dry. Once in the Twin Cities, she drove with scribbled directions clutched in one hand. She only got confused a couple of times before finding the bridge to Nicollet Island, in the Mississippi

River. She parked in front of a cottage painted yellow and purple and patted the Pinto's dashboard in thanks.

Two people came outside to greet her. The woman was almost lost in a bulky fisherman's sweater. She was slight, with big gray eyes and dark hair wound into a bun. Her features were delicate, even fragile. But the hug she gave Chloe was a bone-crusher.

"You're *here!*"

Chloe grinned. "It's great to see you too, Ariel."

"Do you remember Toby?"

Toby Grzegorczyk, a head taller that his sister, looked like a lumberjack. Chloe extended a hand. "We met in Cooperstown once, right? Good to see you again." She and Ariel had gone through the Museum Studies program in New York.

Toby smiled. "Nice to see you also." He kissed his sister's cheek. "I need to get on the road, kiddo."

"Thanks for the help."

"That's what big brothers are for."

Chloe and Ariel waved as he drove away. "I hope he didn't leave because I was coming," Chloe said.

"Not at all. He came down from Duluth yesterday because an elderly neighbor gave me an antique china cabinet, and I needed help getting it into the house." She gestured toward the cottage. "Welcome to my place."

Chloe was diverted by a chicken pecking for grubs in the next yard over. "Funky neighborhood!"

"It's quite bohemian. That makes rent affordable for someone racking up student loans like pinball points." She led Chloe inside.

"How's the Ph.D. program going?"

"I'm at the stage where the end seems nowhere in sight and I can't figure out what the heck I was thinking." Ariel hung their coats on a hall tree. "How long has it been since I've seen you? It was before you moved to Switzerland."

"Geez, seven years or so, then. I've been back in the states for a couple of years."

"I want to hear all about *everything*." Ariel checked her watch. "We're set to meet a couple of people at the mill this afternoon, but we have time to eat first. Just give me a minute to throw the salad together."

While Ariel worked, Chloe studied her friend's home. Like her own place, the décor was largely thrift-shop chic, with a few honest antiques, including the spectacular cabinet now displaying Ariel's collection of flow blue china. Degas prints and black-and-white photographs of contemporary ballerinas provided an unexpected accent.

"Are you still dancing?" Chloe asked.

"I try to squeeze in a couple of classes a week."

Chloe studied a shot of Ariel. The photographer had captured her suspended in the air, one leg forward and one stretched behind in an impossible split, arms graceful, face serene.

"This picture is amazing," Chloe said. Her dancing of choice involved ethnic folk costumes, hand claps and foot stomps, and sweet tunes scratched from old fiddles or squeezed from accordions.

"I was seventeen, I think." Ariel smiled wistfully as she set a bowl on the table. "A long time ago."

"Did you become a ballerina because your parents named you Ariel? Or were they just prescient?"

"I think my mom was trying to counterbalance Grzegorczyk," Ariel said dryly. "Let's eat."

Chloe dug into the wild rice salad with pecans and dried cherries. "*So* much better than road food," she mumbled. "Now, tell me about your new job."

"I'm a curatorial assistant in the Historic Sites department of the Minnesota Historical Society." Ariel dabbed at her mouth with a cloth napkin. "I'd hoped I'd be helping oversee collections or programming at the state's historic sites, but the big project right now is the abandoned flour mill the society wants to turn into a museum."

Chloe eyed her friend. "Kind of a stretch for the woman voted Most Likely to Work in a Victorian Mansion in grad school."

"Kind of," Ariel agreed. "My advisory committee decided I should write my dissertation about women mill workers." She picked at a nubbin in her sweater, then looked back at Chloe. "Actually ... I'm hoping you'll brainstorm with me this weekend. On Friday I have to present an interpretive plan proposal during a special reception and tour of the mill site for partner agencies and donors. I've been working on it, but I just ... it just ... I don't know. I'm having a hard time."

"Sure, I'll kick some ideas around with you."

"*Thank* you."

"Not that I know diddly about the flour industry."

"That doesn't matter. I've learned so much about it that I've lost my perspective. And this deadline has me anxious. My proposal will go to granting agencies, so it's a big deal."

"You'll do fine."

"I hope so. At least the job got me to the Cities, and that was my first goal. When I was working at the county historical society west of here, I was commuting over an hour to get to classes. And I'm less than three hours from Toby and his wife. They have a baby now, and they're all the family I've got."

"I wasn't thrilled to be returning to Wisconsin when I took the job at Old World," Chloe admitted. "Now that I've settled in ... I must admit, it is nice to be closer to my folks. Mostly, anyway." She speared an errant pecan. "I bet this mill thing turns out to be more interesting than you expect. There are a gazillion old farm and house museums in the world, but industrial sites are rare."

"The Washburn A Mill is on the National Register of Historic Places," Ariel said. "Jay Rutledge—he's with the preservation office—is working to get it listed as a National Historic Landmark. You'll meet Jay at the mill this afternoon. And the opening reception for that photograph exhibition is tonight. I told you about that, right?"

"It's a fundraiser," Chloe said promptly.

"We're raising money and raising awareness. Dr. Everett Whyte, one of my professors, is an amazing photographer who's taken some fascinating shots of the mill."

"Sounds intriguing. I'm looking forward to seeing the site."

"And so you shall." Ariel, having eaten about a quarter-cup portion of salad, pushed her plate away. "Ready to go?"

Back outside, the wail of a distant siren made Chloe think of Roelke. He was scheduled to work today. Maybe he was on a call, too. She was still mildly miffed that he'd gotten all snappish on her the night before, but they'd get past that. It helped to imagine Roelke assisting someone good or arresting someone bad, happy as the proverbial clam, right this very minute.

———

Roelke watched the impromptu wake at Rick's parents' house in Milwaukee. *Rick is gone*, his brain announced over and over. *Rick is dead. Rick is gone.* He couldn't grasp it.

The doorbell kept ringing. Deliverymen with downcast eyes offered bouquets of flowers before fleeing back to their trucks. Women with drawn faces arrived carrying foil-wrapped dishes or Tupperware bowls in shockingly bright colors. Someone had brought a crystal plate of cupcakes—who brought cupcakes to a house in mourning?—and someone else brought something smelling of cabbage. It clashed with smoke from the scented candles burning in every room.

A priest had come and gone. The chief of the Milwaukee Police Department and the captain of Rick's district had come and gone. Sergeant Conrad Malloy, Roelke's field training officer back in the day, had come and gone, too. "Hell of a thing," he'd said to Roelke.

"What—who—"

"Not here," Malloy muttered gruffly. He'd paid his respects to Rick's parents and left.

In the living room, Rick grinned down from a portrait over the mantel. He was posed in front of an American flag, looking sharp in his light blue uniform shirt, dark jacket, and visored hat. Mrs. Almirez sat on a flowered sofa, clutching her haggard husband with one hand and Jody, who looked stunned, with the other.

When Roelke had arrived at Jody's apartment that morning, all he'd known to do was fold her into his arms and hang on while she sobbed. He tried to find words of comfort. None came. Finally she'd pulled away. Roelke had driven her to the Almirez house in numb silence.

Now Roelke's shock was giving way to rage. He trembled to get facts. Who did this? What happened? How did it happen? He wished he'd followed Malloy, maybe caught him in the yard. He used to work for Malloy. He understood why the sergeant hadn't wanted to have a conversation in the living room, but Rick had been dead for what, five or six hours already? Roelke wanted to leave this suffocating house of crying people. He wanted to drive to Rick's district station and demand answers.

16

A gray-haired woman with red-rimmed eyes appeared at Roelke's elbow. "Would you like some enchilada casserole?" She waved a weary hand toward the dining room table. "Or—"

"No thank you, ma'am, I—pardon me."

Dobry Banik had stepped inside, wearing his own dress blues. Roelke waited until Dobry offered condolences to Jody and Rick's parents before catching his eye and cocking his head: *Follow me.*

He led the way through the kitchen and outside to a patio. The air was brisk, but the sun made the sheltered corner tolerable. Roelke blinked at the sheer normalness of the scene: a stack of empty flower-pots by the wall, a Weber covered with a fitted cover, two wooden recliners—all waiting for a spring that would never come. Not for this house. Not for this family.

Dobry offered one of those awkward gestures men make, half hug and half back-slap. "I don't believe this," he muttered. "I don't fucking believe it."

"What *happened*?"

"I had my hands full with a drunk when the call came through." Dobry pounded one fist against his palm. "Officer down at Kozy Park."

Roelke winced. Kosciuszko Park, thirty-five acres of gently rolling land scattered with trees, was the heart of the Lincoln Village neighborhood in Milwaukee's Old South Side. It was a place for games and picnics. Even the local numbnuts generally respected the precious green space.

"In the park itself?"

Dobry shook his head. "He was in the road. Lincoln Avenue."

Roelke's stomach muscles clenched. Lincoln was one of the busiest streets in the district.

"By the time I got there, the ambulance was gone and guys were crawling over the neighborhood. Word is that based on the way Rick was lying, he'd probably approached a parked car. He was killed by a single shot to the back of the head. The shot could have come from the driver."

"Rick never would have turned his back on the driver unless he felt totally secure."

"Yeah."

"He was walking the beat alone?"

"We were short because of the wedding, and it was after bar time."

That was about what Roelke had expected. In the city, two guys usually patrolled together until the bars closed. Then each traveled alone.

"A 'shot fired' call came in from a civilian at 3:45 a.m. The clerk tried to raise Rick but couldn't. He was already dead."

"Where on Lincoln?"

"Just west of the statue." The General Kosciuszko Statue, he meant. "But Roelke ... " Dobry glanced over his shoulder, and lowered his voice. "Something hinky was going on last night. Today, on the surface, it's all about one of Milwaukee's finest being killed on duty—"

"*On the surface*? What the hell does that mean?"

"Sergeant Malloy ... " Dobry fumbled in his pocket for a pack of cigarettes.

Roelke thought he might explode. "Sergeant Malloy *what*?"

"Malloy says Rick screwed up."

"Rick screwed up?" Roelke stepped closer. "Rick is dead, and Malloy says *he* screwed up?" The ache in his chest turned molten. Now he *really* wished he'd followed Sergeant Malloy after his perfunctory condolence call. Followed him and tackled him and pounded his head against the ground.

18

"Rick missed his mark at 1:50, and—"

"At *1:50*? And nobody found him until four?"

"Would you let me finish a sentence? He wasn't shot that early, he just missed his mark."

"He wasn't carrying a handy-talkie?" Roelke asked, although he knew the answer.

"Rick always said it slowed him down." Dobry hitched one shoulder up and down. "I don't carry one either."

During the time they'd worked together, Roelke's buddies had often chided him for being an "early adopter." When police vests came on the market, he got one. Radios had been in the cars for years, but when personal radios were made available, he carried one of those too—despite the annoyance of an eight-pound weight on his belt. In Milwaukee, handy-talkies were optional. Lots of the beat men still relied on the old call boxes sprinkled through the city instead.

Would carrying a handy-talkie have made a difference for Rick? Roelke closed his eyes. With a handy-talkie, Rick might have had time to squeeze in a 10-78 call, which basically meant *I'm getting my ass handed to me out here*. Every cop in the area—and plenty who were not—would have descended.

But ... shot in the back of the head, Dobry had said. Rick never knew what hit him.

Then something else Dobry'd said penetrated, and Roelke opened his eyes again. Rick was required to use one of those call boxes to check in every hour. His mark time was ten minutes before the hour. Cops on patrol were only given a five-minute grace period to hit their mark, and sergeants got cranky if that window passed without communication. Unless Rick was wrestling a violent felon to the ground or something, he *never* missed his mark.

"So, what happened at 1:50?" Roelke asked.

"No call from Rick. The guy on the desk flashed the blue lights."

The blue lights were on top of the call boxes. "That should have gotten Rick's attention."

"But Rick still doesn't call in. The clerk, he's a good guy—Cox, remember him? So Cox wants to keep the sergeants out of it." Dobry sucked one last bit of tar and nicotine from the cigarette before grinding it out on the cement pad. "He flashes the lights again, I get on the line, and he says 'Hey, I can't roust Almirez. See if you can find him.' So…I find him." Dobry paused.

Roelke ground his teeth again. For the love of God, if Dobry dragged this story out any longer, Roelke would throttle him. "Where?"

"In a bar."

"Trouble on a bar check?"

"No. Roelke, Rick was having a Policeman's Coke."

*"What?"* Roelke stared at Dobry. *Policeman's Coke* was a euphemism for alcohol. "No way."

Dobry held up his hands. "I saw Rick through the window, tossing back a cold one at the Rusty Nail."

Roelke's eyes narrowed. Even if Rick had been off-duty, the Rusty Nail was not the kind bar he would have chosen to relax in. "Was he with somebody?"

"I don't know. I grabbed my flashlight and shined it inside to get Rick's attention." Dobry pantomimed holding a phone to his ear, the signal for *You got to call in, NOW*. "I waited until he came out, and basically asked what the hell he was doing. He just thanked me, and said he'd go call in." Dobry wiped a hand over his face. "That was the last time I saw him. He hit his next mark at 2:50, right on time. Nobody would have been the wiser except…you know. After Rick got shot, Cox figured he better come clean."

"I don't see why," Roelke snapped, although honestly, he probably would have done the same himself.

"Look," Dobry said grimly. "You know, and *I* know, that Rick must have had a real good reason for what he did. But the sergeant—and probably now the captain and chief too—they don't necessarily see it that way."

Roelke wouldn't have guessed that anything could be worse than what Jody had said: *He's dead, Roelke.* But this…

Dobry stared over the yard. "They kept it from the press for now, but…" He lit another cigarette and inhaled like a man in need. "If reporters discover that Rick had been tossing back a cold one earlier that night, they'll make the entire shooting look like officer error."

Roelke's hands clenched. A growl came from somewhere deep inside. "God*damn* it!" His foot connected with the stack of flowerpots—some plastic, some clay—in a soccer kick. They flew into the yard with an obscene clatter.

---

"Geez." Chloe planted her feet on the sidewalk and grabbed the chain-link security fence so she could study the enormous ruin inside—a hulk of limestone walls covered with cracked concrete, grimy and grafittied.

"Welcome to the Washburn A Mill," Ariel said. "The whole complex was made up of ten buildings, constructed between 1866 and 1908. The museum is being planned for the A Mill, which is the largest." She pointed to a series of cylindrical grain elevators, maybe 100 or more feet tall. "The head house on top of the elevators is five stories itself."

Chloe shielded her eyes from the sun. Atop the head house an iconic sign spelled *GOLD MEDAL FLOUR* in huge yellow letters. "Is this where Gold Medal Flour got its start?"

"It is. And after a couple of mergers, Washburn became Washburn-Crosby Company in 1879, and then General Mills in 1928," Ariel said mechanically. "Listen, Owen and Jay are supposed to meet us here. We should wait in the car. It's not safe to wander around alone."

"It looks like any one of these walls might crumble at any moment," Chloe agreed. Ariel had parked in a lane on the bank of the Mississippi River, in the industrial heart of Minneapolis. The landscape was bleak: weeds, heaps of gravel, railroad tracks, abandoned buildings, crumbles of rubble that only hinted at the industry once powered by the mighty river.

"It's not just that," Ariel said. "This is a bad area. I know we're not far from my place, but those few miles matter. Lots of vagrants, and drug dealers and—oh *good*. There they are."

Chloe watched two men emerge from a station wagon. The driver was a compact man with salt-and-pepper hair. His companion, a blue-jeaned beanpole in his late twenties, jumped from the passenger seat with an air of endless energy. He wore coat and gloves but no hat, displaying an untidy mess of sandy hair. Both men retrieved daypacks from the back seat before joining the women.

"Hey, guys," Ariel said. "This is my friend Chloe Ellefson. We went through grad school together."

The younger man offered Chloe a warm smile. "Owen Brinkerhoff."

His handshake was firm but not crushing. Chloe considered that a good sign. "Good to meet you, Owen. And your role on the team is … ?"

22

"I got involved because of a class in Historic Building Research and Documentation I took at the U of M last fall," Owen said. "Now I'm doing an independent study, surveying the milling equipment still in the building. It's an amazing opportunity."

"Sounds like it," Chloe agreed, although she had no idea what kind of equipment was still in the building. Owen's enthusiasm made her want to encourage him.

The second man introduced himself as Jay Rutledge. "I'm documenting the physical condition of the structures." Jay had thoughtful gray eyes and an air of calm competence.

"I thought Everett might join us," Owen told Ariel. "I called his office a couple of times, but he never picked up." He looked at Chloe. "Professor Everett Whyte specializes in industrial history. He's also my Ph.D. advisor. He knows this mill as well as anyone."

"He's probably setting up for the exhibit opening tonight," Jay said. He smiled at Chloe. "No problem. We can give you a tour."

Owen waved one arm, embracing the landscape from blighted factory to harnessed river. "Everything happened because of St. Anthony Falls. Chloe, did you know it's the only waterfall along the Mississippi?"

"I did not," Chloe confessed, humbled by the magnitude of her ignorance.

"In the US, the falls here are second in power only to Niagara," Owen told her. "In 1874 the Washburn A Mill, the world's largest flour mill at the time, was completed. The production of a basic food item was industrialized for the first time in history. Isn't that awesome?"

"It is."

"The mills needed cooperages, railroads, sawmills, foundries—all kinds of support industries. Immigrants poured into Minneapolis for the jobs." Owen pointed downriver. "We should drive past Bohemian

Flats later. There used to be a whole neighborhood crammed on a floodplain between the river and the bluffs. It was a place for immigrants to get started, and it became quite a vibrant and close-knit community."

"A bridge went in right over the neighborhood," Ariel added. "Wealthy Yankees would stop on the bridge and stare down like tourists. They thought Bohemian Flats was quaint."

"So they could gawk without getting their shoes muddy," Chloe said dryly. "I would like to see the place. I work at an outdoor ethnic museum, but we pretty much stick to the farmstead and crossroads village experience." Something about the notion of a come-and-gone community at Bohemian Flats called to her. After spending so much time considering the lives of immigrants who settled in rural areas, it was intriguing to consider the people who'd made a different choice.

# THREE
# MAY 1878

MAGDALENA STOOD KNEE-DEEP IN the Mississippi River, waiting for a log to drift within reach and dreaming of hats. One day, she thought, I shall own a hat. Perhaps a bonnet, covered with silk and adorned with ribbons. Or perhaps something woven from straw, with a perky brim and a cluster of artificial flowers. Either would be glorious.

Although she purposefully stood with her back to the bridge, she sensed the sightseers high above her. The city's well-to-do often promenaded to the bridge to literally look down on the immigrants making their home on the low tableland cradled by a bend in the river. Magdalena knew that if she did peek, she'd be able to make out the silhouettes of parasols against the setting sun—and hats.

She smoothed the kerchief knotted beneath her chin. She'd covered her hair this way back in central Poland, and on the ship across the Atlantic, not yet knowing that her black headscarf would represent her *otherness*. She lived in the community the

Yankees called the Cabbage Patch, or Little Connemara, or Bohemian Flats. Magdalena suspected that the Yankee women up there knew very little about the Flats. She'd never seen anyone wearing a stylish bustle dress actually descend the seventy-nine steps that separated the Flats from the rest of Minneapolis. She only knew about the nicknames because the weary men who ate and slept at her boardinghouse told her.

"Mama?"

Magdalena turned and felt the sun rise in her heart. "Yes, Frania?" She'd named her daughter Franciszka, but the diminutive endearment was sweeter.

The four-year-old on the bank pointed proudly to a small pile of sticks nearby. "See?"

"Good girl," Magdalena called. "Keep looking, all right? I need to wait a little longer. We're almost out of firewood." And food. And money. But—one thing at a time.

Frania renewed her search, and Magdalena turned back to the river. The evening smelled of muck and wood smoke. The last feeble rays of spring sunshine slipped away from the worn wool shawl knotted over her shoulders. She should head to the boardinghouse soon; she wanted to make soup for the men trudging down from the flour mills. But she'd let her woodpile get dangerously low, and she needed to salvage one good log before heading home.

Life had been easier when her brother Dariusz was alive. They'd immigrated together, among the first Russian Poles to settle in Minneapolis. She'd considered his ill-suppressed disgust about her swelling belly the price for her escape—from the clacking tongues in their tiny village, from the disappointment in her mother's eyes, from the sharp words of rejection from the boy she'd expected to marry. Most of all she needed to escape her father's brother, with his sour-beer breath and grabbing hands and boots caked with pig manure. He'd left those boots on when, three weeks before her fifteenth birthday, he'd shoved her down in the straw stack and jerked his trousers to his knees, grunting like one of his boars. Three months later, she knew the life she'd planned was gone. When Dariusz suggested they emigrate, she'd agreed at once.

After the grueling trip, she and Dariusz had settled here in the Flats and moved into an abandoned shack right on the Mississippi. Dariusz found work in one of the lumber mills by St. Anthony Falls. Magdalena had scrubbed the shanty and declared it open for boarders, eager to contribute and determined to raise well the infant who'd been born halfway across the ocean. Seven weeks later, two strangers knocked on the door—the Irish foreman from the lumber mill and a Polish sawyer who understood a bit of English and tried to translate. Magdalena hadn't understood all of their babble—and she didn't want to—but she did grasp that her brother had been killed in a sawmill accident.

*"Mama!"* Frania pointed upriver, quivering with excitement.

Jerked from her memories, Magdalena saw a stray log, escaped from one of the mills, floating near the shore. A couple of planks bobbed against it. Magdalena's eyes narrowed with determination. Firewood *and* lumber. With enough planks she could build an addition onto their home. She was tired of stepping over snoring men when she made her way to the stove at first light every day.

As the log floated closer, Magdalena slogged into deeper water, almost hobbled as her heavy wool skirt soaked through. I must do this, she thought, suppressing a shiver. She carried a long staff with a crotch on the end and waited until just the right moment before snagging the log and pulling it closer. She wrapped one arm around the log, pivoted, and thrust it straight toward shore with enough speed to lodge on the bank.

Frania clapped her hands. "Stay back!" Magdalena ordered her daughter sharply, before turning and floundering after the planks. She managed to wrestle them from the current as well and staggered to shore, soaked but satisfied.

Then she glanced at her daughter and felt fear. Frania's bony little wrists poked from an old dress. Her cheeks were hollow, which made her dark eyes look huge.

Magdalena sagged, hands on wet knees. She was tired. So very tired.

Then she straightened her spine and set her shoulders. *Tired* was a luxury she could not afford. I must go to the flour mill tonight, Magdalena thought. Even if the idea made her want to weep.

# FOUR

"READY FOR A TOUR?" Jay asked. "Watch your step." He unlocked a gate in the security fence and led the way over abandoned railroad tracks to a door made of rusty corrugated metal. "This way."

Ariel zipped up her coat. Owen turned on a powerful flashlight, and they all stepped inside. "Take a moment to let your eyes adjust."

Chloe heard water dripping, and a cold dampness leached through her parka. The building exhaled something stale and stagnant. Dim yellow light leaked through grimy windows as Owen and Jay played their flashlight beams over the vast floor. Concrete pillars with surprisingly graceful lines rose from broken bricks, limestone rubble, twisted bits of metal, and rusty machines. The mill's enormity felt overwhelming.

"This was the packing floor," Owen explained. "In the 1880s, men packed barrels that held almost two hundred pounds of flour. This mill produced four thousand barrels of flour every day."

"That's amazing," Chloe murmured, distracted by the necessity of considering this space. She had perceived sensory echoes in old buildings since she was a child, and energy still lingered in the mill. In this place she sensed the busyness, the vibrating pulse of industry, the jumble of human beings who'd once walked this floor.

And within the faint hodgepodge of emotions resonating through time, she sensed a thread of fear. Chloe tried to hide a shiver that had nothing to do with the cold air clenched within thick stone walls. She understood better, now, why Ariel didn't like coming here alone.

"We're not cops!" Jay hollered. His words echoed.

"Who are you talking to?" Chloe asked.

"Anyone who might be listening. This place is a magnet for winos, runaways, drug dealers … Last week I chased out two ten-year-old girls playing hooky. The fence and door locks don't do much good, not with so many broken windows."

"Not to mention the sewer tunnels," Owen added. When Chloe gave him a dubious glance, he shrugged. "It's how some of the kids get in. They like to run around and drop smoke bombs down the empty grain bins."

Chloe could imagine this place beckoning anyone wanting to find shelter, fade from sight, or get rowdy. She sincerely hoped that no one expected Ariel to patrol the sewers.

As they moved into the building, the men aimed their lights along the walls and into corners. Amid the ruin were surprising splashes of vivid color—graffiti painted on the cracking walls. Jay sighed when the light found a couple of ratty old sleeping bags, neatly folded and shoved into a corner beside grocery bags and a cardboard box. "Unfortunately Minneapolis does not have facilities for our population of homeless people," he told Chloe. "Most of the people who come here have nowhere else to sleep."

That explained the faint stink of urine mixed with mice droppings and decay. Sad to think this is their best option, Chloe thought.

"Let's climb up to the top of the wheat house," Jay suggested. "The stairs are safe."

"Just don't touch anything," Owen cautioned. "A chunk of concrete might fall from the walls."

Chloe obligingly thrust her hands into her pockets.

Owen provided commentary as they went. She wanted to ask questions, but the climb shortened her breath and she didn't want to sound like a worn-out weenie.

When they finished the ascent, an eruption of movement and sound shoved her pounding heart into her throat. Pigeons disturbed by the intruders noisily fled through broken windows. Pigeon poop and feathers covered the floor, and the air stank of ammonia. Geez Louise, Chloe thought, this is not the gig for Ariel.

Jay scribbled a note on his clipboard. "We've got to get this area cleaned up before Friday."

Owen didn't seem to notice. "The story begins with wheat arriving from farms all over the Upper Midwest and Great Plains. Imagine: in the mill's heyday, seventy-six boxcars of wheat arrived every single day." He paused expectantly.

"That's a lot of wheat," Chloe agreed.

Jay led the way into a room on the south side of the narrow building. A huge metal monster that made Chloe think of a rusty octopus dominated the space. Sunlight filtering faintly through a high row of small windows showed ample evidence of more pigeon parties.

"We're on the eighth floor of the wheat house," Owen said. "Grain arrived with stones, dirt, iron filings from the train cars, bugs, mouse poop—"

This is *so* not the gig for Ariel, Chloe thought.

"—and it came into the wheat house to be cleaned. The head miller chose the mix to grind every day. Different batches of wheat had different protein levels, but each barrel or sack of flour had to be blended to produce identical results."

"It is *essential* to watch your step in here." Jay's flashlight beam lingered on scattered metal trapdoors in the floor. "We haven't had a chance to weld the hatches shut. I suspect they've been used to dump trash, and last year some frat boys decided to haze their newbies by making them rappel down through one of them."

"Where do they lead?" Chloe asked.

"Each of those trapdoors in the floor leads into a nine-story storage bin that held twenty thousand pounds of grain."

"Sometimes wheat seeds would stick together in a bin," Owen added soberly. "A worker would climb down a rope with a shovel or pitchfork to break up the clog. The guy was supposed to stay on the rope, but so many men were killed that the mill owner started insisting they wear harnesses."

"Falling on grain is like falling into quicksand," Jay added. "Every movement makes you sink."

Chloe was starting to think that this was not a gig for her, either.

"There are stories of men dying in these bins well into the twentieth century," Owen said. "Some suffocated. But even if a guy got buried just up to his waist, he'd have eight hundred pounds of pressure per square inch against his legs. It would have been impossible to pull him out."

Ariel, standing with shoulders hunched and arms crossed, gave Chloe a look: *Isn't this just loads of fun?*

Chloe stepped closer to the wall. Even standing on top of a bin felt creepy. "Are the bins empty now?"

"Most are," Jay said. "We haven't crawled through everything yet, though. I wouldn't be surprised if one or two still do hold grain."

Chloe hoped that one day exhibits might help visitors reflect on the inherent danger of working at a mill. But right this minute, she really didn't need hear any more about it. "What's the octopus thingie?" She gestured to the apparatus that took up most of the room: a round structure that reached from ceiling to about six feet above the floor. Rectangular chutes angled down from that central bin.

"This is the turn head distributor," Owen said, patting the metal beast with affection. "Millers used those metal chutes to distribute grain from a conveyor into the bins. Those sliding doors you see about knee level in each chute allowed workers to check for proper grain flow."

Jay stepped closer to one of the chutes, eyes slightly narrowed. This man knows the mill, Chloe thought. She'd seen that look before—in their passion to document and preserve old buildings, architectural historians came to know every cracked brick, every sloping floorboard, every corroding scrap of metal.

Ariel stepped closer too and studied the square metal door in the nearest chute. "That was open last time I was here," she said, interrupting Owen's enthusiastic description of bolters, middlings, and endosperm.

Owen shrugged. "Probably some homeless guy hiding his stuff. Once I found a knapsack tucked away in one of the chutes. Somebody had hammered out a corner of a metal plate so it made a hook."

"With luck it's just a bundle of clothes and blanket." Jay sighed. "But if someone's stashed their baggies of crack in here, we'll need to call the cops."

"Maybe we should call the cops anyway," Ariel suggested uneasily.

Chloe nodded, not keen on the idea of some crazed cocaine dealer wandering in while the history nerds were examining the goods.

But Jay clasped the handle. The door moved with a reluctant, rusty groan of protest. He leapt backwards. *"Christ!"*

Chloe instinctively craned her head to look. Don't *do* that! came some voice in her brain, but too late. She'd already seen that the grain chute, which should have been empty, was stuffed. All that showed in the little open space was the head and shoulders of a man. A man who was quite obviously dead.

She pressed one hand over her stomach, fighting nausea, trying to make sense of what she was seeing. "What ... who ... "

But Ariel was screaming hysterically, and no one could hear.

————

Jody slid open the patio door about three seconds after Roelke punted flowerpots all over the Almirez family's back yard. She studied the debris. "Wish I'd thought of that," she said. "Thanks for coming, Dobry."

Dobry hugged her. "God, Jody, I'm so sorry."

"I know." Jody wiped her eyes. "Roelke, could you take me home? Rick's parents are dear, but I can't—I just ... "

"Let's go."

Once in the truck, Jody leaned her head back and closed her eyes. Roelke was relieved. Dobry's words echoed in his brain: *Malloy says Rick screwed up.*

No way, Roelke thought. Rick didn't make dumb mistakes, and he sure as hell didn't drink on the job. So ... what the devil *had* happened?

Jody didn't open her eyes until Roelke parked in front of her apartment building. "Thank you, Roelke. After I got the news, I didn't know what to do except call you."

"You need anything, Jody, you just call."

She squeezed his hand.

"Jody… did you talk to Rick at all after he went to work last night? Did he mention what he was working on? Anything unusual?"

"He did call me, a little after one a.m." Jody began shredding a tissue. "There's a payphone in the lobby of an apartment building. He can see a call box across the street, but it's unlikely that a sergeant would spot him there. He said he wanted to hear my voice, tell me that he loved me."

"Did he usually call?"

Jody drew in a shuddery breath. "He—we—Roelke, after we got home from the wedding last night, Rick asked me to marry him."

Something brittle beneath Roelke's ribs splintered into a thousand pieces. *I'm hanging on to Jody,* Rick had said. *You better hang on to Chloe too, dumbass.* And what had he done? He'd gotten in his truck and picked a fight with her.

Pain made Roelke realize he was gripping the steering wheel way too hard. He *was* a dumbass, he really was, but he couldn't think about Chloe right now.

"I didn't know," he said. "At least you know he really loved you." Rick had never said *love* when talking about Jody. At least that wasn't surprising, Roelke thought. Guys like Rick and him didn't really use that word.

He turned to Jody. "Did Rick say anything about the shift? Calls? Anything?"

"Nothing out of the ordinary. I asked how the night was going. 'Okay,' he said."

Not a whole lot there to go on.

"There was just one more thing," Jody said. "I think somebody asked him something—I couldn't hear what they said or who it was—and Rick said he was about to do a bar check. Then he said 'I gotta go' to me, and that was it."

"Did Rick mention a tavern by name?"

"No."

Roelke tapped his thumb on the steering wheel. Bar checks, walking the beat. Typical Friday night.

"Everybody from the department is being nice. Chief Bliss called Rick a hero. But I heard some whispers." Jody stared straight ahead.

*Malloy says Rick screwed up.* Roelke cursed whoever had done that whispering in the Almirez living room.

"Rick would *never* drink on duty," she insisted.

"I know."

After a long moment she said, "They said it was quick. Are they lying? Trying to protect me?" Her voice broke. "Oh God, Roelke, what if Rick didn't die right away? I can't bear to think of him hurt, lying there—"

"*Don't.* Dobry said Rick never knew what hit him. And Jody, the district is all over this. *Everybody* liked Rick, and cops go a little crazy when they lose one of their own."

She nodded.

Roelke held her gaze. "And I swear to God, Jody, if the local guys don't find out who is responsible, I will."

"You're a good friend." Jody managed the ghost of a smile. "Thanks for being there for me today, but I need to be alone now. You go on home. Spend some time with Chloe."

"Chloe's in Minneapolis."

"Oh. Well, call her then." Jody kissed his cheek and got out of the truck.

Roelke watched until Jody was safely inside. He *could* call Chloe. He wanted to hear her voice. Still...

*Don't be a dumbass, McKenna.*

Still, he had more to do before leaving Milwaukee. Chloe was off having fun with her friend. Calling Chloe could wait.

# FIVE

THIS, CHLOE THOUGHT, IS one god-awful mess.

She was sitting on a wide stone windowsill inside the mill. When she put one arm around Ariel's shoulders, she felt uncontrolled shudders spasm through her thin frame.

"It was Professor Whyte," Ariel whispered, for about the two hundred and thirty-seventh time.

"Yeah," Chloe said. "I know." Professor Everett Whyte was one of the key players in the plans to save, restore, and interpret the mill. How the hell had he ended up where he did?

They were waiting for the police to say they could leave. Owen was pacing. Jay was still in the wheat house, talking to the detectives. The ambulance team had removed Everett Whyte's body. But through dirty windows, the cop cars' flashing lights pulsed a dire pronouncement: *Death, death, death.*

Chloe felt cold, hungry, and tired. She longed for a swig of something strong enough to purge her mind of what she'd glimpsed in that grain chute. But she didn't have the luxury of self-indulgence—not when Ariel was shivering and white-faced.

"We've already given statements, so why do we need to stay?" Owen exploded. "I'm going to see what's taking so long."

Chloe was relieved to be rid of Owen's agitation. She needed to calm herself so she could help calm Ariel. Folding her arms, Chloe hunched over her knees. Breathe in, breathe out…

Two sturdy black shoes appeared in front of her. "Would you like some coffee?" a woman asked gently.

Chloe straightened again. "I beg your pardon?"

"It looks like you two could use some hot coffee." The woman held up a silver thermos. She was maybe thirty-five, with short dark hair styled in a blunt cut possibly designed as homage to Dorothy Hamill, and wise brown eyes behind glasses with blue plastic frames. Jeans showed beneath her coat. "I heard what happened up there. I'm sorry."

"Are you with the police?"

"No. But the officers know me, and said it was okay if I stepped inside." The woman set up shop in the next windowsill and produced cardboard cups with little fold-out handles from a hamper. "I'm Sister Mary Jude."

"You don't look like a nun." Chloe's cheeks flamed. "That is— I—sorry."

Sister Mary Jude smiled as she unscrewed the thermos lid. "I get that a lot."

Ariel roused herself. "Sister Mary Jude takes care of the homeless people who live in the mill."

"I'm afraid 'takes care of' is a bit of a stretch." Sister Mary Jude poured a steaming cup. "But I do what I can. I have cheese sandwiches too, by the way."

Chloe introduced herself before sipping gratefully. "Aren't the sandwiches for the people who live here?"

Sister Mary Jude sighed. "We won't see a soul again today. Not until people are sure the police aren't hanging around."

"Yeah, well, one of those vagrants probably killed the professor."

The three women turned to the police officer who had made that blunt—and, Chloe thought, premature—assessment. He leaned against a rusty sack-packing machine with crossed arms.

Sister Mary Jude crossed *her* arms. "Do you have reason to believe that, Officer Crandall?"

Crandall shrugged. "We all know it's not the first time a body's been found in the mill." He looked at Chloe, evidently recognizing her as a newcomer. "A month or so ago we found some dead homeless guy dumped into one of the empty grain bins."

Chloe winced. Sister Mary Jude stood straighter. "He was not 'some dead homeless guy,'" she snapped. "William lived a life much like yours until his family died in a car crash two weeks after he was laid off from his job. When the money ran out, he ended up here. William deserved much better from our society than death in an abandoned mill. His friends put him in the grain bin because they didn't know what else to do."

"Look, Sister, a lot of people who hang around this place would be a whole lot better off if you didn't encourage them to stay here—"

"Do you think people *want* to sleep in a rat-infested hulk like this? You pompous—"

"O-*kay*," Chloe said loudly. She admired the nun, she really did, but this debate was fraying her very last nerve. Ariel was giving her best impression of a turtle trying to disappear into a worsted-wool shell.

"Hey, Crandall." A female police officer with dark chocolate skin and an expressionless face paused nearby. "Let's go."

Crandall swaggered away. If he's that woman's partner, Chloe thought, I do not envy her in the slightest.

Then again, there wasn't anyone in this mammoth mill that she envied today.

Something in her chest ached. Strange. She'd had a bad shock, but she hadn't known Professor Everett Whyte. So why did she feel grief?

It wasn't grief balling up beneath her ribs, though. It was longing.

Chloe was a strong and capable woman. But at that moment, nothing would make her happier than seeing Roelke McKenna, over-protective boyfriend and take-charge cop, walk through the door.

———

After leaving Jody, Roelke drove east through Milwaukee. His brain was a slide carousel flashing pictures of him and Rick, fresh from twenty weeks at the recruit academy. Although they'd formally been hired by the city, districts—each with their own buildings and staff—operated almost like individual police departments. Rick and Roelke had been giddy with glee when they were assigned to the same district.

That was in 1975. Just eight years ago, Roelke thought. It felt like eighty. He felt an odd sense of the unknown-familiar as he entered the building and talked his way beyond the lobby. Compared to the Eagle PD, the district was a busy place, with twenty or thirty beat men on a shift, a few detectives, and clerks working the desk.

He hadn't gone far when Captain Heikinen, who ran the district, and Chief Bliss, who ran the city PD, emerged from a meeting room and strode down the hall toward him. Roelke instinctively stepped aside and became fascinated with the floor tile. Back in the day when he'd answered roll call here, he—like all beat cops—avoided the top brass. It was always better to take problems or questions to the sergeants. After eighteen months away, that same instinct kicked in now. The two men passed Roelke and parted with a quick, muttered conversation.

Then the captain backtracked, walking so fast he overtook Roelke. Heikinen was a tall man with brooding eyes under a craggy brow and hands big enough to strangle a hog. He'd worked his way into a command position the hard way, and he knew the streets as well as anyone. The district cops would never have said they liked the man, but they respected him.

"McKenna, isn't it?" Heikinen barked.

Muscle memory brought Roelke's hand up in salute. "Yessir."

"Where are you assigned these days?"

"I'm out in Waukesha County now, sir."

Heikinen scowled, as if Roelke's move was a personal affront, then went on his way. Okay, Roelke thought. Everybody is operating from a bad place right now, and at least the captain didn't toss you from the building. Get on with it.

Sergeant Malloy was on the phone when Roelke approached, so he paused a respectful distance away. Memory flashed Malloy's greeting when Roelke had first presented his rookie-self way back when: "Get in the car, kid. Don't touch anything, don't break anything, don't say anything unless we're alone. If I want coffee, you get it. If a drunk pukes in the car, you clean it up. Got all that? Yeah? Well then, we'll get along fine."

Now Sergeant Malloy slammed down the phone and regarded him. "McKenna. I figured I'd see you again today."

"I don't want to take a lot of your time."

42

"Good." Still, Malloy gestured vaguely to a chair beside the desk.

Malloy was a bulldog—short, squat, muscular, intense. The former Marine was a master at command presence and excelled at talking his way out of trouble. "I know what you're thinking," he'd once told a gun-waving whacko, while rookie-Roelke looked on, trying desperately to figure out what the hell to do. "Listen, neither one of us wants to get hurt. Let's both put our guns down."

And they both did.

Now Malloy regarded his old trainee. "So. You want to be a pallbearer?"

The question sucked air from Roelke's lungs. "What I want," he managed, "is to understand what happened to Rick."

"We all want that."

"So, what do you know?"

"Not a whole lot. Yet. He was shot in the back of the head at close range."

"Why are you saying that he screwed up?"

Malloy's gaze skewered Roelke to his chair. Roelke remembered something Malloy had taught his trainees: *Always look bad guys in the right eye. If they're right-handed—and most of 'em are—it's their dominant eye. You can stare 'em down that way.* It took every ounce of Roelke's control to not look away.

Finally Malloy said, "I believe my exact words were, 'Almirez may have been too trusting.' "

"Rick was *always* careful—"

"And I imagine you've heard he missed a mark and was found drinking in a tavern."

Damn. Roelke had assumed that Dobry hadn't told anyone exactly where he found Rick.

"This," Malloy was saying, "was after he attended a wedding reception, where I imagine he had one or two cold ones. Just how careful do you suppose he was at 3:45 in the Goddamn morning after all that celebrating?"

Roelke thought of something he should have considered before. Rick had gotten engaged right before starting his shift. If there was ever a time he might…

*No.* Roelke's right knee began pumping. "Rick was a good cop."

"Damn straight. But your friend made a mistake. Have you ever made a mistake on duty, McKenna?"

Roelke gripped the arms of his chair. Short answer: Yes. Too many to count. A few qualified as monumental.

"Being a cop means making a million decisions every day. Some you make in a split second, like reacting if someone you trust pulls a gun. Some you think about, like drinking on the job. Sometimes even good cops make mistakes. I have, you have, Almirez did."

"I don't think Rick—"

"Shut up, McKenna. It's my job to call things straight. A good cop is dead. The chief and the mayor and all my guys got blood in their eyes. The rookies are shook up. Rick Almirez is a fallen hero, but if mistakes were made, I've got to say so. Stupidass mistakes can get you killed out there. This is a reminder for everybody else. I've got to protect the living."

Roelke opened his mouth, shut it again.

Malloy leaned forward. "Officer McKenna, I know that you and Almirez were tight. I know you want to charge out there and help nail the asshole who shot a cop. Well, you can't."

"But—"

"We're going to do this, but we're going to do it right, and *you*"— Malloy jabbed a finger toward Roelke's chest—"don't even work here anymore."

"But—"

"Your friend got killed. That ain't easy, but sometimes it comes with the job. So do us both a favor and go home."

"But—"

"Go *home*, McKenna. A full investigation has been launched. We'll find the bastard who did this. Right now, I've got nothing else for you. What I do have is a funeral to plan. So I'll ask one more time. Do you want to be a pallbearer?"

Roelke tried to stare Malloy down, sending a mental message: *I'm not that kid you ordered to clean the squad car. And I've helped out on a homicide investigation or two.*

Malloy stared back.

"Yeah," Roelke finally said. "I do want to be a pallbearer."

"I'll be in touch, then." Malloy picked up the receiver on his desk phone and began dialing. Translation: *You are dismissed.*

Roelke left the office. He left the building.

He also left Malloy's brick wall behind. The sergeant had said his piece. Most of it even made sense. But I'll be damned, Roelke thought, before I drive back to Eagle and twiddle my thumbs, waiting by the phone for news.

Rick's sardonic voice echoed in his mind: *Don't be a dumbass, McKenna.*

"You'd do the same for me," Roelke muttered and headed for his truck.

# SIX

WHEN THE DETECTIVES INVESTIGATING Everett Whyte's death finally released the dejected little band of historians, Owen announced his intention to drive the women back to Ariel's apartment. Since Owen had arrived in Jay's car, and since Chloe wasn't keen on urban driving at the best of times, she decided to let him. Ariel curled up on the back seat. Chloe and Owen made the short drive in silence.

The phone started ringing as they walked into the house. Maybe it's Roelke, Chloe thought, before remembering that she hadn't given him the number. Ariel stared at the phone like she'd never seen such a contraption before.

Chloe picked it up. "Ariel Grzegorczyk's home."

"Chloe?" The voice was male.

Maybe it *is* Roelke, Chloe thought, before realizing that the voice belonged to Jay. I really need to knock off that waiting-by-the-phone thing, she thought irritably. "We just got here," she said. "Any news?"

"The police issued a preliminary statement. A wound on Everett's head matches a gear wheel up by the distributor."

"Maybe he tripped," Chloe suggested. "Or had a heart attack and fell."

"They don't know if that injury caused his death."

"I think it takes more time to get an official ruling."

"Yeah. And actually, that's not why I called. Word is spreading like wildfire. Everett's exhibition will still open tonight, but his friends are going to gather early for a potluck/wake kind of thing."

Chloe shared that news with her companions. "You guys want to go?"

"Absolutely," Owen said.

"Yes," Ariel echoed. "We definitely should do that."

"We'll be there," Chloe told Jay. "Thanks for calling."

Ariel shrugged out of her coat and tossed it on the sofa. "I should make a hotdish."

Chloe almost smiled. Hotdish—a good Minnesota woman's instinctive offering. "I'll give you a hand, but do you mind if I use your phone first?"

Ariel waved a hand: *Help yourself.* Owen followed her to the cubbyhole-kitchen, giving Chloe a semblance of privacy.

She dialed the operator and explained that she wanted to charge a long-distance call to her home number. The call went through quickly. "Eagle Police Department, Officer Deardorff speaking."

"Skeet? It's Chloe Ellefson. I thought Roelke was on duty this afternoon."

"He called in sick."

"He did?" Chloe's eyebrows rose. "Okay. Thanks."

She disconnected, dialed zero, and placed another call. After the eighth ring the operator said, "Your party isn't answering."

"Yeah," Chloe said. "Thanks."

When she wandered back to the kitchen, Ariel was staring into her cupboards. She turned, blinking as if surprised to see Chloe in her home. "Um … no luck?"

"I was trying to check in with a friend of mine, but he didn't answer. What are you looking for?"

Ariel looked dazed. "Well, my mom made hotdish with ground beef, frozen corn, tater tots, and canned mushroom soup."

"You're missing an ingredient?"

"All of them. I could make red jello with sliced bananas and green grapes instead, but I don't have any jello." Ariel looked stricken. "I don't have any jello! I should always have jello and tater tots for when somebody dies!"

Chloe hugged her friend. "Sweetie, jello and tater tots don't matter."

Owen watched with concern. "Ariel, do you go to church? Maybe we could call your pastor."

"I haven't been to church since moving to the city." Ariel pulled away from Chloe's embrace and swiped at her eyes.

"Why don't you call Toby?" Chloe suggested.

Ariel nodded slowly. "Well … yes. I should do that. He'll be home by now." Clutching her elbows, arms folded across her chest, she headed toward the phone. A moment later the murmur of conversation drifted to the kitchen.

Owen said quietly, "She's in bad shape."

"Just being in the mill made her anxious enough without … you know."

"It feels like we walked into *The Twilight Zone*." Owen settled onto a barstool. "I just can't imagine what happened to Everett."

"Would he have gone to the mill alone?"

"He's been going there for years." Owen took an apple from a bowl and began turning it in his hands. "Jay knows the buildings as well as anybody, but all he sees are the historic structures and the stories they can tell."

Chloe leaned against the sink. "Doesn't that about cover it?"

"Everett's take was unique. He took hundreds of photographs to document the Washburn Mill and everything left inside. But he also sees beauty there ... " Owen faltered. "He *saw* beauty there. He was an industrial historian with an artist's eye."

"This sounds like a cliché, but can you think of any reason why somebody would want to hurt him?"

"*No.* He was a great guy." Owen's eyes glistened, and he blinked furiously. "His courses were tough, but he was a good professor. Nothing made him happier than seeing his students get excited about historic buildings and stuff ... *God.* Where am I going to find a new advisor?"

Owen's bewildered grief hurt Chloe's heart. "The police will figure out who did this. I'm dating a cop and believe me, once they start an investigation, they don't let go."

"Everett didn't deserve something like this. I want his killer caught. *Fast.*"

"Maybe nobody actually killed him," Chloe said. "Maybe Everett had a heart attack in the mill, and the ... the tenants didn't know what to do, so they hid the body. Sister Mary Jude said that happened once before."

"Sister Mary Jude wants to believe the best about everyone, but I have a feeling that Everett happened to cross the wrong path at the wrong time. Maybe he startled some frat boys who'd snuck into the mill for a party last night. Or maybe one of the homeless people went berserk. Some of them are mentally ill." Owen shook his head.

49

"A cop named Crandall seemed pretty sure that one of the residents attacked Dr. Whyte," Chloe said. "Have you met Officer Crandall?"

Owen rotated the apple again. "Sure. The cops patrol through when they can. And Sister Mary Jude is there almost every day, trying to talk one more crazy into leaving the mill or something."

Chloe profoundly wished that Ariel had been given another project to work on. *Any* other project. It was hard to imagine a task that her friend was less suited for.

Which is why I'm here, she reminded herself. She and Ariel were friends, but at the heart of Ariel's invitation to visit was a plea for help. Their class at Cooperstown had been small—just fourteen people. During the two-year Museum Studies program they'd learned to work collaboratively, letting each member of the group shine in his or her own way. It was nice to think that the bonds forged back then still remained strong.

Ariel plodded back into the kitchen. "Thanks for suggesting the call, Chloe. Talking to my brother helped a lot." She pushed a loose strand of hair away from her face. "I still don't know what to take to the potluck, though."

"We'll improvise," Chloe said firmly. "What are those?" She pointed at a pile of old cookbooks on the counter.

"I've been collecting Gold Medal cookbooks. And some are from the Pillsbury Bake-Off. Pillsbury's mill is right across the river. We can't exclude their story just because they were a Gold Medal competitor. Both helped make Minneapolis the flour-milling capital of the world."

"I'll tell you what," Chloe said. "If you throw together a salad, I'll bake something."

While Ariel rummaged in the crispers, Chloe began shuffling through the cookbooks. Halfway through she paused. "Oh *my*. Look at this." She held up a booklet featuring the 1966 champions of the Pillsbury Busy Lady Bake-Off. A color photograph of a chocolate Bundt cake, cut to show gooey chocolate oozing from the center, graced the cover.

Ariel emerged from the fridge with a glorious purple cabbage in hand. "That's the Tunnel of Fudge Cake. It's probably the most famous Bake-Off recipe of all time."

"This is the one, then."

"I actually bought all of the ingredients a while ago. I thought it would be fun to serve at a planning meeting. But I don't really bake."

"I do." Chloe skimmed the instructions, glanced at the clock, and nodded. She had just enough time. Since Ariel had the nutrition end of things covered, she'd take charge of comfort food.

———

Daylight was fading when Roelke parked on Lincoln Avenue. A news van from the local ABC affiliate was parked near the Kosciuszko monument. A young man talked into a microphone while a cameraman panned from reporter to an impromptu memorial. Roelke didn't move until the reporter had finished his standup and the van pulled away.

Something cold squeezed Roelke's chest as he got out of his truck. The statue, depicting General Tadeusz Kosciuszko seated on a prancing horse, had long been a place for Polish-Americans to congregate on festival days. A place for the more recently arrived Mexican and South American parents to rendezvous with their kids after playtime. A place for friends and romantics to meet. Now, this was where Officer Rick Almirez had been murdered.

Bouquets of flowers lay against the statue. Candles flickered in *luminarias* and glass holders. Someone had thrust a simple cross into the hard pile of snow left by the last plow. The flowers were good. And maybe the cross would comfort Rick's family. Roelke stared at it, trying to find some drop of solace for himself. Nothing, nada, zip. Although he'd lapsed years ago, he too had been raised in the Catholic Church. So, he thought, where was God when somebody executed Rick? He looked at the basilica, kitty-corner down the street. The golden dome, which towered over the working-class houses surrounding it, glowed on sunny days. Now, at twilight, even the dome looked bleak. Cars whizzed past, the drivers uncaring.

Finally Roelke turned away, trying to figure out why he was here. Seriously, what could he accomplish that the detectives, with all their resources, could not? Well, maybe keeping busy would keep him from going nuts. Maybe getting a complete picture of his friend's last moments would make him feel better. I just need to understand what happened, he thought.

He stared at the street. As soon as Rick had been found, all hell would have broken loose. The first responder would have made that most dreaded call: *Officer down.* With an ambulance on the way, everybody within phone or handy-talkie or blue light range would descend—patrolmen, detectives, sergeants, captains. Somebody would establish a staging area for the press. Somebody would set a perimeter and organize officers for yard searches, because bad guys were often too panicked or too dumb to hide incriminating evidence well. With any luck ...

A gray sedan pulled over and parked nearby. Two people were in the car but only one emerged—Dobry. He added a bouquet of flowers to the shrine, stood for a moment with head bowed, and crossed himself. Only then did he acknowledge Roelke's presence. "Hey."

"Hey. Didn't expect to see you again today."

"Tina bought the flowers. She thought we should ... you know." Dobry pulled out his cigarettes and tapped one from the pack.

"I talked to Malloy a while ago. You reported that Rick was drinking?"

"Had to. I told you that Cox reported the missed mark."

"You could have—"

"What? Lied? Rick would never have expected that."

Roelke struggled to make his tone more conversational. "No, he wouldn't. I just hate having people saying he did something wrong."

"Yeah. You hear anything new from Malloy?"

"Malloy told me to take myself home like a good little police officer."

"Me too, more or less. He put me on desk duty for a while. Said I was too close to Rick." Dobry scowled. "I should be out there."

"You should," Roelke agreed. Dobry was a good cop. He knew he looked like Opie on *The Andy Griffith Show*, and from the day he'd started the academy, he'd worked extra hard to prove himself.

"There is some good news. One of the guys crawling over the neighborhood found the gun in a trash can a couple of blocks from here."

Roelke felt a tiny spark of hope. "That's great!"

"It's a start, anyway." Dobry turned his back to the wind and lit up.

Roelke stared at a bouquet of frozen roses. "Listen, Dobry ... will you keep telling me what you hear around the station? Being on the outside is making me crazy."

Dobry exhaled a plume of smoke. "Of course."

"Jody said Rick called her at one and said something about going to a bar."

"Probably just a routine bar check." Dobry shook his head. "But *something* weird happened. I wish to God I knew what was going on with Rick last night."

"I found out he proposed to Jody."

"He did? He decided to pop the question, and he didn't tell us about it?"

Roelke didn't want to admit that the secrecy bothered him, too. "I guess he wanted to see what Jody said first," he said.

Dobry's eyes narrowed. "Well, if ever a guy might decide he deserved a cold one—"

"No."

"Stuff like that happens, Roelke. We all had a good time at the reception, Jody agreed to marry him, and *then* Rick started a shift. Would you blame the guy for celebrating with a brewski?"

"Shut it right there." Roelke wished he'd kept news of the proposal to himself.

A bus belched to a stop at the next corner. Half a dozen people emerged and began trudging home.

"Listen," Dobry said, "I can't leave Tina sitting in the car too long. She's pretty shook up."

"Sure." Roelke glanced at the car. Tina sat looking out the side window, smoking a cigarette of her own. He didn't know Dobry's wife well, but she struck him as aloof, brittle, hard to please.

Or, he thought, maybe she just doesn't like hanging around with cops. Sort of like Chloe. But he didn't have room to think about Chloe right now.

"Hey," Dobry said, "we're good, right?"

"Sure. We're good."

After the Baniks drove away, Roelke shoved his hands in his pockets, thinking. What bar had Rick been planning to visit after hanging up with Jody? Maybe someone there had called in a problem. Maybe that problem hadn't ended at the bar. Maybe some pissed-off asshole had followed Rick after he left. Or maybe Rick had spotted a car that belonged to somebody with a warrant, parked outside the bar. It was amazing how many seriously bad guys—dealers, kidnappers, killers—got arrested because of an expired registration, a missing taillight, or a recognizable vehicle parked in plain sight.

Roelke balled his fists. There's nothing more I can do here, he thought. Dobry will keep me posted. I might as well go home.

Just one problem. He still didn't feel like going home.

Roelke got back into his truck and pulled an old map from the glove box. He hadn't worked the district in a while, but he knew this area—knew it well.

It was time to reacquaint himself with the old neighborhood.

# SEVEN

As Owen drove to the gallery that night, Chloe struggled with a nagging sense of concern about Roelke. He'd been in a strange mood after the wedding, he'd called in sick, and he wasn't answering his telephone. She didn't know what was going on, and she didn't like it.

People were gathering in the atrium by the time they arrived. Ariel and Chloe found room for their culinary offerings on a table near the door. Ariel had concocted a colorful salad, and when Chloe cut pieces of the Tunnel of Fudge Cake, two young men grabbed the paper plates out of her hand. "We done good," she assured Ariel.

A photograph of Everett Whyte sat on an easel near the food table. Ariel turned away, with Owen on her heels, but Chloe stepped closer. She wanted a mental picture of the living professor to nudge aside the image currently lodged in her brain. The photo showed Dr. Whyte with a thick thatch of white hair, blue eyes, and a ruddy, sun-creased face. He was a small man, standing in front of a grimy door, holding his own camera. He was half-turned, as if someone had called his name and snapped the shot. The professor's grin resembled that of a young boy about to enter an amusement park.

"I can't believe he's gone."

Chloe found Jay at her shoulder holding two glasses of white wine. When he offered one, she gratefully accepted.

"This is a great picture," she said. "Professor Whyte looks like a man who spent his years doing work he loved."

"That he did. And he wasn't slowing down. He'd been dreaming about preserving the mill site for years. Where other people saw obstacles, he saw only opportunity."

"I wish I'd had a chance to meet him."

"I just hope the whole consortium doesn't collapse now."

Chloe sipped her wine, regarding the mourners over the rim. The people talking in hushed clusters ranged from college kids to octogenarians. The group was predominantly male, which wasn't surprising; more men than women specialized in architectural history, and industrial history probably skewed even farther in that direction. But those gathered were of different races, dressed in Sunday finery and blue jeans and everything in between. The diversity said good things about Everett Whyte.

"I'll bet every person here will work to keep his dream of a mill museum alive," Chloe said. "What better way to honor his memory?"

"You're probably right, but even a short delay could cause enormous problems. We've developed a timeline that takes various grant deadlines into account."

"Is Ariel's interpretive plan proposal part of that?"

"It's the foundation. The very first step. Everything else flows from that."

"Ah." Chloe searched the crowd and saw Ariel talking to a beautiful young woman with long black ringlets wearing a purple ankle-length peasant skirt. "I'm worried about her," Chloe admitted. "Ariel has always been a bit … fragile. I promised to help brainstorm ideas, so we'll do that before I head home tomorrow evening, and I'll keep in touch with—"

"Everybody?" A young man with Asian features tapped a beer bottle with a spoon. "Thanks for coming. I'm one of Dr. Everett's graduate assistants. Was one." He cleared his throat. "He worked us hard, but he also made us think. The man could read an old building like a book. He … I … Thank you." He turned away.

A man wearing a gray suit and a truly ugly bowtie clapped the student on the shoulder before turning to the crowd. "All of us in the Public History Department are stunned by this tragedy. Professor Whyte can never be replaced. But his accomplishments will live on in the work of his students and friends, and in his photographs. In a few moments we'll open the doors to the public. On this terrible night, Everett's work will speak for him."

Formalities complete, Jay and Chloe wandered into the gallery: white walls, discreet lights, and a few black-and-chrome benches scattered about. An interpretive panel introduced *Beauty in Blight* with an artist's statement from Everett.

"Someone referred to the exhibit as *Beauty AND Blight* once." Jay chuckled. "Everett bellowed, 'Those things are one and the same! I'm trying to show why old buildings *matter*!'"

"I think I would have liked him," Chloe said wistfully.

She studied a large framed photograph of the towering Gold Medal Flour sign at sunset. The slanting rays struck not the letters, but a broken window in the top story of the head house just below. The juxtaposition of bold pride and cracked decay was poignant and evocative. "Wow."

"Everett had the eye," Jay agreed. "He wanted this exhibit to introduce the importance of our city's industrial heritage to a new audience."

Each photograph revealed loveliness and ruin in the same frame. Rusting machinery, crumbling concrete, and dangling belt drives were paired with vibrant graffiti, an iridescent pigeon sitting on a nest, textured limestone walls, a few weeds in a soup can vase left on a windowsill.

"I'm not much of a city person," Chloe murmured, "and I admit that before today I would never have used the word *beautiful* to describe urban blight, but…"

"Yeah."

She blew out a long breath. "Oh, I *really* hope Professor Whyte died of natural causes."

Jay lowered his voice. "The police asked me if I could think of any reason why someone would want to harm Everett."

"Can you?"

"Not really, but…" Jay looked pained. "I can't say the mill project isn't controversial."

"I assume the price tag is, shall we say, high?"

"Certainly some people would rather see the entire mill complex turned into high-rent condos or offices. Everett agreed that our project was only a part of a revitalization plan that's bigger than the mill museum itself, but he argued with anyone not ready to agree that the main mill structures provide a rare—unparalleled, really— opportunity to preserve and interpret a vital part of history." Jay rubbed his forehead wearily. "Lord, it's been a long day."

"It *has* been a long day." Chloe scanned the crowded room. "I imagine Ariel's more than ready to go home."

And so am I, she added silently, feeling the day's full weight press down. She'd had a late night at the wedding, an early drive to the Twin Cities, and then ... this. A hot bath and the dubious comfort of Ariel's sofa sounded too good for words.

And with any luck, she'd even get Roelke to pick up his telephone before she turned in.

———

At almost eleven p.m., Roelke admitted defeat. He'd visited the Rusty Nail, quickly flashing his EPD badge. The bartender's attitude had bordered on surly: Yeah, Rick Almirez had shown up in the wee hours of Saturday morning. Yeah, he'd ordered a beer.

"What time did he get here?"

"I don't know. And I got customers waiting."

Roelke glared at him. "I asked what time Officer Rick Almirez arrived. Think—*hard*."

"Lulu!" the man shouted. "What time did you leave on Saturday morning?"

A brassy blonde wiping the bar paused. "One forty-five. My ride was waiting."

"Didn't you bump into that cop when you left?"

"Yeah. He was coming in, I was going out."

The bartender turned back to Roelke. "There you go. He came in at one forty-five."

One forty-five, Roelke thought. That made no sense. Five minutes before his mark? No cop in his right mind would settle down for a Policeman's Coke five minutes before he was due to call in.

"You done here, officer?"

Roelke was getting very tired of this asshole's tone. "No, I am not. Did Officer Ramirez often come in and drink?"

"There's a first time for everything."

"Who did Officer Ramirez talk to while he was here?"

The bartender shrugged. "I have no idea."

Yeah, Roelke thought, and I'm the Pope. He'd never met a bartender who didn't know exactly what was going on in his or her tavern.

"I'll be back," Roelke said. He liked having the last word.

Outside, he leaned against the wall, feeling the cold creep through his parka. Rick had been drinking in that grubby bar while on duty, just moments before he should have been at the call box; just hours before he was shot in the head. Why? *Why?*

There were seven other bars in Rick's beat area. Roelke visited every one. Most were largely indistinguishable from any other Milwaukee tavern, where locals gathered for a cold brew or a fish fry or a game of darts. Some of the bartenders remembered him, some didn't, a couple were new. One of the old-timers glared when Roelke asked if Rick had ever ordered a drink. "I oughta punch you in the mouth. Rick Almirez was a good cop. You were his friend. You should know better than to ask a question like that."

The man's anger was a comfort. "I'm still Rick's friend," Roelke said. "And I had to ask."

Rick had hit several taverns after his shift started at midnight. He'd been called to one to break up a fight between two brothers. He'd been called to another to handle a young couple's screaming match. At another he'd escorted a few underage drinkers to the door. Each situation had been resolved without evident complication. No one remembered seeing Rick between one and two in the morning. No one told Roelke anything that would explain where Rick had gone after he called Jody.

Okay, Roelke thought, Plan B.

He drove back to the district office and parked where he could see people coming and going. Eight minutes later an orange AMC Gremlin pulled in. The woman who emerged was heavyset, with a helmet of gray hair and a purse the size of Rhode Island.

Roelke got out and went to meet her. "Olivette? It's Roelke Mc—"

"Oh, *hon.*" Olivette put a hand on his arm. "I'm so sorry about Officer Almirez."

"Yeah." Roelke swallowed, cleared his throat. Olivette was a former prison matron who'd transferred to the district after an inmate threw her against a wall, and her husband insisted that the MPD find something else for her to do. When it came to Olivette, no-nonsense and straightforward worked best. "Did you work graveyard shift last night?"

"Yes."

"What was Rick's last call?"

"I don't know."

"Will you get a list of his calls for me?"

Her eyes narrowed. "You should leave this to the detectives. They know what they're doing."

"I know they do. But Rick was my friend, and I've got to ..." He spread his hands, out of words. The com center was staffed mostly by old guys easing toward retirement, plus any female cop temporarily benched for being pregnant, but there wasn't a soul who wouldn't want to help if Olivette snapped her fingers. She knew all the cops at the district—their quirks, their habits. When rookies screwed up on the radio, she quietly explained the problem instead of scolding or complaining to a sergeant. She'd helped Roelke out of his share of bungles in his early days with the MPD. Either she'd help him now or she wouldn't.

After a moment she opened her purse and pulled out a notepad and pen. "Write down your phone number," she said. "I'll get back to you."

———

"I was looking forward to girl talk tonight," Ariel said when she and Chloe got back to the apartment. "But I'm ready for bed. Do you mind?"

"God, no," Chloe assured her. "It's been a long and horrid day."

After Ariel disappeared up the stairs, Chloe tried calling Roelke again. What the heck? she thought, listening through ten, eleven, twelve rings. No answer.

Chloe brooded about that as she pulled her sleeping bag from its stuff sack and settled on the sofa. Her relationship with Roelke McKenna had its difficult moments, but he was unfailingly steady. This unexplained disappearance was starting to scare her.

She nibbled her lower lip for a moment, then placed another call. "Hey, Libby?" she said, when Roelke's cousin answered. "Sorry to bother you, but I was just wondering if you'd heard from Roelke today." Libby and her two kids were all the family Roelke had. If he was sick or hurt, Libby would know.

"Nope," Libby said. "But I was out on a winter hike with Justin's scout troop all day, followed by a pizza party. Why? Is everything okay?"

"He and I just miscommunicated somehow. I'm visiting a friend and have been trying to reach him."

"If you're away, he's probably hanging out with friends, too. Just a sec." Her next words were muffled. "Justin, I told you to get ready for your bath. You are making a very bad choice right now." Then to Chloe again, "Sorry."

"No, I'm sorry to bother you. Talk to you later." Chloe hung up thinking, Libby's probably right. Roelke had reconnected with old buds at the wedding. Maybe they'd made impromptu plans to continue the reunion. She smiled, remembering him joking gleefully with Rick and Dobry.

Then she remembered the grin Roelke and Lucia Bliss had shared onstage during her seductive rendition of "Slow Hand." Had that glance been friendly, or salacious? Maybe—

"Oh, screw that," Chloe muttered. She was not going to wade in that water. What she *was* going to do was keep calling Roelke until she reached him.

———

Weariness pulled at Roelke's eyelids as he left the interstate and hit the secondary highways that would take him home. Well, no surprise there. Twenty hours had passed since the phone rang. Twenty hours since he'd heard Jody crying over the line. Twenty hours since he'd learned that his best friend was dead.

He slowed when he saw flashing lights ahead. A Waukesha County deputy had pulled over a dark van. As he drew close he recognized Deputy Marge Bandacek. There were at least two guys in the van, maybe more.

Roelke stopped and rolled down the window. "Need help?" he asked quietly, praying that she did not.

Marge hitched up her duty belt. "I got it."

Roelke nodded and drove on. He was too exhausted to be of much good to anybody, especially Marge. She could be a pain in the ass, and he had no energy to deal with that right now. None.

When he finally reached Palmyra, he parked in the lot behind his walkup flat. He heard his phone ringing as he trudged up the stairs. "Jesus," he muttered. It was almost two in the morning. He unlocked the door and walked back to his tiny living room. "McKenna here."

"Roelke?"

He dropped onto the sofa and pushed one knuckle against his forehead.

"It's me," Chloe said.

"Yeah."

Another pause. "I'm sorry to call so late." Chloe's voice had grown stiff. "But I was getting worried. I knew you were expecting me to call, and—"

"Rick is dead."

The sharp intake of her breath sounded over the line. "*What?* Oh my God. What *happened?* He was on duty?"

Roelke's eyes began to sting. "Yeah. Listen, Chloe, I—I just can't—I've been up since—"

"It's okay. I can hear the details later, it's just that … I'm sorry, Roelke. I'm so, so sorry."

"Yeah."

"I'll get on the road first thing in the morning. If I leave by—"

"You don't have to."

"I want to be there."

Another pause stretched over three hundred miles of phone line. He knew she was waiting for him to say something. But he couldn't find the right words, and besides, his throat ached so much he could hardly speak. "I've got to get some sleep," he managed. "I'm on at eight."

"Okay. Get some rest. I'll see you tomorrow."

This time he couldn't push even a monosyllable from his throat. Seconds ticked by. Then he hung up the phone.

# EIGHT

CHLOE WOKE SUNDAY MORNING to a percolator's burble. All of yesterday's horror and sadness flooded back. Her eyes filled and she curled down in the sleeping bag, wishing she could stay there all day. Comforting Ariel had been a struggle, but she'd failed Roelke. Chloe flexed her fingers, remembering how she'd clenched the receiver, willing her strength to somehow travel through the line to him. Damn, she thought, cursing the phone, the distance. She hadn't known Rick Almirez for long, but she'd liked him a lot. *Be patient with that guy*, he'd whispered. *You're good for him.*

*I'll be there for Roelke*, she promised Rick silently. *If he'll let me, I'll be there.*

The scent of coffee wormed through her nylon cocoon, and she had a long drive and difficult homecoming ahead of her. She unzipped the sleeping bag and stumbled to her feet.

Ariel turned from the counter. "I hope I didn't wake you."

"I needed to get up." Chloe wriggled into jeans and padded into the kitchen. "Did you get any rest?"

Ariel handed her a glass of orange juice. "Some. Say, do you talk in your sleep? I thought I heard you in the middle of the night."

Lovely. "Sorry I disturbed you," Chloe said. "I was on the phone, actually. I'd been trying to reach this guy I've been seeing."

Ariel's eyebrows lifted. "Sounds serious."

"It's kinda serious," Chloe admitted. "His name is Roelke McKenna."

"Keep talking. Fruit and yogurt okay for breakfast?"

"Perfect."

"So, Roelke McKenna." Ariel disappeared behind the refrigerator door. "Does he work at Old World?"

"No. He's a police officer."

"Really?"

"Really."

Ariel took that in. "Not what I would have guessed."

"Nor anyone else. Including me."

Ariel began slicing bananas. "He must be a good guy."

Something beneath Chloe's ribs tightened, like a knot being cinched tighter. "Yeah. He's a good guy. Speaking of guys, is it just my imagination, or does Owen have a crush on you? Anything going on there?"

Pink spots appeared on Ariel's cheeks. "He hasn't asked me out or anything."

"Would you say yes if he did?"

"I don't know. It might complicate things. He doesn't work for the MHS, but he's very involved in the mill project. And ..." She shrugged. "He's younger than I am."

"Roelke's four years younger than I am," Chloe told her. "And at least Owen's a history nerd. He's a born interpreter."

"True." Ariel almost smiled as she slid onto a stool at the breakfast bar. "But back to your middle-of-the-night phone call. Is everything okay?"

"He had terrible news. His best friend Rick, also a cop, was killed on duty sometime early Saturday morning."

"Oh, *no*." Ariel squeezed Chloe's hand. "I'm so sorry."

"Thanks." Chloe wiped her eyes. "Me, too. Roelke is really torn up. And ... I feel like I need to be there."

Ariel's eyes widened slightly. A flash of—what? Disappointment? Anxiety?—appeared, then was gone.

Chloe rubbed her forehead. Shit. "I'm sorry, Ariel. After what happened yesterday ... and we haven't had a chance to catch up, much less talk about the interpretive plan."

"Of course you have to go. Don't worry about the interpretive plan."

The percolator's little signal light turned from red to green. Chloe got up and poured them both a mug of steaming coffee. "Do you have spare copies of any of the research material?"

"I do, actually. I've kept a master file *and* a working file where I can scribble."

"If you're willing to loan me the master, I'll read through it when I get home. We can kick ideas around over the phone." Chloe sat back down. "This isn't the weekend we'd planned."

"Not quite." Ariel looked wan. "But I understand. Maybe we can try again sometime."

"We will," Chloe said firmly. She added silently, As soon as I'm sure Roelke is okay.

———

Roelke scowled at the typewriter in the EPD's cramped squad room. He was not a great typer at the best of times. Which this was not. He was about ready to heave the machine through the window.

He got up and poured himself another cup of stale coffee. It was after one o'clock. Chloe must be getting close to home, if she'd truly gotten an early start. If she came at all, after he'd practically hung up on her.

Well, if she's mad, she'll have to be mad, he thought. He had to focus on getting through this shift so he could get back to Milwaukee. An Eagle citizen had called earlier, concerned about a vacuum cleaner salesman. "When was the last time you heard of someone selling vacuum cleaners door-to-door?" she'd demanded. "He might be casing the neighborhood." Roelke had found the salesman and informed him of the village policy against soliciting. The guy had apologized respectfully and driven away.

Filling out the damn form was taking longer than handling the incident itself. Roelke dropped back into the chair, reached for the bottle of Wite-Out, and unscrewed the lid. The tiny brush emerged dry, scattering white crumbs. "Dammit!" he exploded. He got up again and stormed to his locker. He didn't like to mess with the clerk's stuff and always kept a few basic supplies stashed for emergencies.

*You are such a Boy Scout!* Rick hooted in his memory. A longstanding joke.

*I try to be prepared, like you were NOT when whatever SOB pulled a gun on you*, Roelke snapped back silently.

And immediately felt worse.

You have to focus on Eagle right now, not Milwaukee, he told himself. But when he wrenched open the locker door, the woman in the photo on the shelf smiled down at him. Erin Litkowski was a pretty redhead he'd met on a domestic call back in his Milwaukee days. Her sister had given Roelke the photo after Erin fled the state to escape her husband. Roelke kept it in his locker as a reminder that for every victim of violence, there were loved ones who suffered, too.

Like I need a reminder of that, Roelke thought. He stared grimly at the photo. Maybe he should have stayed in Milwaukee instead of moving out to Eagle. He'd wanted to be close to his family—Libby and her kids—but Rick was family, too. Like a brother, really. And—

He twitched when the phone rang, both relieved for the interruption and dreading another call about errant salesmen. He dropped back in his chair and grabbed the receiver. "Eagle Police Department, Officer McKenna speaking."

"Hi, hon. It's Olivette. I've got that list of Rick's calls. Pretty ordinary stuff." She ran through the calls Roelke had already discovered in his own round of neighborhood bars. "And I have his last call. The owner of Gus's Market was worried about some kids loitering in front of his shop."

Roelke knew the place. "What time was that?"

"Three-seventeen in the a.m."

Roelke beat a pencil against the counter, unable to find anything meaningful in the new info.

"I'm on days this week. You need anything else, you just call."

"Thanks, Olivette. I really appreciate it."

Roelke hung up and pulled a pack of index cards from his pocket. On one he wrote what he knew of Rick's last hours:

*Midnight—shift starts*

*12:50—calls in on mark*
*1:00—calls Jody from payphone*
*1:50—misses his mark; spotted drinking at the Rusty Nail*

*2:50—calls in on mark*
*3:17—responds to last call at market*
*3:45—report of shot fired*

Just one shot fired, Roelke thought. A single shot to the back of the head. Had Rick turned his back on someone he trusted? If he was hurrying, as the timeline suggested, had he not been as attentive as he should have been?

But Rick was careful. Never sloppy. *Never.*

Roelke slapped another index card on the counter and began to write.

*1. verify Rick was actually drinking at Rusty Nail*
*2. check call box history—pattern?*
*3. FI reports?*
*4.*

A man wearing a Sunday suit walked through the front door. Roelke shot to his feet. "Chief! Is there a problem?" Sometimes the good people of Eagle, who liked the chief as much as his officers did, called him at home instead of contacting the PD.

"I came to see you, McKenna," Chief Naborski said. He pulled over the clerk's chair and sat down. "I heard about what happened. I know that was your old beat, and that this officer was a friend. How are you holding up?"

Chief Naborski was not a man for empty pleasantries or BS, so Roelke had no idea how to answer that. "I'm holding it together," he said finally. "But I'd like to take a few days off. I called some of the part-timers and got all my shifts covered for the week."

Naborski looked pensive. He was of medium build, but one look at his eyes would deter anyone stupid enough to consider taking him on. "What do you have in mind?"

"I need to be in Milwaukee."

Naborski ran a hand over his gray hair, which was buzzed military style. It reminded Roelke that the chief had survived the Korean War, and therefore nothing in Eagle—or Milwaukee—was likely to faze the man now. The chief said, "You know they've got their best guys working the investigation."

"But the thing is, sir, I really don't give a rat's ass who's working the case. I need to be part of it."

The older man tipped his chair back on two legs. "Why?"

"Because Officer Almirez was my partner once, and my best friend."

"Not good enough."

Oh, I'm just getting started, Roelke thought. He leaned forward, elbows on knees. "I know the way Rick worked. How he thought. How he interacted with people. Also, I know the beat. I haven't been gone all that long—people will remember me. Some of them will be more willing to talk to me now, since I'm not MPD anymore."

Naborski eyed him for another long moment. Then his chair thumped back to neutral. "Okay. I'll give you a week. After that, I want you back here on duty with your head screwed on straight."

"Yessir."

"But I do not know a thing about this, got it?"

"Yessir."

"And you listen to me." Naborski's gaze was intense. "Do not do anything illegal. Do not do anything that will cause trouble for the Milwaukee guys. Do not do anything that will reflect poorly on this department."

"I won't."

"And do not let the way you feel make you stupid."

Roelke swallowed, wondering if that ship had already sailed. "I won't."

"Switch the phone to the sheriff's line and skip the rest of your shift." Chief Naborski stood. He let his hand rest on Roelke's shoulder for a moment before leaving.

Roelke turned back to the typewriter, figuring he should at least finish the report before taking off. He had just claimed victory when Chloe walked in. Her coat was unzipped and her cheeks were flushed. Her eyes were uncertain.

"Hey," he said.

Chloe wrapped him into a hug. He felt her arms squeezing his shoulders and smelled her hair, and it was all so good that it scared him. He pulled away. "You didn't have to cut your trip short."

"I wanted to be here for you."

He didn't have room for that. No room for her. Not while Rick's killer was still roaming Milwaukee. But he didn't know how to explain, so he didn't say anything.

Chloe bit her lip and looked away. Finally she said, "I also wanted to visit Jody. Were you planning to see her today?"

"I was, but…" He waved a vague hand. "I can't take you. I'll be staying in Milwaukee for a while. I don't know how long. I've got some people I need to see tonight."

"How about if I follow you there?" she said evenly. "I know you're off duty. I ran into Chief Naborski outside."

Roelke didn't want to imagine what that conversation might have covered. "Sure," he told her. "I'm going to change out of uniform. Then we can go."

*Be patient with that guy. You're good for him.* Rick's final words to Chloe rang in her head as she drove to Milwaukee. "I'm trying," she said, on the off-chance that Rick was hovering nearby, "but I sure could use some help. You knew him a lot longer than I have. What do I say to the man?"

She waited, but evidently Rick wasn't ready or able to whisper advice. Or maybe, she thought, he doesn't know what I should say to Roelke right now either. Chloe felt fatigue tug at her. Maybe she should have stayed in Minneapolis after all. She'd left a friend who wanted her company and driven five hours to be with one who, evidently, did not. Well, at least she could offer condolences to Rick's girlfriend.

Jody lived in an apartment complex in the southwest suburbs. Chloe managed to reach the parking lot without losing her guide, and parked her Pinto next to Roelke's truck. They got out of their vehicles.

"Shall we go in?" Chloe asked.

"Sure," Roelke said, but he was watching a beat-up gray Datsun turn into the lot. Sergeant Lucia Bliss emerged.

"Chloe, you go on ahead," Roelke said. "Jody's apartment is the first on the left. The one with artwork on the door. I'll be along."

———

"Hey, Bliss." Roelke strode across the lot to meet her. They met with a quick hug, a reminder that Bliss was not actually one of the guys.

"McKenna. Good to see you."

"You, too." Being around people who had known Rick helped, somehow. Bliss wore her uniform, but her usual attitude of capability was gone. Her eyes were red. The knot of hair behind her head looked haphazard. She raised a hand to brush an escaping strand from her eyes.

Roelke blinked as something winked in the sun—a diamond ring, worn above a gold band. "Bliss, did you get married?"

"Hadn't you heard?" She regarded the rings. "Almost a year now."

"Is he a cop?"

"He's a real estate agent."

Roelke glanced to the door where Chloe—the smart, strong, and beautiful woman he cared so much about—had disappeared. "Is it hard, being married to someone who doesn't work law enforcement?"

"Yeah," Bliss admitted. "It can be."

"But you think it can work?"

She sighed. "I sure as hell hope so."

Hardly a ringing endorsement, Roelke thought.

Bliss leaned into her car and retrieved a glass serving dish. "I brought a tuna casserole. I can do notifications on the job when I have to, but when it's personal, I never know what to say. Were you on your way in or out?"

"In, but—hold on a minute, will you? I haven't talked to anybody from the MPD today. What's the news?"

"You heard they found the gun?"

"Dobry told me that last night, but he didn't know the details."

"An American Derringer, twenty-five auto."

Not surprising, Roelke thought. On the street, .22 revolvers or .25 automatics were cheap and available, and he'd pulled a lot of them off bad guys. Crooks rarely bothered to clean their guns, so they were generally pieces of crap. But they were sturdy enough to work anyway and small enough to hide in a pocket.

"Any prints?" he asked.

"Nope."

"Damn."

"Yeah." Bliss watched passing traffic. Roelke watched her, alert to something in her expression. Finally she said, "There's something else. They ID'd the gun."

"They did?" Roelke blinked. That was more than he'd expected.

"It came from Evidence."

A door slammed behind them. A siren wailed in the distance. A delivery truck pulled into the lot. And all the while Roelke tried to process those four little words. "It came from Evidence?"

"Yeah."

"The gun that killed Rick came from Goddamned Evidence? *Our* district Evidence?"

"Yeah," she said bleakly. "Perfect match. Ballistics and serial."

Roelke's fist came down on the roof of her car so hard that a white flash of pain streaked his vision. Bliss flinched. He turned away.

"McKenna," Bliss tried.

He kept walking, beyond the end of the parking lot this time, not stopping until confronted by the indifferent brick of an apartment wall. He leaned over, hands on knees, struggling to find enough oxygen. *Jesus*. The gun that killed Rick came from Evidence.

Whenever cops took a gun away from a bad guy, it was fired once and inventoried. Cops recorded the unique tool markings made on the casings when the bullet left the barrel. The inventory noted what was known about the gun's make and provenance, including the serial number. The record would show who'd owned the gun when it came into custody.

But that wasn't the point.

When he could, he straightened again and walked back.

"It's not just you," Bliss said quietly. "Nobody knows what to think. What to do."

"Does the press have that juicy tidbit?"

She shrugged helplessly. "Not if the brass can help it, I'm sure."

"Because you know what this means," Roelke said flatly.

"Maybe not. There might be some other explanation."

Roelke shook his head. Nice try, he thought, but, no. Once a gun was inventoried, it was kept in the locked room until guys from the Property Bureau downtown came to collect it.

That meant the SOB who shot Rick Almirez in the back of the head and left him to die in the road, was a cop.

# NINE

"I GUESS WE KNOW why Rick turned his back on the shooter," Roelke said bitterly. "It probably *was* someone he knew. Someone he worked with."

Bliss jerked her head toward the apartment building. "Should we tell Jody?"

The idea of telling Jody that her fiancé had been killed by another cop made Roelke feel nauseated. "No. Not until there's more to tell. Like, the bastard is in custody."

"Okay. I won't say anything."

Roelke leaned against the car and folded his arms. "What the hell is going on, Bliss? What could Rick have done to make someone want to do this? Everybody *liked* Rick. Didn't they?"

"Yeah, everybody got along with Rick."

"Was he working on something sensitive? Drug stuff?" It wasn't unheard of for a cop to seize six bags of cocaine and inventory five. Or for a couple of guys to bust some underage drinking party, confiscate the booze, and go back to the garage for a party of their own. It didn't happen often, but it happened.

"Not that I know of."

"If Rick saw somebody on the take, he would have gotten in their face about it. He had no tolerance for that kind of crap."

"That would be easier to believe if he hadn't been caught boozing it up himself right before he died." Bliss raised both palms to deflect his glare. "If Rick was hanging out at a bar, there must have been a good reason. But that's not what people are saying. Word's out that he'd just gotten engaged."

Dobry Banik has a big mouth, Roelke thought irritably.

"It's easy for some people to conclude that he was celebrating while on duty," Bliss was saying. "And if he'd do that…"

"Let's get back to the gun." Roelke squeezed the words past clenched teeth. "Who had access to the Evidence room? Did a key go missing?"

"I don't know."

"Well, can you ask around?"

Bliss worried her lower lip. "Heikinen came to roll call and barked at the whole shift. Basically told us to keep our mouths shut and our noses where they belonged until the killer gets caught. I can't just go poking around."

Roelke stared at her right eye. "For God's sake, Bliss! It's Rick we're talking about here."

"I *know* that," she snapped. "But even if I did manage to hear something, just what exactly would you do with it? Go and question somebody you don't have any right to question? My butt would end up on the kicking end of Heikinen's boot."

She had a point, but he wasn't willing to let go. "Could you ask your dad?"

"Are you out of your mind? My dad would never discuss anything like that with me. When it comes to police work, I'm just a lowly sergeant."

Roelke ground his teeth. Word was that Chief Bliss was a tightass. *His* dad had been a cop, too. Roelke understood that Bliss needed to protect her career. Still... "Just keep your ears open, okay? Please. Let me know what you hear."

"I will," Bliss promised. "He was my friend, too."

———

Chloe hadn't been sure what to make of "artwork" on someone's door, but when she saw a dozen masterpieces created by young hands and fingerpaint, she knew she'd found the right place.

Jody answered the chime, and her eyes lit with appreciation. "Chloe! It's so sweet of you to come."

The six-plus hours Chloe had spent behind the wheel that day were instantly worthwhile. "I was admiring the artwork. Nieces and nephews?"

"I teach kindergarten."

"You teach kindergarten?" Chloe's throat swelled. For some reason that made everything seem worse.

"Please, sit down." Jody indicated a plump sofa. "Want some coffee or tea? Or something to eat? People have brought all kinds of food."

"Tea would be great."

After Jody disappeared into the kitchen, Chloe sized up the apartment. The décor held muted tones of beige and rose, but more student art provided cheerful splashes of color. Two easy chairs matched the sofa, the twin bookcases hadn't been banged together from particle board, and the print of Lake Michigan shoreline on the opposite wall had been beautifully framed. A picture on the end table showed Rick and Jody facing each other in a crowd. Rick was holding Jody's waist and smiling at her with intense joy. Jody's hands rested on his shoulders, her head tipped back to meet his gaze.

Jody returned with steaming mugs. "That was taken at Summerfest. I think Rick decided to propose that day, even though it took him seven more months to work up the nerve."

Chloe felt a new fissure in her heart. "You two were engaged?"

"Oh, sorry—I assumed Roelke had told you." Jody reached for a tissue and blew her nose. "Rick asked me after the wedding reception, right before he went to work, actually. And you know what's terrible?"

*Everything,* Chloe wanted to say. "What?"

"All those months, I kept hoping that Rick wouldn't buy me a ring. I wanted to help pick it out, you know?"

"Sure."

"So he didn't buy me one. We were going to go look together. Then a few hours later he gets killed. Now I wish like *anything* I had a ring that he'd picked out for me."

Chloe reached for a tissue and blew her nose, too.

Jody used a spoon to squeeze her teabag. "Chloe, I want to say some things that I probably won't have the nerve to say later."

"Um, okay."

"Rick didn't propose for so long because he's—he was—a cop. And I'm not." Jody gave Chloe a level gaze. "You understand what I'm talking about?"

"I think so," Chloe said, although she wasn't sure.

"Once our relationship got serious, I thought about it a lot. We even took a couple of weeks away from each other because I needed to decide if I could handle it. And knowing that the person you love most might get killed every time he goes to work is only the beginning."

Do I want to hear this? Chloe wondered, but wanting didn't count; she needed to hear this. "Go on."

"Cops work all kinds of hours. They can get called in for emergencies, so it's hard to make plans. They don't make a lot of money, so they pick up odd shifts when they can."

Chloe thought of all the times she and Roelke had struggled to find time for a date. "I do know a little about that."

"All guys like Rick and Roelke and Dobry want to do is help people, you know? That's why they became cops. But they get sucked into all kinds of human misery, day after day after day. They don't want to bring it home, but they can't help it. And that can take a toll on the people they love."

Chloe remembered Dobry's wife, polite but distant.

"There are things they won't talk about. I don't mean secret stuff, I mean all the things they believe to their bones that no one can understand except another cop. Do you know what the divorce rate is for cops?"

"I do not."

"It's sky-high. Highest of all is a cop married to someone who isn't a cop—*God*." Jody abruptly put her mug down and tea sloshed over the rim. "I shouldn't be talking like this."

"It's all right," Chloe said quietly. "If this is what's on your mind, it's exactly what you should be talking about."

Jody blotted the spill with tissues. "I know you and I only just met, but I knew right away we could be good friends, and … and I thought you should know. I don't know how serious things are between you and Roelke—"

Neither do I, Chloe thought.

"—but maybe you need to do what I did. Take some time to really think things through before it goes any further."

"I'll do that," Chloe promised. "But Jody? Although I haven't been around cops as long as you have, I know a few things, too. I know that coming here"—she gestured at the peaceful, feminine space—"was good for Rick. I know you were a good partner for him. I know these last months were the happiest of his life because of you."

Jody summoned a watery smile. "No wonder Rick spoke so highly of—"

The doorbell cut off the rest of her sentence, which Chloe thought was just as well. She wiped her eyes while Jody went to the door.

It was no surprise to see Lucia Bliss follow Jody back to the living room. It *was* a surprise to see Lucia alone. Where was Roelke?

"Did you two have a chance to meet on Friday night?" Jody asked. "Lucia, this is Chloe Ellefson. She's a friend of Roelke's."

Chloe offered a very polite smile. "We didn't officially meet. Hi, Lucia."

"Hi." Lucia put a CorningWare dish on the coffee table. "Jody, I brought you a tuna casserole."

The Wisconsin version of hotdish, Chloe thought. Probably tuna, noodles, and cream-of-something soup. It was hard to know what else had been included—a can of peas maybe?—beneath the crust of crushed potato chips. She wished she'd had time to make a Tunnel of Fudge Cake. Maybe she could bring one over later. Jody probably already had three tuna casseroles in her freezer, but surely no one had brought such decadent chocolate comfort. Roelke might like it too …

*Roelke*. What the heck was taking him so long? Chloe glanced out the front window just in time to see him drive out of the parking lot, turn onto the main street, and disappear.

Roelke drove straight to the old neighborhood. A district cop had killed Rick—or, at the very least, provided the gun. He had to find out who, and why.

*Don't be a dumbass, McKenna.*

"Too late to change now, buddy," Roelke muttered. He parked on Lincoln and got out of the truck.

He'd patrolled these streets for six years and been away less than two. He still knew this beat—the bad corners, the homes most vulnerable to robberies, the spots most enticing to homeless adults and runaway teens. He knew where to warm up on frigid nights. He knew where to hole up if a smartass sergeant came out to check up on the beat men. Most just wanted to know their guys were safe, but every once in a while some overzealous newly promoted sergeant went looking for someone to report. It was fun to play cat-and-mouse with those guys. Usually they calmed down quick enough.

It wasn't just the place that felt familiar, though. It was the people who lived and worked in this neighborhood—Poles, Latinos, American Indians, others, too. Roelke knew the knuckleheads and the drunks. He knew the people who'd go out of their way to help the police, the people who didn't want to get involved, the people who simply didn't give a damn. He knew who spoke English and who could translate for the Hispanic people who did not. He knew who had a telephone, who locked their doors, who looked out for their neighbors.

Roelke zipped up his coat and tugged on gloves. He might need to talk to any number of people before finding all the answers. Right now, he was only looking for one.

It didn't take long to find the man in a pocket park in Lincoln Village, near the basilica. Roelke heard tuneless harmonica chords before spotting a figure in tattered military fatigues sitting on a bench, puffing away while pigeons pecked at the ground around his feet.

Roelke approached slowly. "Hey, Sherman."

The man broke off abruptly and sat up straight, his bright blue eyes wide with alarm. Then he nodded vigorously. "Officer McKenna!"

To Roelke's relief, Sherman looked relatively sober. Aside from a few more gray streaks in his beard and matted hair, he hadn't changed since they'd last talked.

Sherman had drifted around Milwaukee's Old South Side for years, drinking too much, always wearing military camouflage. Word was he was a 'Nam vet who'd spent time as a POW. Roelke hated seeing him live on the streets, but he'd never been able to pry any information about family from the guy. Maybe he didn't have any. Maybe they'd given up on a returned soldier who couldn't find his way back to his prewar self.

The older man suddenly frowned. "Where's your uniform?"

"I don't work for the MPD anymore. I'm still a cop, though."

"That's good." Sherman looked relieved. Then his expression turned hopeful. "Say, do you feel like eating a cheeseburger? I feel like eating a cheeseburger."

Roelke almost laughed. "I do," he said. "Let's go."

Five minutes later they entered a local diner, a narrow space with counter service on one side and booths along the other wall. Roelke chose the back corner, glad there were few other patrons. He wanted a private conversation. Besides, he'd forgotten how bad someone with no access to a shower smelled. He didn't want to inflict that on other people.

Roelke ordered coffee, cheeseburgers, fries, and double helpings of cole slaw—God only knew when Sherman had last eaten any vegetables—and let the man enjoy his meal. When the last morsel had disappeared, Sherman wiped his mouth politely with a napkin. "Thank you. Do you think they might have an extra bun or two in the kitchen? I'd like to take something back for my pigeons."

"I'll ask."

"You were always nice to me. Some of the new guys, all they want to do is blue card me."

"Yeah." Roelke sighed. The standard procedure after finding a drunk on the street was to haul him in to sleep it off for five hours. A blue card was filled out to document the offender—time in and time out. And in his day, Roelke had found Sherman falling-down drunk more than once.

Trouble was, even in winter, blue carding him was the worst possible response. Sherman freaked *out* if he sobered up and found himself in a holding cell. After one such experience, Roelke avoided hauling the guy in if at all possible. A cup of coffee and a cheeseburger were sometimes enough to ward off a binge.

"Officer Banik is okay, too," Sherman amended. "He doesn't buy me cheeseburgers, but he usually leaves me alone. And Officer Almirez is nice. But…I heard about what happened to him."

"What did you hear?" Roelke asked.

"That he got shot and killed."

"Well, I'm trying to find out what happened to him." Roelke's knee began to bounce beneath the table. "And I need you to do me a favor."

"Sure," Sherman said. No hesitation.

"Real early yesterday morning, someone saw Officer Almirez sitting at the bar in the Rusty Nail, drinking beer. He was on duty."

Sherman frowned. "That doesn't sound right."

Roelke felt a surge of raw affection for this lost soul. "No, it doesn't sound right. I really want to know if Officer Almirez was talking to someone in particular, and what they talked about. I asked to the bartender, but he ain't sayin'. Can you check around for me?"

"Sure."

Just like that. In the old days, Sherman had come through for him many times. It had been little things, mostly—what kid broke the butcher shop window, who was selling pot, who was bragging about a new color TV right after the electronics store got ripped off. Sherman was familiar, no threat to anyone, just a homeless guy nobody paid attention to. But while Sherman had his share of problems, his hearing was just fine.

"Thanks," Roelke said. "Do you think they'll let you into the Nail?"

He nodded. "I go there sometimes."

No surprise there. The Rusty Nail's barkeep was the type who'd take a dollar from whoever walked in the door. Roelke pulled out his billfold and extracted a twenty. "Don't spend this all on booze, hear me? And listen, I don't know what this is all about. Back off if somebody pays attention. There might be drug dealers involved or something. You understand?"

Sherman nodded, looking unperturbed. Maybe he wasn't able to fully grasp the situation, the potential. Or maybe after his time in Vietnam, Milwaukee drug dealers just weren't that scary.

"Thanks, Sherman. I'll find you again in a day or so."

"Okay," Sherman said. "Don't forget to ask about the buns. And before we go, how about a milkshake?"

Roelke caught the waitress's eye and ordered. Sherman waited patiently for his shake. When it arrived, he dug in with the fervor of an eight-year-old on his birthday.

I hope I'm doing the right thing, Roelke thought. A bad cop might prove more dangerous than any drug dealer. But there was no going back now.

# TEN

CHLOE SAID GOOD-BYE TO Jody soon after Lucia Bliss arrived. "I've got to get going too," Lucia said. She stood, wiping her palms on her trousers. "I'm just so damn sorry."

She and Chloe walked down the hallway and outside without speaking. Awk-ward, Chloe thought. She wanted to ask if Lucia had been giving Roelke lusty looks on Friday night, but it didn't seem like the time. She wanted to ask what Lucia had said in the parking lot that sent Roelke back onto the road, but that didn't feel right either.

Chloe was about to turn toward her car when she heard the other woman sniffling. Chloe swore inwardly and tried to think of something to say. "I... I'm sure Jody was glad you came."

Lucia blew her nose and wiped her eyes. "I didn't have a clue what to say to her."

"Just knowing that good cops like you are trying to solve Rick's murder must provide some comfort," Chloe said. "You must be a good cop. You're a sergeant, right? It can't have been easy to earn that. Being a woman and all, I mean."

"Well … it was tough," Lucia admitted. "It's hard to say who was harder on me, my dad or my fellow cops."

"Your dad didn't want you to have a career in the police force?"

"My dad told me when I was six that I would be the first female police officer in Milwaukee. When I missed that by a few years, he decided I'd be the first woman district captain in Milwaukee."

"Ah. No pressure, though."

"Right." Lucia almost cracked a tiny smile but seemed to think better of it. "See you around." She lifted a hand in farewell.

Chloe looked around, giving Roelke another few seconds to drive back into the parking lot. He didn't appear.

"Well, this completely sucks," she muttered. She was tired, she was hungry, she was sad, and she didn't know how to get back to the freeway. Most of all, she was hurt that Roelke had taken off like that.

———

After making arrangements with Sherman, Roelke drove back to Jody's apartment. Bliss's car was gone from the lot. Chloe's, too. I can't think about that right now, he thought again. After hearing Bliss's news, he'd needed to *do* something. Now that he'd gotten his top-performing informant of old on-task, he felt calm enough to talk to Jody.

She answered the door looking weary but composed. "Hey, Roelke."

"I don't have to stay if you don't feel like more company."

She took his hand and tugged him inside. "You were so close to Rick that having you here is good, somehow. You know?"

"Yeah." He did know.

They sat in the living room. "It was sweet of Chloe to come."

"She wanted to," Roelke said. "Listen, Jody... I need to ask you again about that phone call you got from Rick."

She spread her hands, looking puzzled. "I've already told you everything. We couldn't have been on the phone for more than a minute or two."

"Do you know what phone he called from?"

"Well... not for sure." She tipped her head, considering him pensively. "What's this all about?"

Roelke struggled to keep his rage—and what he now knew about the gun—locked down. "I have to do something," he said at last. "So I just keep going over stuff."

"Rick would be doing the same thing. You're both such *cops*."

Roelke cleared his throat, willing the lump to subside. "When he called you at one a.m., he said his next stop was a bar. I've been trying to reconstruct his timeline, and as far as I can tell, he didn't do his first bar check until forty-five minutes later." Not that tossing back a cold one at the Rusty Nail counted as a bar check, but that was not up for discussion. "Have you remembered the name of the bar he was going to hit after hanging up with you?"

Jody leaned back against the cushions. "I'm positive Rick didn't mention a name. Somebody called to him while he was talking to me. Rick answered. His exact words were, 'I'm going to the bar as soon as I leave.'"

Roelke felt a new flash of hot anger—this time aimed at himself. Jesus, he thought. How stupid can I be?

"I'm really sorry, but—"

"You have nothing to be sorry about. In fact, you've been enormously helpful."

A little frown pulled lines into her forehead. "I have? How?"

Roelke was tempted to tell her everything. But if he did, he'd have to swear her to silence. The ugly fact that the killer's gun had come from the district's Evidence room wasn't public knowledge yet. And if he admitted to Jody that she'd given him the glimmer of a fresh idea to pursue, there was always the chance it might slip out.

She sat up straight. "Roelke? What's going on?"

"I swear I'll tell you, but only after I pursue a couple of things. It may all come to nothing."

"Roelke," she protested, "I deserve—"

"I gotta go." He kissed her on the cheek before getting to his feet. "I may be hard to reach on the phone, but I'll stop back soon."

She looked unhappy, but she let it go. As she closed the door behind him, though, she muttered something about "damn cops."

Roelke strode away. The thing was, he'd missed something.

Back in the day, he and Rick never unwound in their own district. It was way too dicey to drink in the same place they'd been busting up fights. They'd ended up with a favorite tavern the next district over. After becoming friendly with the owner, they'd gotten to calling the tavern after him. "Let's hit Kip's," they'd say. It was a classic Milwaukee tavern—small, nothing fancy, just good burgers and cold beer and a fish fry on Friday nights. The sign above the sidewalk was nothing fancy either. Nor was the name painted on it: THE BAR.

Roelke got into his truck and cranked up the heater, trying to think. Would Rick have had time to make a quick detour to the Bar after calling Jody, and before turning up at the Rusty Nail? Depending on where he'd called from—yeah, it was possible. It would have been a quick trip. It made no damn sense. But it was possible.

Roelke briefly considered driving straight over there but discarded that idea. A cop barging in to ask questions on a Sunday night might be noticed, remembered, discussed. Better to wait until tomorrow. He'd hit the place early, before things got rolling.

He suddenly realized how exhausted he was. Even anger's buzz was fading. He didn't relish the hour-long drive back to his apartment in Palmyra... but Rick's sofa wasn't available for crashing on anymore. The reminder was a weight against his ribs, a stinging in his eyes. Sometimes the pain of Rick's death was enormous and blunt: my best friend is simply gone, forever. Sometimes the pain came tiny and sharp: I will never eat Rick's huevos rancheros for breakfast again.

Roelke waited until he felt able to suck air into his lungs again. Then he turned his truck toward home.

———

Chloe had fallen asleep on the sofa, but she'd left a lamp burning, and she woke when the apartment door opened. She sat up, rubbing her eyes as his footsteps sounded in the hall.

Then Roelke stood in the doorway. "What are you doing here?"

"I do have a key," she reminded him mildly.

He didn't move.

"I wasn't even sure if you were coming home tonight," she began but stopped when his fists clenched. Okay, for some reason that was the wrong thing to say. "I wanted to see you. I care about you, Roelke. That's what people do when they care. They show up."

He didn't answer. She forced herself to wait, letting the silence stretch. At length he walked to a chair and dropped. He put his elbows on his knees and rubbed his face with his hands. She waited some more.

"I can't do this right now," he said finally.

"Can't do *what*? I'm not asking you for anything. I just don't want you to be alone right now."

He still didn't meet her gaze. "But I need to be alone. I have to do this thing in the city. For Rick."

God, this was hard. She felt as if she were tiptoeing over broken glass. "What is it you're trying to do for Rick?"

"He was my friend, Chloe," he said, with a blaze of heat.

I do know that, she thought.

"And he was a good cop. You don't know—he would never— look, we always watched out for each other. We have to take care of our own. There's nobody else."

Another silence descended. Chloe nibbled her lower lip. Clearly she was still missing things, important things. "Is somebody saying Rick wasn't a good cop?"

He stared at the carpet.

"Please don't do this, Roelke. Please don't shut me out."

He didn't answer. Instead, Jody's voice rang in her memory: *There are things they won't talk about. I don't mean secret stuff, I mean all the things they believe to their bones that no one can understand except another cop.*

Chloe counted to a hundred, letting the seconds tick by. Then she stood. "There's a pot of sweet potato chili in the fridge," she said quietly. "I know you like it, and you have to eat. Take care of yourself, okay?"

This time she didn't wait for an answer. She turned her back on the man she cared so much about, and left him alone.

———

That night Chloe took solace from the unconditional adoration of her cat, Olympia, but got little sleep. "Great start to the week," she muttered as she drove to work the next day. She was sad, worried, and not looking forward to her day even a little bit. Monday morning staff meetings at Old World Wisconsin were the bane of her professional existence.

The huge historic site was closed at this time of year, but the pace didn't slacken. The permanent employees—a pitifully small band of about eight overworked souls—were expected to appear in the director's office each week. Chloe's relationships with other permanent staff members ranged from pretty good (Byron Cooke, curator of interpretation) to strained (Stan-the-Man Colontuono, maintenance chief) to god-awful (Ralph Petty, director). When she surveyed the assemblage this Monday morning, however, she was surprised to feel more affection toward her colleagues than usual. If these people were annoyed, frustrated, unhappy, resentful, or just plain pissed, they generally didn't hesitate to tell her *all* about it.

In other words, they were not cops.

Petty excelled at creating agendas that contained at least one item sure to spark trouble. This week's Petty Atrocity had to do with scheduling the interpretive staff—the underpaid and underappreciated seasonal frontline educators who interacted with the public. "We need to reduce the budget without reducing any services," Petty announced.

Byron shifted uneasily in his chair. He was a young man with little wire-rimmed glasses, shaggy dark hair, and a passionate devotion to the site. "I'm not sure how to accomplish that."

Petty looked over his own half-glasses at Byron, tipping his head in a manner that might have been necessary or might have been calculated to be as patronizing as humanly possible. "You will adjust the hours in each building to reflect traffic patterns."

"It may not be quite that simple," Byron said carefully. "I appreciate the necessity of controlling expenses, but before we commit to making cuts, I'd like to at least discuss—"

"There's nothing to discuss. I'm looking at trends. Clearly, there are periods of time when interpreters have nothing to do. I'm not willing to pay people to read romance novels and eat bonbons."

Byron's cheeks flushed.

Oh, the hell with this, Chloe thought. "I expect a lot of the interpreters," she announced.

Petty frowned at her. "This is an interpretive matter, Ms. Ellefson."

Actually, Chloe thought, this is one more example of why you shouldn't be sitting behind the director's desk. "It's also a collections matter," she assured him, in her best *we're all in this together* voice. "When the interpreters don't have visitors, they dust for me. They vacuum for me. They black stoves and soak wooden vessels for me. They visually examine the most vulnerable artifacts in their buildings and report any problems to me."

Byron had marshalled his own arguments. "They also use quiet time to help in the gardens. And they practice their skills. It's impossible for a beginner to become a competent spinner if she's interpreting for visitors every moment."

"They warp looms," Chloe added cheerfully. "They practice using drop spindles and making hair flowers."

"They—" Byron began.

"That's enough!" Petty snapped. "Byron, I expect you to take a close look at your schedule for the coming season and report back next week with recommendations for cutting hours."

"I will take a close look," Byron promised. He flashed Chloe a grateful look.

Chloe rolled her eyes in response: *No problem. What a jerk.* Everyone understood that tight budgets meant cutbacks, but insulting interpreters in the process was despicable.

The meeting rolled on, with people reporting recent accomplishments. When Chloe's turn to shine came, she dutifully noted the collections work she'd accomplished: visiting a potential donor, completing the cleaning and inventory of another batch of woodenware in storage, meeting with a retired carpenter who had volunteered to reproduce an artifact wheelbarrow for use in the garden program. For good measure, she added a carefully-excerpted version of her trip to Minneapolis. "It's important to build bridges with other institutions in the Upper Midwest," she concluded sagely.

Ralph Petty was frowning at her again. "You were at the mill over the weekend? I heard about the professor's death."

"It's tragic," Chloe agreed, for once with complete sincerity. "But fortunately, there's a broad coalition being formed to help develop and interpret the property. There are some wonderful opportunities for collaboration. The mill's history has relevance for the stories we tell here."

"MHS is highly respected," Petty mused. "Collaborative efforts might bring more Minnesota visitors to Wisconsin sites."

"I'm delighted that one of the staffers reached out to me. I've offered to consult on the interpretive plan." Chloe beamed at Ralph, which always messed with his head. "On my own time, of course."

Last up to report was Stan. "We've got enough snow for another day or two of skiing," he reported. "I groomed the trails this morning. If they're good, we could open tomorrow. But I had to cut a new trail between the Village and German because of that big tree that came down. Somebody really needs to ski that section before we send visitors out there."

When conditions permitted, Old World Wisconsin allowed cross-country skiers limited access to the site. Guests adored the unique opportunity to ski among historic structures within a state forest. But maintaining the trails in ever-changing conditions put a strain on the skeletal staff.

Everyone looked at everyone else. Suddenly Chloe realized that she was being an idiot. "I'll do it."

Petty frowned at her again.

Oh for God's sake, Chloe thought. I'm trying to be helpful. "I've explored a couple of trails in the state forest over lunch breaks, so my skis are already here. Also, I don't want to ruin the visitor experience by leaving tire tracks on site, but I've been needing to get to the German area anyway. The oven in the Schottler stove isn't heating evenly, so I can ski out and check it." None of the stoves on the site heated evenly, actually. That's what happened when century-old stoves were pressed back into service. But she doubted that Petty would think that through.

He did not. "Very well, Ms. Ellefson. Coordinate with Stan."

*Score*, Chloe thought. She'd had a horrible weekend, a good friend was freaking out, and Roelke had all but slammed the door on their relationship. A peaceful ski out to Schottler was just what she needed.

———

From the outside, the Bar didn't look to have changed a bit. Roelke stopped across the street. That hard-to-breathe heat flamed in his chest. God, how many times had he and Rick come here? It was close enough to their district to be convenient, far enough away that most of the neighborhood regulars were not people they'd questioned, arrested, or otherwise annoyed. Sometimes he and

Rick blew off steam in a gripe session at the corner table, sometimes they just grabbed a meal. All in all … good times.

Roelke had timed his visit carefully, arriving fifteen minutes before Kip would flip the CLOSED sign to OPEN in the window. He slipped down the alley and let himself in the back door. The tiny kitchen was empty, and he walked quietly to the barroom door. Two women were racking clean glassware behind the bar. A bleach bottle blonde who looked vaguely familiar must have been working here back when. The brunette, who was not familiar, must be a more recent hire. He remembered the beer signs on the walls but not the bowling trophy. Roelke and Rick had played darts in one corner, but in their day, shooting pool in another had not been an option.

Darts were good enough for us, Roelke thought. He did not approve of the changes, which made him feel old—and that did nothing to improve his mood.

A side door opened, and Kip emerged from his office. He stared at Roelke. A slow smile spread across his face. "Officer Roelke McKenna!" he bellowed. "A friend from the past."

Kip, who owned the Bar, was totally bald, of medium stature, and somewhere in his sixties. He looked harmless, but Roelke had seen him whip a baseball bat from beneath the bar with lightning speed. Command presence. It wasn't all about bulk. "Hey, Kip."

Kip's smile faded. "Aw, Roelke. Come on into the office. Danielle and Joanie can open up for me."

Roelke followed the older man into the claustrophobic confines of his workspace. The only writing surface was the top of a two-drawer file cabinet. Ledgers, boxes of envelopes, and other administrative clutter lived on high shelves. Kip opened two wooden folding chairs propped against the wall.

"I'm just sick about Rick Almirez," Kip said. "I'm sorry, Roelke. You two were tight."

"We were." Roelke's voice cracked. He cleared his throat. "That's why I'm here, actually."

"Yeah?" Kip leaned back in his chair. "Want to have a wake here? Nothing official. Just a chance for his friends to raise a glass in his honor."

Roelke's throat grew thick. Again. "That's a great idea, Kip."

"You name the date, and we'll make it happen."

"Okay. The thing is … I've been trying to piece together what Rick's last duty shift was all about. And there are a couple of things I can't figure. Kip, did Rick ever come in here and drink while he was on duty?"

"What the hell are you talking about?"

"Rick was spotted at a bar a couple of hours before he was shot. Drinking. He missed his mark, even."

"What bar?"

"The Rusty Nail."

Kip snorted with scorn. "It didn't happen. Not *any*where, but *especially* not a dive like that."

"Well, evidently it did. I'll figure out what that was all about, but I've got another question. For a short time Rick was totally off com. No one tried to reach him from the station, but no one saw him on the beat, either."

"I see."

"The last person he talked to was his girlfriend. He said he was going to 'the bar'"—his tone made clear he was quoting—"as soon as he hung up. He didn't hit any of the taverns on his beat within the next forty-five minutes. I was wondering if he was referring to your place. Did you see him early Saturday morning?"

"No. He didn't come in at all."

Roelke's feeble hope thudded to the ground. He hadn't realized just how much he'd counted on learning something new here.

Kip rubbed his jaw. "Rick came in only one day last week. Him and Dobry."

Rick and Dobry? The three of them had come in together a few times, way back when. But Roelke had never imagined Rick and Dobry coming here.

Suddenly he had to get out of there. "Thanks, Kip."

Kip grabbed his arm. "Roelke. I'm really sorry I couldn't help you." His eyes were dark with concern. Roelke wondered if there was something else, something Kip wanted to say. But the moment passed. Wishful thinking, Roelke thought.

Back on the street, he shoved his hands into his coat pockets. His long exhale puffed white. Keep moving, he told himself. You've eliminated one possible source of information, so move on to the next.

Trouble was, he couldn't remember what he needed to do next. *Rick*, he thought, *I don't know that I can do this. Nothing is stacking up.*

*Don't be a dumbass, McKenna.*

"I *am* a dumbass," Roelke muttered quietly. For some reason he thought of Chloe. Then he made himself stop thinking of Chloe.

He walked to a Polish diner that served *pierogi* and strong coffee. Once he'd ordered, he pulled his stack of index cards from his pocket and found his to-do list.

1. ~~verify Rick was drinking at Rusty Nail~~
2. *check call box history—pattern?*
3. *FI reports?*

Right. He could tackle both of those this afternoon. Getting back to an action plan, and a plate of pork-and-cabbage *pierogi*, gave him new energy. I might be a dumbass, Roelke thought, but I'm a long way from giving up.

———

Old World Wisconsin was magnificent in any season, and Chloe enjoyed her ski to the Schottler Farm, one of three farms in the German area. The other two were half-timbered structures built by Pomeranian immigrants. While they had much to commend them, they were not cozy. But the Schottler farmhouse, a glorious structure built unabashedly of big logs, had a kitchen with a door that closed. Once she'd built a fire in the stove, the room warmed up nicely. She used the hidden telephone to let Stan know that the trail was fine.

Then she settled in for some quiet time. On a lark, she'd even brought out the ingredients to make *kuchen*, a staple in the Schottler foodways program. After all, she did need to see if the oven heated unevenly.

As it turned out, as long as she turned the pan halfway through baking, the oven worked fine. By early afternoon Chloe was relaxing in the toasty kitchen, eating warm apple *kuchen* (she'd promised to bring some back to Byron if he sacrificed the fruit in his sack lunch), and doodling in the journal she'd tucked into her daypack.

Although she didn't talk about it much, Chloe loved to write. She'd taken creative writing classes in college and had almost finished a historical novel while living in Europe. That chapter of her life had not ended well, and she'd destroyed the typewritten manuscript.

Since starting work at Old World last June, Chloe had scribbled a few poems and even joined a writers' group. And although she hadn't admitted it aloud, she was toying with the idea of a new novel. A historical mystery, actually. She was of Norwegian descent, and in the interest of ploughing fresh ground, she'd decided to write about a German immigrant. So being here, alone, was good for all kinds of reasons.

When the muse subsided and thoughts of Roelke began to intrude, Chloe reached into her daypack again. At the last minute she'd grabbed the files Ariel had given her, cramming them in beside the old plastic butter tubs she'd used to transport flour, milk, and eggs from Byron's stash of foodways program supplies. Time to think about interpretive themes for the mill museum.

Chloe contemplated a morsel of *kuchen* before popping it into her mouth. It's all about flour, she thought. The staff of life. Everyone needs flour, be it baked into moist loaves, rolled into crisp crackers, molded into dumplings dropped into soup—or yes, even formed into *kuchen*. Everyone needs flour.

# ELEVEN
## MAY 1878

I need flour, Magdalena thought. Of all the brutal injustices Polish immigrants left behind, most summarized the reason for leaving their homeland in two words: *Za chlebem*. For bread. And here she was, in the new world, with not even a morsel. So she would go to the mill. But first, chores—hauling the sodden log and planks home, making soup for her boarders.

Magdalena left Frania guarding the planks while she dragged the heavy log away. Snowmelt had come late this year, but soon the river would rise, the Flats would flood, and she and Frania would be forced to camp on the hill for a week or so. But tonight, she could cook knowing that as soon as the log dried, she'd have firewood to last for a while. Her boarders would pay their rent in two days. She'd done laundry for a bachelor neighbor and received a catfish in exchange. She had the occasional egg from her lone chicken. She had a bit of fresh watercress, a few dried peas and barley left, and two wrinkled heads of cabbage she'd packed in a barrel of sand last fall. She had garden seeds ready to plant in the patch behind the cabin. For the moment, she and Frania were safe.

———

The sun was setting, Magdalena had changed into her other dress, and soup was bubbling on the stove by the time the men came home. She had four boarders, newly arrived Polish men who worked as loaders at the Washburn Mill. Before taking them in, she had explained the situation bluntly: "My daughter and I sleep in the loft. If I hear a footfall on the ladder, I will meet the intruder with a butcher knife. Understood?"

Wide-eyed, the young men had nodded. And she'd never had a bit of trouble.

"Wash up," she ordered now. The men looked like ghosts. Flour dusted their hair, their skin, their clothes. Tiny balls of sweat-caked flour caught on the hairs along their arms. Once they'd done their best with basin and washrag, she dished up soup. Three of the boarders retired to a bench outside to eat in the fresh air of a spring evening.

Pawel settled at the split-log table near the stove. "Come sit with me, my *kwiatuszek*," he called to Frania. My little flower.

The little girl climbed onto his lap. When Pawel bounced Frania on his knee, she laughed joyfully.

Magdalena felt a bittersweet ache beneath her ribs. She was used to tending Frania by herself—burdens, blessings, all rolled together. Seeing her daughter with Pawel made her wish...

"More!" Frania crowed.

"You've worn me out!" Pawel protested. "And my soup is getting cold." Instead of sliding to the earthen floor, Frania leaned against Pawel and let him eat.

"You're good with her," Magdalena said. The words slipped out before she could weigh the wisdom in speaking.

Pawel ducked his head, cheeks flushed. "I like children."

Magdalena regarded him. Pawel was a big man with massive shoulders and corded muscles. He spent his twelve-hour shifts rolling 196-pound barrels of flour from the packing machines into train cars. He was part of the Polish Eagles, a six-man crew that usually bested other packing teams when challenged to a race. No one would pick a fight with Pawel.

But unlike some of the other laborers, Pawel had a gentle manner. His face was broad and plain, his hair the color of dried mud, his hands huge. No one would call him handsome, but Magdalena liked him. She thought he liked her. Maybe, she thought, just maybe…

Pawel pulled a rag from his pocket and dabbed at his eyes. "Was the dust bad today?" Magdalena asked. The men often came home with red-rimmed, watering eyes.

"As bad as I've ever seen it," Pawel admitted. "So thick in the air that I couldn't see my hand at the end of my arm." He picked a morsel of fish from his soup and handed it to Frania. She accepted eagerly.

"Pawel!" Magdalena protested. "You are kind, but you need—"

"Ah." He waved her protest aside and smiled at the child. "I have a gift for you and your mother, Frania." He pulled a piece of pale blue paper from his pocket.

Frania snatched it and beamed at her mother. "Mama!"

Magdalena took the treasure. One side was covered with English writing, but the other was blank. This paper, such a lovely blue, was a rare gift. She looked at Pawel with wonder. "Where did you come across such a piece?"

Pawel shrugged, looking both pleased and embarrassed. "One of the managers tossed it away. And I thought…" He waved his hand toward the delicate paper cuttings pasted on her whitewashed walls. "You do such fine work."

Magdalena's cheeks grew warm. It was a small thing, really, the *wycinanki*. Years ago her mother had taught her to make intricate designs from tiny snips of paper, patiently layered, just so. Here in Minneapolis it was hard to come by colored paper, but she enjoyed carefully taking her sheep shears to what she could find. Her best piece, a bright spray of flowers with a rooster on each side, hung over the door.

"What shall I make with this, Frania?" she asked.

"A rose!"

"Yes. I shall cut a lovely blue rose." Magdalena looked at Pawel, about to thank him, but his expression caught her by surprise. "Pawel? You look sad."

He hitched one shoulder up and down. "I've been thinking of my mother. If she still lives, today is her fortieth birthday."

"I'll say a prayer for her," Magdalena offered softly. There weren't enough Polish immigrants here yet to support their own church, but she attended mass with some of the German Catholics. The priest had not—at least so far—lectured her for immoral behavior, as the priest in her village had done.

"What do you miss most about the old country?" Pawel asked.

The question startled her. "I try not to think about the old country," she said after a moment.

"Sometimes I can't help it. I miss my mother most, I think. And oh—her *pierogi*! I do miss those. She made them for special occasions,

stuffed with sauerkraut, or cheese, or mushrooms... all delicious."
Then a look of horror nudged the reminiscent smile from his face. "I
do beg your pardon! You provide excellent meals. I did not mean—"

"I know." Magdalena smiled, but an awkward silence settled over
the room. I could make *pierogi*, she thought. I have cabbage. I have
eggs. I just need flour.

# TWELVE

CHLOE FINISHED HER *kuchen*, still thinking about flour. During her career she'd helped tell the beginning of that story (planting, growing, and harvesting grain) and the end of that story (creating baked goods from scratch) at historic farms from Wisconsin to Switzerland. She'd never had opportunity to consider the middle phase, though—turning grain into flour. The mill's interpretive possibilities really were exciting.

She read the research reports, scribbling ideas as they came. An hour later she reluctantly acknowledged that she should be going. She made sure the fire was out, bundled up, and fetched her skis from the front porch. The cast iron skillet she'd baked the *kuchen* in, which now needed cleaning, was a heavy addition to her pack.

But it was worth it, Chloe thought, as she kicked off. My love life might be falling apart, but I do enjoy my work.

Her optimism carried her back to the Education House. She'd endured her assigned workspace in a dilapidated trailer through the fall, but once the weather turned cold, she humbly begged Byron for corner space in the cottage he shared with the curator of research. She'd found an old wooden desk in a storage shed, scrubbed away all evidence of mice, and bribed a maintenance guy to help her haul it to her new digs. She had no privacy at Ed House. Byron was on the phone a whole lot, potential interpreters came for interviews on a daily basis, and she now was expected to help answer the museum's main phone line if it rang more than twice. Still, the move had been good.

Byron's car was the only one in the Ed House lot. "I come bearing *kuchen*," she called as she walked into the main room.

"Good," Byron said. "Say, somebody's been trying to reach you."

Roelke, maybe? Chloe's heart rose, making her *I'm an independent woman* psyche nervous. But Byron added, "A friend from Minnesota." He handed her several little *While You Were Out* slips.

"Ariel," Chloe said automatically. Then she frowned. The *From* line on each slip was blank, and the number listed below was unfamiliar.

Chloe went to her own desk and placed the call. A man answered after one ring. "Hello?"

"This is Chloe Ellefson."

"Oh, thank God," he said. "This is Toby, Ariel's brother. I need your help."

Chloe felt every muscle go taut. "What's the matter?"

"It's Ariel," Toby said. "She's been arrested."

———

Fortified by his *pierogi*, Roelke drove to his old district building. He sat in his truck until shortly before second shift started. Inside, he gave the desk guy a friendly wave—*Hey, it's just me*—as he walked by. Sergeants would be busy with roll call—inspecting uniforms, checking weapons, handing out lists of stolen cars' license plates, sharing whatever the beat guys needed to know.

He reached the communications room as Olivette was shrugging into her coat, which was an astonishing orange number. Her eyes narrowed, but she didn't speak until joining him in the corridor. "You want another favor."

"You did offer," Roelke reminded her.

She sighed. "I did. What do you need?" She began walking. Her old-fashioned boots, the kind that came to mid-shin and fastened on the side with button-and-loop closures, made rubbery whispers.

Roelke fell into step beside her. "I need the list of specific call boxes Rick used for his mark calls during his last shift." A cop couldn't make a mark from the same box twice in a row, and a record was kept to prove he was covering his beat. "I know what Rick's habitual pattern was. Maybe comparing his mark locations with the call list you gave me will present something new."

"That's out of my jurisdiction, hon. Did you ask the clerks?"

"I'm trying to be low-key here, Olivette."

"Right." She mulled that over. "Okay. I'll see what I can do."

"Thanks. What's the mood in the building?"

She glanced over her shoulder. "You know about the gun?"

"Yeah. Anything new come to light?"

"Nothing that's been announced. The mood around here?" She shook her head. "It's ugly."

———

"Ariel's been arrested?" Chloe repeated.

Toby sounded frantic. "I've never heard her so hysterical before."

111

"But why on earth was Ariel arrested? What can the cops possibly think she's done?"

"I don't *know*! She said she'd been arrested, and then she hung up."

"Did you try calling back?"

"Of *course* I tried calling back!" Toby said. "The cop I talked to said she had terminated the call herself, and wouldn't provide any further information. I'm desperate to get down there, but my wife's sick and can't really take care of the baby, and—"

"Let me see what I can do," Chloe said. "I'll call you back."

She dialed Ralph Petty to request time off. Maybe I shouldn't have been *quite* so helpful at the staff meeting this morning, she thought. The site director had never liked her. Baiting him and *then* asking for a favor was not a good strategy.

When he picked up, she plunged in. "My colleague in Minneapolis needs help. She's trying to finish that interpretive plan proposal in time to meet a grant deadline on Friday—"

"Go ahead. We'll consider it a professional favor to a sister institution."

"—and I'd like to …" Chloe realized belatedly what Petty had said. "Um … Okay. Thanks."

She hung up and looked at Byron. "Petty only agrees to my ideas if they involve me leaving town. Coincidence?"

"I think not. But I'd just go with it."

Chloe waited until she got home to her rented farmhouse to make personal calls. Her friend Dellyn said she was happy to kitty-sit Olympia again. "Sorry," she murmured to Olympia, who clearly understood that Chloe was going to leave *again*, and was clearly aggrieved. "Lots of lap time when I get home, I promise."

Then Chloe dug out Toby's phone number and used a pencil to dial. "Hey, it's me. I told my boss that I have a wonderful opportunity to consult with the Minnesota Historical Society on the mill project, and I got permission to take a few days off. I'll leave for Minneapolis first thing in the morning and call you when I know what's going on."

Her last call was to Roelke's cousin Libby. "I wanted to be sure that you'd heard about Rick's death."

"I saw it on the news," Libby said grimly. "This is straight out of my worst nightmare."

"Have you talked to Roelke?"

"I haven't been able to reach him. How's he holding up?"

"I'd have a better idea," Chloe said, "if he would actually talk to me. He's in Milwaukee. My company is not wanted."

"Oh."

"That being the case, I'm going to Minneapolis for a few days. A friend of mine is having a hard time. Here's the number, in case you need to reach me." She dictated the digits.

"Got it."

Chloe nibbled her lower lip. "Will you ... I don't know ... could you keep trying to get in touch with Roelke? Maybe he'll talk to you."

"Probably not." Libby paused. Chloe pictured her in her kitchen, thinking. Finally Libby said, "Time with the kids would do him good. Their dad just let Justin down for the zillionth time, and that will give me an opening. I'll see what I can do."

"Thanks. I'm worried about him."

"Yeah," Libby said. "I'm worried about him, too."

————

After leaving Olivette, Roelke drove downtown. While the MPD district stations operated with a large degree of independence, the Police Administration Building served as a clearing house and repository for all records. The central property guys circled through the districts every couple of days, picking up firearms, knives, baseball bats, croquet mallets, pot, cocaine, and everything else that cops had seized from bad guys and stored temporarily in their own inventory room. Even dinky stuff got moved here. A gun that had killed a cop? That would be locked down tight.

Roelke made his way to the clerical division, an enormous room filled largely with files designed to hold five-by-seven-inch cards. One of the police aides looked up from a typewriter. "Can I help you?"

This guy can't be more than seventeen, Roelke thought. The aides were kids who wanted to be cops, high school graduates waiting to turn twenty-one so they could apply to the academy. Roelke fought the urge to grab this kid's shoulders and say *Are you sure you want to be a cop? Really sure?* Instead he said, "I'd like to see Fritz Klinefelter."

"Here I am." A heavyset man with a Santa Claus beard wheeled himself from a passageway between banks of files. "Hey, McKenna."

Fritz Klinefelter had once been a field training officer. Tough but fair, his rookies said, which was the best a guy could hope for. His FTO career ended when a drunk driver plowed into his squad car. Now Klinefelter used a wheelchair and ruled the clerical division.

When the older man rolled around the desk, Roelke pulled one of the visitors' chairs over and extended a hand. "It's good to see you."

"You, too. You remind me of good times in the bad old days. Remember the car wars?"

Roelke laughed—actually laughed out loud. Milwaukee cops, if they were assigned a car at all, were lucky to get one with four wheels. Still, there was nothing worse than coming out of a tavern and discovering an empty spot where the car used to be. "I figured I was off probation when you moved my car around the corner."

Klinefelter's grin faded. He looked over his shoulder. "Hey, guys? Take ten."

The baby-faced kid looked up from his typewriter. "But I haven't finished—"

"Take ten." He didn't raise his voice, but all three aides filed silently from the room. Klinefelter turned back to Roelke. "First of all, I'm sorry about Almirez."

Roelke was looking forward to the day when every conversation did not begin with expressions of sympathy. "Yeah."

"You know the gun came from district Evidence?"

"I do." Roelke's knee began to piston. "Somebody inside that building broke into Evidence, snatched the gun, and shot Rick in the head."

"It seems so."

"Rick got along with everybody. You ever hear otherwise?"

"No."

"I've talked with Banik and Bliss, and neither of them can think of anyone who had a beef with Rick. He'd just gotten engaged to a wonderful girl, so I guarantee you he wasn't sleeping with somebody's wife. But something's going on. Maybe somebody got sucked into drug stuff, and Rick saw something."

"Did he report anything like that?"

Roelke made a frustrated gesture. "If so, nobody would tell me. I talked to Sergeant Malloy but didn't get very far."

"Try talking to one of the detectives?"

Yeah, right, Roelke thought. "There's nobody I know personally. Besides, I'm trying to work back channels."

"So you came to me?"

"I did," Roelke said, hoping Klinefelter would understand that he meant it as a compliment. To be sure he added, "I don't know who to trust right now. I thought you might let me check through Rick's FI cards." Field investigation cards, he meant. An information-gathering form printed on rectangles of yellow cardstock. Active cops turned in a lot of FI cards, and they ended up here for long-term storage. "I don't know what I'm looking for, but maybe he recorded an incident that might give me something to go on."

"Could be," Klinefelter said. "But somebody beat you to it."

"Well, I figured that might happen," Roelke admitted. "It's been two days already. Standard procedure for the detectives, I guess."

Klinefelter leaned forward in his chair. "But here's what's not standard procedure. I was home when I heard about what happened. I came in Saturday morning to pull all of Almirez's cards for the detectives. It's what I could do, you know? When I got here, all of those cards were gone. Somebody had pulled every damn card with Rick's name on it, going back six months."

Roelke did not like what he was hearing. "Did you check in with the detectives working the case?"

"Straight off. The guy I talked to thanked *me* for pulling the cards and leaving them on his desk. I have no idea who put them there, or what cards might have been removed from the stack first."

Roelke felt a prickling sensation on the back of his neck. "What does that mean?" he asked, although he knew.

Klinefelter's eyes flashed with anger. "It means that while some beat man may have pulled the trigger, somebody higher up is involved. Somebody with access to a key to our records."

Roelke pressed a knuckle against his forehead. What the hell was going on inside the MPD?

"Now, I got something to say to you. I don't like it, but facts are facts." Klinefelter worked his jaw. "I've got a twenty-nine-year old daughter with Down Syndrome. She's going to need expensive care after me and my wife are gone. A lot of cops work security when they retire, but once the MPD puts me out to pasture, I'm not going to have a lot of job offers come my way. You understand what I'm telling you?"

A warning throbbed in the back of Roelke's skull. "I'm a Lone Ranger here."

"I'm sorry, McKenna." Klinefelter looked torn up. "You deserve better, and so does Almirez. But that's the way it is."

"It's okay, really." Roelke tried to focus. "Just a couple of things before I go. Do you have any idea what might have been in the records that made somebody so nervous?"

"No. The kids do the actual filing. It's unlikely they'd remember anything, and I'm not asking them. I do not want them involved, even a little bit. They got their whole careers ahead of them."

And Fritz Klinefelter believed that meddling in this investigation—even something so mild as trying to remember who Officer Rick Almirez had written up recently, and why—might end those careers before they even entered the recruit academy.

"Watch yourself, McKenna," Klinefelter said grimly. "We already got one dead cop."

———

*Jesus, Rick,* Roelke thought as he drove west from Milwaukee. *What the hell did you stumble into? And why didn't you tell me about it?*

They'd had opportunities to talk. Roelke often spent the night at Rick's apartment after band practice. They'd wasted the usual amount of time grumbling about work stuff—repeat-offender drunks, cranky sergeants, a change in the overtime policy. Rick had not hinted at anything more dire. Maybe he was trying to protect his friends, Roelke thought. Maybe he'd sniffed out something dangerous, and he didn't want me or Dobry anywhere close to it.

But Rick hadn't said he was about to ask Jody to marry him, either. Roelke remembered Dobry's disappointment when he heard that news: *He decided to pop the question, and he didn't tell us about it?*

By the time Roelke left the interstate, his head hurt. His eyes were gritty. His nerves felt pan-fried and crispy. All he wanted to do was go home, take a hot shower, and hit the sack. But as he neared Eagle, it occurred to him that he hadn't heard from Banik or Bliss since he'd asked each to keep him posted. Could be that a message was waiting at work.

Roelke drove to the EPD. The squad car was gone, thank God. He wasn't up to chit-chat. Inside, he found two message slips in his mailbox. The first: *Libby called. Urgent. Trouble with J.*

"Oh, hell," he muttered. He did not have time or energy to deal with new problems. But... *Trouble with J.* The hard times Libby and her two kids faced after an ugly divorce were the reason he'd left the Milwaukee PD in the first place. Justin was a great kid who had a lot of problems, all—in Roelke's opinion—stemming from the fact that his father was an asshole.

Roelke called his cousin. She answered on the first ring. "Roelke? I know what happened. Are you okay?"

"I'm holding it together."

"Come over for supper."

"Can't. What's going on with Justin?"

Libby exhaled audibly. "He's got a huge social studies project about ethnic heritage to do. Dan promised to take him to the Milwaukee Public Museum tomorrow after school, but he canceled. Justin is hurt and angry and taking it all out on me and his little sister."

"Put him on. I'll talk to him."

"What I really need is for you to take him through the exhibits at the museum."

"Libby, I *can't.*"

"Why not? Chloe said you were spending most of your time in Milwaukee."

"You talked to Chloe?" Roelke tried to figure out why that bothered him.

"She's going back to Minneapolis, by the way."

He didn't have to figure out why *that* bothered him. Holy toboggans, what the hell was *wrong* with him? His best friend was dead and he'd just sent his girlfriend packing.

"So, will you take Justin through the museum? Just the history part."

"I'm not the best person to spend time with Justin right now." His voice was husky.

"Justin needs guy time. He needs *you.* Look, we can meet you there. Just give him an hour, okay? I wouldn't ask if I didn't really need your help."

"I know you wouldn't." He cleared his throat. "Okay."

After finalizing logistics Roelke hung up and looked at the second message slip. *Dobry Banik called. No message.* Dobry probably wanted to be sure that Roelke knew about the gun coming from Evidence. Well, he'd touch base with Dobry tomorrow.

Roelke rubbed his forehead. After what he'd learned from Fritz, he'd also warn his friends to watch their backs. I need to take better precautions myself, he thought. He'd spent the past couple of days in jeans and flannel shirts. Time to add his bullet-resistant vest.

He opened his locker. The photograph of Erin Litkowski, the woman who'd gone into hiding to avoid her whacko-brute husband, caught his attention again. Something niggled at the edge of his mind. He frowned, struggling to grasp it. Then he snatched the photo.

For the first time, Erin reminded him of somebody else. He flipped through a carousel of mental images. It wasn't that long ago that he'd seen *someone* who …

Knowledge came like a punch to the gut. This morning, at Kip's, two waitresses had been getting ready for first shift. One had looked familiar. She had short, straw-colored hair, not the red curls in the photo. But the face—the face was older, but the same. He was sure of it.

Erin Litkowski was back in Milwaukee. Erin Litkowski was working for Kip at the Bar.

# THIRTEEN

ON TUESDAY MORNING ROELKE drove back to Milwaukee, still brooding. Erin was back in the city. He'd spent much of the night trying to make sense of that, and his brain felt ready to explode. Erin had gone to some lengths to disguise her appearance and identity, and Kip had referred to his employees as Danielle and Joanie. If Erin didn't feel safe in Milwaukee, why would she return? Roelke had contact information for Erin's sister, but he didn't want to call her—at least not until he talked to Erin and found out what was going on.

I really need a place to stay in Milwaukee, he thought, as he tried to slide a Styrofoam cup of bitter gas station coffee into the little plastic cup holder without sloshing it. Maybe he could crash on Dobry's sofa tonight. But... no. How would Tina Banik react to a silent and angry houseguest? Plus, Dobry was working graveyard shift. Too awkward.

Roelke rolled his shoulders, trying to ease aching muscles. He'd managed to catch Dobry on the phone the night before, right before his friend left for his shift. "They know where the gun that killed Rick came from," Dobry had muttered. "And it's bad, Roelke."

"I know. I ran into Bliss at Jody's place, and she told me. Hear anything else?"

"No."

"Dobry, you knew more about Rick's calls and stuff than anybody. Can you think of *anything* Rick saw or did that might have threatened another cop? Drugs, anything like that?"

"I have been racking my brains ever since Rick got shot, and I've—got—*nothing*. I can't think of a single damn thing that would make somebody want to … do this."

"Yeah," Roelke said grimly. "Me either. Does the name Erin Litkowski mean anything to you?"

"Um … don't think so. Should it?"

"No reason it would. It was someone I met briefly years ago. Listen, watch your back, okay? And tell Bliss that."

"You, too. You going to keep poking around?"

"I don't know," Roelke had said, tasting something acidic in his mouth as he lied to his friend. But there was a bad cop in the district. The less said, the better.

It was too early to visit the Bar, so he stopped first at the district station and managed to catch Olivette in the parking lot. "Hey, Olivette, I was wondering if you'd had a chance to—"

"Oh, Roelke, *hon*," she exclaimed, throwing her arms around him. While he tried to interpret this unprecedented affection she whispered, "Don't come around here again. Captain Heikinen called me at home this morning and wanted to know what we'd been talking about."

Roelke's bones grew cold. "What did you tell him?"

"That you were all torn up and it helped to trade stories with an old friend." Olivette stepped back again, but hung on to both of Roelke's hands, as if offering moral support. "Look, it may not mean anything. He chewed out a couple of rookies yesterday during second shift roll call—had them quivering like jelly. I'm sure he's getting screamed at by the chief. I'm sure he's furious that he doesn't know who killed one of Milwaukee's finest Saturday morning. Still…"

"Still, I need to stay off his radar," Roelke finished. "Thanks, Olivette. We're done."

"*I'm* not done," she said indignantly. She rattled off a string of numbers. "Got that?"

Roelke mentally repeated the call box ID numbers several times, imprinting them on his brain. "You're a peach, Olivette. Thanks."

"You take care." For an astonishing moment she looked misty-eyed. She turned abruptly and marched toward the building.

Roelke drove to a coffee shop in the next district, where he was unlikely to be recognized by anyone. The menu offered nothing more nutritious than homemade kringle, croissants, and other pastries—Chloe would love this place, he couldn't help thinking—but their coffee was perfectly brewed. He slid into a corner booth and flipped his cup over for the waitress: *Fill 'er up and keep it coming.* Once settled with a single plain doughnut and a steaming mug, he whipped out his index cards.

He wrote *Captain Heikinen* on one card, and *Questioned Olivette re: her conversations with me* on the line below. What the hell was that all about? Captain Heikinen, like Sergeant Malloy, was an old-school copper with no tolerance for whiny rookies or crooks. They expected their guys to handle themselves on the street but not think too much about decisions being made by their superiors. When

Roelke worked at the district, he'd never done anything good enough or bad enough to get called to Heikinen's office.

Finally Roelke wrote, *Heikinen involved in the sweep of Rick's FI cards downtown?*

On another blank card he wrote down the mark numbers Olivette had supplied. The location of each call box in the beat was still branded in his brain, and he compared them with what he'd learned about Rick's shift. There were two kinds of calls: Rick's marks, when he'd called *in* to the station from a known location; and the outgoing calls, when someone in the Communications room at the station had called *out* to send him to a known location.

Roelke used a red pen to follow Rick's route on his neighborhood map, noting the times for each. He traced the routes with his finger, picturing Rick patrolling the familiar streets in a logical pattern, interrupted whenever he was sent to respond to some problem.

There was nothing in the data he had to account for Rick's time between his call to Jody and his two a.m. sighting at the Rusty Nail. But just a few blocks away from the call box he'd used at one a.m., in the next district but easily accessible, was Kip's place. The Bar.

*Rick Almirez, you son of a bitch*, Roelke thought.

A week ago, Roelke would have sworn on all that was holy that if Rick learned that Erin Litkowski was back in Milwaukee, he would have been on the phone to Roelke, his best friend and former partner, about five seconds later. Now? Roelke wasn't ready to swear a damn thing.

———

Chloe was so worried about Ariel that she actually hit the highway before dawn. I should never have left the Cities, she thought, as she tried to slide a Styrofoam cup of bitter gas station coffee into the little plastic cup holder without sloshing it. She felt as gray at the morning sky. She'd spent a restless night trying to guess why the police would arrest Ariel, and imagining the petite ballerina sharing a cell with street-hardened druggies or hookers.

Chloe wanted desperately to talk with Roelke about this police stuff. Just sharing what she knew would have helped. Having him come along would have helped a whole lot more.

He's doing what he needs to do right now, she reminded herself. She thought of Rick's words, and her heart began to ache. *Don't give up on that guy.*

"I won't," she promised Rick. "But do me a favor, okay? Don't let him give up on me."

———

Roelke found Sherman huddled on the sidewalk near a heating grate, his breath frosting white in the air. "Once the sun comes up I can't lie on the grate anymore," he said. "They make me sit up."

Cops, Sherman meant. Roelke had listened to many good people explaining why having homeless people lying on their walkways was bad for business. He also knew that people like Sherman didn't have a whole lot of options if they wanted to survive a Milwaukee winter.

"Okay, Sherman," he said. "Let's get you a hot breakfast."

Back at the diner, Roelke ordered scrambled eggs, bacon, orange juice, and coffee. Sherman sighed with happy anticipation. Then he said, "I found out some stuff about the guy."

Every nerve quivered to attention. "What guy?" He had to be sure.

"The guy Officer Almirez talked to in the Rusty Nail," Sherman said patiently. "His name is Mr. Lobo."

That struck Roelke as odd. "Lobo?"

"Mr. Lobo. Yes. He doesn't live around here."

"Where does he live?"

Sherman shrugged. "Nobody knows. Mr. Lobo just got out of Waupun."

Roelke's jaw went tight. Waupun was a maximum-security prison northwest of Milwaukee. If the mysterious Mr. Lobo had been incarcerated there, he might be the kind of SOB willing to kill a cop. Maybe he had some old score of his own. Maybe Rick had spotted a familiar face at the Rusty Nail that night, and sat down to see if Lobo seemed poised to go straight or not. It would be just like Rick, Roelke thought, to offer some friendly advice to someone he'd helped send to prison.

Of course… maybe that wasn't it at all. Maybe the cop who'd stolen the gun from Evidence had hired Lobo to pull the trigger.

Roelke leaned across the table. "Is Mr. Lobo the person who killed Officer Almirez? Does he know somebody on the police force? I mean, does he have a friend on the force? How did he get the gun? How—" He stopped abruptly when he noticed growing panic on Sherman's face. Sherman would answer any question to the best of his ability, but he couldn't handle more than one at a time.

The waitress arrived with their food. Roelke gave the man time to dig into his meal before starting again. "Sorry. I didn't mean to rush you."

"That's okay." Sherman was eating with mechanical efficiency.

"So… are people saying that Mr. Lobo killed my friend?"

"People think maybe he did."

"What else did you hear?"

Sherman looked at Roelke sadly. "Mr. Lobo is gone again. Nobody knows where he went."

Roelke felt better and worse at the same time. It fit, in a way. After a quick talk at the Rusty Nail, Rick and Lobo might have agreed to meet for a more private conversation at Kosciuszko Park. If Rick thought the guy was trying to go straight, he might have turned away at the end of that conversation, allowing Lobo to shoot him in the back of the head. Once the job was done, Lobo would make himself scarce. Rick had been dead for three days. Lobo could be *anywhere* by now.

Sherman said, "I bet if you talk to someone at Waupun you could find out more stuff."

No, no, *no*, Roelke thought.

Sherman drained his orange juice. "You know somebody at Waupun?"

"Yeah. I know somebody at Waupun."

"That's good."

But I have no intention of going to Waupun, Roelke added silently. "Did anyone say what this Lobo guy looked like?"

"He looks like Officer Almirez."

Latino, then. Roelke nodded slowly. His beat in Milwaukee's Old South Side had once been home to the most densely populated community of Polish-Americans in the state, but urban renewal and highway construction had pushed some of them out to the suburbs. New immigrants had moved into the gaps—Bolivians, Guatemalans, Mexicans...

Roelke's eyes narrowed. He'd picked up a bit of Spanish before leaving the city. And he was pretty sure that *lobo* was the Spanish word for wolf.

# FOURTEEN

CHLOE HAD TAPED A list of directions to the dashboard. That system worked only until she missed the first turn, but eventually she arrived at the police station ... only to learn that Ariel wasn't there. "Miss Grzegorczyk is no longer in custody," the desk officer informed her.

"She's not? When did you release her? Why was she arrested in the first place?"

"I'm sorry," the man said with detached courtesy. "I am not able to provide that information."

Chloe found a payphone and dialed Ariel's home number. No answer. She chewed her lip for a moment, then called the Minnesota Historical Society and asked for her friend.

"This is Ariel Grzegorczyk."

"Ariel? It's Chloe. I drove up this morning—"

"*Really*?" Ariel's voice quavered. "I can't believe you did that for me. What about that guy you're dating?"

"He's kinda busy. But—what the hell is going on? Why did you get arrested? Can you take the afternoon off?"

"I … um …" Ariel's voice was barely audible. "I can't really talk about it here. And I can't leave, I've got too much work to do."

"Does Toby know you got released? He sounded frantic."

"I talked to him this morning. He said he'd call you, but you must have already left."

Courtesy of my oh-so-early departure, Chloe thought. "Look, why don't I just plan to meet you at your place after work. Sound good?"

"*Very* good. Thanks."

So, what now? Might as well go to the mill, Chloe thought. After working through Ariel's files, she could look at the building with new insight.

She managed to find the mill with only a nominal amount of driving in circles, and parked near the river. Then she stood by the chain-link fence surrounding the hulking compound. Her gaze flinched to the top floor of the wheat house, where she'd seen Professor Everett Whyte's lifeless body stuffed into that wretched grain distributor thing. Geez Louise, she thought, rubbing her arms with mittened hands. I didn't even know the man, and I'm having a hard time. How can anyone expect Ariel to ever return?

Chloe made a deliberate effort to think new thoughts. Once, hundreds of train cars had rattled in and out, bringing grain and taking flour. She imagined the burly, sweating loaders; the men working the packing machines …

"Want to go inside?"

Chloe jerked away from the fence with a yelp.

"Sorry," Sister Mary Jude said. "Didn't mean to startle you."

Chloe put a hand over her suddenly racing heart. "I was daydreaming. I'm rather good at it."

"My friends in the police force would say that daydreaming in this part of town isn't the best idea." The other woman smiled wistfully. "Me, I can't think of any better place for it."

Chloe wasn't sure what to make of this nun with a wedge haircut, blue jeans, sensible shoes, and a huge picnic basket held in each hand. She's got to be a strong woman, Chloe thought, to do good work in such a daunting place, day after day. "I think you're right."

"So. Want to go inside?"

"Is it safe?"

"I believe it is."

"I don't have a key."

Sister Mary Jude gave Chloe an *Oh, you sweet little thing* look. "Come on."

Chloe followed her around the corner, along the fence, around another corner. If she heads into a sewer, Chloe thought, I am outta here. But Sister Mary Jude abruptly stopped and grasped the bottom corner of the chain link section and pulled, showing how a row of the metal pieces connecting the section to a post had been neatly severed. "Here we go." Once both women had crawled through the opening, Mary Jude carefully realigned the edge to its intended position.

Chloe squinted at the secret gate. "I would never have known it was there."

"The cops will find it soon enough. But by then, there will be a new entrance."

Chloe eyed the grubby walls, trying to spot another hidden entry. "You must spend a lot of time looking for the access."

"Not at all. They always let me know."

"Who does?"

Sister Mary Jude glanced over her shoulder with a quizzical look. "The tenants, of course."

Of course, Chloe thought. The tenants. The sister came daily, bringing food and trying, in Owen's words, to talk one more crazy into leaving the mill. Chloe said humbly, "I lead a meaningless life."

"Oh, I doubt that very much. Come on—oh, wait." The nun looked over Chloe's shoulder. "Hello, John!"

Chloe turned and saw a man with long hair and a matted beard approaching. He wore a ragged coat that might have been army surplus, and gloves that hadn't started as fingerless, but were now. He lifted a hand to Sister Mary Jude, but his intense gaze bore into Chloe like twin lasers. It took everything she had not to take a step backward.

"We'll be setting out lunch in a few minutes," the nun said. "Want to come inside with us?"

The man walked past without replying.

"One of the tenants?" Chloe asked.

"People call him 'Camo John' because of the fatigues. I brought him a warmer coat, but he gave it away." Sister Mary Jude watched Camo John disappear around a corner. "I often find him circling out here. Walking the perimeter, you know?"

A veteran, Chloe thought. What the hell is the matter with our society?

Sister Mary Jude led the way through a partially blocked doorway and down narrow passageways, flashlight in hand. She seemed confident; Chloe felt the walls closing in. Perhaps plunging into the bowels of the abandoned mill wasn't the brightest idea, even with the imperturbable Sister Mary Jude as a guide.

Maybe the nun is aiming for sainthood, Chloe thought. Or martyrdom. She didn't aspire to either, but she didn't want to whine now. Besides, she truly was interested in the mill's occupants, past and present. She fought off her heebie-jeebies and searched for something more banal to say. "Sister Mary Jude—"

"Why don't you just call me Mary, all right?"

"Okay. I was just noticing all the graffiti in here." The walls were marked with stylized letters, pictures, symbols she didn't recognize.

"Does that surprise you?"

Chloe realized that she'd somehow blundered. "No, that is—I guess the kids who come here to party do it. I mean, homeless people probably don't spend money on spray paint."

"But homeless people have no voice," Mary said. "No power. Graffiti might be a way of combating that helpless feeling, don't you think?"

"I guess so."

"Some of the homeless people here speak of tribes. Groups of people who join forces. Graffiti lets one tribe communicate important information to others."

Chloe peered at some oversized letters as they passed. "Like what?"

"Like, *Keep out of here*. People who have nothing might mark a wall or a corner to say, *This space is mine.*"

"I'm sure you're right." Chloe was starting to suspect that Sister Mary Jude had her own reasons for bringing her into the mill. "Um … where, exactly, are we?"

"On the second floor. I don't recommend the lowest level, by the way. The machinery down there transferred the power of St. Anthony Falls to all the floors of milling machinery. You wouldn't want to fall into one of the big turbine pits. Besides, the people who go there generally don't want to be found. Drug dealers and the like—those are the ones I avoid."

"Okay." Chloe closed the already short distance between her and her guide.

"Most people here really are harmless. A few people have pets. The teenage girls tend to band together. Moms sometimes take turns with child care."

Child care, Chloe thought bleakly.

They climbed stairs and emerged into a cavernous room. Dim, dusty light filtering through cracked windows illuminated the remains of rusting machinery. "Watch your step," Mary cautioned. She trained her flashlight beam ahead to illuminate the danger. "A few rooms still have electricity, amazingly enough. But this isn't one of them."

Chloe recognized Owen's sack-packing machines. "Oh, I see where we are!"

The other woman checked her wristwatch. "I'm right on time. If you don't mind hanging back a bit..."

"Sure. I don't want to startle anyone."

"Oh, they already know you're here." Mary began unpacking her hampers on a deep windowsill. "The detectives tried to interview the residents, so everyone's on edge."

"Ah." Chloe crossed her arms against the pervasive, damp cold. Were people watching from unseen corners? *Someone* had watched Professor Whyte during his final visit...

She was distracted by a gray-haired man who shuffled from an aisle between machines. His hands twitched, and his gaze never lit long in one place. "You got sandwiches?"

"Bologna or cheese."

He accepted a cheese sandwich and a paper cup of coffee. Over the next twenty minutes or so Chloe watched a parade of wary people appear for lunch. Men and women, elderly and teenaged; a few in office attire, but most clothed in filthy tatters. A few lingered, chatting with each other like elders enjoying social hour after church. Most snatched food and melted back into the shadows.

The nun spoke to everyone: "Is your cold any better? ... You should have a doctor look at that cut, Joe. I can give you a ride to the ER ... I did look for chocolate chip cookies, but the pantry was out. Will Fig Newtons be okay?" Sometimes she paused to lay a palm against someone's cheek. Sometimes she offered a quick blessing.

The last to arrive was a teenaged girl with stringy brown hair, a narrow face, and hunched shoulders. She burrowed deeper into her coat when she noticed Chloe.

"Hi, Star," Mary said calmly. "That's just a friend of mine."

Star glared at Chloe. "Are you a social worker?"

"Nope. I just like old buildings."

Evidently reassured, Star turned her back and accepted a sandwich.

"Have you considered that GED program I told you about?" Mary asked.

Star scratched at a streak of electric blue paint on the sleeve of her grubby parka. "I don't want to go into some stupid program!"

"You could just go for classes. Think about it, okay? You need *some* plan to get—"

"You're talking like that stupid guy." Star snatched the last handful of Fig Newtons and ran.

Mary pensively watched her go. Chloe began gathering empty coffee cups. "What guy was she talking about?"

"She doesn't like Officer Crandall."

"That makes two of us," Chloe muttered. Crandall was a jerk. "What was the thing about a social worker?"

Mary screwed the lid back onto her thermos. "When Star ran away from home, she ended up in a temporary shelter. The social worker called Star's parents. *Huge* breach of trust."

"I get that," Chloe said slowly. "But still ... that girl doesn't look more than fourteen. Fifteen tops. Have you reported her to the police?"

"What do you think will happen if I do?" Mary's eyes narrowed. "If Star gets dragged back home, she'll just run again. And next time she won't be willing to talk to me at all."

"It's just that ..." Chloe blew out a long breath. "It breaks my heart. An industrial site is no place for a child."

"No, it's not. But at least here she's got a few friends."

"How do they survive? One cheese sandwich a day—"

"I'm not the only one who comes. Some churches offer meals. Star does some panhandling, too. A couple of the other girls are prostitutes."

"Prostitutes!"

Sister Mary Jude spread her hands, palms up. "Look, I don't pretend for one moment that this is okay. But all men like Officer Crandall want to do is haul them downtown and stick them on a bus home. The kids who end up living here—*wanting* to live here—didn't run away because of some squabble over allowance. Star's got all the hallmarks of a victim of sexual abuse."

Chloe thought about this woman who came into the ruined mill day after day, hauling baskets of sandwiches through holes in the fence and creeping through dark corridors. "You're doing very good work here," she said, "but ... how can you face this, day after day?"

Mary stared at the floor. "Once upon a time, I was fourteen and needed some help. I was lucky enough to find it. Now, I can't imagine anything more important than looking out for girls like Star—and everyone else who finds themselves here, with nowhere else to go. Somehow it seems especially fitting to serve food in this mill." She met Chloe's eyes. "Give us this day our daily bread."

Chloe remembered her grandmother reciting the same words in Norwegian: *Gi oss i dag vårt daglige brød*. She remembered telling Roelke during a difficult trip to Iowa a few months earlier that she craved baked goods when she was stressed. She remembered thinking about flour as she munched *kuchen* in the cozy Schottler kitchen. She remembered Owen's enthusiasm: *This was the first time in world history that the production of a basic food item was industrialized.*

And now Sister Mary Jude brought Wonder Bread sandwiches to the mill that had once produced enough flour to make twelve million loaves of bread every day. Technology had changed, but that most fundamental human need—*our daily bread*—had not.

Chloe thought about Camo John and Star and everyone else she'd seen that day, each with his or her own story. And she thought about Everett Whyte. "Mary, is there any news about Professor Whyte's death?"

Mary balled a paper napkin. "Not that I've heard."

Chloe hesitated, then came out with it. "Do you think it's possible that one of the residents here killed Professor Whyte?"

"Some of them do struggle with mental illness. Some are addicted to drugs. I can't pretend that I know *any* of them well. Beyond that..." Mary made a gesture of futility.

"Was there tension between Professor Whyte and the tenants? Might somebody have resented him because he represented the forces intent on turning this place—their home—into a museum?"

"The police asked me that, too. But Dr. Whyte actually advocated for the homeless population. Most people just want them to disappear quietly. But he suggested that a permanent shelter be included in the master plan for the heritage corridor rede-velopment."

Chloe considered every master planning meeting about some historical building project she'd ever attended. "I can't imagine that notion was met with rounds of applause and open checkbooks."

"I wasn't there, but—no."

Chloe leaned against the stone wall, feeling the chill leach through her parka. Homelessness was an enormous and complex problem, but nobody should have to live in an abandoned mill.

Mary sighed. "Certainly many of the residents do resent plans for redevelopment. All I can say for certain is this: I use caution, but I've never felt frightened here."

And yet Ariel won't come inside alone, Chloe thought. And in the silence, if she allowed her senses to open, Chloe perceived a frisson of fear amidst the sense of hustle and labor lingering in the rusting ma-chinery and crumbling stone.

# FIFTEEN

ROELKE FORCED HIMSELF TO wait until an hour after opening to present himself at the Bar. He wanted to see the place busy, the workers preoccupied. He followed a noisy group of construction workers into the tavern. Kip was behind the bar. The brunette waitress he'd seen the day before plunged from the kitchen with a tray of red plastic baskets holding burgers and fries.

No blonde. No Erin.

Roelke walked to the kitchen door, startling a Latino man working at the sizzling grill. "*De nada*," Roelke said. He checked the single bathroom. The door was open, the room empty.

No Erin.

"Hey, Roelke," Kip called from behind the bar.

Roelke took a stool at one end of the polished expanse, away from other customers. Kip finished filling three mugs for the brunette before grabbing a towel to wipe his hands and walking over to Roelke. "What's up?"

"Where's the other waitress I saw here yesterday? The blonde?"

Something in Kip's face changed. It was almost imperceptible, but Roelke saw the shift. "Why do you care?" the bartender asked.

"I think she's an old friend of mine. Just wanted to say hi."

"Joanie doesn't work here anymore."

*Damn.* "Since when?"

"Since last night. The end of the shift she comes to me, says she's got to quit."

"That's what she said? Exactly? 'I've got to quit'?"

Kip looked down and seemed startled to see that he was still drying his hands. He tossed the towel beneath the bar. "Yeah. That's exactly what she said. Completely out of the blue."

"Kip!" the brunette—Danielle—called impatiently. "Two more Millers."

Left alone, Roelke stared numbly at the wall. Had Erin quit because of *him*? But—why?

Roelke had met Erin Litkowski only once: the night her husband ignored his restraining order and tried to kick in her door. Since the husband was gone by the time Roelke arrived, there hadn't been a whole lot he could do. The call had come in the middle of a very busy shift, and when a woman had come to see him at the station a week later and identified herself as Erin Litkowski's sister, Roelke—to his shame—hadn't been able to summon a mental picture of the woman.

Then the sister pressed the photograph into his hands and explained that Erin had fled Wisconsin. "Thank you for trying to help. Erin said you were kind." Roelke had always regretted that he hadn't been able to do more. The only salve had been those final words: "Erin said you were kind."

If that's so, Roelke thought, why would she run again only *after* I show up?

He was still trying to figure that out when Kip returned. "Sorry you missed your friend," he said. "Can I get you something to drink?"

Roelke stared at Kip's right eye. "I don't want anything to drink, Kip. I want to know what's going on."

Kip met his gaze without blinking. "Nothing's going on."

"Bullshit!" Roelke's curse was a small explosion. A woman at the nearest table turned her head with a disapproving frown. Roelke struggled to control both his voice and his growing fury. He leaned closer. "C'mon, Kip, it's me. I'm off duty. Tell me what you know."

"I don't know what you're talking about."

Roelke reached into his coat pocket and pulled out the photograph of Erin Litkowski. "Look familiar?"

Kip studied the photo. "There's a resemblance, but I don't think it's the same girl."

"Well, I do." Roelke slipped it away again. "I also think that Rick Almirez dashed off his beat on Saturday morning between one a.m. and one forty-five and came here, which means you lied to me yesterday."

"Roelke—"

"*And*, I think those two things are connected."

"Roelke!" Kip's voice was low, but sharp. "Shut your mouth."

The brunette was back at the bar. "Kip?"

"Just a minute," he called, his gaze never leaving Roelke's. Then he lowered his voice again. "Leave. *Now*. I do not want you back in my bar. You got that?"

Roelke blinked. "You don't want—*what*?"

"You heard me. This is my bar, and I decided a long time ago that I would not take crap from anybody. Get up, walk out of here, and do not come back."

The words *make me* quivered on the very tip of Roelke's tongue. He slowly rose to his feet and clenched his fists. Rick was dead, Erin was in Milwaukee, and people were lying.

He thought, I have—*had*—it. He needed to punch somebody. He didn't really want to punch Kip, but right that moment, he'd do.

———

Before Chloe could ask Sister Mary Jude more questions about the mill's residents, someone shouted, "We're not cops!" A few moments later Owen and Jay emerged from the shadows. "Hey, ladies," Jay said. He gave Chloe a quizzical glance. "I thought you'd gone home."

"I came back."

"Have you talked to Ariel today?" Owen asked.

"I called her at work a little while ago to let her know I'd arrived." She left it at that, since the men didn't seem to know that Ariel had been arrested and released. "Anything new from the police?"

Owen and Jay exchanged a sober glance. Jay said, "Still nothing. It seems like we should know *something* by now."

Chloe was still hoping that despite the bizarre entombment, the cause of Dr. Whyte's death was natural. In the brooding stillness, she sensed listeners in the shadows. A shiver flicked over her skin.

O-*kay*, enough of this. "Well, I'm sure the police will find answers soon," she said briskly. "In the meantime, I'm here to help Ariel develop ideas for the interpretive plan. You guys want to weigh in on educational themes, stuff like that?"

"I'd focus on the heyday for the Minneapolis milling industry," Owen said. "This city led the world in flour production between 1880 and 1930. All the technology was perfected during that era. It was the beginning of the end for rural gristmills."

Jay nodded. "All of the mill structures still standing date to that period, and there's still a lot we can use." He patted an iron beam fondly. "We've got the engine house and rail corridor, grain elevators, a wheat house with nine storage bins, and of course the milling rooms and machinery. It will take decades and dollars to get everything stabilized, but with even a small portion made accessible, we'll have plenty to interpret."

"I think you're overlooking something."

Chloe had almost forgotten Sister Mary Jude. "What do you mean?"

"I hope you'll include the entire continuum," the nun said. "The mill's story didn't end in 1930, or even the day it shut down in 1965. There are still people here. Their stories matter, too."

"Good point," Chloe told Mary quietly. "I'll suggest to Ariel that recent history is part of the plan."

"That's all I ask." Mary nodded. "Since you three obviously have work to do, I'll leave you to it."

"I'll walk with you," Jay said. His voice was casual, but Chloe didn't miss the undercurrent. Jay didn't want Mary walking alone through the mill's dark corridors.

The nun didn't miss that either. "Oh, for heaven's sake. I've been visiting this mill for years."

Jay picked up her baskets. Sister Mary Jude looked exasperated. Jay returned her gaze, imperturbable. After a moment the stiffness left her shoulders, and she relented. "Very well. I suppose an escort isn't a terrible idea."

Chloe and Owen watched them walk away. "She's right," Owen said. "We need to tell the story of all the people who have spent time here."

I do like this guy, Chloe thought. She hoped Owen would follow his instincts and ask Ariel out.

As if reading her mind Owen asked, "So, how did Ariel sound when you talked to her earlier?"

Chloe considered her response carefully. "Shaky, to be honest."

Owen frowned. "I wish her brother didn't live in Duluth. I met him on Friday, and he seemed like a stand-up guy."

"Good thing she has friends in the Cities who care, too."

"Yeah." Owen smiled.

Chloe wanted to steer the conversation away from Ariel. "It's been fun to help with the interpretive proposal. The mill represents a phenomenal opportunity. Even historically, the conversation can't be just about process. It's about people."

"Jobs in the flour mills gave many people a chance to move from poverty to middle class," Owen said. "Wages were better here than at nearby factories, but the work could be brutal, especially in the early years. I think part of the story has to be the dangers workers faced."

"You mentioned the problem with workers getting trapped in grain."

"Mind if we walk while we talk? I've been working on the dust collectors, up on the eighth floor."

"Sure!" Chloe said with as much false cheer as she could find. Her first foray to the eighth floor hadn't ended well.

Owen led the way back to the stairs and they began the climb. "Actually, the mill itself was a single machine."

Chloe figured she better participate in the conversation now, before she was gasping for breath. "A single machine?"

"The vibrations were so great that the builders designed two structures, with free-standing wooden walls inside the limestone exterior to absorb the movement." They rounded a corner and started up the

143

next flight of steps. "I wish I could go back in time and see it, just for a few moments," Owen added wistfully. "Everything was connected. Mechanics replaced belts on the fly, without shutting anything down."

"Seriously?" The thought made Chloe's toes curl.

"And believe me, the machinery was powerful enough to chew up anyone who got distracted for even a second. But all the dangers weren't mechanical. There was also the dust."

"Dust?"

"I'll show you."

They wound their way up several more floors. When they emerged from the stairwell, Owen flashed his light on a labyrinth of pipes and gears overhead. The beam illuminated a rainbow of graffiti that defied the gloom too—a solar system near the floor, as if created by a child; stick figures soaring near the ceiling, as if painted by a giant; elaborate initials proclaiming at least transitory occupation of the space.

Owen gestured toward several large funnel-shaped things. "Those are dust collectors. Nobody paid much attention to the build-up of flour dust in those early days, but it was an enormous danger. Did you know that flour dust is flammable?"

"My grandfather always reminded my grandmother not to put flour sacks into the burn barrel, back in the days when people burned their trash."

"In a burn barrel, a bit of flour dust would cause some popping. The starch molecules in flour expand rapidly in the presence of heat. You know this building isn't the original mill, right?"

"Um…I'm not sure I did know that." Chloe thought back to her first tour of the mill, abruptly aborted when Jay discovered Dr. Whyte's body. "What happened to the first mill building? Did it burn down?"

"No," Owen said soberly. "It exploded."

# SIXTEEN
## MAY 1878

*Pierogi* WOULD CHEER EVERYONE, Magdalena thought. Her board-ers were new-comers to Minneapolis. They never complained, but surely each man longed for familiar food.

The murmur of conversation drifted through the front door. Mag-dalena stood and fetched her last candle from the shelf. "I can't burn this for long, but we can at least have light enough to finish our meal."

Once the tiny flame was flickering, she sat down again. Pawel met her gaze. "I have … that is … I have a small gift for you."

Magdalena put down her spoon. "Another gift?"

"It's nothing, really, I—I just like to keep my hands busy at lunchtime." He scrabbled in his pocket, pulled out his hand.

Magdalena accepted his offering: a wooden crucifix about three inches tall. Pawel had strung it on a chain braided from thin leather cords. "How very kind." She put the cord over her head and let the cross fall against her bodice. "Thank you, Pawel."

"Well." Clearly embarrassed, Pawel gently put Frania aside. "I believe I'll sit outside with the others before sleep time. Anastazy offered to share some tobacco he received from home."

Magdalena put her hand on his arm. "Pawel, if I put Frania to bed, will you listen for her? I have an errand to run."

He frowned. "Of course, but ... an errand? By yourself? *Now*?"

"Yes, now." Magdalena stood. "Just leave your bowl in that kettle, all right? I'll wash up later."

In the loft, she kissed her daughter's forehead and tucked her under the sheet. "Sleep, little one," she whispered. "Tomorrow you shall eat bread."

Back downstairs, she pulled her shawl over her head and walked outside. Her boarders tipped their hats politely, and she felt Pawel's worried gaze following her. She turned northwest and didn't look back.

A half-moon in the cloudless sky lent pale blue-gray light to the night. The fat Czech woman next door was pulling laundry from her line. One of the Danish women was shooing her chickens into their coop. Magdalena exchanged waves and greetings—they didn't speak the same language, but they understood each other. She sidestepped to avoid a goat trotting down the narrow lane, and again as a boy raced past in apparent hopes of getting home before full dark.

A nervous twinge fluttered in Magdalena's stomach as she left the Flats. She had vowed never to return to the Washburn A Mill. It's not too late to turn back, she reminded herself.

Her fingers found the wooden cross, and she took strength from the gift. She would not waver. Frania needed bread. And Pawel missed his mother's cooking.

The huge stone building loomed solid and forbidding. It ran night and day, but only a few millwrights worked through the dark hours—making rounds, listening, watching, making sure nothing was amiss among the rattling machines.

Magdalena picked her way across railroad tracks and slid through the shadows to the mill. Maybe, she thought, no one will see me. Maybe I can get what I came for and slip quickly away.

The doors were locked at night, but the black-haired man had shown her the key hidden beneath a loose stone. "If you don't find the key, that means another girl beat you to it," he'd said, laughing.

Magdalena's fingers trembled as they traced along the rough stones. Maybe the decision had been made for her. Maybe she could scurry back to the Flats knowing she'd done her best...

But the key was waiting.

She crept to the door, worked the lock, slid inside. He must keep the hinges oiled, she thought, for the heavy door moved silently. The huge water-powered turbines were spinning a level below the ground floor. Magdalena walked quickly to the closest stairs. She paused, listening for footsteps or a man's voice, but heard nothing but the machinery. Pawel had once told her that the entire mill operated as a single machine, all the smaller machines yoked together by pulleys and belts. Entering the mill this way felt like creeping into the mouth of some great beast.

She climbed to the packing floor. Rows of tall machines stood silent here, gears still, empty barrels left in place under big black funnels. This is where Pawel works, she reminded herself. She imagined him tipping a heavy barrel the instant its lid had been pounded into place, rolling it away from the packing machine to the rail corridor, running back for the next... hour after hour after hour.

Even now, flour dust hung in the air. She could see it in the glow cast by a kerosene lamp bracketed high on a wall, taste it with every inhale. She felt it beneath the soles of her shoes, too. No matter how careful the men were, a mill producing four thousand barrels every day spilled a lot of flour.

Magdalena knelt and pulled out the sack she'd tucked under the waistband of her skirt. The cleanest piles of flour were along the walls, out of the main walkways. Sweepers shoved it there and left it. Even in the gloom, the leavings glowed like snow drifts. She'd never seen such pale, light flour before moving to Minnesota. It occurred to her that the fine ladies of Minneapolis in their bonnets and dainty hats likely ate white bread every day.

She was scooping flour into her sack when she heard footsteps. Her heart sank like a stone in the river.

"Well now," he drawled. "I have a visitor."

She scrambled to her feet. "*Please*. I need just a little flour, and there's so much going to waste—"

"Oh, I don't mind about the flour." He was a big man. Not strong like Pawel but paunchy, jowly; a Pole hired to patrol the mill so the millwrights could tend their machines without worrying about intruders. Magdalena didn't know his name.

She'd met him soon after her brother, Dariusz, was killed, when the pantry shelves were empty and Frania whimpered in her sleep. Magdalena had left her child with the fat Czech woman and trudged to the mill, desperate. They say flour drifts on the floor inside, she'd thought as she pounded on the door. He'd answered the door; she'd begged. "I think we can come to an understanding," he'd said.

Magdalena had looked into his eyes and heard her uncle, grunting like a hog while she beat his back with her fists. "No."

He'd considered her, shrewd and appraising. "I thought you said your girl was hungry?"

And so began their dangerous game. She had bartered and bargained and, that first night, gone home with flour purchased with only a long, disgusting kiss. But he raised the price with each visit. The last time, he'd left her breasts bruised green and purple. She'd strode home blinking back tears and promising God and herself that she'd never go back to the mill again.

But Frania needed bread, and Pawel dreamt of *pierogi*.

"So," the black-haired man said. "You need flour. And I need something, too."

"I can't. I *won't*. I only need flour. Not so much, just a little."

The corners of his mouth quirked. "I could lose my job just for letting you come in here. You got to make it worth my while."

She clutched Pawel's wooden cross. "*No.*"

He shoved her roughly against the wall. She gasped as her head struck stone. Planting his feet, he pressed against her. "You've been trying to play a fancy game, and I'm tired of it."

*One day I shall own a hat.*

He grinned. With movements almost lazy, now, he pulled a cigar from one pocket, and a packet of Lucifers, too. "You and I are going to get to know each other better."

"You," Magdalena spat, "are going to hell."

He struck the match.

In the half-instant remaining, Magdalena somehow understood that hell had come to get him.

Then the Washburn A Mill exploded.

———

Two miles away, the Polish men sitting in front of their boarding house were knocked to the ground by the explosion. Pawel staggered to his feet, watching a ball of fire rage into the sky and consume the darkness. "Holy Mother of God," he whispered, crossing himself. He felt a sense of dread like he'd never known. In that instant, Pawel somehow understood that his heart was about to break.

# SEVENTEEN

"THE MILL EXPLODED?" CHLOE repeated blankly. "Because of *flour dust*?"

Owen nodded. "On the second of May, 1878. The dust inside this mill was so thick the workers couldn't see more than a few feet in front of them. We know now that flour packed densely into containers is generally safe, but when individual particles get suspended in the air in confined spaces, and they're exposed to oxygen, the risk is enormous."

"I had no idea."

"All it took was a spark. The explosion and fire destroyed much of the commercial area along the riverfront, and it cut the city's milling capacity in half. It also killed fourteen men working the night shift here, and four more nearby. A daytime explosion would have been *much* worse. After the explosion the mill was rebuilt with safer machinery, but the danger of fire and possible explosion never completely went away. There was always the chance that if a motor caught fire, flames could get sucked into the whole system. That could have led to another massive fire and explosion."

My God, Chloe thought. That explains the fear lingering in this place. It wasn't just the machinery, or the danger of suffocating in a grain bin.

"We interviewed a former employee who worked until 1965, when the mill closed," Owen added. "He always feared that a fire might start and not get noticed right away. He worked the night shift, when just a few guys were on duty."

Chloe's eyebrows rose. "Just a few guys in this whole place? At night? Spooky."

"Once there was a flour dust explosion in the next room. The man described the sound of it, and his eyes…" Owen shook his head. "Even years later, I could see terror reflected in his eyes."

"Geez." Chloe hoped that there wasn't a cloud of flour dust inexplicably lingering in the next room now.

"There was another bad fire in 1928. The building was remodeled after that, and some of the milling machinery goes back to that time as well." He gestured at the dust collectors. "For years the flour dust was considered a waste product. The local mills dumped three thousand pounds of bran, germ, and dust into the river every single day."

"Wow," Chloe murmured absently, but her mind was stuck in 1878. *Everyone needs flour.* She hadn't realized that flour could also be deadly.

————

Roelke stood glaring at Kip, hands balled into fists, every muscle poised to spring. He had no idea how he and his old buddy had gotten to this place. He had no idea what to do about it. All he knew was that he needed to pound somebody into the pavement.

Kip reached beneath the bar, where he kept the damn baseball bat.

*Don't be a dumbass, McKenna!*

The words were so clear that Roelke jerked his head, half-expecting to see Rick Almirez hooting with laughter because he'd just pulled the mother of all practical jokes on his best friend. Instead Roelke saw four women at the closest table, watching with expressions ranging from indignation to apprehension. The next table went quiet, then the next. Soon the tavern was silent.

Roelke turned and walked out of the Bar.

He kept walking, faster and faster, trying to outpace the thoughts banging around in his brain. Rick and Erin. Rick and Erin. There had to be a connection. There *had* to be. And that meant that Erin's husband had just pole-vaulted to the top of his suspect list.

A passing taxi threw up a spray of slush. Roelke barely noticed it, or a car horn's distant blare, or anything else. He was trying to understand the incomprehensible. Why was Kip lying? He *had* to be lying—

"*Hey!*" Someone grabbed the back of Roelke's coat. He whirled and saw Danielle, coatless and panting. "Didn't you—hear me?" she gasped. "I've—never seen Kip—go nuts like that. I said I was just—taking a ciggie break."

Roelke felt his cop brain snap back to attention, angry that he'd let himself be oblivious to his surroundings. "Sorry. Why do you want to talk to me?"

"I heard part of what you said to Kip. And the thing is, I really liked Joanie."

Roelke whipped out his photograph of Erin. "Is this her?"

Danielle covered most of the red curls with her thumbs. "She looks different now, but yeah. That's definitely her."

"Do you know why she quit?"

Danielle glanced nervously over her shoulder. "I didn't even know she *had* quit until I got in today."

"Do you know where I might find her?"

"I don't know where she lived. She didn't talk about herself at all."

"How long did she work for Kip?"

Danielle shrugged. "I started three months ago, and she was already here."

"Can you think of anything that might help me find her? I really am an old friend. I'm worried about her. I just want to be sure she's safe."

"I'm worried, too. I could tell she was scared of somebody."

Her SOB husband, Roelke thought.

"All I have is this." Danielle scrabbled in her pocket. "I found a sort of business card thing this morning under the coat hooks we use."

Roelke felt his nerves quiver as Danielle extracted a creased business card. An address, a phone number—he'd be grateful for even the tiniest scrap of information.

He didn't get an address. He got chickens. Two very pretty chickens, flanking a bouquet of flowers, printed in vibrant colors. It was all very artsy, and not the least bit helpful.

Danielle must have noted his disappointment. "There are two words on the back."

Sure enough. Someone had penciled *Linka-Małgorzata* on the back. "Do you know what that means?"

"Nope."

Roelke didn't either. *Linka* might be a name. The whole thing sounded vaguely Polish. Dobry's family was Polish, so at least he had someone to ask. "Did Erin—Joanie—ever mention art school? Anything like that?"

"No. She didn't say much of anything personal, though. Look, I gotta get back."

"Here." Roelke fumbled for one of his own business cards. "If you hear from her, or hear anything else about her, please call me."

# EIGHTEEN
## MAY 1917

FRANIA STOOD KNEE-DEEP IN the Mississippi River, watching for floating driftwood and remembering the kerchief that her mother, Magdalena, had worn over her hair. It was Frania's clearest memory—her and Mama, gathering wood while the city women watched from the bridge above, as if the Flats residents were zoo animals.

She spotted a floating log with stocky trunk and smaller branches. *Perfect.* Papa Pawel came home from the mill exhausted, and she didn't want him taking on chores that she or her daughter could do instead. Pawel had been a champion loader—first with barrels, later with 140-pound sacks—at the Washburn Mill for over thirty years now. But the brute labor was becoming too much, and he'd developed a dry, hacking cough. Miller's lung, they called it.

After the horrible explosion in 1878, Pawel had managed the boardinghouse during the two years it took to build a new mill. Frania had been only four years old when her mother had disappeared in what the newspapers called "The Minneapolis Horror." Pawel and the neighbor women had raised Frania, who gradually took over the boardinghouse. No one knew what Magdalena had been doing by the mill, but Pawel was certain she'd been killed.

At seventeen, Frania had married a millworker of her own—a quiet, gentle Pole with a lopsided smile and kind eyes and dreams of returning to the old country. Two years later, a month before Lidia was born, his sleeve had caught in a piece of machinery. After the funeral, Papa Pawel had painted *Widow Frania's Boardinghouse* on the sign by the front door of their whitewashed cottage. Frania became famous for her poppyseed cakes, gingerbread, and especially *pączki,* the filled doughnuts Poles held dear. Sometimes as many as a dozen newly arrived Poles paid two dollars a month for sleeping space, meals, and clean laundry.

But the Great War brought changes. Fewer European men arrived in the Flats these days. More women, war widows of one sort or another, were taking in boarders. If only—

"Mama!" Frania's daughter, Lidia, stood on the shore, waving wildly. Tomasz, the black-haired boy with her, lifted a polite hand. Like Lidia, he'd been born in the Flats to immigrant parents.

Frania grasped a branch and towed the deadwood, trying to smile. Tomasz made her nervous—always talking about leaving the Flats. He'd tried to enlist when the United States entered the war, but his limp—legacy of a childhood injury—kept him out of uniform. Now he labored at the flour mill, courted Lidia on his free day, and spoke hungrily of "life above."

Before Frania reached land, Tomasz said something to Lidia and limped away. Frania untucked her skirt's hem from the waistband and kissed her daughter's cheek. "Were you and Tomasz walking out?"

Lidia nodded happily. "I'm sorry I wasn't here earlier to help, but it's such a fine spring day..."

"What do you two speak of?"

Lidia took a deep breath. "Mama, I've been thinking about college."

"College?" Frania repeated blankly.

"Some girls do go, you know. I could get a good job after graduating. Tomasz thinks it's a fine idea."

Frania was tempted to ask if Tomasz going to pay for these classes, but she realized in time that she might not like the answer. Tomasz was smart, hardworking, and ambitious. It wasn't surprising that he would encourage Lidia to dream of something so unimaginable.

Frania sighed. All men wanted to do better for themselves and their families. Tomasz, though, seemed particularly eager to leave all things Polish behind.

# NINETEEN

TWENTY MINUTES LATER ROELKE sat in his truck with engine on and heater blasting. Right now he couldn't face even a friendly waitress. He didn't want any more coffee. He didn't want anything to eat. He just wanted to figure out what the hell Rick had gotten himself into.

He pulled his stack of three-by-fives from his pocket, gathered the *People* cards, and set the rest aside. First, Captain Heikinen. Heikinen had access to call sheets, Evidence, probably even the downtown records. He'd also made a private and inappropriate call to Olivette to ask what the heck Roelke McKenna was doing. "More than you know," Roelke muttered, before turning to the next card.

Next, Kip: *Hired Erin. Lied about Rick. Hiding something.* Roelke underscored that last word savagely.

He reached for a blank card, trying to dig the name of Erin Litkowski's husband from his memory. Steve, wasn't it? Steve Litkowski. Had Erin turned to Rick for help? Roelke didn't have any trouble with the picture of Steve Litkowski going after a cop who tried to assist Erin. But how could Litkowski have gotten his hands on a gun locked up in police Evidence? Roelke wrote, *Check up on Steven Litkowski.* Time to learn what the asshole was up to these days.

On another blank card he wrote *Lobo/Wolf. Sherman says Lobo was talking to Rick in the Rusty Nail shortly before the shooting. Recently released from Waupun. Seems to have disappeared from MKE.*

Roelke lined these four cards up neatly on his dashboard—Captain Heikinen, Kip, Steve Litkowski, Lobo. He willed his brain to find a link, some connection. None of it made sense. He'd never heard even a *hint* of any shady stuff about Heikinen. Same with Kip—he was straight as a signpost and ran a clean place.

Litkowski was a bully and a wife-beater. Lobo was a felon. How might those two have connected? And how did Erin fit into this? Why had she come back to Milwaukee? How did she end up working for Kip? And why, Roelke demanded silently, did she run from *me*?

Maybe it was time to contact Erin's sister. Roelke considered, then decided against it. If she was hiding Erin, she probably wouldn't say anything. If she hadn't known Erin was back in Milwaukee, she'd be devastated to discover that her sister had come back but disappeared again.

Roelke wondered once more if drugs were in the middle of this mess. Cocaine didn't discriminate. Some people got involved for the money; some for the kicks. Maybe Lobo had been a dealer, and Litkowski had a secret habit. It wasn't unheard of for some big-time dealer to manage his business from prison. Roelke still couldn't fit Kip into the puzzle, but if Rick had discovered that Captain Heikinen was on the take, maybe he'd been trying to get Lobo to flip. Roelke could almost hear Rick: "Come on, man, you just got out! You want to go back to prison? Or do you want to help take down a dirty cop?"

Just one problem with that theory: he hadn't found any evidence of drugs. Somebody had stolen a gun from Evidence, and somebody had used that gun to shoot Officer Rick Almirez in the back of the head. Everything beyond that was conjecture.

Roelke felt a wave of loneliness as he watched pedestrians pick their way over snowbanks. *I'm a Lone Ranger,* he'd said to Klinefelter. Well, he was still discovering what that felt like. During his days as a Milwaukee patrolman, he'd always had Rick to kick ideas around with. More recently, he'd had some good conversations with Chloe about investigations. She hated being in the middle of crime stuff, but she was smart. She approached things differently, and she'd helped him a lot.

But he couldn't think about Chloe right now.

Instead he made a new to-do list:

1. *Call Jody & ask about Lobo and Heikinen*
2. *Ask Dobry to check Steven Litkowski's address, and check for arrest record*
3. *Ask Dobry about Linka-Małgorzata*

Roelke stared at the next blank line for a long time before cursing, gritting his teeth, and finishing:

4. *Go to Waupun*

He stuffed the cards away, found a payphone, and called Jody. "It's me," he said. "How are you doing?"

"I never know what to say when people ask me that."

"Me either. Listen, I need to ask you a couple of things. Do you know if there was any bad blood between Rick and Captain Heikinen?"

"As far as I know, Rick didn't have any direct dealings with the captain. He would have been more likely to talk about that with you."

"He never said anything to me. I was just wondering. Here's another one: did you ever hear Rick mention a bad guy named Lobo? It could be a nickname."

"I don't think so. Is it important?"

"It could be. I just found out that Rick was talking to a guy called Lobo in the Rusty Nail that night."

"Wolf," Jody murmured. "Is that who shot Rick?"

"It's too early to know that," Roelke cautioned. "But it's a start. Evidently this Lobo guy just got out of prison, so maybe Rick had arrested him."

"You can check that, right?"

"I'm going to try. The thing is . . . it's possible that some of Rick's records are missing."

"*Missing*?"

"Somebody got to Rick's field reports before they could be officially pulled. They ended up on the detective's desk, but I've got no way to know what, if anything, disappeared on the way."

Silence.

"Listen, Jody. It looks like a cop is involved. Maybe more than one."

"What? I don't understand!"

"Me neither. But I'll get it. I swear I will."

"I didn't think I could possibly feel any worse." Jody's voice was hollow. "But I do now."

Roelke pressed one knuckle against his forehead. "Maybe I shouldn't have told you."

"*No.*" The hollowness was replaced with a gritty strength. "I need to know, Roelke. Don't try to shelter me."

"Just don't mention any of this to anyone, okay? I don't know who to trust anymore."

162

Chloe kept Owen company for the rest of the afternoon. She had no-where else to be, and she was interested. Besides, she was pretty sure she'd get lost if she tried to leave the mill on her own. If she even had the nerve to try.

On the way back down, they paused on the fifth floor. Owen opened an interior door. "Take a peek."

Chloe walked into an office that might have been vacated moments earlier, not almost two decades. The desk still held a big blotter, typewriter, pens. A woman's sweater dangled from a coat tree. A placard—*Every day is safety day!*—hung on the wall. A sign on a time clock reminded workers that cards could be punched no earlier than ten minutes before shifts started.

"It looks like the employees just stepped out," Chloe said.

"When the mill shut in 1965, the workers got no notice. Some of them learned about it on the evening news." Owen studied the room. "When I'm here alone, I half-expect one of the old millers to tap me on the shoulder."

"Yeah." Chloe was glad that she wasn't the only one tuned to the workers who had come and gone.

They stopped next on the second floor to see rows of roller stands. "The grinding floor," Owen said. "They called it 'the money floor.' These rollers were so much more efficient than millstones that they revolutionized the entire process. Groups of roller mills were designed to grind grain into finer and finer flour."

"Ah," Chloe said sagely.

He tapped a roller mill. "I've isolated this one so we can simu-late an operating machine. Fortunately I've had help from a couple of undergrads, and a millwright who got laid off in 1965. He loves tinkering with the machinery."

"Is he bitter about the mill closing so abruptly?"

Owen considered. "It broke his heart, but I wouldn't say he's bitter. Now, there were some ugly labor problems in the early 1900s. Union men versus owners, that sort of thing. Some guys lost their jobs, so I imagine that caused hard feelings."

Some things never change, Chloe thought.

They left the complex as the afternoon sun sank in the west. "Say," Owen said as they passed—legally—through a gate in the fence. "Did you ever see Bohemian Flats?

"That community down by the river?"

Owen clicked the gate's padlock. "Right. Even with all the automation, two million pounds of flour a day did not make itself. The city's population increased by something like thirteen hundred percent between 1870 and 1890. A lot of immigrants found work in the mills. And some of them lived down on the Flats." Owen glanced her. "I'd feel better if we go down together, okay? I'll drive."

"If it will make you feel better," Chloe said magnanimously.

He drove no more than a mile or so before Chloe saw a low flatland between the river and the road. Owen pulled over. "This was Bohemian Flats, although there's not a lot to see now," he said apologetically.

Chloe didn't care. There was *something* here, something that compelled her to get out of the car. Behind them, steep bluffs rose to the city proper. A bridge ran almost overhead, connecting the highlands here on the western bank of the Mississippi with the equally impressive bluffs on the east side.

Owen got out, too. "At one time this was a community of maybe five hundred people. Lots of Slovaks, Czechs, Irish, Swedes, Germans,

Poles…" He hunched his shoulders against a knife-like wind. "It's hard to imagine, now that everything—and everyone—is gone."

"Oh, I can imagine it," Chloe assured him. It was strange to be here in this silent, windswept pocket. The bustling modern city on high seemed more than a steep climb away. She squinted into the growing shadows and had no trouble at all imagining the people who had once called this place home.

# TWENTY

## AUGUST 1917

LIDIA STOOD KNEE-DEEP IN the Mississippi River's cold muck, waiting for a few more shingles to drift within reach and dreaming of hats. One day, she thought, I shall own a hat. Perhaps it would be a bonnet, covered with silk and adorned with ribbons. Or perhaps it would be woven of straw, with a perky brim and a cluster of artificial flowers. Either one would be glorious.

She'd climbed the ninety-seven steps to the top of the hill. She knew how Yankee women dressed. Now that she was seventeen, she needed to find good work. She'd dreaded the prospect of hiring out to clean floors or mind babies for the very gawking women who came to look down on the Flats. But now, she thought, perhaps I'll be able to earn money for a hat without going into service as maid or nanny...

A floating shingle bumped into her. She snatched it quickly, and the two more close behind. There, that was enough to fill her basket—which was good, because the lumber business was in decline, which meant the pickings were, too. Lidia waded ashore and headed home.

She had the shingles drying in the sun by the time Grandfather Pawel trudged home from the mill. Through the window she watched him nod with satisfaction before turning to the washbasin by the front door.

He came inside as she set the table for dinner. "Well done, Lidia." He paused, coughing. When he could, he continued, "Now I can mend the ridgeline."

Mama turned from the cookstove. "Not until you've had a good meal and some rest," she scolded lightly. "You're too tired."

Grandfather Pawel sank down at the table. "Frania, I don't think I can last much longer." He stared at his big hands. "I'd hoped to last another year or two. We'll hurt for my salary."

Mama began dishing up the soup. "We'll get by." Her tone was light, but her mouth settled into a worried line.

Their anxiety made Lidia's heart ache. She took a deep breath. "Perhaps things won't be quite as difficult as you imagine. I want to apply for a job."

Mama's eyebrows lifted. "What job is this?"

Lidia took great care to set the spoons out with precision. "At the mill."

"At the *Washburn* Mill?" Mama's eyes went wide. "There are no jobs for women at the mill."

"There will be soon," Lidia told her. "The company is going to begin packaging flour in small sacks, which are more convenient for homemakers. They are going to hire forty women to handle the bags!"

Mama looked accusingly at Grandfather Pawel, who raised both hands defensively. "She didn't hear about it from me."

Lidia slid into her place. "Tomasz told me about it," she said, as innocently as possible. Tomasz had, in fact, urged her to apply. "We must be good Americans," he'd said. "Especially now with the war, and so much hatred toward foreigners. We must be one hundred percent Americans."

Lidia suspected he was right, but her mother and grandfather didn't share that view. Well, right now she didn't want the conversation to get diverted to a discussion of her choice of beau. "Mama, the pay is good! Fourteen dollars a week, and Sundays off. *Please*. I want to apply."

Mama set the last soup bowl down on the table with such force that broth spilled over the brim. "That mill has brought this family nothing but grief!" Tears glinted in her eyes. Grandfather Pawel looked stricken, too.

Lidia hated bringing pain to the two people she loved most in the world. But the deaths of my father and grandmother have nothing to do with me, she thought. "I won't be doing anything dangerous. With the dust collectors, the chance of fire is very small. I won't be working near the train tracks or big machines. The sacks will be just five pounds."

The silence was heavy.

"I could look for a position as maid, or a nanny," Lidia allowed, "but there is little future in such work. The world will always need flour! At the mill, there might be room for advancement. They say they want women to become supervisors on their floor. They say that women might be able to move into clerical jobs too, especially with men leaving for the war. I would need more education for something like that, of course …"

She paused again. Mama didn't move. Through the open door came the normal evening sounds: boys playing, women laughing, a few distant shouts, a dog barking.

Grandfather Pawel had been staring at his soup, but he finally looked at her. "There is trouble in the mill you may not be aware of. Some men want to form a union. They figure that with the war, there is more need for flour than ever, and now is the time. The boss men are against it. There is talk of a strike."

Lidia sucked in her lower lip. Everyone knew that in 1903, over a thousand Washburn Mill employees had gone on strike—and lost. Managers hired new workers, swearing they'd never bargain with a labor union. Some of the strikers had eventually been re-hired, but none of the organizers. Growing up on the Flats, surrounded by immigrants working the most grueling, dangerous, and poor-paying jobs, Lidia had heard plenty of grumbles and complaints. And she sympathized.

Mama's mouth tightened. "I don't want you in the middle of such trouble!"

"A strike wouldn't have anything to do with me," Lidia insisted. "They are setting aside a special place for the women to work. We won't be anywhere near the men."

"My *kwiatuszek,*" Grandfather Pawel said sadly. My little flower. "I know you are a hard worker. I know you want to help the family and get ahead. But I don't think the mill is the right place to do it."

Lidia twisted her spoon in her fingers. "I want to be part of something important! Minneapolis is the flour milling capital of the world. Every day, these mills produced enough flour to bake twelve *million* loaves of bread." She was quoting Tomasz, now. She couldn't fully grasp that number, but his eyes shone when he spoke of it, and the enormity of it excited her. "So … may I apply for the position?"

Grandfather Pawel hitched one shoulder in a tiny, helpless shrug. Mama lifted her chin and stared at the paper cutting tacked like a blessing above the front door. Grandmother Magdalena had made the beautiful *wycinanka* shortly before her death.

Finally Mama turned her gaze on Lidia. "You are old enough to make your own decisions."

"Oh *Matka*, thank you—"

"I'm not finished," Mama snapped. "Think hard before giving the mill men your application. Tomasz has filled your head with big ideas, but I fear that working in the Washburn Mill will bring you sorrow."

# TWENTY-ONE

ROELKE'S COUSIN LIBBY AND her kids were waiting in the lobby when he arrived at the Milwaukee Public Museum. Time to switch gears, he told himself. In a major way.

Libby was a blunt, no-nonsense woman. After divorcing her scumbag husband, she'd done an impressive job, in Roelke's opinion, of creating a new life for herself and the kids. She was bemused by, but tolerant of, four-year-old Dierdre's passion for Disney princesses, girlie-girl ruffles, and dolls with long curls. But Libby didn't always know how to handle her son.

"Hey, guys," Roelke said. He hoped his hearty tone sounded more normal to their ears than it did to his.

Libby smiled. "It's good to see you."

Roelke kissed the top of Dierdre's head—carefully avoiding the plastic tiara—before turning to Justin. "I understand you've got a school project to do. Ready to see the museum?"

"Just you and me." Justin glared at his mother and sister. "Not *them*."

"Hey," Roelke said sharply. "That kind of talk is not okay. I want to see the exhibits with you, but we're not going anywhere until you apologize to your mother."

He thought Justin might refuse, possibly at the top of his lungs. Finally the boy muttered, "Sorry."

"Thank you," Libby said, and she thanked Roelke with her eyes. "You can take the camera, Justin. The exhibits close in an hour, so how about Dierdre and I meet you guys in the snack shop then?"

Roelke followed a sign pointing toward the museum's most beloved exhibit, The Streets of Old Milwaukee. "So," he said to Justin, "what is your assignment exactly?"

"We have to do a project about an ethnic group that settled in Wisconsin."

Roelke had visited the museum for the same reason when he was in fourth grade. The exhibit had been brand-new then. "Any group? Aren't you supposed to study your own ethnic background?"

"No. We get to choose."

"Well, hunh." Evidently, Roelke thought, a few things *have* changed since I was in fourth grade.

"It's better this way," Justin explained earnestly. "Suppose some kid in my class was adopted? Or suppose some kid's parents don't know where their ancestors came from? That's why we get to pick. No one ends up feeling bad."

"That sounds like a good plan," Roelke agreed.

They'd reached the exhibit. "Come on!" Justin cried.

Roelke was relieved to see Justin shaking off his bad mood. Roelke would never understand how Dan Raymo could be so callously indifferent to his kids. Dierdre had no real relationship with her father. She also was easygoing and adaptable by nature. But Justin … Justin was a sensitive kid. He wore glasses and was not good at sports and didn't make friends easily. And he still tried hard to believe that his dad was a nice guy who loved him. I'm glad Libby called me, Roelke thought, and followed Justin into the dim corridor.

Museum curators had created a glimpse of the city at the turn of the last century. Roelke felt a sense of his own boyhood awe return as he strolled down a narrow cobblestone street complete with horse troughs, fireplugs, lampposts simulating gaslight, and even trees. Sidewalks bordered maybe two dozen businesses, including a candy shop, movie house, tea shop, and tavern. Manikins dressed in old-timey costumes were visible through the windows of shops and homes.

"Ooh, look at this one!" Justin called, his nose pressed against the window of a butcher shop. Inside a woman appeared to be arranging fresh sausages on a plate. More sausages hung on the wall behind her. Justin stared hungrily for a moment before racing on. The museum was quiet at this hour, and they had the exhibit to themselves.

Was the city ever really like this? Roelke wondered as he ambled along. Quaint, quiet, peaceful? Maybe for some—good Germans and Irish and Polish folks in their middle-class neighborhoods. Maybe life was still like this for some people. Not for cops, though. Never for cops.

Roelke's heart squeezed into his throat when he spotted a re-created restaurant: THE COMFORT SALOON AND RESTAURANT, CHAS. MADER. BOTTLE BEER 5 CENTS. He and Rick had wanted to take Chloe and Jody to Mader's. Now they never would.

"Hey, Roelke!" Justin called. "Is this an old-fashioned phone booth?"

Roelke joined the boy in front of a round, white-painted wooden structure with a fancy pointy roof. "Do you see a telephone inside?"

"Nope," Justin reported. "And there's no windows."

"Imagine that I walked a beat in Milwaukee a hundred years ago and arrested somebody. Back before public phones and handy-talkies."

"Oh!" Justin's face lit with understanding. "Is this where you'd put a bad guy? Like, if you were really mad at him?"

"I think the idea was that I could lock a bad guy in this holding cell until the paddy wagon came to take him to jail. But it *would* help if I was mad." Roelke could think of several people he'd like to lock in that dark, cramped holding cell—forever.

The Streets of Old Milwaukee flowed into the European Village, where each house was devoted to a different ethnic group. "This is where you'll get some good ideas for your project," Roelke told Justin. "Look in all the windows and see what house you like."

As Justin began his study, Roelke stared up at the wooden EUROPEAN VILLAGE sign. A fancy heart and two roosters were painted above the words. He thought of the card Erin had dropped at the restaurant, with its chickens.

"Roelke!" Justin gestured wildly from the window of a white-washed home with thatched roof. "I like this one."

Roelke joined him and found the identification label: *Polska Chata*. POLISH HOUSE. "Why this one?"

Justin tipped his head, considering. "It's really cheerful."

Roelke peered through the window. "It is," he agreed. "But you should look at all the houses before you decide."

When Justin wandered off, Roelke stayed at the Polish House window. A female manikin wore red shoes, a green shawl over a lacy white blouse, and a vivid skirt adorned with flowers. Bright flowers were painted on the white walls. The yellow ceiling was covered with painted strings of flowers. More flowers decorated the green furniture and the white chimney above the stove. Flowers were even painted around the windows on the outside walls.

Roelke pulled Erin's card from his pocket and studied it. The card's flowers were similar to those decorating the Polish House. But although a plate hanging on the back wall featured two blue roosters, and a metal rooster sat in one windowsill, there were no chickens in sight.

So ... is the design on this little card really Polish? Roelke wondered. Does it have some meaning? Does all that fancy stuff in the Polish House have meaning, or is it just decoration? He had no idea. But he knew who might. All this ethnic culture stuff was right up her alley.

Suddenly Roelke missed Chloe so badly that he had to sit down. He wanted to show her the chicken card. He wanted to show her the Polish House. He wanted to talk with her about Rick. He wanted to crush her into his arms and bury his face in her hair. He wanted to drift off to sleep with her head on his shoulder.

"Roelke? I like the German House best." Justin appeared beside his bench. "It's got ..." The boy's voice trailed away, and his eyes grew wide. "You're *crying*."

Roelke swiped at his cheeks and felt wetness. He drew a shuddery breath into his lungs, blew it back out. "I guess I am," he said. "My best friend got killed a few days ago, and Chloe is visiting a friend in Minnesota. I'm very sad."

"I've never seen you cry before," Justin whispered.

"I don't *like* to cry. But every once in a while, when you're feeling really awful, it's okay to cry." Roelke didn't know what else to say. Part of him was horrified for letting tears spill over in front of Justin, and part of him thought that it might be okay. He gave Justin time to say something. Speak of his father, maybe, and how sad he felt about Dan backing out of this museum trip. Justin stayed silent, but he nodded once and patted Roelke's arm gently. Maybe that was enough.

"Did you say you liked the German House best?" Roelke asked.

Justin nodded again. "It's got a whole lot of toys."

"Sounds good. We better take some pictures."

When they met Libby and Dierdre, Justin told them all about the cool German house. Dierdre was busy with a coloring book, but Libby listened intently. "Sounds like a winner," she told him. "On the way home, we'll drop your film off at the drugstore to be developed."

"Can we please buy some posterboard too?" Justin asked. "I can make a display with the pictures."

"Sure thing, buddy. And you know what? I've got an old German cookie recipe at home. If you like, we can bake some for your class."

Justin's face lit up. "Okay!"

Libby fished a couple of dollar bills from her jeans pocket. "The gift shop is right over there. Go see if they have some good postcards." When Justin disappeared, Libby turned to Roelke. "I can't thank you enough."

"It's okay. I'm glad I could help."

She peered at him. "Are you all right?"

"I never know what to say when people ask me that."

Libby wrapped her arms around him. *Don't do that,* Roelke almost said, because she wasn't Chloe, and because he was afraid he might leak another tear or two if she was too nice to him. But in the end he kept his mouth shut and hugged her back.

"You've always been there for me, Roelke," she told him quietly. "*Always.* You know I'd do anything for you. All you have to do is let me know."

"I just miss Rick. And I miss Chloe."

"Chloe will be back."

"I don't know. She... I think I screwed things up."

"She'll be back," Libby repeated. "Trust me. I know."

Roelke shrugged.

Libby handed over a small piece of notepaper. "Here. This is her friend's phone number. Give her a call."

Roelke stuffed the slip into his pocket.

"When was the last time you had real food?" Libby asked. "Come over for breakfast tomorrow. Or lunch. Whatever you want."

"I can't come over tomorrow."

"Why not?"

Roelke watched two older ladies hurry through the lobby, zipping up coats and pulling on gloves. "Because I'm going to Waupun tomorrow," he said. "I need to talk to Patrick."

# TWENTY-TWO

WHEN CHLOE FOUND HER way to Ariel's cottage, lights glowing inside gave the illusion that all was well. But as soon as Chloe got inside and shed her parka, Ariel folded her into a tight hug. "I can't believe you drove all the way back up here. Toby shouldn't have called you."

"I'm glad he did." Chloe stepped back and surveyed her friend. Ariel appeared even smaller than she had just two days earlier, more fragile. Dark crescents shadowed her eyes. "When was the last time you ate a decent meal? I brought some potato soup I had in my freezer. Let's get that on the stove."

Once Chloe had the soup melting over low heat, she set out a plate of crackers, sliced cheddar, and walnuts. She poured two glasses of wine and set one in front of her friend. "Okay, talk. Why on earth did you get arrested?"

Ariel hung her head. "I did something really, really stupid."

"What did you do?" Chloe asked, as calmly as humanly possible. She'd been waiting for twenty-four hours to hear the tale, and she wanted it. Now.

"My dissertation outline is due in a couple of weeks. Dr. Whyte offered to review a draft. I gave it to him last week."

"I think I know where this is going."

Ariel nodded. "The police have a sign on Dr. Whyte's office door, saying it's off-limits. I guess they're not finished going through everything in there. I was afraid I wouldn't get my outline back. At least not for a long time. And I didn't make photocopies of anything, which was incredibly dumb, I know…"

Chloe made a cracker-nut-cheese sandwich with one hand, and a circular *go on* gesture with the other.

"So I just sort of… panicked."

"Why didn't you just ask the police if you could have your outline back?"

"I was afraid they'd say no."

"So you decided to break into his office?" Chloe asked, trying really hard to sound nonjudgmental.

"I didn't actually break in," Ariel said defensively. "I had a key."

"You had a key to Dr. Whyte's office? I didn't realize you worked that closely with him."

Ariel studied a walnut. "I didn't. But Owen did."

"Did Owen know you borrowed his key?" Chloe got up to stir the soup.

"Oh, yes. In fact, he wanted to come with me. I wouldn't let him." Ariel sighed. "That's the only thing about this whole mess I did right. I told the police I borrowed the key without Owen knowing anything about it.

Chloe stabbed a frozen chunk of soup with a bit more effort than necessary. Lying to the police was always a bad idea. And now *I* know Ariel lied, she thought. Lovely. She remembered Owen's oh-so-casual question at the mill that afternoon: *Have you talked to Ariel today?* Ariel had probably been too unnerved to call him herself.

Ariel put her elbows on the counter and buried her face in her hands. "I can't *believe* this happened."

"So, what actually did happen?" Chloe asked.

"On Sunday night I just kept stewing and worrying and tossing and turning...so finally, about three a.m., I got up and drove over to campus. Owen's key got me in a back door. Then..."

"Then you made a dash for Dr. Whyte's office?"

"I slipped inside the office, but I couldn't find the file. A security guard saw my flashlight through the office window. He called the cops." She hunched her shoulders, staring at her lap. "And they came."

"That must have been awful."

"'Awful' is an understatement."

"Oh, sweetie, I'm so sorry." Chloe considered something along the lines of "Someday you'll laugh about this," but Ariel looked so stricken, it didn't seem wise. Finally Chloe said, "So you got arrested. And you called Toby. Why did you hang up on him?"

"Because I didn't know what to say. I was humiliated."

Chloe opened cupboards until she found soup bowls. "But obviously after questioning you, the cops let you go. They must have believed that you didn't have anything to do with Dr. Whyte's death, and that going into his office—while not the best idea in the world—wasn't intended as a criminal act."

"I guess so," Ariel said dully. "I don't really know what they think. They questioned me in this grubby little room that smelled like mildew, and then all of a sudden they said I could leave. I called a cab and got here about four thirty in the morning. I did let Toby know I was home, but neither one of us wanted to bother you at that hour. We didn't expect you'd leave home so early."

"I was a tad concerned." Chloe checked that there were no more frozen bits of leek or potato. "Did you at least get your outline back?"

"No. The police didn't offer it, and at that point, I wasn't going to ask."

"Probably wise," Chloe agreed, although honestly, the fact that the cops hadn't at least promised its return seemed a little petty. "Where's a ladle? Oh, I see it." Chloe dished up two bowls of soup, set one in front of Ariel, and settled down across the breakfast bar from her.

"Academically, I'm screwed. I'll end up paying tuition for an extra semester while I try to re-create my work." Ariel picked up her spoon, stirred, put it back down. "I'm really not hungry."

"I don't care. Eat it. All of it."

Ariel managed several gulps. "What about your boyfriend? I thought you needed to be there." She looked ready to cry. "I'm *so* sorry, Chloe. I made things worse for everybody."

"It actually worked out okay, sadly enough. It turned out Roelke didn't want my support."

"No?"

"It's complicated." Chloe sighed. "We're still figuring out what kind of couple we are. We've been together for a while now, but we've never used the L-word."

"The L-word is a big deal," Ariel agreed. "Once you tell someone you love them, everything changes."

"Rick's girlfriend told me it's really hard to be with a cop. There's stuff they won't talk about. And literally, while she was telling me this, I looked out the window and saw Roelke drive away." Chloe shook her head. "Maybe it's time to decide what we want from a relationship."

"Do you want something more?"

And that is the million-dollar question, Chloe thought. "The night Rick was killed we went to the wedding of two Milwaukee police officers. It was the first time I'd really spent time around a lot of Roelke's friends, and it was…different."

"Hard to fit in?"

"I didn't know how to behave. I didn't say anything, but Roelke could tell I didn't really have a good time. And in fairness, he's bent over backwards to try to learn about the things that are important to me. He's even spent time with my family. Voluntarily."

"An acid test." Ariel scooped up another bite of soup.

"I tried, Ariel. I really did. But me trying to fit in at a cop party is like—"

"Like me trying to fit in at an industrial historic site." Ariel made a rueful gesture. "Are you sure you shouldn't be back home with Roelke?"

Chloe shook her head. "Roelke has shut me out. His best friend is dead, and nobody's caught his killer. There's no room for anything else. No room for me."

"I'm sorry."

"It's complicated," Chloe repeated, considering her wine as if hoping to find clarity among the bubbles. Finally she realized the illogic in that and drained the goblet instead. "Back in December, we were on vacation in Iowa and Roelke got involved in a murder case. He did a lot of really good police work, but in the end, he thought he should have done more. That he missed some clues. He lost some confidence."

"Once you've lost your confidence," Ariel said, "it's really hard to find it again."

There was a peculiar note in Ariel's voice, an intonation Chloe couldn't define. "Why do I feel like we're not talking about Roelke anymore?"

"I'm thinking about quitting the history biz. Maybe I'm meant to teach ballet to five-year-olds."

"No, no, no." Chloe put her spoon down. "Listen to me. Dr. Whyte's death was horrid. Us finding him made it a thousand times worse. And I can imagine how you feel after your little … excursion to the police station. But you can't let what happened drive you out of the field. Industrial history may not be your thing, but this mill represents an awesome opportunity, and you get to be involved in planning the interpretive programming—"

"Not if I don't meet the stupid deadline! I tried to work on the interpretive plan today, and I couldn't string two coherent thoughts together. If I don't do a good job with this proposal, it won't just be bad for me. It will be bad for the historical society. They've gone way, way out on a limb to save the mill, and I'm supposed to turn in the proposal on Friday. *Friday*, Chloe! That's just three days away."

"You can do it. You've already got some great ideas. And I've got some additional suggestions. We can kick ideas around this evening, and I can even start typing some things up."

"I suppose."

Chloe sat back. She'd delivered a pretty darn good pep talk, but Ariel didn't look even a little bit cheered. "What? Is there something else?"

Ariel blinked. "What?"

"Look, spill it," Chloe said. "I'm your friend. I want to help. I'm *here*, for God's sake. But I keep getting this feeling that you're not being completely honest with me." She carried their bowls to the sink, giving Ariel time to make up her mind. She needed to give herself time, too. It ticked her off to think that after everything she'd done to be supportive, Ariel was keeping secrets.

"You're right," Ariel said.

Chloe left the dishes and sat back down. "Yeah?"

Ariel took a deep breath. "Last week, Dr. Whyte asked to photograph me dancing in the mill. Toe shoes, gauzy tutu, the whole thing."

"Okay," Chloe said slowly. Having seen *Beauty in Blight*, Dr. Whyte's current photo exhibit, she got the concept.

"I didn't really want to do it, but … he's my professor, one of my advisors. Was, I mean. He was an important member of the inner circle involved with saving and interpreting the mill."

"So you did the photo shoot?"

"I thought we'd just take a couple of pictures—it was freezing in there—but he wanted a lot." Ariel had been studying her thumbnail, but now she met Chloe's gaze. "Everything I said before is true. I want my dissertation outline back. But I also wanted to find the photographs."

Chloe rubbed her temples. "I understand why you want the pictures back, but why hide that? Why the secrecy and sneaking around?"

"I … It just didn't seem right."

"*What* didn't seem right?"

"The whole photography session. I was sorry I'd agreed. I had this strange feeling the whole time, like some of the residents might be watching us."

"I've had that feeling in the mill myself," Chloe admitted.

"It seemed crass to be posing *en pointe* in a tutu while people in the next room were hungry and sick."

"I can see that," Chloe said. Sort of, anyway. She still didn't quite get why Ariel had felt a need to hide the whole photo shoot from her. She was still trying to figure out what to say when the telephone rang.

Ariel stared at the phone through two more rings before she seemed to remember that action was required. She jumped up and grabbed the receiver. "Hello? Oh, hi, Toby. … What? No. Chloe and I were talking, and we didn't have the news on. … They did? What did they say? ... They said *what*?" To Chloe's surprise, Ariel burst out laughing. She stifled it immediately, and threw Chloe a guilty look before telling Toby, "I'm sorry, that was horribly inappropriate. It's just so—so—unexpected. How in the world could Whyte have—"

"What?" Chloe demanded.

"I'll talk to you later, okay?" Ariel told her brother. She hung up and stared at Chloe. "You are not going to believe this."

"For the love of God, Ariel, *what*?"

"The police released Dr. Whyte's cause of death. And according to the medical examiner, he drowned."

# TWENTY-THREE

AFTER LEAVING THE MILWAUKEE Public Museum, Roelke walked Libby and the kids to her car, promised to get some rest and eat a decent supper, and waved them off. Then he went in search of a payphone. He had to walk several blocks, because he wanted a booth, not just an open wall mount. He stacked up his coins, extricated the scrap of paper Libby had given him, and placed the long-distance call.

A woman answered on the third ring. "Hello?"

"Is this Ariel…" Roelke squinted at the paper in the dim light and decided not to attempt the last name. "Is this Ariel? My name is Roelke McKenna. I'm—"

The phone clunked down. "Chloe! It's for you!"

I guess she knows who I am, he thought, not sure if that was reassuring or not.

Chloe came on the line. "Roelke?"

"Yeah. It's me."

"Um … how are you?"

"Managing. How are you?"

186

"Okay." She sounded cautious.

He didn't really blame her. "I miss you."

"I miss you, too." Her voice softened. "I really do."

"I'm sorry things are like this."

"Me, too."

"But I'm doing what I need to do."

"Have you found anything?"

"I'm working on it. Spending time in the old neighborhood. After a crime, it's important to go back to the people who live in the community. They know the place, the people, better than anyone."

"I'm sure that's true. I just worry about you going it alone."

"Libby's ordering me around. And I've still got a few friends on the MPD. You haven't met them all, but you know Dobry Banik. And Bliss."

"I had a chance to talk with her a little bit on Sunday, when I went to see Jody," Chloe said. "She must be good at her job to make sergeant, so ask for help if you need it. And I'm sure Dobry wants to find out who did this horrible thing as badly as you do." She hesitated. "I'm not a cop, and I didn't know Rick well, so I guess I couldn't be of much help to you…"

You could, he thought, but he didn't know how to assure of her of that *and* explain why he'd refused her company—at least not without a much bigger pile of dimes and quarters—so he kept his mouth shut.

" … so let people like Bliss and Banik help," she was saying. "Please."

Roelke pressed his knuckle against his forehead. He hated this. He hated the telephone, the distance, the uncharacteristically tentative tone in Chloe's speech. Most of all he hated the reason he was standing in a damn Milwaukee phone booth on a cold February evening.

"You still there?" she asked.

187

"Yeah. Listen, can I ask you a question? Somebody gave me this little card thing. It's the size and shape of a business card, but instead of a name and address, it just has artwork on the front."

"Artwork?"

"Two chickens and some flowers. Very colorful. I have no idea what they mean. If anything." He rolled his eyes, feeling stupid.

"Is the card somehow involved with Rick's murder?"

"It might be. But I was in the Milwaukee Public Museum this afternoon with Justin—"

"Oh, good."

He frowned, momentarily distracted. "Why is that good?"

"I know how much Justin loves spending time with you."

The operator cut in and asked for more coins. Keep it moving, McKenna, he told himself. "Anyway, a lot of Polish people live in my old district—"

"Polish? Or Polish-American?"

He wasn't clear on the distinction. "Both, I guess. *Anyway*, I was looking at the Polish House in the museum, and it had a lot of painted flowers on the walls and furniture and stuff that sort of reminded me of the flowers on the little card. You know, folk art. And I wondered if there might be a connection. Do you know anything about Polish folk art?"

"Not very much," Chloe said doubtfully. "Let me put Ariel back on."

The phone clunked down again. "He's got a question about Polish folk art," Chloe said in the distance.

Ariel spoke into his ear. "Hi, it's Ariel again."

He repeated what he'd told Chloe. "The style seemed similar to what I saw in the Polish House."

"It might be *wycinanki*."

188

Roelke had no idea what vee-chee-non-kee was. "You think?"

"The Polish folk art of paper cutting is called *wycinanki*. Or *wycinanka*, for a single piece. Does the artwork on your card look like it might be cut from paper? From layers of different-colored paper pasted one on top of the next? I know your card was printed, but does the style look like the original might have been constructed that way?"

"It's kind of hard to tell."

"You said the design shows two chickens? Not roosters?"

"They're chickens."

"Roosters are very common motifs in Polish *wycinanki*. Roosters symbolize vigilance, or aggressive resistance to intruders. Something like that. Are you sure your birds aren't stylized roosters?"

Roelke was sorry he'd ever mentioned the damn card. "They—are—*chickens*. Short tails. No combs."

"Hmm." She sounded dubious. "Well, it's hard to know for sure."

"One more question, if you don't mind. Do you speak Polish? Do you know what *Małgorzata* means?"

"Sorry," Ariel said. "I only know a few words, and that's not one of them."

"Thanks anyway. Can you put Chloe back on?"

Chloe returned. "Was that helpful?"

"Maybe," he lied. "Look, I'm sorry, but I'm in a phone booth and about out of coins—"

"Want me to call you back so we can talk longer?"

*Yes*, he thought. "No," he lied. "I'm meeting Dobry in a bit."

"Oh." Pause. "I'm glad you called, Roelke. I'll probably be here for another couple of days. Take care of yourself."

"You too," he began, "and—" But his time and coins ran out, and the line went dead. Just as well, maybe. He didn't even know what he'd been going to say.

# TWENTY-FOUR
## JULY 1918

"You really should consider moving," Tomasz said, looking from Lidia's mother to her grandfather. "Rent is higher on the hill, to be sure, but the advantages—"

"I don't believe we will," Grandfather Pawel said. Again. They were all speaking English because Tomasz preferred it, but that wasn't the only reason his voice was stiff.

Lidia flushed. Tomasz meant well. He wanted the best not just for her, but for her family. And she agreed with him, really. It was unusual for a family to stay in Bohemian Flats for so long. The spring floods this year had been as bad as any, and lugging all their valuables to a friend's house higher up the hill had been a struggle. No one down here had electricity or indoor plumbing. Would Mama and Grandfather Pawel be able to manage once she was married and gone?

"We just worry for you," Lidia said softly. "That's all." She finished drying the last of the dinner dishes and draped the cloth near the stove.

Some of the tension eased from Mama's face. "We can talk about houses another time," she told Lidia and Tomasz. "It's your engagement night! We should be celebrating."

Grandfather Pawel looked to Mama. "Frania? I think this would be a good time to ..."

Mama nodded and hurried into the next room.

Lidia saw Tomasz's apprehension. "*Matka* likes the old traditions," she whispered. "It's harmless."

Mama reappeared with a loaf of bread on a plate and two white scarves. She put the plate in the middle of the table.

Grandfather Pawel cleared his throat. "All right, you two. Stand across the table from each other and clasp your right hands."

Lidia stepped into place and reached over the bread. Tomasz took her hand. His grip was firm, steadying. He was a handsome fellow, with muscular arms and tiny black curls at the nape of his neck. His eyes glinted with pleasure whenever she walked into a room, and what girl could resist that?

Then Pawel used the scarves to tie Tomasz's and Lidia's hands together—once, twice. "May you always work together to prepare your bread." His voice was husky.

Lidia knew one wild moment of panic and almost jerked her hand against the loose bond. Tomasz squeezed harder, as if to say, *Oh, no. We shall face the rest of our lives together.*

I will remember this moment forever, she thought: the intensity of Tomasz's eyes in the lamplight, the warmth of his skin pressed against hers.

Mama cut two pieces of bread from the loaf. "The larger is for Lidia," she said. "May she always have bread for her children."

Lidia ate her piece, feeling every crumb on her tongue, her gaze still locked with Tomasz's. *Children*. It was hard to imagine.

Grandfather Pawel slipped the scarves off and handed one to each of them. She was to keep her white cloth forever. In hard times, it would remind her that she'd pledged her life to Tomasz.

Mama began cutting the rest of the loaf into small pieces. "I'll put these bits into a basket," she told Lidia and Tomasz. "Take them to our neighbors so they may bless your upcoming marriage as well."

"I'm afraid Lidia and I must be going," Tomasz said.

Mama looked startled. "So soon?"

"I'm due at the mill before long." Tomasz stood up. "Now that I'm a millwright, I work longer hours. Lidia keeps me company." He walked to the peg where she'd left the adorable hat he'd given her as an engagement gift. "Lidia?"

Lidia could feel the intensity of her mother's gaze. "Why don't you go along," she suggested. "I'll be along shortly."

Pleasure and ... was it relief? ... spread over her mother's face, but the muscles in Tomasz's jaw tightened. She could tell that she'd disappointed him. But I can't take it back now, Lidia thought. She'd have to apologize later. Surely Tomasz would understand.

"Very well," he said. He bowed formally to Mama and Grandfather Pawel, picked up his own hat, and walked out the door.

Mama reached for the coffeepot. "That one will never be content, I fear."

"*Matka*, that's not fair," Lidia protested. "He just wants the best for us. For all of us."

"I understand that he has to work," Grandfather Pawel put in, "but why must you be there too? It seems a lot, when you've already put in a full day."

It *was* a lot, actually. Like all the other women packers, she worked every day except Sunday. Her quota was six five-pound bags filled, sealed, and packed in a crate per minute.

"All for thirty-five cents an hour!" Tomasz complained. "To earn an extra dollar, you'd need to pack a thousand more sacks!"

"I'm content," Lidia had said mildly, and it was mostly true. She was proud of her crisp white cap and apron, proud of how fast she could pack. She liked earning money, liked the other girls working with her, liked that everyone called the fifth floor No Man's Land. The girls had their own private sitting room there, which was quite pleasant.

"Well, my sweet, innocent, and most beautiful girl, I am *not* content." Tomasz had taken both of her hands in his. "And I promise you, I will work to get the life we deserve." And he'd delivered one of his long and delicious kisses, which had left her too breathless to speak.

Now Lidia said, "The promotion to millwright was a good one, but with staggered shifts, Tomasz and I have little time together. I like keeping him company while he works."

"Young love," Grandfather Pawel said. He kissed Lidia's cheek and walked stiffly toward the door. "I believe I'll sit outside."

Both women watched him leave. Through the front window Lidia saw him settle onto the bench. He'd done so every fair night for as long as she could remember. Sometimes he visited with friends who stopped by. Sometimes he whittled. Sometimes he gazed up toward the Washburn Mill, as if waiting for someone to come home.

Lidia swallowed hard. Pawel wasn't related to her by blood, but no man could have been a better father to Mama, or grandfather to her. He was a dear man, and she'd miss seeing him every day after she married. Mama too, and even the little house that smelled of mud and *kiełbasa* and roses.

Mama spoke into the quiet. "Must the wedding take place so soon?"

"Yes," Lidia said firmly. "Now that the horrible war is over, we don't want to waste a moment. Life can be too short."

"I know that well."

Lidia knew Mama was thinking of her own mother, her own husband, both gone much too soon. "I know you *do* understand. Tomasz and I want to snatch happiness while we can."

"Well, then." Mama pressed her lips together as if to hold in further objections, and nodded. "We must make plans for a *kołacz*."

The wedding bread, she meant. The traditional ornate loaf was prepared with tender care and watched over with worry and ceremony. If the top cracked while baking in the oven, the omen was bad for the marriage. Lidia couldn't help smiling as she pictured the small kitchen crowded with old Polish women, each with her own opinions.

Then she pictured Tomasz rolling his eyes when confronted with yet one more old-world custom. "Please don't fret about a *kołacz*," Lidia said. "We are Americans now."

"*Bez kołacy nie wesele*," Mama said firmly: Without a *kołacz*, there is no wedding.

"Fine! Fine. Whatever you and the other women prepare will be lovely."

Mama nodded. "Yes, we shall take care of it. But tonight, I have some bride-gifts for you."

She fetched a basket and they sat down together. Mama stroked Lidia's temple with a gentle finger. "You've grown into such a fine young woman."

"*Matka*, please," Lidia said. "You're going to make me cry."

"That is not my intent." Mama smiled and pulled a square of folded wool from her basket. "This shawl belonged to your grandmother Magdalena. It's nothing fancy. Pawel says she was wearing her best shawl the night the mill exploded. Still, I'd like you to have it."

"Thank you." Lidia pulled the shawl into her lap. Tomasz would shudder if she ever wore something that had come across the Atlantic with Grandmother Magdalena. But it was sweet of Mama to pass it on to her.

Mama reached into her basket again. "These also belonged to your grandmother." She placed sheep shears on the table.

"But Mama … I don't plan to raise sheep!"

"My mother didn't have sheep either. Not here, in the new country. I do remember her, you know. She was very beautiful. I can still see her, leaning toward the fire and snipping at bits of paper with these sheep shears. I so wish you could have known her."

"Me too, Mama," Lidia said.

"When I look at these shears, I see both strength and beauty. She used a rough tool to make the most lovely *wycinanki* flowers. I want you to have them, and this, too." Mama placed a paper cutting gently beside the shears.

Lidia caught her breath. This *wycinanka* had always hung over the front door.

"I imagine that my mother learned to make such lovely cuttings from *her* mother, and so on," Mama said. "I want you to put this one up over your own door. Let it remind you of your family, and where you came from." For the first time, Mama's voice trembled. "I'm afraid you might lose your way, up there on the hill."

Lidia threw her arms around her mother, not caring now that tears spilled down her cheeks. "I won't lose my way," she whispered. "I promise."

# TWENTY-FIVE

"So," Ariel said. "That was your policeman."

"That was him," Chloe agreed, trying not to reveal that the conversation with Roelke—unexpected, over the phone, with Ariel standing three feet away, with that inexplicable detour into Polish folk art—had been extraordinarily frustrating.

"My grandmother gave me a wonderful piece of *wycinanki*, but it's packed away somewhere. I can show you some examples, though." Ariel ran her finger along the spines on a nearby bookcase, removed a heavy volume, and began leafing through it. "Paper cutting is one of the best-known Polish folk arts."

"*Scherenshnitte*," Chloe said. "That's the Swiss word for paper cutting. They're pretty good at it, too."

"Polish work from some regions is one color, like the Swiss usually do," Ariel said. "But some of it … here." She held up the book.

Chloe's jaw actually dropped with awe. "That's *spectacular*." The spread showed an intricate circular piece featuring two roosters and lots of flowers. The design had been formed layer by painstaking layer, each a different, rich color. The result was vibrant and cheerful.

"As I told Roelke, roosters are very common in Polish work. But he said the birds on the card he has are chickens."

"He spent summers on his grandparents' farm," Chloe said, "so I'm pretty sure he knows the difference. But—what was he trying to discover?"

"I think he wanted to know if the artwork he had was Polish." Ariel looked chagrined. "I couldn't say without seeing it, so I don't think I was much help."

Chloe dropped onto the sofa. "I don't understand what's going on in his head right now. But I do know he'll keep searching for answers until he finds them." She sighed. Rick's death was personal, and being kept out of what was going on in Milwaukee made her feel lonely.

The loneliness also came from not being able to talk to him about what was going on here in Minneapolis. Like finding a dead man on the top floor of a huge flour mill. A man who had somehow drowned before being hauled to the mill's eighth floor and hidden away. She wanted to plunk all the information down in front of her personal cop and hear what he had to say. But her personal cop was not available. He would not be available until he learned who had shot Rick. She didn't even want to *think* about what would happen if the murder went unsolved.

Chloe gave herself a long moment to feel very sad. Then she straightened and looked at Ariel. "Okay. I think it's time we get to work on that interpretive plan."

———

Dobry and Tina Banik lived in Bayview. Roelke parked at the curb just as Dobry pulled into the detached garage.

They met on the driveway. Dobry approached with a grocery bag in his arms and a quizzical expression on his face. "What are you doing here?"

"I need to talk to you."

Dobry put the sack down. "Let's talk out here so we don't disturb Tina."

Roelke pulled his notebook from his pocket and turned to the page where he'd copied the two words penciled on the back of the card. "You speak Polish, right? Are these Polish words?"

Dobry leaned toward the light mounted on the garage. "*Linka* is a name. I think *Małgorzata* has to do with painting, redecorating, something like that."

So maybe Erin met a Polish folk art painter named Linka, Roelke thought. That was not even a tiny bit helpful.

Dobry pulled the ever-present pack of cigarettes from his pocket, followed by a lighter. "What's this all about?"

"I have no idea," Roelke admitted. "Did Rick ever mention someone named Joanie?"

"Don't think so. Who is she?"

"Remember I asked you about Erin Litkowski? It's the same woman. I met Erin back when I worked for MPD. Evidently she's changed her name to Joanie. I don't know what last name she's using." He should have asked Danielle.

Dobry shook his head. "Sorry. Doesn't ring a bell." He lit up and slid the lighter away.

Roelke felt half disappointed and—childishly—half relieved that Rick hadn't left *him* out in the cold while confiding whatever there was to confide about Erin to Dobry. "Her husband's name is

Steve Litkowski. He's a first-class asshole. Could you check and see if any calls have come in about him in the past few months?"

"Sure, I can do that. You think he tangled with Rick?"

"It's possible."

"How does that jibe with the gun coming from Evidence?"

"It doesn't," Roelke admitted. "Yet, anyway. Maybe he has a buddy on the force." A sickening thought.

"Shit," Dobry muttered.

"Yeah. When was the last time you went to the Bar?"

"Just last week. Wednesday, I think. Rick and I grabbed a bite there. Why?"

"Anything odd about Kip when you were there?"

"Not that I noticed. I didn't really talk to him. All I cared about right then was a burger and onion rings."

Roelke clenched his teeth, watching two cooler-than-cool teenaged boys slouch down the street. If Rick didn't confide in me about Erin coming back to Milwaukee, he thought, and he didn't confide in Jody, and he didn't confide in Dobry... there's no one else to ask.

He forced himself to let Erin's return to Milwaukee go, for the moment. "Listen, don't mention any of this to anybody, okay?"

"No problem."

"Anything new?"

"No." Dobry glanced over his shoulder, as if someone might be lurking on the lawn. "It's gone quiet. Too damn quiet."

"What do you mean?"

"Just that. The sergeant on graveyard shift last night said at roll call that we all need to put Rick's death behind us—"

"*Behind* you? Rick's killer is wandering around out there, and everybody is supposed to—"

"I know, I know. Don't kill the messenger."

"Is Con Malloy saying that?"

"He is," Dobry said soberly.

"Damn," Roelke muttered. Sergeant Con Malloy was not one to hush himself. Roelke heard the sergeant's terse comment in his memory: *I've got to protect the living.* "Is Malloy covering something up, do you think? Protecting somebody?"

"I wish I knew."

"What about Captain Heikinen?"

"How should I know? He doesn't talk to us grunt coppers, and he hasn't made any press statements."

If that had some meaning, Roelke didn't know what it was.

"I'll tell you, walking into that building feels like walking into a powder keg." Dobry inhaled like a man in need. "The heat's on the detectives, but even more on Heikinen. Rick died on his watch, and four days later, we don't seem to know squat."

That reminder—*four days*—pounded Roelke like a mallet. With every passing day, the trail got colder. With every passing day, the killer could be farther away. "Could you sniff around? Maybe ask Malloy if he thinks Heikinen might—"

Dobry threw his butt to the cement. "This is not a good time for me to 'sniff around' anything. I am certainly not asking Malloy about the captain."

"If you just—"

"Roelke? Maybe you should back off."

"And maybe you should do more than sit on your ass behind a desk while the bastard that killed Rick is still out there!"

They stared at each other in the gathering gloom. Roelke felt a weary sense of déjà vu—hadn't he just been through this with Kip? What the hell was the *matter* with everybody? Dobry's little-boy face looked hard. Roelke felt his hands curl into fists.

A light over the back steps flicked on. Tina opened the door. Roelke turned and stalked to his truck.

"Roelke," Dobry began.

Roelke got in the cab, slammed the door, and drove away.

———

Roelke didn't have any place left to go in this city, so he drove aimlessly and tried very hard not to think. He turned on the radio, hoping to drown out the questions banging about his head. Pat Benatar sang with gritty enthusiasm, inviting someone to "fire away" at her. He punched the knob off again.

Left alone with himself, he had to acknowledge that he'd screwed up. Again. He'd been out of line to suggest that Dobry ask a sergeant about anything, much less an ongoing murder investigation, *much* less the district captain. Out of line when he'd accused Dobry of sitting idly on his ass. Out of line to get so angry. He'd have to make things right. "But not tonight," he muttered. He did not have the energy to go back to the Banik house and apologize.

He ended up back in Lincoln Village and parked by Kozy, on Becher Street—the edge of his and Rick's old beat. Roelke remembered his friend laughing with kids, slamming a mouthy drunk against the wall, buying Christmas gifts for a family that had been robbed, checking in on a nervous shopkeeper, barking orders in Spanish to cool down a few testy Latino teens, comforting a weeping woman after her grandson had been hit by a car. Rick was dead now. It felt like an Independence Day sparkler had just fizzled out.

"And I've got *nothing*," Roelke muttered.

He'd spent time trying to make sense of a card with two chickens on it, but honestly, there was no proof that Erin had been the one who dropped it. There was no proof that Rick's murder had anything to do with Erin or her husband or the mysterious Lobo. Rick's FI cards disappearing was evidence of something, but he didn't know what. Some cop had taken the murder weapon out of Evidence, but he didn't know who. He was at a total loss.

Roelke's cheeks grew warm when he remembered convincing Chief Naborski that he, Roelke McKenna, needed to be in Milwaukee: *I know the way Rick worked. How he thought. How he interacted with people. Also, I know the beat. I haven't been gone all that long, so lots of people will remember me. And I'm pretty sure that a couple of people I know in the neighborhood will be more willing to talk to me now, since I'm not MPD anymore…*

Roelke sat up straight. I, he thought, am an idiot who does not deserve to wear a badge.

His first instincts had been good. He knew Rick, and he knew this neighborhood, as well as anyone. He'd gotten sidetracked with speculation about Mexican cocaine rings and chickens and the glimpse of Erin Litkowski, but he was *not* out of options. It was time to do what he did in the old days: start walking the streets and wait for something to present itself.

It was a cold night, but being here felt as familiar as an old sweater. I love this neighborhood, he thought. He loved the tidy rows of narrow houses on narrow lots, gable walls facing the streets so the steep-pitched roofs zigzagged like saw teeth. He loved the fact that it was an actual neighborhood, where men walked to work in factories, women walked to corner markets to buy groceries, and families walked to the Basilica of St. Josaphat for mass on Sunday mornings. He loved the sense of community in an area that included a European butcher shop, a restaurant featuring Mexican food, and a boxing gym run by an Ojibwe man.

He walked south toward the Kinnickinnic River, nodding at pedestrians. He was about to turn west when a woman trudged past with a murmured "Good evening," then stopped and turned back. "Officer McKenna?"

He turned, too. "Mrs. Dombrowicz! How are you?"

"Good, all in all. But just sick at heart about what happened to Officer Almirez."

"Yeah."

Mrs. Dombrowicz was a widow with a tired set to her shoulders, hands reddened by her work at a local dry cleaner's, a face creased with worry, and kind eyes. She gripped Roelke's gloved hands in her mittened ones. "You were partners, weren't you?"

"Yeah." Not for long, but there at the end of Roelke's time in the MPD. What they'd always hoped for.

"What are you doing in the old neighborhood?"

"Just walking, Mrs. D. Thinking about my friend and walking."

"You come along home with me," she said briskly. "I'll put on the teakettle."

Roelke couldn't think of anything finer right now than a mug of hot tea served by Mrs. Dombrowicz. "Thank you, ma'am. I'd like that."

Mrs. D had lived in Lincoln Village all her life. After her husband died of cancer she'd raised five children alone. Her youngest child, Donny, was constantly in trouble. "Is Donny still living at home?" Roelke asked as they turned a corner.

"He is. He's got a job, cooking burgers at the sandwich place over on the Grutza block." She flapped one hand in a helpless gesture. "We'll see if he can hang on to this one."

Roelke had his doubts. Donny wasn't really a bad kid, but the numbnut had not inherited his mother's work ethic, and he was constantly screwing off. Roelke had arrested him for stealing hubcaps, for spray painting a bakery's window, for smoking marijuana on a school playground. Stupid stuff like that. More than once Roelke had responded to a call and thought, *Donny D.* More than once he'd knocked on Mrs. D's door and explained he was looking for her son. If Donny was home, Mrs. D marched him from his bedroom by the ear and handed him over. If he wasn't home, she promised to call when he showed up. He always showed up, and Mrs. D always called.

Now Roelke found himself back in the familiar living room— small, crowded, spotless. A picture of the Virgin Mary graced a small shrine in one corner. A television on a rolling stand filled another. Framed family snapshots covered the walls. A coffee table held a knitting basket and a paperback romance novel.

Mrs. D served tea with a plate of store-bought chocolate chip cookies. "Thank you for your kindness," Roelke said. The simple but heartfelt gesture meant more than he could say.

Then he noticed the mugs themselves: tall, cream-colored, and adorned with two blue roosters and *Polish Fest 1982*. He pulled the chicken card out of his pocket one more time. "Mrs. D, does this mean anything to you?"

She took it from him. "It's quite pretty."

"Somebody found it and gave it to me. Does it look like a Polish design?"

She nodded. "Oh, yes. It reminds me of old Polish paper cutting."

"*Wycinanki*?"

She beamed. "Yes! That's it exactly."

# TWENTY-SIX
## OCTOBER 1920

"THAT'S PRETTY, LIDIA," SUE said. "What is it?"

"*Wycinanki.*" Lidia stood back to admire the paper cutting she'd just tacked over the door in No Man's Land. "My grandmother made it. It hung over the front door while I was growing up, like a blessing on everyone who came inside."

"I like it," one of the other girls chimed in. "But don't you want to put it up at your house?"

"I figured a little extra cheer here at the mill wouldn't be a bad thing," Lidia said lightly. She didn't add that her husband wouldn't tolerate any hint of "old-world nonsense."

"I'll take all the blessings I can get," Sue agreed. "I declare, Lidia, you have transformed our lounge into the prettiest parlor in Minneapolis."

Lidia gazed with pleasure at the women's room. She missed the overflowing window boxes and bursting gardens lovingly tended by the Bohemian Flats women. But Thomas—he insisted on the American spelling now—wasn't fond of flowers either, so she'd brought gardens indoors here by planting geraniums in cans in front of the windows. When one of the girls mentioned getting new curtains, Lidia had asked for the old ones. After mending a few frayed hems, she'd embroidered more flowers on the panels and hung them over the windows here. Putting up the *wycinanki* Mama had given her as wedding gift added the final touch of charm.

Well, no, she corrected herself. The real charm lay in the name of this place: No Man's Land. All the girls came here to eat lunch, play the piano, giggle and sigh over movie and fashion magazines, knit and crochet. They planned outings and celebrated engagements. It was pleasant here. It was safe.

"Will you be able to join us for the croquet tournament on Sunday afternoon?" Sue asked.

"It's such a busy time," Lidia said. "My garden—"

"Oh, do come." Sue tipped her head, giving Lidia a pleading look. "You never join us anymore. Surely you can pull weeds another day."

"It's not that I wouldn't love to come," Lidia added honestly. "I'll have to let you know."

"Well, I'm ready for a picnic," Sue said. "All my fiancé wants to talk about is the union and all the trouble with managers."

Harriet, who worked in the bag factory, came through the door in time to hear that last. "*Labor and capital are partners, not enemies,*" she quoted sarcastically. "Does anyone actually believe that?" She tossed the question out like a dare, but she smiled, too. Harriet was a tall redhead, opinionated and bold and full of fun. Some might not agree with her views, but everyone liked her.

"What does Thomas think, Lidia?" Sue asked.

Lidia hesitated. The labor struggles Mama had worried about were growing. The National War Labor Board had recently ordered all the mill owners in Minneapolis to negotiate with their employees. The mill managers told workers to elect representatives to meet with directors about safety concerns and other workplace issues. Very few Washburn-Crosby employees had bothered to vote. Most didn't believe the Labor Board's ruling would actually lead to cooperative discussions between workers and employers.

"He doesn't say much about it," Lidia said, which wasn't true. Thomas had been furious about the low turnout. "We have to give management a chance," he'd fumed, stalking back and forth across their parlor floor. Lidia didn't agree, but she didn't say so, even here with her friends.

"The union men say the representatives won't have any actual power," Harriet said. "The company men will listen and nod and then do nothing. It's all a pretense."

Lidia knew that Grandfather Pawel thought it was all pretense as well. She reached for her empty lunch bag. "I best be off."

She left the lounge before anyone else could add their entreaties. Her shift was over, but her husband had two more hours to work, so she made her way to the massive dust collectors on the eighth floor. She found Thomas eyeing a rotating auger overhead, arms crossed. When he saw her he held out one arm, squeezed her close against him, and kissed her cheek. "There's my beautiful girl."

She kissed him back. "Trouble with the dust collectors today?"

"Listen. Hear that?" Thomas understood these machines the way her mother understood zinnias and roses.

She listened dutifully. "I think so."

"Just a small adjustment ..."

Lidia had never gotten used to watching her husband make repairs with mechanical parts grinding and belts rattling at high speed. Accidents were all too common. The men joked—without humor—that after flour and lumber, the city's biggest business was the production of artificial limbs.

She waited until Thomas was wiping his wrench with a greasy rag before speaking. "Some of the girls have planned a croquet tournament for Sunday afternoon," she said, striving for an off-hand tone. "I thought we might go."

"Sunday is the only day I get you all to myself."

"I like that too, but just this once…"

"No." He shook his head. "We'll go window-shopping downtown instead. You can pick out a new hat."

Lidia didn't want a new hat. She wanted to play croquet. "But Thomas, I—"

"You will not defy me, Lidia!" He hurled the wrench to the floor with a harsh clang.

Lidia felt her heart thump against her ribs. She stared at her husband, too shocked by his sudden rage to speak.

His fists slowly uncurled. He picked up the wrench and put it back in the toolbox.

"I … I've got cucumbers to pickle," Lidia said. "Do you mind if I head home a bit early today?" With a side trip to Bohemian Flats on the way, she thought. She wanted to visit Mama and Grandfather Pawel. It had been too long.

"Don't go yet. I like your company."

Lidia opened her mouth to protest, but swallowed the words. She didn't want to provoke another outburst. "Very well. I'll stay."

Thomas gave her a satisfied smile. "I imagine every wife wishes she was so lucky as to have an adoring husband."

Lidia leaned against the wall, shifting her weight to ease one knee, then the other. She'd been on her feet packing flour sacks all day. Sometimes while keeping Thomas company she could find a crate or bench to perch on, but here there was nowhere to sit. Still, she couldn't complain. Some of her friends lamented that within a few months of marriage, their husbands didn't seem to care if they spent time together or not. Sad thought.

"Yes, Thomas," Lidia said. "Every wife should be so lucky."

# TWENTY-SEVEN

Mrs. D studied the chicken card. "A couple of the ladies at church still sell paper cuttings at the holiday bazaar. They say peasant women in the old country made designs to brighten up their little hovels. All they had was sheep shears in those days."

"I understand that chickens aren't common, though," Roelke said.

"Well, no, I don't recall ever seeing chickens before." She looked pensive. "But the flowers—those look real familiar."

"How about the word *Małgorzata*?"

"*Małgorzata* is a girl's name. The Polish form of Margaret."

"Well, hunh." Dobry had been *way* off. Of course, Dobry was also what, third-generation Polish? Evidently his vocabulary wasn't so good. Roelke was glad that he'd double-checked, but the new translation didn't help. He had no idea why this card might have two women's names on it. He had no idea if the card had anything to do with *anything*.

They drank their tea and ate their cookies and were talking of changes in the neighborhood when Donny came home. He looked startled to see Roelke, but then he smiled. "Hey! It's Officer Mc-Kenna!" Donny tossed his coat onto a hook by the door.

The kid never did hold a grudge, even back when Roelke had been the one hauling his sorry ass into the station. "Good to see you, Donny. I uFnderstand you've got yourself a job."

"I do, yes sir."

"See if you can hang onto it, all right? Don't give your mother any more grief."

"I won't," he said, so cheerfully that it almost sounded believable. "You coming back to work here?"

"Officer McKenna is just visiting," his mother explained. "He came back to the old neighborhood to pay his respects to Officer Almirez."

Donny sobered. "Oh, yeah, that was *bad*. Right there by Kozy Park. Was he undercover, do you think?"

"No, he was in uniform and walking his regular beat," Roelke said. Honestly, this kid was just not too bright.

Donny shrugged. "Well, last week I saw him out of uniform up north of Mitchell Street. I tried saying hello, but he dissed me."

Roelke's knee began to bounce. "He dissed you? That doesn't sound like Rick."

"I know! I mean, he had to take me in a few times, but that doesn't mean a guy can't be friendly, right? But when I said 'Hey,' he acts all like he doesn't know who I am. So I said, 'Hey! Officer Almirez!' And he says, 'Wrong guy, buddy,' and just keeps walking."

"You're sure it was Officer Almirez?" Mrs. D asked.

"Ma, the guy arrested me three or four times, so I do know what he looked like." Donny gave Roelke a *Sheesh, can you believe that lady?* look. "I was kind of pissed, but then I figured he must be working undercover, right? Like on TV. If I'd known, I never woulda said his name out loud like that."

"So, where exactly was it that you saw him?" Roelke asked.

"Near St. Stanislaus." Donny looked proud. "I've got a new lady, and she lives on the corner there."

Not part of Rick's beat. "What time did you see him?"

Donny shrugged. "It was after dark. That must have been why he felt safe walking down the sidewalk, hunh? He probably figured that nobody would recognize him away from his usual turf." He looked from Roelke to his mom and back again, clearly pleased. "Undercover, eh? Pretty cool."

But Rick didn't work undercover, Roelke thought. Or did he keep me in the dark about that, too?

———

Ariel, curled like a cat on the sofa, stretched and yawned when the clock struck ten. "I better get ready for bed. I want to get in to work early tomorrow."

Chloe surveyed the jumble of files, notebooks, and other reference materials with satisfaction. "We accomplished a lot this evening."

"I do feel more optimistic about making the deadline." Ariel's face wasn't quite so pinched with worry and stress.

"I'm loving the major interpretive themes we've identified," Chloe said. She picked up her notebook and went down the list: the importance of St. Anthony Falls over time, the growth of the flour industry, changing technology, marketing, agriculture and connections with Midwestern farms, the worker experience, recent history. "I'm sure they'll evolve, but for now, people will have a lot to think about."

"*Thank* you, Chloe."

"It always helps to bounce ideas around. One of the biggest challenges is having so much to work with. The mill's story is as big as an industrial innovation that literally changed the way human beings ate, and as small as the challenges facing a new-come immigrant worker loading barrels into train cars."

"Lots of change over time," Ariel agreed. "Right up to the day the mill closed in '65."

"And people have used the mill ever since," Chloe added, mindful of Sister Mary Jude's request.

"Right." Ariel carried their dirty tea mugs into the kitchen. "Tomorrow, I'll try to fill the research holes at the archives, and you can start typing up the preliminaries here. You're sure you don't mind staying another day or two?"

"My boss encouraged me to collaborate with the Minnesota Historical Society," Chloe said. And nothing about my conversation with Roelke last night suggests I should be driving east, she added silently. Evidently he only called to discuss Polish folk art.

Which probably told her something she needed to know.

Chloe bit her lip. She knew Roelke truly cared about her, but would he ever want a long-term commitment? Is that something she wanted herself? Jody had advised her to take a break and really think about whether she could handle the reality of being with a cop. Roelke's withdrawal had handed her that opportunity on a crystal plate.

So, Chloe thought, can I handle the reality of being with a cop? For the first time, she wasn't sure. The danger inherent in Roelke's job had become a whole lot more real. She'd spent an evening watching Rick Almirez laugh, play jazz, kiss his girlfriend. Hours later someone shot him and left him to die in the street. The risks Roelke took every single day were suddenly very visceral.

Chloe didn't want to live in fear. But ... she also wasn't ready to conclude that she and Roelke should break up.

Well, enough brooding about that for now. Ariel had plenty of problems without a depressed roommate.

Chloe began tidying the stack of old cookbooks, then paused. "Hey, I just got a great idea. Why don't you serve baked goods at the reception? Old Pillsbury Bake-Off favorites, stuff like that."

Ariel looked at her blankly. "I don't bake."

Chloe beamed. "No, but I do!"

"If you're sure…"

"Of course I'm sure. This is the fun part! Look at it this way. You're not responsible for making a few rusty old machines operable again, like Owen. You're not responsible for stabilizing that massive crumbling complex, like Jay. You're not responsible for raising millions of dollars, or holding together a consortium of agencies, or working with the architects."

"Thank God."

"This museum is going to be awesome. I can hardly believe that the Minnesota Historical Society has the vision to even attempt this project—but it does, and you get to be part of the educational planning! No matter where you go from here, this is going to be one mighty plum on your resume."

Ariel raised both palms in surrender. "You're absolutely right. I've had a bad attitude about this assignment from the beginning. I'll do better from here on, I promise." She flicked off the kitchen light. "You have everything you need?"

"I'm good. I'm just going to work a little longer."

Ariel disappeared up the stairs. Chloe picked up the *Gold Medal Flour Cook Book,* 1910 edition. "Like this is work," she scoffed under her breath. She thumbed through the yellowed pages, flagging intriguing recipes. Squash Muffins, Delicate Cake, Doughnuts, Ginger

Cookies… She'd have to save a few of those for Roelke. He loved ginger cookies…

*Roelke.* Chloe sighed as worry bubbled back to the surface. Where was he, right this minute? Was he getting some sleep, or was he still in the city? Were grief and exhaustion making him insensitive to danger?

Before turning back to the cookbook, she sent a thought over the icy miles to Milwaukee. *Be safe, Roelke. Please be safe.*

———

Roelke left the Dombrowicz house and walked back toward Kozy Park, trying to understand this new snippet of information. Donny D wasn't clever enough to make up the story. Rick was the kind of cop who'd stop to chat with a guy like Donny—even something quick like, "Hey, Donny, keeping your nose clean?" Why would Rick say, "Wrong guy"?

Roelke reached the park without finding any answers. Rick was killed on the south edge of the park, near the statue of Polish-American hero General Kosciuszko. Floodlights illuminated more bouquets and a formal funeral wreath at the base, but the flowers—frozen and brittle—provided no comfort.

A taxi's headlights glared past. Roelke walked to the far side of the monument so the fourteen-foot marble base shielded him from Lincoln Avenue's heaviest traffic. He put one hand high against the stone. Cold seeped through his leather glove. "Rick," he mumbled, "I can't figure out what was going on with you. Help me out here, buddy. I need *help.*"

He waited. Nothing. He hadn't really expected anything, had he? That would have been dumb.

Still, Roelke tried again. "I miss you really bad. The thing is … the thing *is*, I am also really pissed. What were you mixed up in? Did you find a cop on the take? Did Erin's husband find out she was back in Milwaukee? Were you really working undercover? How could you not *tell* me?"

Roelke's throat ached. His eyes were stinging. Dammit, he thought. He'd told Justin earlier that it was okay to cry if you were really sad, but he was more than sad now, and—

A rifle shot cracked the night. Something struck against Roelke's right side like a freight train. He stumbled and whirled at the same instant, ending up on one knee with his back to the monument, peering across the park. Nothing, no one.

Something hot and furious gave way inside him. Roelke launched across the snow-covered grass—slipping, stumbling, running on. After leaving the pool of light surrounding the statue, the wooded ground ahead seemed black as pitch. Where the hell was the shooter?

Just as he reached the base of a tree-studded rise, Roelke heard Chief Naborski's voice in his memory: *Do not let the way you feel make you stupid.*

Roelke dove toward the closest tree, heart pounding, breath coming in noisy heaves. The shooter had cover. The shooter's eyes were accustomed to the darkness. Running across the open lawn *toward* the shooter definitely qualified as stupid.

In the middle of Wisconsin's most densely populated community, Roelke suddenly felt very alone. Prickles raced over his skin. Every hair on the back of his neck quivered. Every muscle felt tight. He waited for the second shot.

Instead he heard a car door slam on Becher, an engine roar, and the screech of tires spinning on ice before finding traction. That had to be the shooter. *Had* to be. His own reckless plunge toward the sniper must have spooked the guy into running instead of taking a second shot.

A siren wailed, coming closer. Roelke stood and began backing toward the statue, gaze still scouring the dark wooded rise in case he'd been wrong about the car. *You will not shoot me in the back,* he told the SOB silently.

He reached the statue as the MPD car jerked to a stop. Flashing lights flared over the snow. Roelke raised his hands just so nobody got confused. "I'm an off-duty police officer," he called.

The responder was a new guy. They retreated behind the car, and Roelke displayed his badge. "We had several citizen calls about a shot fired in Kozy Park," the kid said, his voice pitched with excitement. Two more cop cars screeched to a halt. More sirens wailed in the distance. "And after what happened last Friday night—"

"Yeah." Roelke was still panting, but trying not to show it. Somebody tried to kill me, he thought. *Somebody tried to kill me.*

"So, what happened? You heard the shot? Where were you?"

"I was over by the statue, paying my respects, and..." Roelke became aware that his right side throbbed. He raised his arm and fingered the tear in his coat. He felt nothing wet, warm, or sticky, so—no blood.

The kid stared. "Jesus Christ! Did you get shot?" He whirled around. "Sarge! Over here!"

Sergeant Malloy approached with a curse. "McKenna? What are you doing here?"

"He got shot!" the kid cried.

"My coat got grazed," Roelke said. It seemed very important that he not mention the protective vest he was wearing. "I'm not hurt."

"What are you doing here?" Malloy repeated.

Roelke gestured at the memorial at the base of the statue. "I was paying my respects—"

"It's almost eleven p.m. You chose this hour to pay your respects?"

"Yeah. I did."

More cops were descending. One shooed away a few civilians. Somebody barked orders. Another officer angled the spotlight mounted on his car so the beam slashed the park. You won't be able to track him, Roelke thought. In the flashers' surreal pulse, he saw a thousand sets of tracks crisscrossing the snow.

"Did you see the shooter?" Malloy demanded.

"I didn't see a damn thing."

"Where was he?"

"Somewhere…" Roelke waved a vague arm.

"Where? Where were you standing?"

Captain Heikinen cut through the crowd. "What have we got?" he snapped. "Is anybody hurt?"

"Just—just give me a minute." Roelke leaned against the car with hands on knees, as if waiting for dizziness to pass. He wasn't dizzy. Everything seemed to be in extraordinarily sharp focus.

The only thing that wasn't clear was whether he should speak truth to the familiar blue uniforms. The idea that he *wouldn't* was extraordinary. But someone had pulled Rick's Field Investigation cards before Klinefelter could do it. And someone had killed Rick with a gun taken from police custody.

A hand clamped Roelke's shoulder—Captain Heikinen. "You're not hurt?"

"No sir."

"Then pull yourself together. Every moment counts. You were standing by the statue when the shot was fired?" He gestured, and light glinted red on his wedding ring. Roelke thought about Chloe.

He thought about the conversation he'd had with Lucia Bliss. *Is it hard, being married to someone who doesn't work law enforcement? Yeah, it can be. But you think it can work? I sure as hell hope so.*

Captain Heikinen had to be what, sixty? Sixty-five? How long had he been married? Was it a good marriage?

"Officer McKenna!"

Okay, Roelke told himself. It's time to make a gamble. A gamble that could end his own career. A gamble that might help nail Rick's killer—or might give the killer room to shoot again.

# TWENTY-EIGHT
## JUNE 1921

"WHAT ARE YOU MAKING for dinner, my dear?" Thomas came to stand behind her, both hands on her shoulders. "Everything must be perfect for our guests."

Lidia worked the rolling pin on a mound of dough. "Roast chicken with green beans and biscuits." His favorites.

"I know the Windoms will enjoy the meal as much as I will." He nibbled her earlobe. "I'll be proud to introduce you as my wife. And if all goes well, I'll soon be promoted. I can do much more for the mill than I'm doing now."

"I know you can." Lidia liked this mood—optimistic, energetic. "Thomas, when do you think I might be able to start taking home economics classes at the university? The Gold Medal Home Services women get to develop recipes, and give advice when housewives write in with questions. They even travel to demonstrate modern cookery methods to—"

"Soon I'll earn so much that you won't have to work at all."

But I *want* to work, Lidia thought. The thought of being trapped in this house all day made her feel dizzy.

Recently the advertising department had invented a woman named Betty Crocker to represent Gold Medal Flour to consumers. All of the mill's female employees were invited to write *Betty Crocker* in their own handwriting. Lidia had practiced and practiced before submitting her sample. Although it hadn't been chosen as the official Betty Crocker signature, just the possibility had made her hungry for better opportunities.

"Let me do the talking this evening," Thomas was saying. "I'll impress the man with my knowledge and ambition. All you need to do is smile and charm."

"I'll do my best," she said, "but if you don't let me finish, I won't have everything done in time."

"Of course." He released her at once.

Lidia studied the rolling pin and suddenly saw Mama's hands, preparing dough for *pierogi*. My, Lidia thought, how long has it been since I've eaten *pierogi*? Not since she'd lived in the Flats, surely. Funny—as a child, she'd never particularly liked them, but now...

She gave herself a mental shake. Don't be a ninny, she scolded herself. *Pierogi* were heavy things, and her biscuits were light as air. Thomas always said so.

As a young millwright, Thomas wouldn't normally have cause to chat with a manager like Mr. Windom. But Thomas had somehow found an opportunity, and impressed the man so much that Mr. Windom had accepted an invitation to dinner. Lidia wanted this dinner to be perfect as much as her husband did. If Thomas could just obtain a low-level management position, surely he'd be happy.

Lidia reached for her biscuit cutter and realized that Thomas had retreated only to the kitchen doorway. "Oh!" she gasped. "I thought you'd gone."

"I need to talk with you about something," he said. "But I can wait until you're finished." He gestured at the dough.

"I can talk while I work."

"Very well. It's about your job at the mill."

Lidia's hand stilled. Most of the girls left when they got married, but she and Thomas had agreed that her salary was too important to lose. Had he decided that it didn't look good for a man on the rise to have a wife bagging flour in the factory? She felt a flicker of panic. She needed her job. She needed her mill friends. She needed No Man's Land. "Yes?" she managed finally, focusing on the biscuit dough.

"You must never repeat what I'm about to tell you."

"All right," she said cautiously.

He stepped closer, as if someone might be lurking outside the window. "Management has hired detectives to work in the mill."

"What? Why? What are they doing?"

"They are working as loaders or packers. Even one miller. And they are quietly learning which men are secretly agitating in support of the union."

"But … what for?"

"Oh, come now, Lidia." He leaned against the table, arms crossed. "You're a smart girl. Management can't get rid of troublemakers if they don't know who they are."

Lidia thought of Grandfather Pawel, so worn down after years of heavy labor. She thought of other men, today, who only asked for a chance to negotiate for good working conditions in return for their commitment to the mill. She and Thomas had differing views on this subject. She wished he hadn't told her about the spies.

"One of the detectives has even been elected to office within the union," Thomas was saying. "So things are proceeding as planned."

Lidia felt a twist in the pit of her stomach as she realized how Thomas had ingratiated himself with Mr. Windom. Had his promotion to millwright only happened because he supplied information about other workers?

"There is only one problem," Thomas said.

"Oh?" Lidia carefully pressed the cutter into the dough.

"No Man's Land."

Lidia cut another perfect sphere, lifted the cutter carefully, and placed it again. All the while a single word buzzed in her brain: *No, no, no.*

Thomas grasped her wrist. "Lidia! We need your help."

"Thomas, you can't be asking … I can't. I can't! Please don't ask me to spy on my friends."

Irritation flashed on his face. "It's not so much to ask. No one will ever know."

"I will know!"

"I wouldn't ask if it wasn't so important." He pulled her close, pressing her head against his shoulder. "This is for us! Everything we've worked so hard for is within our grasp. Mr. Windom is already pleased with me. This was his idea, actually, not mine. If you do this, I can advance farther within the company. You won't have to work so hard. We can move out of this tiny place, maybe in time even hire someone to help you with chores. This is just one more piece of the plan …"

His words washed over her, and his hand gently stroked her hair. Lidia thought of her friend Harriet, and some of the other girls who chattered freely behind the closed doors of No Man's Land—as they *all* did, believing that there, at least, they were safe.

After a moment he stepped back and grasped her shoulders. "Well, Lidia?"

"Oh, Thomas, I just don't want to …"

"Mr. Windom expects an answer this evening, my dear. Think about what it would mean to us, and to our future. How much it would mean to me." His fingers pressed into her skin.

Lidia couldn't hold his gaze. "Very well, Thomas. I'll do it."

He smiled and released her, kissed her forehead, and walked out of the kitchen.

Lidia got back to her dinner preparations, thinking about her promise, thinking back over her three years of marriage. When, she wondered bleakly, did I start lying to my husband?

# TWENTY-NINE

I JUST LIED TO the cops, Roelke thought as he drove away from the chaos at Kozy Park. He'd told them the shot came from the east side of the park, near the lagoon and new community building, instead of due north. He knew he should feel really bad about that, but honestly, he just felt numb.

Malloy had wanted him to stick around. "Sit in my car, for Chrissakes," he'd barked. "Get warm. You can write down what happened back at the station." But Roelke didn't want to stick around. *Like you said,* he'd retorted silently, *I don't work here anymore. I don't take orders from you anymore.*

He looped through traffic for a while to shake off any tail—*somebody* had tailed him to the park—and drove to a truck stop out on the interstate. He bought a few necessities and checked into a nearby motel, paying cash and giving a fake name. The sleepy clerk handed him a key attached to a plastic oval with the room number stamped on it, no questions asked.

Inside, Roelke eased off his shirt and vest. The right side of his chest was swelling green and purple—probably a cracked rib, but nothing worse. If he hadn't put his hand up on the statue, the bullet would have hit his arm, maybe shattered a bone.

He taped the rib, pulled his clothes back on, and sat on the bed. The cinder block walls made him think of a jail cell. Was his brain just preparing for the dreaded trip to Waupun tomorrow? Or was it suggesting that perhaps he should start imagining himself in custody?

"Yeah, well, fuck that," he muttered. He'd figure this out. He *would*.

So, back to work. He dumped grounds into the tiny coffeemaker and pulled out his index cards. He slapped a blank one on the desk and wrote, *Someone tried to kill me. Must have been tailing me.* That notion made him furious—at the SOB who'd shot him, and at himself for not being more alert.

He tried to move on. *Not a handgun. Sniper—possibly a vet?*

The machine stopped burbling, so he poured some coffee. He added powdered creamer and instantly regretted it. That stuff never dissolved very well. He sipped, grimaced, sipped some more.

He underlined the last word he'd written, but identifying the shooter as a probable military veteran did little to tighten his net. Half the guys on the MPD were Vietnam vets. Half of the rest had served in Korea. Malloy for sure, maybe Heikinen, too. It was impossible to picture either man shooting at him or Rick. If one of them was involved in a cocaine ring or something and things got out of hand, he'd surely hire someone to do the dirty work. Someone like Sherman's Mr. Lobo?

Okay, next suspect. Roelke glanced at his watch, called the station, and asked for Dobry. "Hey, it's Roelke," he began when his friend picked up. "I—"

"Roelke?" Dobry's voice was low and urgent. "What the hell is going on? Are you okay? It's officially mum, but word around here is that somebody took a shot at you in Kozy Park."

"I'm okay, but that's not why I called. First, I'm sorry I blew up earlier. I was out of line."

"Forget it."

"Did you have a chance to check on Steve Litkowski?"

"I did, yeah. Just a sec." The faint sound of papers rustling came over the wire. "Here it is. Want his address?"

Roelke jotted it down. "He's moved."

"Yeah, he's up in Shorewood now, but I got the records."

"Was there any indication that Litkowski served in the military?"

"No, but about three months ago he knocked his live-in girlfriend around pretty good. A neighbor heard screams and called it in."

"Did the girlfriend press charges?"

"Nope."

Roelke sighed. He hated domestic calls. Most of the women were too scared or demoralized to turn the law on the men who had turned on them. There was nothing worse than trying to talk to a beaten woman with her boxer-boyfriend listening from the next room. "It's just a family thing," she'd most likely whisper. If she wouldn't press charges, there was nothing he could do but lecture the guy and walk away. Calls like that made him sick.

"Is there anything else you need?" Dobry's voice dropped, as if someone else was nearby. "I truly want to help, Roelke. Just as long as it doesn't, you know, draw the wrong kind of attention."

I know all about drawing the wrong kind of attention, Roelke thought. He heard again the distant crack of the rifle. He touched the bruise blossoming on his rib cage. He couldn't ask anyone else to draw that kind of attention. "I appreciate the info on Litkowski, but there's nothing else."

After hanging up, Roelke considered his resources. He'd brought his gun inside. He always carried emergency cash, hidden beneath the seat in his truck. One thing was certain: until the shooter was behind bars, no way was he spending any more time with Libby and the kids.

Or Chloe. The missing of her brought an ache to rival the bullet's punch against his vest. Still, he was profoundly glad that she was well away in Minneapolis, hanging out with a girlfriend, busy with curator stuff. He hoped all over again that he or somebody would nail the shooter *fast*, because until then, he couldn't be with Chloe, either.

# THIRTY

ROELKE WAS BACK AT the Kozy statue before dawn Wednesday morning, his off-duty revolver a comforting weight in his coat pocket. His determination to think through what had happened kept lingering willies at bay. He believed the shooter had been due north. It was easy to follow the footprints from his own crazy run, which ended when he belatedly dove for cover.

Now he walked on. A big old maple stood on top of the slope. Snow behind the tree was well trampled. Roelke studied the muddled prints—nothing distinctive. Then he picked up a stick, leaned against the trunk, and squinted down the impromptu rifle barrel toward the statue. Yep, a clean line of fire. And he, standing beneath the lights, had provided an easy target.

He poked around without finding a rifle shell casing. Well, he already knew the shooter was good. Roelke pictured him making the shot, drawing back the bolt, catching the shell as it ejected—all quick and quiet.

Roelke found a line of footprints leading straight north from the maple. *That's* why he hadn't been able to detect any movement the night before—the shooter had kept the maple between them, not veering right or left while retreating. Roelke followed the tracks until they ended at a shoveled walkway. No way of knowing where the SOB had gone after that. Roelke walked on toward the north border of Kozy Park, but he couldn't connect any tracks to the shooter.

He stopped by an old building used by park maintenance staff, staring at Becher Street, piecing together the likely scenario. The guy had tailed Roelke to the park. After Roelke stopped by the statue, the shooter had circled around and parked here on Becher Street, poised to hit the nearby interstate on-ramp for a fast getaway.

I, Roelke thought bitterly, might as well have put a neon target on my back.

He turned to head back through the park. While skirting the maintenance building, he noticed a deep disturbance in the snow. It looked like somebody had fallen. Probably too much to hope that the guy who shot at me fell on his ass, Roelke thought, and kicked angrily at the snow.

His foot grazed something. He found another stick, poked around, and ... Holy *toboggans*. He'd uncovered a gun.

It was a Smith and Wesson .38, Model 60—similar to his own gun, but smaller. He hooked the stick through the trigger guard. This was not the gun that had been used to shoot him the night before, though. Whoever had shot Rick execution-style and took aim at *him* with sniper-style precision did not seem the type to accidentally drop a handgun in the snow. Probably some other bad guy had rid himself of a gun used in an unrelated crime.

Roelke glanced over both shoulders. A faint blue-gray light was creeping through the trees. He saw headlights, heard a commuter bus wheeze to a stop. If local cops were going to come beat the proverbial bushes at first light—which they surely would—they'd show up any minute. He had another choice to make, and he was out of time.

He pulled an evidence bag from his pocket and dropped the .38 inside. He slid the bag into his left coat pocket. Then he walked away.

But Jesus, something was wrong. An iron band began squeezing his chest. Sweat dampened his shirt, his palms. Could he even make it back to his truck? He'd parked blocks away.

Very slowly, Roelke trudged to Lincoln Avenue and crossed the street. His chest grew heavier. The two guns, one in each pocket, thumped against him as he climbed steps and slipped inside the Basilica of St. Josaphat.

The main sanctuary was empty. He slid into a rear pew, closed his eyes, and concentrated on breathing. In, out. In, out. After a few minutes the pain in his chest eased a bit.

Roelke didn't really know what was freaking him out. He'd lied to the cops last night. Picking up the .38 this morning wasn't any worse than that.

Except, it kinda was. The gun was an actual thing, a weight in his pocket. Not only might it have nothing to do with Rick's death, it could be evidence in another crime. If he didn't turn it in, another bad guy might get away.

Roelke leaned over, elbows on knees, face in his hands. I don't know if I can see this through, he thought. All he'd wanted to do was help find whoever shot his best friend. Now things were spiraling way, *way* out of control.

On the one hand, he must be doing something right. Whoever murdered Rick was evidently getting nervous. I can't quit now, Roelke thought. Digging just a little deeper might let him nail Rick's killer.

On the other hand, digging just a little deeper might cost him his career. Or his life. Even if he took that risk, it wasn't fair to Libby, to Justin and Dierdre, to Chloe—

"Are you all right, son?"

The voice was so close that Roelke almost went for his gun. He jerked upright, but before he could draw, his brain identified the intruder as an elderly priest—black robe, white hair, thin face, intelligent blue eyes, surprisingly rosy cheeks.

"I didn't mean to startle you," the man said. "I just wondered if you needed help."

Roelke hiccupped a mirthless laugh. What would the nice Father say, he wondered, if I confess that I have a gun burning a hole in each of my coat pockets? "I'm sorry," he managed. "I just wanted to sit here for a while, but I can leave if—"

"There's no need for that." The priest stepped into the row and sat down beside Roelke. "I often do the same thing. A place of such beauty and peace encourages rest and reflection. Is this your first visit?"

"It's the first time I've been inside." Roelke had scarcely noticed his surroundings when he entered, but now he took in the glory: soaring arches, gilt paint, magnificent murals, marble columns. The altars looked to be carved of marble too, as well as the pulpit and the stations of the cross. Morning sun streamed through stained glass windows, bathing the sanctuary with warmth.

"St. Josaphat was named a Minor Basilica in 1929," the priest said with quiet pride. "That honor is awarded only to the most lovely and historically significant structures. And it's on the National Register of Historic Places."

"I know what that is," Roelke said. Chloe had told him about it. God, how he wished she was sitting beside him, chattering incomprehensibly with the priest about the basilica's architecture.

"A century ago, poor Polish immigrants donated their pennies and built this church as a testament to their faith."

"That must have been a whole lot of pennies."

The priest laughed. "Yes, indeed. Those good Poles made enormous sacrifices. The basilica is a monument to their faith and their hope of better times to come."

Roelke wouldn't mind a good dose of faith and hope right now. He was running on empty.

"Are you a religious person?" the priest asked.

"No," Roelke said. His faith had faded somewhere between altar boy and cop.

"I won't invite you to the confessional, then. Still, perhaps it would help if you talked about what's troubling you."

"The police officer who was killed in Kozy Park was my best friend," Roelke heard himself say. "And I've discovered that he had kept some important things secret."

"So you are carrying a sense of betrayal as well as grief. I hope you'll find it in your heart to forgive your friend his secrets. Maybe he had good reason."

"Maybe."

"I will say a prayer for you both."

"Thank you." Lapsed or not, that actually made Roelke feel a little better.

Suddenly he realized he was overlooking the obvious. He reached into his coat pocket—carefully, not showing the gun—and found the envelope holding Erin's photograph. "I've also been looking for another friend of mine. She might have attended services here a few years ago."

The priest studied the photo carefully before shaking his head. "I'm sorry."

"I think she needs my help, but she's disappeared. I can't figure out why she needs to hide from me."

"Ah." The priest nodded pensively. "More secrets. Well, perhaps she's stronger now. Perhaps she's reached a point where she is more interested in giving help than receiving it."

I wouldn't mind getting a little help from Erin right now, Roelke thought. He realized that he was angry at her, too.

"I'll leave you now, but please, linger as long as you wish," the priest said. "May you find solace." He paused before adding, "*I consecrate this house you have built, I place my name here forever; My eyes and my heart will be here for all time.*" He smiled. "First Book of Kings, ninth chapter, third verse. It's written in old Polish at the base of the dome." He pointed overhead. Then he squeezed Roelke's shoulder in farewell and left him alone.

When Roelke stood sometime later, he knew that he would not turn the gun he'd found over to the police. At least not right away. He'd see what happened in the next day or so. He had also decided not to show the gun to Banik or Bliss. He couldn't drag either of them down with him.

Bottom line: A cop had taken the weapon used to kill Rick from Evidence. A cop had pulled Rick's records. There was at least one bad cop in the district, and he didn't know who it was. He would see this thing through to the best of his ability, alone.

Roelke found an alcove where votive candles were arranged in rows. Several were already burning. Roelke lit four more: one for Rick, one for Erin, one for Libby and the kids, and one for Chloe. Then he left the basilica.

He kept a basic evidence kit in his truck, and after looping through traffic for fifteen minutes, he found a quiet parking lot and checked the gun he'd found for prints. Not a one.

"That's suspicious right there," Roelke muttered. Then he hid the gun beneath the seat and squared his shoulders. It was time to go to Waupun.

# THIRTY-ONE

FROM THE WARM DEPTHS of her sleeping bag, Chloe became aware of Ariel tiptoeing to the front door. "What time is it?" Chloe mumbled. It was still dark.

"Six-thirty. Go back to sleep."

"Did you eat breakfast?" Chloe rose on one elbow, rubbing her eyes. She was developing a new appreciation for Roelke, who had been known to observe that she didn't eat well enough. He should try keeping a stressed ballerina fed. "At least take some fruit with you."

"Okay, okay." Ariel darted across the room and grabbed an orange from the bowl on the breakfast bar. "Call me at work if you need anything." She let herself out the door.

To her annoyance, Chloe found herself too awake to stay in the sack. Might as well get to work, too. The more she accomplished, the better Ariel would feel.

After her own breakfast, Chloe settled down to type up the list of primary interpretive themes. Ariel's portable typewriter was electric and even had a backspace function that transferred mistakes to a thin band of correction tape, so that task was accomplished quickly. Between now and Friday, she and Ariel needed to type up a longer narrative summary of each theme.

Just for kicks Chloe started with Marketing, a topic she wouldn't have thought interesting until she delved into flour milling history. There are a zillion ways to look at this, she mused. There was brand development to consider. Advertising. Promotional giveaways. Competition between Gold Medal and Pillsbury. The pioneering use of radio. The meteoric rise of Betty Crocker.

She was sitting on the sofa with feet tucked up, scribbling away, when the phone rang. She picked it up. "Ariel Grzegorczyk's home."

"Chloe?"

"Libby?"

Libby laughed. "Did I catch you at a bad time?"

"I was reading about Betty Crocker. She was an invention, which sort of duped a lot of people. But the staff behind the name really helped homemakers figure out how to feed their families, and how to cope with shortages during the Great Depression and World War II." Chloe sighed happily, then remembered that Libby hadn't called to discuss Betty Crocker. "How are things down there?"

"I saw Roelke last night. He helped Justin with a school project at the Milwaukee Public Museum. I think it was good for everybody."

"I heard a bit about that," Chloe said. "Roelke actually called me after. Not that he said much. I know he's doing what he feels he needs to do, but I worry about him. He holds too much stuff inside."

"No kidding," Libby said. "God only knows what mood he'll be in after visiting Patrick today."

"Who's Patrick?"

The line went silent. Finally Libby muttered, "Oh, *hell*."

Chloe untucked her feet and sat up straight. "Libby? Who is Patrick?"

"God, I'm sorry, Chloe. It never occurred to me that you didn't know. But I shouldn't be the one to—"

"*Who—is—Patrick?*"

Libby's sigh echoed through the wire. "Patrick is Roelke's brother."

———

The sun warmed the truck cab so well that Roelke rolled down his window as he drove into the city of Waupun. Just your everyday Wisconsin town, he thought. A main street with a variety of shops, many housed in historic buildings. The sound of geese flying overhead, probably heading for nearby Horicon Marsh. Schools, churches, playgrounds. And, oh yes, a maximum-security prison tucked away in a residential neighborhood.

He parked near the Waupun Correctional Institution. As he plugged the meter a jogger called, "Just so you know, the meters here have a two-hour limit. If you go down a block, you'll get an extra hour."

"Thanks, but this should do it." Roelke profoundly hoped he'd be in and out in twenty minutes or less.

He studied the facility. Some of the limestone buildings inside the compound were well over a century old, with castle-like turrets. Despite the razor wire topping the fence, the prison had an antique look to it, and a plaque proclaimed its status on the Wisconsin Register of Historic Places. I've probably been to more historic sites today than Chloe has, Roelke thought. It seemed safe to assume that she had not visited a basilica and a penitentiary.

Okay. Time to focus.

He left the guns in the truck. At the first gate he showed his police ID and explained his reason for visiting. Ten minutes later he passed through the second gate and on to the building.

Corrections Officer Detrie was waiting. He seemed like an upright guy—mid-forties, direct gaze, good command presence. "What can I do for you, Officer McKenna?"

"I'm working a case that may involve someone recently released from here. The man is known as Lobo. Latino guy, maybe in his thirties."

"The name doesn't ring a bell, and we've got lots of Hispanics in here." Detrie cocked his head. "Let's go check the records."

Roelke tried not to get his hopes up. Good thing, too. "Sorry," Detrie said some minutes later. "No record of a Lobo. It's probably a nickname. We know a lot of 'em. Hell, half of the guys have their gang name or whatever tattooed in big letters. But evidently not your guy."

"Thanks for checking." Roelke beat a tattoo against his thigh with one thumb. That was about what he'd expected. He took a deep breath and straightened his shoulders. "I'd like to visit one of your inmates, if that's okay."

"Visiting hours don't begin until two, but we can make an exception. Who do you want to see?"

"Patrick McKenna," Roelke said. "He's my brother."

Detrie passed him off to another CO, who escorted him to another building. Roelke signed in on a clipboard and emptied his pockets for the guard at the admittance desk. He deposited a quarter in a little locker and stashed his coat and gloves. The guard stamped his hand and gave him a slip of paper with his name and a table number on it, then buzzed him through a locked door. On the other side, another CO checked Roelke's stamp before ushering him into the visitation room. "Table Six," he said. The room was empty, but Roelke dutifully found Table Six and sat down to wait.

His knee was working like a piston once again and he felt wound tight. Calm down, he told himself. It wasn't so bad in here, really. With its rows of institutional tables, the room was vaguely reminiscent of a school cafeteria, except the tables were really low. A carpeted square in one corner marked a children's play area, with a couple of playpens and bins of battered toys. There were vending machines, flyers advertising various programs and services taped to the walls, a couple of bubblers, and shelves holding books and board games and packs of playing cards.

After maybe fifteen minutes the door buzzed again. A CO escorted Patrick to the table and left.

Roelke stared at his older brother while a big wall clock ticked noisily away. He hadn't seen Patrick in over five years. He looked older, oddly subdued. He was thinner, but his chest and arms were more muscular. The standard blue jumpsuit looked strange. The dark hair and eyes, the strong chin, cheekbones curved just like his own—those hadn't changed.

Finally Patrick said, "It's good to see you, Roelke."

"You too," Roelke lied.

"Libby comes every once in a while, but I gave up looking for you a long time ago."

"I guess I never knew what to say."

"You didn't have to say it. I screwed up. Well, I'm paying for it."

"Yeah."

Patrick shifted in his chair. "So, how are you doing?"

"Good," Roelke lied.

"You got a girlfriend?"

"No," Roelke lied. No way was he even mentioning Chloe's name in this place. "So, are you … um … doing okay?"

"As okay as somebody can be in a prison," Patrick said. "I went into the hole a couple of times after I got here, had to start over on earning privileges and stuff, but I've been doing good for a while now. I don't know what Libby's told you—"

Not much, Roelke thought, because I never let her.

"—but I am trying. My social worker got me into AA and an anger management group. And I go to church services."

"That's good," Roelke said, although he was pretty sure that most of the inmates who found Jesus on the inside left Him on the inside when they got out.

"I earned my GED two years ago. And I got into a production welding training class. I like it."

"That's good."

There was another pause. The CO circled casually past, took a drink at one of the bubblers, finished his circuit.

"It was the booze, you know," Patrick said. "Just like dad."

"Yeah. Just like dad."

Anger glinted in Patrick's eyes, but he kept his voice level. "It could have been you, Roelke. Did you ever think of that? Did you ever think that maybe we both had issues with alcohol and anger management—"

Issues with alcohol and anger management? Roelke was tempted to ask this guy who he was, and what he'd done with Patrick.

"—and that maybe you were just luckier than me? I got caught up in some bad shit, I know that, but I might have straightened myself out. I might have been like you."

"You're not like me."

"It must be very comforting to think that," Patrick said, "but we're more alike than you want to believe. Can you honestly sit there and tell me you've never lost control? Made mistakes? Done something that you regretted?"

Roelke flashed on the stolen gun hidden under the seat in his truck, the lies he'd told the police the night before. Last summer he'd kicked a handcuffed prisoner. Still, not *quite* like Patrick, who had lost control for the last time in a tavern, with a knife in his hand, in a tangle that included several cops.

But Roelke had more than once worried that he was exactly like Patrick. That scared the absolute shit out of him. He used that fear as a deterrent, doing his best to get through life without self-destructing like Patrick and their father had.

Patrick sighed. "Why did you come here, Roelke?"

"Libby told me once that I need to make peace with you," Roelke said, which was astonishing, because he hadn't planned to say anything like that. Until this minute he hadn't even remembered that.

Patrick thought that over. "I guess all I can ask for is a second chance. You're still my kid brother."

"Okay." Roelke scrubbed his face with his palms, desperate to move on. "I was also hoping you could answer a couple of questions for me."

"What about?"

"A guy who, I'm told, was released from here not too long ago. A Latino guy named Lobo. You know who that is?"

Patrick shifted uneasily in his plastic chair again, and looked over both shoulders. "Yeah, I know who that is. He got out maybe three weeks ago. Why do you ask? Is he in trouble again already?"

"He might be. I'm looking for him."

"Better you than me, then." Patrick shook his head. "He's not somebody to mess with. Lobo didn't like one of my cellies, and the guy ended up with a shiv in the back. Needed thirty-three stitches."

"The CO didn't know who I was talking about. Lobo must be a nickname, right?"

"His real name is Alberto Marquez. The COs are decent guys, mostly, but there's a lot they don't know."

Roelke didn't doubt that. "So what was Lobo in for? Drugs? Still calling the shots, so everybody in here had to pay him respect?"

"Drugs had nothing to do with it." Patrick sat back in his chair, looking surprised at Roelke's ignorance. "Lobo got sent to prison after some guy hired him to kill his wife."

# THIRTY-TWO
## JULY 1921

"You must do better, Lidia," Thomas said curtly. "Mr. Windom is waiting."

Lidia concentrated on the tiny replica of a Gold Medal Flour sack she was stitching. The company had offered the pincushions as premiums, and when demand had far surpassed expectations, all the women employees had been asked to help out. "I have been asking questions, Thomas." Lie number one. "But even in No Man's Land, the girls are uneasy about discussing union activities." Lie number two.

They were on the grinding floor this evening. The Money Floor, the men called it. The place where 150 roller mills marched in rows right above the mighty turbines that harnessed the river and powered the whole works. The floor vibrated. The miller on duty was circulating, grabbing handfuls of flour from each machine with a little metal spatula. He could tell if a machine wasn't working properly just from rubbing the flour between his fingers.

Routine problems fell to the millwrights like Thomas. He knelt before one of the roller mills, listening to the whirring gears. "We know some women are supporting the union," he said. "We just don't know who they are."

"I'll try harder." Lie number three.

"See that you do. Do you want to jeopardize all that I've worked for? I'm trying to make a better life for us. For *you*. Union agitation here at the mill will only bring trouble. Don't you see that?"

"Yes." Lie number four.

"Then for God's sake, *do* something about it." Thomas's face was taut as he slowly slid his hand through the maze of moving parts.

Lidia had to look away as she pictured a belt snapping, a shirt sleeve tangling in gears. Marriage had proved more difficult than she'd expected, but she still loved this man: the curls on the back of his neck, his dream of creating a better life, his energy. When he gave her one of his old smiles, something still tingled inside. When he worked on these machines, she still worried.

If only he weren't *quite* so driven, she thought. If only he weren't so moody. If only the bad tempers weren't growing more commonplace. If only he didn't make her feel as if—aside from working her shift—she didn't dare leave his side.

Thomas held his breath, making the mechanical adjustment by feel alone. Lidia's mind shivered, and she imagined her own hand easing toward the gears. Not to help her husband, but to—

Lidia crossed herself almost convulsively. God forgive me, she thought. She leaned against the wall—trembling, sick to her stomach. Where had such an evil thought come from?

Thomas sat back on his heels. "Hand me the oil can." He gestured to the long-spouted can resting on top of his wooden tool box.

"Thomas. I . . . I would like to go back to the Flats for a little while."

He rose slowly, turned to face her. "What did you say?"

"Just for a visit," Lidia said quickly.

"Absolutely not."

"I just want to be with my mother for a couple of days."

"And what will everyone think of me if you do so?"

"Perhaps we could say that my mother is ill. *Please*, Thomas. I need to see Grandfather Pawel and *Matka*."

The Polish word was a mistake. His face hardened. His fingers closed around her wrist with such strength that she had to bite back a whimper. In the middle of this enormous mill, she felt very alone.

"I said no," Thomas hissed. "If you leave my house, I will kill you."

# THIRTY-THREE

CHLOE CLUTCHED THE TELEPHONE, struggling to parse Libby's words. Roelke had a brother? How could she not have known that?

"Are you still there?" Libby sounded worried.

How could Roelke have kept something like that a secret?

"Chloe?"

"I'm here."

"I am so sorry. I can't believe Roelke hasn't—I never dreamed—"

"Where is it, exactly, that Roelke is visiting his brother today?"

"Look, I should let Roelke tell you—"

"Libby," Chloe said, "I swear to God, if you don't tell me where Roelke is going today, I will drive to your house and shake it out of you."

Another long sigh. "Patrick is in prison. He's at Waupun."

Chloe had trouble wrapping her brain around that, too.

"Chloe?"

"You know what? You're right. This is something that Roelke and I need to discuss."

"I am *so* sorry."

"It's not your fault," Chloe said. "I'll talk to you later." She hung up.

Then she stared at the wall, thinking back through every conversation she could remember about families—his, hers. "It's just me and Libby and the kids," he'd said once. She was sure he'd said that.

Roelke McKenna, cop, had a brother named Patrick, felon.

Chloe prowled the tiny living room, clutching her elbows, getting angrier and angrier. It was bad enough that Roelke had pushed her away after Rick got killed. But this was worse. What else didn't she know about?

There's nothing you can do about it right this minute, she told herself. Go back to Betty Crocker.

She flopped down on the sofa and picked up the article she'd been reading. Two minutes later she put it down. She picked up one of the cookbooks and flipped through the pages. She put the book down, too. Even the glorious Tunnel of Fudge cake held no allure.

Suddenly Ariel's tiny house felt way too confining. Chloe grabbed her car keys, shrugged into her parka, and left.

But where to go? She wasn't going to drive to the Minnesota Historical Society and dump this on Ariel in the middle of a pressure cooker workday. She was too angry to talk about it, anyway.

She spotted a sign for the Red Owl market and dove into an empty parking space. She might as well stock up on flour, sugar, butter, and so on. Once inside, she got an even better idea. "You take credit cards, right?" she asked the clerk. He nodded. She reached for a cart.

Half an hour later she parked by the Washburn A Mill. When she got out of the car, she heard a mechanical rumble coming from the gravel beds on the river side of the complex. A bulldozer and dump trucks chugged along the river while several men in hard hats watched.

One of the men broke away. "Hey, Chloe!" Jay called. "What's up?"

Chloe shrugged with what she hoped was a believable smile. "I needed an excursion, so I came to help Sister Mary Jude with lunch. I didn't know this was going on." She pointed toward the heavy equipment.

"The gravel yard owners agreed to let us clear enough away to expose some of the ruins buried underneath for the big tour on Friday. It's like tearing wrapping paper off a gift."

"What's down there?"

"The mill was the largest direct-drive water-powered operation on the planet! That gravel covers canals, tailraces...who know what else. I've got a handful of students who are happily trading some heavy labor for extra credit."

"This whole place is an archaeological site." Chloe thought of the artifacts Owen had shown her from the day in 1965 when the mill closed, all perfectly preserved in place. "Layers over layers over layers."

"I've never worked on a project like this one, that's for sure. The buildings don't preserve some grand architectural style. They were designed for function. And yet, that function led to something grand." Jay shrugged, looking a little sheepish. "If you see what I mean."

"I do," Chloe assured him. "I didn't at first, but now that I've spent a bit of time here... it's utterly compelling. Professor Whyte captured that intangible sense of hidden stories in his photographs."

"I suppose you heard the latest?" Jay asked. "The cause of death?"

"Ariel and I heard last night. Is it likely that Dr. Whyte would have been walking along the river?"

Jay removed his hard hat and raked a hand through his hair. "Sure. Maybe he wanted to photograph a bit of old wall showing through the gravel. Maybe he tripped, hit his head, and fell into the Mississippi.

The police said from the start that he had a head wound, and maybe they jumped to the wrong conclusion about what caused it. I doubt he drowned in one of the turbine pits—if he'd fallen in, it would have taken a monumental effort to get him back out. But in either case, how do you explain getting his body to the eighth floor?" He made a wide arc with his arm, pointing.

"That question gives me the creeps."

"Yeah." Jay settled the hat back on his head. "Listen, Owen's working in the mill with a couple of undergrads, well within a shout of the spot where Sister Mary Jude serves. If you need any help, just holler." He went back to the excavation.

Chloe headed to the mill. She approached just as a police squad car pulled up to the curb. Officer Crandall and his partner emerged.

"I remember you," Crandall said without preamble. "Where's your pretty little friend? The one who got arrested for breaking into the murdered guy's office?"

"My *colleague* is at work," Chloe told him coolly. Jerk.

The black officer—Ashton, according to her nametag—was standing behind Crandall, and actually rolled her eyes. "Didn't you say you wanted to check around the far side?" she asked him.

"Yeah, yeah. I got it. I'll let you ladies have your confab, or whatever." Crandall sauntered away.

Chloe looked at Officer Ashton. "I don't mean to be disrespectful, but how can you work with that man and not go insane?"

The officer watched her partner disappear around a corner. "At least with Crandall, what you see is what you get. The ones that scare me are the guys who set me up to fail. My first sergeant gave me a quota for parking tickets that was three times the norm."

"Because you're a woman?"

She shrugged. "I'm a woman with black skin. It's hard to know what rankles the good ol' boys the most." Then her impassive cop face slipped back into place. "Forgive me. That was inappropriate. How is your friend?"

"Pretty shook up," Chloe said. "The rest of us too, of course, but Ariel is a bit more fragile. The incident that led to her being arrested was an unfortunate misunderstanding, of course. Ariel made a dumb mistake, she explained the situation to the officers, and that was the end of it." A new worry slid into Chloe's mind. "Officer Crandall doesn't honestly believe that Ariel had anything to do with Professor Whyte's death, does he?"

"I couldn't speak to that."

Shit, Chloe thought, I bet that's exactly what Crandall thinks. "Ariel had nothing to do with it. If you could have seen her face when we found Dr. Whyte, and heard her scream… No *way* she faked it. She was in shock."

"As anyone would be," Officer Ashton said. "Good afternoon, Ms. Ellefson. Let us know if you see anything suspicious."

Chloe was still fretting over that exchange when she saw Sister Mary Jude park a yellow VW Bug down the street and pull her picnic hampers from the back seat. The nun walked briskly toward the mill and smiled when she saw Chloe. "I didn't expect to see you again."

"I'm staying with my friend and came to help you. I've got some groceries in my car. Chocolate chip cookies, among other things. Dog food and diapers, too."

"That's kind of you, and much appreciated. But"—Mary studied Chloe for a moment, head tipped—"are you all right?"

"Oh, I—I was just talking with Officers Crandall and Ashton, and got the impression that Crandall, at least, believes Ariel had something to do with Professor Whyte's death. It's preposterous."

"I wouldn't put much stock in what Officer Crandall thinks."

"I know, he's an *idiot*, but the very idea…" Chloe was astonished to feel tears well in her eyes. She blinked hard, but suddenly she was outright crying.

Mary found a packet of tissues and handed one over. "Is it possible that something else is troubling you?"

"Not really," Chloe sniffled, wiping her eyes. "It's just that… well… I learned that someone I care about has been keeping a pretty major secret. I can't say he out-and-out lied about it, but he sure danced around the truth."

"You must feel a little betrayed by that," Mary observed. "And angry. And hurt."

"Kind of." Chloe blew her nose and took a deep breath. All right, that was enough of sounding pathetic.

"Are you a religious person?"

"I'm a spiritual person," Chloe said with sudden caution. If the good nun starting getting all religious-conversion on her, she'd have to deposit her groceries and go.

"Then you won't mind if I say a prayer for you and your friend tonight?"

Chloe started to cry all over again. "That would be quite nice. Thank you. And… if you don't mind, could you request some extra protection for my friend? His name is Roelke. I'm angry at him, but I'm worried about him, too."

———

Roelke found a little café on Main Street with a decent salad bar and an empty corner booth. He boxed up whatever emotional fallout there was after seeing his brother—he'd deal with that later—and focused on what Patrick had said about Lobo.

Finally, *finally*, a few links were presenting themselves. According to Patrick, a man had hired Lobo to kill his wife, and Lobo had come close to succeeding. So, domestic violence was common to Lobo and Steve Litkowski. Rick had been seen talking to Lobo. And although he still had no proof, Roelke believed that Rick had been helping Erin.

So. Maybe Erin came back to Milwaukee, Steve Litkowski found out and came after her, and Erin turned to Rick for help. Rick might have done some digging of his own, maybe learned that Lobo was still willing to freelance. Maybe, Roelke thought, Erin didn't run away from Kip's to avoid *me*. Maybe she ran away because she feared that after shooting Rick, Lobo was probably coming for her.

What Roelke still didn't know was how any of that involved a cop. Someone took the gun from Evidence lockup. Someone examined Rick's FI cards before they reached the detectives assigned to the case. Those two facts didn't fit with his theories.

Maybe one of Rick's FI cards had referenced Lobo. If a cop had hired the ex-con, that cop would want to be sure that Rick's cards didn't reveal anything that could eventually implicate said cop.

After eating his last tomato, Roelke got out his index cards and added what he'd learned about Lobo the Wolf, AKA Alberto Marquez. Rick must have had a good reason for sharing a brewski in the Rusty Nail with him. Maybe Rick was trying to string the asshole along, get some intel.

Next, Roelke updated his task list:

1. *Ask Dobry to look up arrest record for Alberto Marquez*
2. *Canvass the block where Donny D said he saw Rick*
3. *Check Eve's House*

Eve's House was a battered women's center. It seemed unlikely that Erin would be hiding there. The last time Steve threatened to kill her, she'd felt compelled to flee the state. Still, it was worth checking.

Roelke gathered his cards, tapped the edges, and tucked them away. Then he thought hard about the prospect of returning to the Old South Side. In the course of his police career he'd been punched, kicked, and spit on more times than he could count. Once a woman came at him with a skillet, once a drunk came at him with a knife, and once someone tried to run him over. But it was particularly chilling to picture a sniper taking deliberate aim at his back.

Equally chilling was the knowledge that it had happened in densely-populated Lincoln Village. Roelke did not want to get shot at again. He also didn't want a shot aimed at him to hit somebody else. How reckless was it to return to the neighborhood?

Okay, he decided finally. The shooter had struck twice in Kozy Park in the middle of the night. So—stay away from Kozy Park, and get the heck out of Milwaukee before sundown.

The waitress stopped by his table. "Can I get you some dessert?"

"No thanks," Roelke said. "I've got places to be." Enough thinking, for now. It was time to *do* something.

# THIRTY-FOUR
## SEPTEMBER 1921

LIDIA PICKED HER WAY across railroad tracks and slid through the shadows to the mill. Don't think, she ordered herself. Enough thinking, for now. It was time to *do* something.

"I forgot to give Thomas his supper," she told the night watchman, holding up a lumpy sack. The man let her inside. All the guards knew her, knew she spent many hours in the mill with her husband.

This Sunday night there was a problem with one of the enormous underground turbines that yoked the power of St. Anthony Falls. One of the auxiliary engines was down too, and the millwrights had done the almost unthinkable—halt the entire operation. The enormous building was oddly silent. Lidia faltered, disoriented by the absence of the familiar throb and rumble. But she could still feel Thomas's fingers like a manacle on her wrist, still hear his threat, still see the absolute conviction in his eyes.

Lidia started to cross herself, then checked. That morning, she'd whispered a plea in the confessional: "I—I believe my husband will kill me, Father, if I displease him. What can I do?"

"You must do what God intended," the priest commanded. "Submit to your husband in all things, and pray."

So Lidia knew she couldn't appeal to God, not anymore. She had to help herself.

She hurried down the passage to one of the roller mills, one floor above the turbines where her husband was working. As soon as the mill shuddered back to life, this machine was next on Thomas's list.

Thanks to the hours she'd spent watching Thomas clean and repair machinery, she knew a fair bit about cogs and gears and belts. But with no tools of her own, she'd initially been stymied. And after making his threat, Thomas had kept her in sight every moment that she wasn't working her own shift.

Then came word of the shutdown, and all the millwrights were ordered to assemble. "It isn't appropriate for you to be there," Thomas had muttered. And as Lidia frantically considered this unexpected opportunity, she realized she did have one tool of her own.

Now she sent up another prayer. *I never knew you, Grandmother Magdalena. Please don't think I'm evil. I know I'm doing a terrible thing, but I don't know what else to do. And I don't want to kill Thomas, truly. I just want to slow him down.*

She paused, eyes closed. And she fancied she felt the presence of Grandmother Magdalena there in the mill with her. A woman's voice seemed to say, *Do it.*

Lidia took a deep breath, reached into her sack, and pulled out Magdalena's sheep shears.

# THIRTY-FIVE

Since Owen had left one gate and door unlocked, entrance to the mill today didn't require stealth or acrobatics. "Hello!" Chloe called as she and Sister Mary Jude came inside. "It's Chloe Ellefson and Sister Mary Jude!"

Owen appeared from an aisle of packing machines, carrying a carton. "Hey!"

"Getting set for the reception?" Chloe asked.

He nodded. "I am determined to have that roller mill operational by Friday night. We've replaced all the belts, and cleaned and oiled all the gears. We'll be doing a trial run later." He almost quivered with excitement, like a boy setting up his first train set.

Chloe was again charmed by his determination. "I'll stop down."

Owen held up the carton. "Say, can you pass this on to Ariel? Jay's team found some old stuff while cleaning out the women's floor in the Utility Building. No Man's Land, they called it."

"I'll get it to her."

He set the carton on the floor. "My undergrad mechanics aren't back from lunch yet, so let me help you set up."

They put out the lunch fixings in the deep windowsills overlooking weed-choked railroad tracks. "Did you hear that Everett Whyte drowned?" Owen asked in a low tone. "Pretty freaky."

Mary peeled plastic wrap from a tray of sandwiches. "We may never understand what happened."

Chloe glanced over her shoulder, making sure they were still alone. "Maybe Dr. Whyte tripped, hit his head and blacked out, fell into the river, and drowned. If some of the residents saw what happened, and didn't know what to do, they might have... you know."

"Everett was a small man," Owen said. "Still, it's hard to picture somebody hauling his body over the gravel, up the slope, through the fence, into the mill, and up eight flights of stairs."

Sister Mary Jude sighed. "You're thinking like people who have stable homes."

Chloe and Owen exchanged a glance. "I'm not sure I follow," Owen admitted.

"Every person who lives in this mill has an uneasy relationship with the police." Mary began arranging apples, oranges, and bananas on a plastic plate. "They have no legal right to shelter here. Some have a history of drug abuse or prostitution or mental illness. While the notion of carrying Dr. Whyte to the eighth floor seems bizarre to us, it might make perfect sense to someone who wants only to deflect unwanted attention."

"It's all very sad." Chloe ripped open a bag of cookies, imagining Star or Camo John or any other lost soul trying to decide what to do with the body of a man spotted floating face down in the Mississippi.

As if summoned by her thoughts, a shadow crossed the wall and Camo John approached. His face was impassive, his eyes inscrutable in the gloom, his big hands hanging by his sides. This man makes me uncomfortable, Chloe thought. Did the fact that he was big and dirty and uncommunicative make her feel that way? Or was there truly something to worry about?

"Hello, John." Mary smiled cheerfully, banishing Chloe's momentary unease. "Will it be cheese or bologna today?"

"I better get back to work," Owen told Chloe. "Come down in about ten minutes if you want to see our trial run with the roller stand."

Other residents began slipping from the shadows, hunched into coats that too often seemed inadequate for the mill's damp cold. Chloe was struck again by the diversity—men and women, some elderly people, a few teens. A young woman clutched a baby in her arms. Mary produced disposable diapers and baby food.

A sad ache settled beneath Chloe's ribs. "I'll be back," she called and headed for the closest stairwell with flashlight in hand. She didn't want to disappoint Owen, and if she didn't take a quick breather, she'd start to cry. I don't know how Mary keeps going, she thought. Day after day after *day*.

On the grinding floor she found Owen at the detached roller mill with two younger men. Owen grinned. "Good timing!"

Chloe stopped a respectful distance away. Owen nodded, and one of the young men threw a switch. The belts began their endless circles and the roller mill shuddered up to speed.

Owen reached for a bag of grain. "Watch this—"

The sentence ended in a wordless cry. Owen flew backward. A broken belt slapped the machine with a horrible sound, over and over and over.

Chloe ran to Owen, who lay motionless on the cement. Something buzzed in her brain. Not Owen. Not sweet, cheerful Owen.

"Turn it off!" one of the undergrads yelled. "Turn it *off!*"

"I don't know how!" the other student shrieked frantically.

"Just get away from it," Chloe ordered. She felt for a pulse under Owen's jaw. Please, God. Not Owen, *too.*

"That belt was fine before lunch!" the first student cried. "It's like somebody—I don't know—it's like sabotage or something!"

"Calm down," Chloe told him sharply. "Go get help. *Now.*"

Sister Mary Jude appeared and dropped to the floor beside Chloe. "I heard the shouting—what happened? Is he alive?" She put a hand on Owen's cheek.

Grateful tears welled in Chloe's eyes when she felt the steady beat of life beneath her fingertips. "He's unconscious. I don't see any sign of blood, so the best thing we can do is keep him still and warm until help arrives."

"And pray," Mary whispered, closing her eyes. "Mother Mary, please help us…"

Chloe yanked off her parka and laid it gently over Owen. He'll be okay, she promised herself. Surely he will.

But her brain echoed with the student's dire assessment: *It's like sabotage or something!* Taken by itself, Everett Whyte's death might yet be ruled accidental. But if someone had tampered with the machine Owen had been working on, it would be difficult to believe that someone wasn't trying to frighten or kill the people working to reclaim the abandoned mill.

———

Roelke drove from the city of Waupun back to Milwaukee's Old South Side. Donny D had said he'd seen Rick near Mitchell Street, a bit north of Lincoln Village. St. Stanislaus Catholic Church's glowing copper domes rose above another old-Polish, new-Latino neighborhood. Did Lobo stay here after leaving prison? Was that why Rick had been walking the streets here out of uniform, hoping no one noticed or identified him as a cop? Or had he been secretly meeting Erin?

Roelke parked on a side street and began walking. "I'm looking for a friend," he told shop clerks and cashiers, holding up Erin's photo. "Have you seen her? She's blond now." His hopes rose when a baker nodded. "Maria, isn't this that lady who comes in every day and buys one wedding cookie?"

Maria paused from washing the bakery case to take a look. "No way! That doesn't look anything like the wedding cookie lady."

Roelke pushed farther down the commercial corridor, then branched out to the residential streets. He showed the photo to an elderly man pulling a market cart, the young woman bent beneath her bulging daypack, two moms with babies in strollers, a jogger. At a small house with a hand-painted sign hanging by the door—*Rose Cottage*—his hopes lifted when an elderly woman inspecting her dormant garden studied the photo with interest. *Something* flashed in her eyes, and he held his breath.

"My, she is a pretty one." Her voice held the inflection of someone raised in a community of first-generation immigrants who spoke Polish at home. "She reminds me of an actress on *Dynasty*. Do you watch *Dynasty*?"

"No ma'am." Roelke handed her his business card. "If you do see my friend, will you please give her this?" She nodded and tucked it into a coat pocket. He slipped Erin's photo away and on impulse, pulled the chicken-flower business card from the envelope. "Does this mean anything to you?"

"No, but I do like the colors. This reminds me of the paper cutting some of the old women used to do."

"*Wycinanki*," Roelke said breezily, like he knew all about it and therefore did not need to be informed that Poles preferred roosters. "Right. Thank you, ma'am."

Don't get discouraged, he ordered himself. You're not out of ideas yet.

———

Chloe stood alone as the ambulance pulled away. Jay—after finally shutting the damn roller mill down—had gone with Owen. The grad students had left. Looking shaken, Sister Mary Jude had packed up her hampers and followed.

"Well, this day just keeps sucking more and more," Chloe muttered. The mill would make a fantastic museum one day, but she was going to stay away until that transformation had taken place. She'd sensed a layer of fear the first time she'd walked through the mill. Finding Dr. Whyte's body had been horrid. Owen's injury was just too much.

Chloe hurried to her car with the carton he'd given her for Ariel. Once inside with the doors locked, professional curiosity demanded a peek inside. She pulled one of the corner cardboard flaps free. "Oh!"

The first thing that presented itself was a rectangle of heavy cream-colored paper, corners marked with pin holes. Despite a film of dust, and the passing years' inevitable fading, a collage of cut and layered paper still suggested a vivid rainbow of color. A central bouquet of stylized flowers was flanked on each side by a rooster. She gently lifted the piece. Pride in creation, determination, feminine strength ... all those seemed palpable.

She was pretty sure that this glorious example of *wycinanki* had been made long before the mill closed in 1965. It so closely resembled what Roelke had tried to describe on the phone that an ice chip slid down Chloe's spine. Ariel had said that a motif of flowers and roosters was common. Still, it was uncanny that this piece, left behind in No Man's Land, echoed whatever it was that Roelke had found in Wisconsin decades later.

Was it even remotely possible that the same woman had created each *wycinanka*? "If so," she whispered to whomever might be listening, "why did you leave this beautiful piece in No Man's Land? And how did you get from Minneapolis to Milwaukee?"

# THIRTY-SIX
## SEPTEMBER 1921

LIDIA TOOK THE TRAIN from Minneapolis to Milwaukee. She knew there was a large Polish community there, and although she'd managed to hide away a few coins after grocery shopping these past few months, she couldn't afford to travel any farther.

Best of all, a train east was scheduled to leave fifteen minutes after she arrived at the station. She tried to sound calm as she counted out the fare, but her mind was back at the mill. Had the belt snapped, slapping Thomas with enough force to break an arm or knock him unconscious? The belt was an old one, made of buffalo hide, and she'd used the sheep shears to gnaw at the stitches holding the two ends together. Once the problem with the turbines was fixed and the mill growled back to life, the belt wouldn't have held for long. Perhaps it had given way before Thomas even began to work on the roller mill. Was he fixing the roller stand, fuming because she wasn't waiting for him? Had he grown suspicious of the sabotage, and her absence, and gone looking? He'd go to their house, and probably Mama's as well, before widening the search … wouldn't he? Or would he instinctively know she was trying to escape?

Ticket clutched in one sweating hand, Lidia made her way onto the train and found an empty seat. She watched out the window, braced for the sight of her husband running down the platform, bellowing, coming for her. It was hard to breathe until she heard the whistle shrill and felt the car lurch slowly forward.

But with every clack of the turning wheels she felt herself moving farther and farther from *Matka* and Grandfather Pawel. From Bohemian Flats and Minneapolis and the mill. From her whole world. She'd had no time to say good-bye—and she wouldn't have dared, anyway.

Lidia had to change trains in La Crosse, Wisconsin. She approached a woman in worn clothes who looked to be about her size and offered to exchange clothes. "Why?" the woman asked suspiciously, eyeing her stylish dress.

"I need to disappear," Lidia whispered.

Ten minutes later she emerged from the ladies' room wearing a heavy skirt and faded blouse. "Be careful," the other woman said, before disappearing into the swirling crowd in her new finery.

Lidia pulled Grandmother Magdalena's old shawl over her shoulders and felt surprisingly comforted. She hated leaving Magdalena's beautiful *wycinanka* behind, tacked over the door in No Man's Land. But once Thomas discovered her absence, he might well storm the women's lounge. If one of the girls mentioned that her prized artwork was gone, he'd know for sure that she'd run away. At least, Lidia thought, my engagement scarf—the white cloth binding her to Thomas—has also been left behind. And the stylish hats he'd bought for her, too. How she had once loved them! It seemed ridiculous now.

"All aboard for Milwaukee!" the conductor hollered.

As Lidia climbed onto the train, a wave of nausea brought beads of sweat to her forehead. She'd felt sick for several weeks, now. Awareness had starched her resolve to leave Thomas—if not for herself, for the sake of their child.

Lidia closed her eyes and leaned her forehead against the glass. Oh *Matka*, she thought, fighting tears. And Grandfather Pawel ... how worried you must be.

# THIRTY-SEVEN

Eve's House was an unremarkable two-story home in a quiet neighborhood. Well, Roelke thought, did you expect a neon sign at a shelter for battered women?

Closer inspection revealed the security measures. He heard children's laughter coming from the back yard, which was surrounded by a tall, solid fence. The front door was sturdy; the first-floor windows had been replaced by glass blocks. Men can be so damn toxic, he thought, imagining women inside—terrified, depressed, nursing bruises or broken bones, wondering what on earth they were supposed to do now.

When he rang the doorbell, a thirty-ish woman cracked open the door, leaving a safety chain in place. "May I help you?" She wore jeans and a turquoise turtleneck. She'd captured her honey-colored hair in a long braid that reminded him painfully of Chloe.

He held up his badge and ID. "I'm a police officer, ma'am. I'd like to speak to whoever is in charge."

The woman studied the badge before letting him inside. "I'm Helen," she said, locking the door securely again. "The director of Eve's House. Let's go into my office."

She led him to what had once been a dining room, now divided by a wall. Another woman sat at a metal desk, hunched over a telephone, speaking in a low, calm voice. Helen led Roelke through a door into her private space, which held another cheap metal desk and a couple of file cabinets. The cubicle was decorated with posters. Some were informative—*Ten Common Signs of Domestic Abuse*—and some were reassuring—an earth mother presented in warm hues, toes on the ground and hands reaching for the stars. Roelke removed a one-eared stuffed bear from the chair facing the desk and sat down.

Then he held out Erin's photograph. "I'm trying to find a woman named Erin Litkowski, also known as Joanie. The last time I saw her she was blond." He watched Helen, and *yes*, there it was; a flicker of recognition.

"Why are you looking for this woman?" Helen asked.

"I want to make sure she's safe. She left Milwaukee a couple of years ago when her husband threatened to kill her. She recently returned to the city and began waitressing in a tavern. Her husband might still be prepared to kill her. Erin isn't safe in Milwaukee, even hiding at a shelter like this."

Helen fiddled with a paperclip, assessing him. She had a narrow face and intelligent hazel eyes. Finally she said, "I don't normally discuss the women who come here with anyone but social workers."

"I am a cop," Roelke said, feeling a bit defensive.

Helen's expression didn't change. "I know exactly who you are. Erin said you might come."

Roelke leaned forward eagerly. "She did? She's here?"

"She *was* here. She's gone."

His moment of hope disappeared. He'd missed her. Erin had been here, and he'd missed her. *Again.*

Helen abruptly nodded, as if she'd come to some conclusion. "I can't tell you where Erin has gone. But I will tell you that Erin didn't come here as a client. She came here five months ago as a volunteer."

"A volunteer?"

"She'd heard that her husband was living with another woman. A former friend. Erin came back to warn her against getting involved with him."

"Did the friend take her advice?"

"No." Helen spread her hands in a gesture of resigned futility. "But Erin decided to stay in the city, at least for a while. I was glad to have her help. Women who have endured abuse themselves have instant rapport with the women who come here seeking help."

"Did Erin ever mention another police officer to you? Officer Rick Almirez?"

Helen's gaze didn't waver. "No."

So, still no hard link between Erin and Rick. Roelke tried to hide his frustration. "Well, thank you for telling me. If Erin ever comes back, will you please ask her to get in touch with me? I just . . . I just want to know she's okay."

"I'm not sure that's a good idea," Helen said evenly. "I've already told you more than I normally would."

Roelke was running out of patience. "Look, ma'am, I know you've seen and heard some horrible things, but I am a *police* officer. You, and the women who come here, can trust me. I know it can be hard to share personal stuff with a cop, but—"

"Frankly, Officer McKenna, being a cop doesn't count for much around here."

He sat back, suddenly feeling stupid.

"Erin spoke well of you, so I'm going to be candid," Helen said. "Erin discovered that someone on the Milwaukee Police force, someone in the local district, had been charged with domestic violence. You know what happened next? The DA quietly dismissed the charges. The whole thing got swept into the shadows."

Roelke's right knee began to piston.

"I don't know who it was," Helen continued, "but that officer is still responding to domestic calls. How can I convince battered women to call the police for help when the cop who shows up might sympathize with the abuser?"

# THIRTY-EIGHT
## SEPTEMBER 1921

A CONSTABLE WALKED SLOWLY through the Milwaukee train station, eyeing the crowd, tapping his wooden billy club against his palm. I can't appeal to him for help, Lidia thought. How can I be sure that he wouldn't side with Thomas?

She'd arrived in Milwaukee weary, nauseated, anxious, and broke. Now she sank down on an empty bench, watching other travelers. She seemed to be the only person in the station with no one to meet and nowhere to go. With a surge of panic, she wondered if she'd just made a colossal mistake. Although life with Thomas could be bad, there had been good times too …

But—no. Lidia reminded herself that Grandmother Magdalena had been strong enough to immigrate. Mama had grown up without parents and survived the death of her husband. I must be strong too, Lidia thought, and make my own new life.

Someone had left a newspaper on the bench, and she skimmed the pages. Perhaps she could get a job that included lodging. A nanny, maybe, or a maid...

Then she found an advertisement for a Settlement House—a place for immigrant women to learn what they needed to know in this strange city. I'm an immigrant of sorts, Lidia thought, clutching Magdalena's Polish shawl around her shoulders. She'd start there.

———

Women hurried up the steps of the Abraham Lincoln Settlement House on Ninth Street as Lidia arrived. Two teens in old-world clothes and new-world hairstyles jostled past her, laughing. "Sorry!" one of them called over her shoulder in Russian. Lidia heard more conversations in Russian, and other languages too—Polish, German. The mix transported her back to Bohemian Flats, and that gave her hope.

A heavyset matron with gray hair styled in permanent waves sat behind a table in the entryway. "May I help you?" she asked. "Are you here to register for a class? We offer instruction in hygiene and American cookery, as well as English language."

Lidia thought of the immaculate and oh-so-American house she'd shared with Thomas. "I'm not looking for classes."

"Perhaps you're looking to buy a copy of *The Settlement Cookbook*? It's wildly popular, and sales support our programs."

Lidia thought of the fragrant, floury afternoons she'd helped her mother bake bread and *pierogi* and *pączki*. She cleared her throat. "I just arrived in Milwaukee and have nowhere to go. I was hoping that you might help me find work and a place to stay."

"Oh, dear." The other woman shook her head. "I'm so sorry, but we're not an employment agency. Nor do we offer lodgings. Our main goal is to help newcomers to this country become American." The sound of an instructor counting to ten in English—each numeral repeated by a chorus of foreign female voices—drifted down the hall.

"I see," Lidia murmured. She was so used to the Bohemian Flats' pervasive spirit of helping newcomers that it hadn't occurred to her that she'd be turned away from the Settlement House. I have nowhere else to go, she thought numbly. As she turned away she whispered a prayer to Mary: "*Do Ciebie wolamy wygnancy, synowie Ewy...*" To thee we cry, poor banished children of Eve.

If Jesus didn't understand why she'd fled her husband, maybe his holy mother would.

She left the building, clenching folds of wool. What now? She knew Milwaukee's Polish immigrants had built a beautiful church called St. Josaphat. Should she look for help there? After enduring her own priest's censure, she didn't want to...

Footsteps clicked behind her. "Miss? Please, wait." The woman from the Settlement House caught up to Lidia and lowered her voice. "I can see you need help."

Lidia gestured back toward the building. "I do, but as you said, there is nothing here for me."

"Many of Milwaukee's immigrant women need exactly what the Settlement House can provide. But every once in a while..." Something haunted flickered in the woman's eyes.

"Might you be able to spare something to eat?" It galled Lidia to ask, but she needed to think of her unborn child. "Perhaps just a piece of bread?"

"I'll do better than that," the woman promised. "I found someone to work the desk for me, and I'm taking you home. You'll be safe there while we figure out what to do next."

# THIRTY-NINE

CHLOE SAT IN HER car with the old *wycinanka* on her lap. She knew from reading Ariel's files that some Polish women had worked in the mill. I have to include some Polish baked goods in the goodies for the reception Friday night, she thought. And we need to expand one of our interpretive themes. The old Gold Medal and Pillsbury cookbooks were only part of the story. The mill museum needed to honor immigrant women who had made their way to Bohemian Flats, and possibly found work in the flour mills.

Chloe knew a lot about ethnic food traditions. She'd also brought her battered old copy of *The Settlement Cookbook* along. Using recipes from a wildly popular cookbook that had been published in Wisconsin would spotlight regional connections, and actually lend credibility to the notion that her visit was intended to be reciprocal. She'd brought a few other old regional cookbooks as well. Nothing made her happier than telling stories about the anonymous women who had worked so hard and sacrificed so much to make new homes in the Upper Midwest.

Most of them had left nothing behind. But a Polish woman in Minneapolis had once pinned up this paper cutting in No Man's Land. Now, making Polish foods would provide a tangible link back.

———

When Roelke left Eve's House he drove in erratic circles again, watching his rearview mirror. When he was sure that no one was tailing him, he left the district and parked in a vacant lot, backed against a wall so he could see anyone approaching. Then he confronted what Helen had told him.

A cop in the local district had been arrested for domestic violence. The charge had been quietly dismissed. Now battered women who called the cops might find *another* batterer knocking at the door, badge in hand.

Roelke remembered the fear in his own mother's eyes when his father had exploded in rage; remembered how he'd felt as a child, listening to the arguments, the thumps, the cries of pain. His mother hadn't found the strength to leave with her two boys until Joe McKenna had thrown her against the banister with enough force to break her arm.

*Jesus*, Roelke thought now. He felt sick. Somehow Rick's murder had reached into his own worst memories, dredging up people and events he'd long ago committed to permanent storage.

Roelke thought of all the men he'd known in the district. Sure, lots of them were old-school tough guys. Some cops still believed that domestic arguments should be private, even if the woman got roughed up a bit. Roelke could imagine that a cop might not reach out to help a frightened woman as *he* would, encouraging her to press charges, but it had never occurred to him that one of his fellow cops might be going home and knocking around his own wife or girlfriend.

So ... who was it? How could he ever know? He didn't have any friends in the DA's office, and it would take a *very* good friend to spill those kind of beans. Roelke scrubbed his face with his palms. One thing he was pretty sure about—Rick had known. And Rick had zero tolerance for guys who punched women. He'd probably tried to talk the guy into fessing up, maybe even quitting the force. He'd probably threatened to expose him.

And he'd probably gotten killed for it.

Roelke felt something hot and hard beneath his ribs. Don't get stupid now, he ordered himself. You're getting close. Find the SOB before he finds you.

He reached for his notecards and instead found the brochure for Eve's House folded up in his pocket. He stared at the tri-fold, trying to pull some clue from the text.

*Abusive individuals need to dominate their wives or girl-friends. They often express jealousy, are quick to blame others for their problems, and try to isolate their victims. They may use threats or other forms of intimidation to control their part-ner, and alternate abusive actions with expressions of love.*

*Victims of domestic violence are likely to withdraw from fam-ily and friends, become subservient in an effort to appease their partners, and appear anxious to please. They may also miss work frequently, speak of becoming accident-prone, and wear heavy makeup and clothing intended to hide physical signs of violence.*

Roelke hadn't known all the district cops well even when he'd worked in Milwaukee, and some people had come and gone since.

Still, he tried to think back, to remember any hints he might have missed...

And as he worked his way through that mental inventory, a few facts started to sort themselves into a hard line.

"Oh, *Jesus*," Roelke whispered. It couldn't be. It couldn't really be a friend...

A siren blared, and a police car raced by. Nothing to do with him, but a reminder that he couldn't let his guard down. He surveyed his surroundings carefully.

Then he found a blank index card and wrote two words on the top line: *Dobry Banik.*

1. *Tina wears tons of makeup*
2. *Tina rarely speaks to Dobry's friends*

Roelke tapped his pencil against the steering wheel, thinking. In his memory, he heard Dobry's summation at the Almirez house: *Stuff like that happens, Roelke. We all had a good time at the reception, Jody agreed to marry him, and then Rick started a shift. Would you blame the guy for celebrating with a brewski?* Stifling a growl, Roelke continued with his list:

3. *Dobry tried to shift blame to Rick, and reported the drinking*
4. *D wanted to talk to me in the driveway, instead of asking me inside, the night I stopped by*
5. *D gave me the wrong translation of the Polish word on Erin's folk art card*
6. *D refused to ask Malloy some questions re: Rick's death*

Honestly, that one might not be entirely fair. The guy had a right to protect his career, even if it meant making choices Roelke didn't agree with. Still.

### 7. D was the one who saw Rick drinking on duty in the first place

Maybe Rick *hadn't* been drinking on duty. Sherman had confirmed Rick's presence in the bar, but not the alcohol. Maybe the bartender had lied. Maybe Rick had only been in the Rusty Nail to talk to Lobo. Maybe Rick had blown off his mark call because trying to discover if Steve Litkowski had hired Lobo to kill Erin was more important.

But still ... Dobry? Baby-faced Dobry? Longtime friend Dobry? Roelke stared at his notes, wondering if he'd lost his mind. Was Dobry capable of smacking Tina around? Maybe. But was Dobry truly capable of shooting Rick in the back of the head?

Okay, Roelke told himself. Think this through. All he had was suspicions, possibilities. Before accusing Dobry—or anyone else—of domestic violence or murder, he had to find *proof.*

———

Chloe wanted to tell Ariel in person what had happened to Owen. And now I have a treasure from No Man's Land to give her too, she thought, hoping the find might counterbalance the shock of Owen's accident.

She managed to find the Minnesota Historical Society building, and then she managed to find the Historic Sites Division offices, only to learn that Ariel was tied up in a meeting. "I'm sorry," the young woman at the reception desk said. "Can I give her a message?"

"Have we met?" Chloe asked. The receptionist—Simone, according to her name badge—looked familiar. "Oh, wait. You were at the wake for Dr. Whyte." Simone and Ariel had huddled together for comfort while she'd been talking with Jay.

"You're Chloe, right? Ariel's told me about you."

"I wanted to make sure Ariel knew about an accident at the mill this afternoon."

Simone nodded soberly. "Jay called from the hospital. Owen has regained consciousness."

Chloe's shoulders slumped with relief. "Thank God."

"Yeah. After what happened to Whyte, everybody was pretty shook up to hear about Owen." Simone blew out a long breath, as if ridding herself of bad vibes. Then she nodded at the carton in Chloe's hands. "You want to leave that for Ariel?"

"Thanks, but I'll take it back to her place," Chloe said. "Good to meet you, Simone."

But it wasn't good to meet Simone, not entirely. Something scratched at Chloe's brain as she left the building. She didn't feel like going back to Ariel's cottage, so she locked the carton in the trunk of her car and went in search of an honest cup of coffee.

Fifteen minutes later she took her first sip and tried to relax. What was bugging her? It was more than Owen's accident, but she couldn't put her finger on it.

Maybe I need index cards, she thought. How many times had she seen Roelke scribbling notes on three-by-fives, arranging and rearranging them as he tried to work through some difficult problem? She swiped at tears, missing Roelke so much that her throat ached.

They'd worked through their share of problems together, each contributing ideas and puzzle pieces until the picture became whole.

Maybe Roelke was sitting in a diner too, right this minute, working on his own problem. She sent him a mental message: *Figure it out soon. I have a problem of my own, and I miss you.*

———

Roelke felt tense muscles ease a bit when Lucia Bliss walked into the diner. Cops loved the George Webb chain because the restaurants stayed open all night. No one would think twice about seeing a woman in uniform there.

Bliss slid into the back corner booth across from him. She did not take off her coat.

"Thanks for coming," he said.

"I can't stay long, but when you said you had new information about Rick's death … " She paused when a waitress brought the hot tea Roelke had ordered. "Coffee for me, please."

When both mugs were filled, Roelke leaned forward. "Have you ever heard of Erin Litkowski?"

"I don't think so. Who is she?"

"A woman who fled Milwaukee to escape her psycho husband. She came back, but she's gone into hiding again." Roelke realized he was getting sidetracked. "I'm working on that, but I need a favor from you. Can you look to see who arrested a bad guy named Alberto Marquez? He was in Waupun because somebody hired the SOB to kill his wife, and he might be back in business."

Bliss frowned with confusion. "What does that have to do with Rick?"

"I've learned that a district cop was the cause of a domestic disturbance call."

Her eyes widened. "A cop, beating up his wife? Christ."

"His wife actually pressed charges, but the DA's office dismissed them and hushed the whole thing up. Have you heard anything about that?"

"No, but I could name two dozen possible candidates." She dumped some creamer into her coffee. "You know how it is. Cops get their adrenaline up when some asshole tries to run, and they end up roughing up the guy a bit. If a cop loses his temper on the street, who's to say he won't do the same thing at home?"

"Yeah." Roelke sipped his tea. He understood that heat-of-the-moment urge to inflict street justice all too well. One of the things he liked about the Eagle PD was Chief Naborski's take on that. The chief was old enough to be old-school, but he wasn't. He wouldn't tolerate that kind of thing.

Bliss looked a little sick. "So, you think Rick somehow discovered who it was, and that led to him getting killed? Somebody felt threatened and decided to protect his career by shutting Rick up?"

"I don't know," Roelke said carefully, "but I'm going to find out. Do you have any connections in the DA's office? Someone you know through your dad?"

Bliss made a futile gesture, palms up. "Like I said, my father keeps work stuff separate from family stuff."

"Could you ask around at the station? Maybe bring up the subject of domestic calls and see if—"

"McKenna, I'm a female sergeant on the Milwaukee Police Force. You think the guys treat me like one of the gang?" Bliss rubbed her temples. "They don't."

"I wouldn't ask if I had anywhere else to turn." Roelke stared at her right eye. "It's Rick we're talking about here."

"I *know*," she said, with a little heat. "It's just that ..."

Roelke felt a twinge of unease. Maybe he shouldn't involve Bliss. She was a good cop who knew how to take care of herself. But given what had happened to Rick, and to *him* ...

"Have you asked Banik? He'd get farther, just joking around with the boys."

Roelke had anticipated that question. "I'd rather not ask any of the guys about this. Given the issue, I thought you'd be best."

Bliss's eyes widened with understanding—and shock. She placed both palms on the table and leaned forward. "Do you actually think Dobry Banik might have—"

"I didn't say that."

"No. No *way*. Dobry would never, ever—"

"I didn't say he did," Roelke repeated. "Look, forget it. You're right. It's probably too dangerous to even raise the topic."

Bliss stared at the table for a long moment. "No, I can't walk away from this. I'll see what I can do. For Rick's sake, I'll see what I can do."

Roelke blew out a long, slow breath. "Thanks. Just don't mention this to anyone else. If I'm right—and I'm pretty sure I am—this guy has already killed one cop, and tried to kill me."

They left the restaurant together. Bliss walked away quickly. As Roelke paused, pulling on his gloves, he noticed the dome of the basilica, blocks away but still sending a protective glow over the neighborhood. And Roelke McKenna, who hadn't attended mass in years, found that a comfort.

# FORTY
## OCTOBER 1923

LIDIA SETTLED ONTO A pew in St. Josaphat's sanctuary, finding comfort in the quiet hush. After her priest in Minneapolis had instructed her to submit to Thomas in all things, Lidia had thought her faith was gone. But since arriving in Milwaukee two years earlier, she'd slowly found it again here. The sacrifices local Poles had made to construct such a place touched her. She liked imagining the immigrants who had provided much of the labor—the men learning to use carpentry tools, the women hauling away dirt in their aprons.

I've done as well as I could hope, Lidia thought. She'd never taken a college class, but she now taught home economics at the Settlement House. She'd learned to make *wycinanki*, and sold them at a nearby shop. She'd rented a tiny house and, best of all, she had beautiful two-year-old daughter.

Her mother had once said, *I'm afraid you might lose your way, up there on the hill.* I did lose my way, Lidia thought. But I managed to find it again.

She missed *Matka* and Grandfather Pawel, and she always would. But her closest friends had found a way to let them know that she was safe and well. Through the same furtive whispers, she'd learned that Thomas had broken an arm when the belt she'd damaged gave way, but he'd survived. Lidia was profoundly grateful that she wasn't guilty of murder. Still, as long as Thomas lived in Minneapolis, she could never return to Bohemian Flats…

A woman with a shawl pulled over her head lit a candle in an alcove. Lidia tipped her head. Wasn't that Anna? The young woman had started a cooking class Lidia taught at the Settlement House, but she hadn't finished the course.

Lidia caught up with her by the door. "Anna?"

Anna whirled with a gasp. Lidia saw the green-and-purple bruise on her cheekbone, the haunted look in her eyes, the exhausted set of her mouth.

Lidia had planned to invite her back to class. Instead she said, "Anna, will you come home with me?"

"Oh, no," Anna whispered. "I shouldn't have even … I must get home."

"I don't think you're safe at home."

Anna's cheeks flushed. "It's my fault. My husband—it doesn't happen often."

"It shouldn't happen at all," Lidia said. "I can help you. Do you have children?"

Anna slowly shook her head.

"That makes things much easier." Lidia smiled gently. "If you choose to come with me, I can hide you and help you travel to a new place. You will be safe."

Anna's eyes filled with tears. "You don't know—"

"I *do* know." Lidia held Anna's gaze.

Understanding flickered in her eyes. "*Oh.*" She hesitated, looking fearfully over her shoulder. "If he finds me…"

"He won't. I promise."

The two women walked to Lidia's small house, just two more Polish women in dark skirts with shawls pulled over their heads. "I live alone with my daughter," Lidia explained. "She's with a neighbor today. I'll make some tea, and then we can talk."

An hour later, Lidia knew that her instincts had been good. Anna needed to flee the husband who channeled every frustration and disappointment into punches. "It will take a few days to make arrangements," Lidia explained. "You must stay inside."

Anna's fingers twisted together nervously. She glanced at the door as if expecting her husband to kick it in at any moment.

Lidia was part of a spiderweb of people who helped desperate women escape Milwaukee. It wasn't uncommon for terrified women to return to the men who'd left them with bruises, scrapes, burns, and broken bones. Fear of the unknown could be even more powerful. I must keep Anna busy and calm, Lidia thought.

She fetched two pairs of scissors and the box where she kept scraps of paper. What was better than *wycinanki* to keep Anna's hands and mind occupied?

# FORTY-ONE

AFTER BLISS WENT BACK to work, Roelke called Jody. "Sorry I haven't come by. I think I'm closing in on this thing."

"*This thing*? Roelke—"

"I'll explain everything when I can. Listen, did Rick mention anything recently about a domestic violence case?"

"No. He didn't usually talk about work, though."

"Have the detectives told you anything new?"

"No. They're going through Rick's financial records."

"That's routine," he assured her. "Try not to worry. I'll call again as soon as I can." He hung up before she could protest. The best thing he could do for Jody right now was keep his distance.

Roelke leaned against the phone booth wall, feeling exhaustion pull at his muscles, his bones, his brain. What had Rick discovered? If the detectives knew, they were keeping it quiet. *Think*, he ordered himself. He'd been closer to Rick Almirez than any detective. What did he know about Rick that they didn't?

*I'm still digging, buddy,* he told Rick silently. *I'm getting closer. But if there's anything I need to find...*

*Don't be a dumbass, McKenna.*

Roelke drummed his fingers against his thigh, mentally reviewing Rick's habits and routines. ... *Oh.*

"Thanks," he muttered. "I'll check on that tonight."

He pulled out more change and called his cousin. He didn't think his name had been released in connection with the shot fired in Kozy Park, but best be sure. "Hey," he said when she picked up. "How's Justin doing?"

"Better," Libby said. "How about you?"

"Okay. Just wanted to check in."

"Someone's been trying to reach you." Roelke heard a papery rustle and pictured Libby searching through art projects and mail and drafts of whatever article she was writing. "Here it is," she said. "Fritz Klinefelter called twice. He'd tried at the EPD, and the clerk gave him my number. He wants you to stop by his house this evening."

Fritz? After what he'd said in the Records office, that was a surprise. "Thanks, Libby. I'm sorry that you ended up playing receptionist for me."

"I don't mind. Listen, Roelke, I ... um ... I also talked to Chloe earlier." An odd note crept into Libby's voice. "And ..."

"And what? Did she have a message too?"

The line was silent. Then, "No. No message."

"I'll call her when I get a chance," Roelke promised.

He hung up wondering what had been on Libby's mind. The conversation summoned Chloe from the mental box where he was trying to keep her until he finished up this mess with Rick's death. He put a steadying hand against the cold glass, overwhelmed with the missing of her.

Chloe was in the kitchen when the front door slammed. Ariel shrugged out of her coat and settled at the breakfast bar. She looked inexpressibly weary.

"I baked some Old-Time Cinnamon Jumbles." Chloe put out a plate. "We need to talk."

Ariel looked wary. "What's up? Simone told me you came by."

"Some things started bothering me this afternoon." Chloe slid onto a stool and regarded her friend. "It took a while, but I finally figured out what they were."

"Oh?"

"Simone referred to your former advisor as 'Whyte' this afternoon. Not Dr. Whyte, or Professor Whyte. It seemed odd. Everyone at the wake spoke of him in deferential terms."

Ariel picked up a cookie. "Just a slip of the tongue."

"I don't think so. I've only heard one other person use just his surname. The night Toby called about the cause of death, you said something like 'How in the world could Whyte have drowned?' Pretty disrespectful, under the circumstances. Then I realized that all the people singing Everett Whyte's praises at the wake were guys."

Ariel studied the cookie.

"And speaking of Toby, I was under the impression that he'd made a quick trip down from Duluth just to help haul your antique hutch. But when I was at the mill yesterday, Owen mentioned meeting Toby last Friday."

Ariel placed both palms on the counter as if needing support.

"I am trying really hard not to be furious with you," Chloe admitted, "because you still haven't told me the whole story. Ariel,

288

was Everett Whyte abusive to women? Did he take advantage of his female students?"

"He…I…." A tear spilled down one cheek. "*Yes*. He offered me a small modeling fee—fifty bucks—to pose in a tutu at the mill. That's *all*, and I'm so broke that I agreed. But once we got in there, and he'd taken a bunch of pictures…" She shuddered. "He didn't attack me or anything—"

With relief, Chloe released her most visceral fear.

"—but he asked me to pose in ways that made me uncomfortable. Finally he asked me to slide one strap down over my shoulder. When I didn't do it he walked over and pulled it down himself."

"You should have told him where to stick his camera, and gotten the hell out of there."

"How?" Ariel demanded. "I was afraid to make my way back out of the mill alone, especially in pointe shoes and a tutu. We'd come in his car, so I had no way to get home. And he told me that if I didn't 'participate,' he just might not be able to support my thesis. Do you have any idea how much time and money I've invested into my Ph.D. program? He had the power to take it all away."

Chloe wished that Everett Whyte was still alive so she could knee him in the nuts, really *really* hard. But that satisfying mental picture evoked her second biggest fear. "Did you tell your brother what happened? Did Toby go to the mill last Friday to confront Whyte?"

"I did tell Toby, and he did go to the mill, but he didn't kill Whyte! I swear, Chloe. Toby found Whyte up by the distributor, and he *did* end up punching him. Whyte fell, and Toby left him there. But he was alive."

"Which is why you freaked out when we found the body stuffed into the distributor," Chloe mused grimly.

"I didn't know what to think! I was afraid Whyte died from his head wound, which would mean that Toby *did* kill him. That's why I got a bit giddy when the police announced that Whyte had actually drowned. I was so relieved..." Her gaze implored Chloe to understand.

"Right," Chloe said curtly. Ariel had kept a whopping big secret. Discovering that so soon after learning that Roelke had also kept a whopping big secret didn't help. Chloe remembered what Sister Mary Jude had said that morning: *You must feel a little betrayed by that. And angry. And hurt.*

Right on all counts, Chloe thought, wondering if she was ever going to be able to trust anyone again.

———

"You probably don't trust anyone right now," Fritz Klinefelter told Roelke, "so thanks for coming."

"Sure." Roelke followed as Fritz wheeled himself into a den. A calico cat opened one eye to inspect the newcomer, then closed it again. Family pictures on the walls and a brightly-colored mug that said *I love Grandpa* on the coffee table made the room cheerful. Roelke took a seat on the sofa. "I didn't expect to hear from you."

Fritz's eyes were grim. "I had good reason for telling you that I couldn't help investigate whatever is going on. But honest to God, knowing that somebody in the department messed with my records and had something to do with Rick Almirez getting shot ... it makes me sick. I talked it over with my wife, and she said I need to do what I think is right. She said she and our daughter would be okay as long as I did that."

Roelke swallowed hard. That sounded like something Chloe might say. "You married a good woman."

"I did." Fritz nodded. "So. I've put in over thirty years with the Milwaukee Police Department. I've worked with lots of good men who put their lives on the line every single day trying to help people and get assholes off the street. And I will *not* let one bad cop undo the work of a thousand good ones. I don't know how I might help, but I can't leave you out there on your own."

Roelke's world suddenly felt a whole lot less lonely. "Thanks."

"So, what have you learned since Monday?"

Roelke filled him in about Erin, about what he'd heard at Eve's House, about Lobo. "Bliss checked for me," he said. "He was originally arrested in another district, but he was seen talking to Rick the night Rick died."

Klinefelter rubbed his chin.

Roelke wasn't ready to admit his no-hard-evidence suspicion that Dobry Banik might have been involved with Rick's death, but he did describe getting shot at in Kozy Park. "So I go back out to the park before dawn next morning," he concluded. "And in the woods where the shooter was, I find something." He got the evidence bag holding the gun from his coat and handed it over.

Fritz studied the gun through the plastic. "You show this to anyone else?"

"No."

"The idea of a sniper shot makes me think ex-military."

"Yeah," Roelke agreed. "But a military sniper—or a professional SOB like Lobo—doesn't seem the type to accidentally drop a handgun. So maybe this gun has nothing to do with me or Rick."

"I assume you checked for prints?"

"Nothing. Either the shooter wore gloves or the gun was wiped clean."

Fritz studied the gun with narrowed eyes. "I don't think that grip is original."

"No?" It had never crossed Roelke's mind that the grip might not be original. He'd known a couple of guys with big hands who replaced the originals on their service revolvers with thick rubber grips for ease of handling. Those were easy to spot, but the grip on this .38 wasn't rubber.

"Do you carry a fingerprint kit with you?"

Roelke fetched his investigation kit from the truck. Fifteen minutes later, Fritz had removed the grip and dusted the stub for prints. Roelke watched, knee firing up and down.

"Oh, yeah." Fritz gave Roelke a look of satisfaction. "We got a couple of nice ones here."

"Holy toboggans." Roelke felt like a child who'd just been handed a prize. "But ... I can't just waltz into the station and ask to check personnel records."

"I'll take care of that," Fritz told him. "Call me tomorrow, and I'll tell you if we've got a match. But remember, even if we can match these prints to somebody on the force, we have no reason to believe this gun was used in a crime. A different gun was used to kill Rick Almirez, and a different gun was fired at you."

"You just see if you can find a match," Roelke told him. "I'll take it from there."

———

Roelke waited until well after midnight to drive by Rick's apartment. No sign of his car. Roelke circled back to Rick's parents' house. The familiar Chevy was in the driveway.

After parking around the corner, Roelke walked back, quietly used his EPD-issued door opener tool on the Chevy, and slid inside. With luck the dome light's brief flash hadn't caught anyone's attention, but he only needed a moment. Rick's car was immaculate, so maybe the detectives had given it only a cursory inspection.

He eased down the visor over the passenger's seat. How many times had he watched Rick stash something important here, out of sight but accessible? Roelke felt for the seam made when Rick had added a thin oversleeve behind the visor. *Bingo.* The tip of Roelke's index finger met a corner of cardstock. He pulled it free and made sure nothing else was hidden away before ghosting out of the car again.

He made it down the street and around the corner without prompting even a sleepy yip from anyone's dog. He thought he knew what he had, and he was eager to—

Something pale lay against his truck's windshield, where nothing pale should be.

Roelke dropped to a crouch beside the cab, heart pounding, waiting for another rifle shot to explode the night, cursing. He'd been so careful! Whoever had tailed him here was damn good.

A minute ticked silently by. Another. The SOB wouldn't have left a calling card if he wanted to shoot me tonight, Roelke thought. He took a deep breath before standing, snatching the paper left beneath a windshield wiper, and diving into the cab. His fingers shook as he started the ignition. He pulled out from the curb and screeched away.

He drove in circles for a long time before finally parking in front of another police district office. Only then, in the dim glow of a nearby streetlight, did he read the note.

*Officer McKenna—Please meet me at the entrance to the old chapel at Forest Home Cemetery Thursday evening at 6 p.m. I have to leave Milwaukee again before Steve finds me, but I must talk to you first. —Erin*

Roelke knew three seconds of joy—*Yes!* Then his cop brain kicked in—*Too good to be true!* How had Erin found his truck in the Almirez neighborhood in the middle of the night? Was another cop helping her, as Rick had tried to do? Or was someone setting up a trap? Forest Home was a huge old cemetery just down Lincoln Avenue from the Basilica of St. Josaphat. It was the kind of place a woman on the run might choose to meet, convenient but private. It was also the kind of place to make a sniper giddy with glee.

Well, he had fifteen hours to think about the proposed rendez-vous.

Roelke pulled out the little card he'd found in Rick's car and held it toward the light. As he'd suspected, it was another one of those *wycinanki* things, featuring the familiar flower bouquet flanked by chickens. He flipped the card over and saw another name written in pencil on the back: *Erin*.

Roelke blinked back tears. *Finally*, a concrete link between Erin and Rick.

But he still had no clue what the *wycinanki* cards meant. Had this one been sent to Rick from Erin, or had Rick intercepted something meant for Erin? No knowing.

Roelke held the card next to the note and compared the handwriting. Different, definitely.

Okay, he thought. He knew who to ask about that.

———

Roelke called Erin's sister Pauline just after seven a.m. the next morning. He needed to catch her before she left for work, and he didn't think she'd mind.

She did not. Thirty minutes later he sat down at her kitchen table and began a brief summary of events, just as he'd rehearsed.

Pauline didn't let him get far. "Erin is in Milwaukee?" she gasped.

"I think she *was*," Roelke said carefully. "I didn't recognize her at first. By the time I did, she was gone. She didn't get in touch with you?"

"No." Erin's sister tented her hands in front of her mouth as if praying. "She's obviously still afraid of Steve. He's taken up with Erin's best friend from high school."

"I didn't call you earlier because I had nothing definite to tell you. But something's happened, and I need your help." Roelke held out the note he'd found on his truck, and the *wycinanki* card. "Can you tell me if either of these is Erin's handwriting?"

Pauline glanced at both, then pointed at the penciled name on the back of the folk art card. "That one. See that tiny little loop on top of the E? She started doing that in grade school."

Roelke flipped the card to display the artwork printed on the front. "Have you ever seen something like this before? It's a print of a Polish paper cutting."

"No." Pauline took the card, but she wasn't interested in the artwork. She turned it again and touched her sister's ephemeral signature.

The ache in Roelke's chest seemed to radiate well beyond his likely cracked rib. He hated to involve Pauline without having more to offer. He also hated knowing that the cemetery invite was indeed a trap. A trap set by someone who knew enough about Erin, Rick, and *him* to set it up.

Pauline looked at Roelke with a worried frown. "So—who wrote that note about meeting you in the cemetery?"

"I don't know," he admitted. "But I am going to find out."

# FORTY-TWO

AFTER ARIEL WENT TO work Thursday morning, Chloe found a recipe for Polish doughnuts called *pączki* —just the thing for a depressing morning. Ariel had kept secrets, and Chloe didn't know how to get around that. First my guy, and now my friend, Chloe thought. Lovely.

She also found herself in a difficult spot. Toby would surely become Suspect Number One if the cops learned that he'd gone to the mill to put the fear of God into Whyte. Chloe believed that Toby had only wanted to protect his sister from further harassment. And she believed that Everett Whyte was, despite his many accomplishments, a slimy little jerk. Still, Ariel and Toby had withheld information that might be of critical importance to the detectives working the case. So … what was she supposed to do now?

Chloe was still trying to figure that out when the last bit of sweet dough had been transformed into a filled doughnut. As she cleaned the counter, she unearthed a stack of index cards—and snatched them as if Roelke had transported them there, just for her. She settled down with pen, mug of coffee, and a doughnut. She sampled her handi-work—oh *my*, was it good—before writing *Everett Whyte* on one of the cards.

Toby wouldn't be off the legendary hook until someone discovered the truth behind Whyte's death. The drowning might have been accidental, but knowing what kind of man the professor had been opened up a world of new possibilities. Chloe jotted notes and ideas on cards, surveying them, arranging them, making associations, and arranging them again. She'd met too many men like Whyte, men who used their power to demean women. He had done so to Ariel, evidently without fear that he'd be held accountable. What other women had he abused? Other students? Colleagues?

What about women at the mill? Girls like Star must have appeared particularly powerless and vulnerable. But girls who survived on the street—or in the mill—were tougher than Ariel. Perhaps Whyte had threatened one of them, and the intended victim had struck back.

Chloe wrote, *Ask Sister Mary Jude about the girls*. She knew them best. And, *Talk to Jay*. He may not have noticed any unacceptable be-havior, but if nudged to think back, looking for telltale signs, he might have insights, too.

Chloe called the State Historic Preservation Office. "Jay Rut-ledge is working at the mill site today," the receptionist said.

"Thanks." Chloe hung up and chewed her lower lip. She was *not* keen on returning to the mill, but maybe Jay was working with the crew by the river again, and she could talk to him outside.

She licked jelly from one finger and considered her cards. This system truly is helpful, she thought. And scribbling on index cards did evoke Roelke's presence in a comforting way.

So ... what other bits of cop advice could she retrieve? Chloe replayed the lone conversation they'd had on Tuesday night, when he called to ask about Polish folk art and chickens. *I'm spending time in the old neighborhood,* he'd said. *When a crime occurs, it's important to go back to the people who live in the community. They know the place, the people, better than anyone.*

In this case, the neighborhood was the mill. Sister Mary Jude had mentioned that the detectives had tried to interview people living in the mill, with poor results. But the detectives were men. If homeless women had been harassed by Whyte, they'd be much more likely to talk to the nun. Or to Officer Ashton. Or to *her.*

Chloe glanced at the clock. Ten past noon. She tucked the cards away and reached for her coat.

———

Roelke called Fritz three times on Thursday morning. "Got anything with those prints? Find a match?"

"Nothing yet," Fritz muttered, three times. "Call back in an hour."

The waiting was unendurable. Roelke felt wired and tired and jumpy. After doing what he needed to do at Forest Home Cemetery, he drove aimlessly—east to Lake Michigan, north to Mequon, west to Elm Grove. Everything was the same and everything was different. Rick was gone and Chloe *felt* gone, and one of the few friends he had left might soon be revealed as a killer.

At one o'clock he dialed the now-familiar number again. Fritz came onto the line. "Roelke." His voice was heavy.

"You found a match."

"Yeah. *Jesus.*" Fritz's voice quivered with rage or grief or both. "The gun you found at Kozy Park was definitely handled by a cop."

———

When Chloe arrived at the mill, she wandered down to the riverside ruins. No sign of Jay. "Shit," she muttered. So much for Plan A.

She made her way to a mill window and peered inside, expecting to find Sister Mary Jude cleaning up from lunch. Although her VW was parked nearby, there was no sign of her, either. So much for Plan B.

Chloe retreated to her car. Her theory—that someone had retaliated for Whyte's abuse—didn't explain why someone had tampered with the roller stand that injured Owen. She was not going into the mill alone.

Forty minutes later backup arrived in a Minneapolis Police Department car. Chloe got out to meet Officers Crandall and Ashton, trying to invent Plan C on the fly. "Good afternoon," she said brightly. "I was looking for Sister Mary Jude, but maybe lunch ended early."

"Her car's still here." Crandall scratched his butt. "She's probably in there coddling some nutjob."

Yes, Chloe thought, you are still a jerk.

"She should just—hey! You kids have no business down here!" Crandall scowled as two preteen boys flew around the corner on bikes. The boys, amazingly enough, stopped and waited as he lumbered in their direction.

Chloe turned quickly to Officer Ashton. "Could I get a little of your time? Just yours. I want to look for a young woman in the mill. She'd *never* show herself if Crandall comes, and I'm too chicken to go by myself."

A smile twitched at Officer Ashton's mouth. "I'd call that wise, actually. Sure, we can make that work."

Five minutes later Crandall was off on a coffee break, as suggested oh-so-respectfully by his partner, and Chloe and her escort were inside the mill. Officer Ashton asked, "What's this about?"

"I'm wondering if Everett Whyte hassled some of the runaway girls. I've heard rumors." That understatement sent heat to Chloe's cheeks. "I met a girl called Star the other day. She might talk to us."

"You really should take this to the detectives working the case."

"Are either of the detectives female?"

Officer Ashton sighed. "Okay. I've got maybe forty minutes before Crandall picks me up."

The two women worked upward, floor by floor. "I'm looking for Star," Chloe called. "I just want to talk." By the time they got to the eighth floor they'd found blankets and shopping bags and discarded lighters. They'd heard voices and the sound of running feet. They'd seen exactly no one.

"Either this young woman isn't here, or she doesn't want to talk," Officer Ashton observed.

Chloe wasn't ready to admit failure. They'd stopped near the huge dust collectors. Chloe shone her flashlight in the corners, behind the massive equipment, along the brick walls. Graffiti glowed like neon. Some of it was electric blue.

"Star might have left some of this graffiti," Chloe said, remembering the vivid shade she'd noticed on the girl's coat.

Officer Ashton considered the spray paint. "This is surreal, isn't it? Not what you typically see. Weird how the stick people are up high, while constellations are near the floor."

Chloe felt a sinking sensation. Not constellations. Stars. Fallen stars.

She crouched for a better look. Each star in the little clusters had two letters inked in the center. Initials, probably. These girls had almost lost their collective voice, but one had felt compelled to leave a record. "This must be where the girls sleep at night."

"Sad thought."

"It truly is." Chloe straightened and studied the rest of the impromptu mural. Each floating stick figure had a particular anatomical detail. Male, all of them. Chloe could only speculate about the first two—a father, a teacher, a next door neighbor back home? But the third . . . "Look," she said. "This one is holding—"

"Whoo-hoo!" someone shouted.

*Bang!* A flash glinted in Chloe's peripheral vision. A whiff of smoke induced instant panic. Explosion! Flour dust! Conflagration!

"Smoke bomb," Officer Ashton muttered. "Fool kids! I'll be right back."

"Sure thing." Chloe hoped her thumping heartbeat wasn't audible. Enough with the hysteria, she told herself. Time was ticking by, and she wanted to decipher what she could of Star's pictographs.

She looked back at the third man-figure, holding a small box with something protruding from it. A camera with telephoto lens? If so, Everett Whyte was almost certainly one of the men who'd trampled Star beneath his feet.

Officer Ashton's voice drifted from the next room: "You could break your necks running around in here! Why aren't you in school?"

The vivid blue graphics progressed along the wall. Chloe slowly followed, deciphering what she could of Star's biography. A swing set, a school bus . . . the story seemed to move backwards in time, before Star came to the mill and completed her descent.

The pictographs were about waist-level here. Chloe stepped back to get a better view. Was that a house? She side-stepped—and her right foot met only air. Thrown wildly off-balance, she half-fell. Her right shoulder slammed into concrete. Her left leg was jerked sideways with a painful wrench. Her flashlight flew from her hand, thunked against something metallic, and went out.

What the hell had just happened? Gasping, blinking against tears and the sudden gloom, Chloe tried to make sense of the last twenty seconds. When she did, her mouth went dry. While following the graffiti, she'd wandered into the room where they'd found Everett Whyte's body. She remembered Jay imploring them all to use caution here because of trapdoors in the floor. *Each of those trapdoors in the floor leads into a nine-story bin that held twenty thousand pounds of grain*, he'd said.

Someone had opened one of the trapdoors. She had stepped into the hole and partially fallen through. Her body weight pinned her right arm against the hard edge of the opening. Her left hand was free, but there was nothing to grab.

Why hadn't Officer Ashton come back? Was she in earshot, or had she felt compelled to escort the boys all the way outside? "Help!" Chloe tried to cry, but the word emerged more as a croak than a yell. Her body was starting to tremble.

All right, *focus*, she ordered herself. You haven't fallen yet. You can do this.

Clenching her teeth, she leaned farther to the right. With another painful wrench she bent her left leg and tried to draw the knee closer to the edge of the hole. If she could just manage to kneel … and wriggle her right arm up to brace on the other side of the opening … *maybe* she could rise high enough to get her butt up on the floor.

She was straining to accomplish that when something rustled behind her. "Officer Ashton?" Chloe panted. "Help me!"

Footsteps came closer. Then a foot rammed her left knee. She tried to resist the unyielding pressure, but could not. Her left leg slipped through the hole. Pain burst in her hip, then her left elbow as they hit concrete in fast succession. Her legs pedaled frantically. She felt dizzy. She heard herself panting, too terrified to scream.

Her left shoulder struck the edge of the trapdoor, then her head followed. *Grab hold!* her shocked brain commanded, but she was already falling all the way through the hole and into blackness.

———

Roelke was defeated by a locked garage. Through a side window he could see a Ford Thunderbird—new model, stylish, red. Five minutes inside, and he might have had proof. But he couldn't get at it.

He swore under his breath. Fritz's news had fueled the rage now threatening to devour his self-control, and it took everything Roelke had to *not* kick the door in. You're a better cop than that, he told himself, over and over. You *are*.

Besides, this was a residential neighborhood. He'd taken a risk just in checking the garage door. If some nosy neighbor called the cops, he could probably talk his way out of it. That would take time, though. And he didn't dare risk missing the rendezvous at Forest Home Cemetery. Since he'd failed here, that trap offered his last opportunity to nail Rick's killer.

———

Chloe's plunge lasted a split second and an eternity. She bounced off something hard and unyielding before hitting something hard but pliable. A harsh and metallic *clang* echoed from above. Then—nothing.

Awareness returned with pain and confusion. Chloe knew she must have blacked out. The notion was appealing because everything hurt. *Everything*. Worst was a throbbing pain in her left wrist. She had a headache, too.

Where was she? The air tasted fetid. The darkness was thick and black. Sitting up seemed impossible, so she tried moving her fingers. Miniscule pellets shifted beneath her skin. She froze. The tiny pellets were wheat seeds, poured twenty years earlier into a concrete bin designed to hold twenty thousand pounds. *Falling on grain is like falling into quicksand,* Jay had said. *Every movement makes you sink.*

Did breathing count as movement? Surely it did. With that assessment, Chloe instantly began hyperventilating.

Lovely. She could hold her breath until she suffocated on *top* of the wheat, or breathe until she suffocated *in* the wheat. A surge of hysterical laughter bubbled inside, and she fought to stay calm. And at least this particular bin wasn't empty. If she'd fallen into an empty bin, she'd already be dead.

And, while she had a vague memory of landing on her side, she'd rolled onto her back. That was good, right? If she hadn't bounced against whatever it was she'd bounced against, she might have torpedoed feet-first into the grain. Owen had spoken of that: *Even if a guy got buried just up to his waist, he'd have eight hundred pounds of pressure per square inch against his legs. It would have been impossible to pull him out.*

Her fuzzy brain tried to replay what had happened up there. She didn't know who had actually opened the trapdoor—idiot teen on a dare, idiot kid with a smoke bomb, idiot college student here to clean up the distributor room for the reception. But she remembered the feel of that foot shoving her all the way through the hatch. She remembered hearing that *clang* overhead as she fell. Someone had watched from the shadows as she stumbled into the hole, shoved her on through, and deliberately shut the trapdoor. That someone was probably Whyte's killer.

It was all horribly unfair. "Why me?" she whimpered. "What did *I* do?"

Speaking brought an almost-imperceptible shifting beneath her. No more talking, she mentally commanded. No sniveling. The whys can come later. Right now, you need to focus on getting out of here.

Chloe *did* focus on that, for a good twenty or thirty seconds. But she couldn't come up with an exit strategy that didn't require movement. Maybe her best option was simply to wait motionless for help. Knowing that she must *not* move, however, simply made Chloe twitchy. It also switched her brain to overdrive. Maybe Whyte hadn't been killed because of his deplorable actions after all. Maybe there truly was a maniac roaming the mill, and she made as good a target as any.

And … maybe that maniac was headed downstairs right this minute. This bin's bottom hatch must have been shut since 1965. Suppose the killer was on his way to open it? If so, a billion-zillion kernels of wheat could start flowing any second. She'd be crushed. Or suffocated. Or both.

Chloe felt cold sweat soaking through her clothes. Her heart hammered. Her tongue tasted of iron. Her fingers clenched convulsively, gathering fistfuls of grain, terrified of the power these miniscule kernels possessed. Wheat was supposed to give life, not take it.

Had some poor mill workers died in this very bin? Chloe forced her breathing to slow, tried to become still and open her awareness, to reach out. *Um, guys? I'm terribly sorry about what happened to you, but right now, I could sorta use some help here. Any suggestions?*

Chloe expected to perceive, if anything, a sense of masculine horror lingering from a doomed man's last moments.

Instead she became aware of something strong and calm and feminine. No whispered words, no tugs on her sleeve, no ghostly light illuminating a ladder. But there was something, and it helped.

Okay, Chloe thought. Since waiting passively in the dark didn't work, I need a plan to get myself out of here.

She remembered bouncing against something hard as she fell, right before she passed out. Holding her breath, moving with exquisite stealth, she oh-so-slowly eased her right arm up from the grain. Clenching her teeth against pain she reached through the blackness— back and forth, up and down, cringing against every tiny shift beneath her. *Something* other than wheat was in here…

Her arm was trembling with effort before her hand finally struck something hard. Moving kernels whispered beneath her, but she hardly noticed because her fingers were exploring wood, rough and splintery but beautifully unyielding. Someone over the years had dropped a plank down here. It seemed to be wedged tight at an angle above her.

The lure of something so solid was irresistible, and Chloe's fingers closed over the board in a vise-like grip. She pulled herself to a sitting position and wrapped her right arm around the board. "*Thank* you," she whispered, feeling a sense of reprieve. She had no way of knowing if the lower end was sitting on grain or lodged against the cement wall. She wasn't safe … but she wasn't paralyzed with fear anymore, either.

*All right, damn you*, she told whoever had shoved her through the hatch. *You may think you did me in, but I'm not dead yet.*

# FORTY-THREE

"Don't go to the cemetery," Fritz Klinefelter said.

Roelke hunched his shoulders against the wind. He'd waited for Fritz by his van at the Police Administration Building. "Look, I didn't come here to argue. I just want somebody to know where I'm going. If this goes sour, please—call these women." He handed over contact information for Libby and Chloe.

Fritz tucked it away. "You said you had one more place to look for evidence, right? What—"

"I didn't get it. That means all we've got is a cop's prints on a gun that was *not* used to shoot Rick or me. I have to go to the cemetery."

"It's a trap."

"I *know*. That's one of the things I have going for me. I also learned some things about the killer back in Kozy Park. I've got a plan." He told Fritz what it was.

The older man remained unconvinced. "For Chrissakes, at least take backup!"

"We don't know who else is involved."

"This damn chair," Fritz muttered, pounding his knees. Then he glared at Roelke. "You will call me when you're done."

"Yes sir. I'll call you." Roelke extended his hand. "Thanks, Fritz. Thanks for everything."

———

In the dark, Chloe had no idea how far she'd fallen. Two feet? Twenty? If she could shimmy up the board, would she be able to reach the trapdoor? If she reached it, would she have the strength to push it open? Would her weight on the board make it more secure, or press the lower end into the grain and start a cascade?

"Only one way to find out," she muttered. She leaned sideways, face-down over the plank, and slid her right knee over. The board hitched downward a couple of inches, and grain kernels *shushed* a warning. Chloe waited until everything was still and quiet again before trying another slide to center her weight on the board. The grain muttered with more menace, and the effort brought a wave of dizziness.

This might, she thought, be even harder than I thought. The pain in her left wrist suggested a broken bone. The board was only about six inches wide, and wedged at about a forty-five degree angle. The upward crawl would be a slow process.

Well, there was nothing to do but try. She held her breath, reached higher on the board, and managed to pull herself up—perhaps an inch. Reach, pull. Reach, pull. Reach, pull.

Sometime later she had to stop. Her arms were quivering. Her clothes were clammy. Her fingers felt like sausages, and her wrist pulsed white-hot. She was pretty sure that if she tried one more hitch she'd pass out. Rest, she thought. Rest is good.

At least it sounded good in theory. It was difficult to rest, however, while balanced on a narrow plank over twenty thousand pounds of gluteny quicksand. Focus on something else, Chloe told herself. Friends. Kittens. Polish doughnuts.

But her brain twitched stubbornly back to the mess—her fall, Owen's injury, Whyte's death. What if Star or another young runaway had killed Whyte? Surely the girls would never tell. *Some of the homeless people who live here speak of tribes*, Sister Mary Jude had said. *Groups of people who join forces.* Who better to join forces than teenaged girls who found an abandoned flour mill more appealing than what they'd left behind? Of course they'd protect each other's secrets.

That thought took Chloe down a mental path she hadn't noticed before. One uneasy fact presented itself. Then another. She felt herself getting seriously upset all over again.

"All right, that's it," she muttered. Resting and thinking were not improving her situation. Gritting her teeth, she reached above her head, grabbed the board, and tried the pull-slide maneuver again.

The board lurched, dropping several inches.

She froze, heart thumping, cheek pressed against the musty wood. How close was the board to giving way altogether? Was she closer to the wheat below or to the trapdoor above? *Please*, she said silently to God or the feminine presence or whomever might be listening. *Please*…

A human voice echoed faintly from above. "Chloe?"

Chloe's inner pendulum made a wild swing from despair to hope. "Officer Ashton?" she cried, trying not to shift her weight an iota. "I'm down *here*!"

The metal hatch groaned open above her head. Chloe squinted against the square of dim-but-gorgeous light, dazed. I was almost there, she thought. A couple more hitches and I would have hit the trapdoor.

A head appeared above the opening. "Chloe? How on earth did you get down there? Are you okay?"

It wasn't Officer Ashton. It was Sister Mary Jude. Chloe couldn't find words.

Mary disappeared momentarily. Then her head and shoulders reappeared. Prone now, she stretched one arm through the hatch. "Grab my hand!"

Chloe couldn't move.

Mary wiggled her fingers. "Can't you reach?"

Chloe still wasn't sure that talking was wise, but this silent standoff wasn't accomplishing anything either. "I can reach, but... I don't trust you." Being shoved from the board by Sister Mary Jude seemed a worse fate than simply falling again.

"Why on earth would you say such a thing?" Mary sounded genuinely shocked.

Oh, Chloe thought, she's good. "The day we found Whyte's dead body, you were calm. But you were a wreck the day Owen was injured, even though the paramedics said he was going to recover. Why the change?"

"Look, I don't know what's happened, but we've got to get you out of there."

Chloe closed her eyes. "I think Star, and maybe some of the other girls too, told you that Everett Whyte was a predator. You promised Star she wouldn't have to talk to 'that guy' again. You told me she was referring to Officer Crandall. It's hard to imagine Crandall actually talking with her, though. And in the very same conversation, you said all Crandall wanted to do was stick girls like Star on a bus out of Minneapolis. Star was referring to Whyte, right? He'd been hassling her?"

311

"We don't have time for this!"

"You also told me that Whyte was an advocate for the homeless. But I've seen his report in Ariel's files. He didn't suggest any kind of assistance. After space for the museum is set aside, all he envisioned for the rest of the complex were condos and high-end shops."

Mary's voice became strident. "*Please*, Chloe. Grab my hand."

"Tell me!" Chloe cried. "Did you kill Everett Whyte?"

————

Roelke drove around the perimeter of Forest Home Cemetery's two hundred rolling acres on streets busy with commuter traffic. If he'd guessed right, and timed things right, the shooter was already hidden on the cemetery grounds. Waiting for *him*, Officer Roelke McKenna, to blunder into the lighted portico at the old chapel on the northern side, looking for Erin. Waiting with a rifle and an exit strategy that, based on what had happened in Kozy Park, led back south for a quick getaway...

*Yes.* Roelke felt a flush of triumph when he spotted the car he was looking for, parked inside the cemetery near the Cleveland Avenue bridge. Maybe he really could end this thing tonight.

He parked, approached the red Thunderbird, and destroyed the possibility of quick escape with a couple of screwdriver stabs. He heard air leaking from the tires as he walked north in the fading twilight with compass in hand. Time to track a killer.

He was able to begin on one of the meandering drives, which was good—no footsteps crunching on snow. Despite the biting wind, the landscape was serene. This oldest part of the cemetery was dotted with elaborate monuments, fancy mausoleums, towering trees. When he'd scoped out the cemetery earlier, he'd seen the sign proclaiming Forest Home's status on the National Register of Historic Places. He seemed destined to visit historic places these days.

Or maybe he just hadn't paid attention to historic places before he met Chloe. Despite the coming confrontation, the pervasive sense of oldness here felt surprisingly peaceful. His weeklong efforts to *not* think about Chloe had been stupid. Chloe was part of him now. *When this is over,* he told her silently, *I'll make things right.*

Until then, knowing that Chloe was far away, safe with her friend, made it easier to concentrate on the job at hand.

———

"Did you kill Everett Whyte?" Chloe repeated. She had to know. Before she passed out and fell off the board and drowned in a crushing mass of wheat, she had to know.

"This is crazy!" Sister Mary Jude cried.

The plank jerked beneath Chloe again.

*Go!* someone whispered in her ear.

Chloe scrambled to get one foot planted on the board. She managed one blind, desperate upward lunge, right arm stretched above her head.

A hand clamped around her wrist like forged iron. "Come on!" Mary gasped. "Help me!"

Mary tugged, and Chloe strained with every ounce of grit she had left. Her head cleared the hatch. Mary scrambled onto her butt and braced her feet. Chloe got one elbow braced on the floor.

But she simply couldn't manage the second. "My wrist is broken," Chloe gasped. "I'm falling!"

"No—you're—*not*." Mary had both hands on Chloe's right wrist. She wrenched so hard Chloe thought her arm might pop off, but she didn't care because she was slowly scraping through the hatch.

The two women landed in a throbbing heap on the floor. Mary kicked the metal door shut again. "*Thank* you," she whispered prayerfully, much as Chloe had earlier. Then, "I'll go get help."

"No. Please, before anybody else comes—just tell me what happened. Was Whyte preying on the girls?"

Mary hesitated, then nodded. "He was. They wouldn't have tolerated rape, but he offered things—food, a warm coat, money for a fix, whatever they needed most. And most of the girls were so desperate that they were willing to pay the price. A quickie, nude photographs, whatever. Not Star, but most of them. You don't know what it's like…"

Chloe remembered Mary's earlier brief accounting: *Once upon a time, I was fourteen and needed some help. I was lucky enough to find it. Now I can't imagine anything more important than looking out for girls like Star.* "You were a runaway once too, right? Runaway girls stick together in here. They're a tribe, and you're still a member."

"Perhaps I am." Mary stared blindly at the floor. "I hated Everett Whyte. I hated how he used his power to abuse those girls. I did not kill him." Her shoulders sagged. "But I watched it happen, and did nothing to stop it—"

"Okay, I've heard enough." Officer Ashton walked into the room. The gun held in both hands was pointed toward the floor. "I've been searching high and low for you," she told Chloe. "You all right?"

Not really, Chloe wanted to say. "I'm all right."

Officer Ashton stepped closer, reached for the handcuffs on her duty belt, and started to holster her weapon. "So we can finally identify Professor Whyte's killer—"

An angry roar echoed from within the grain distributor's metal head. A blur of olive drab and dark hair launched at Officer Ashton. The man grabbed her, threw her against the wall.

"No!" Mary screamed. "John, *no!*"

A gunshot exploded.

Camo John whirled, stumbled, went down to his knees with a look of surprise. He pawed at the blood staining the front of his coat. Then he toppled, landing crookedly on one of the distributor's metal arms.

Officer Ashton and Mary looked stunned. Chloe *felt* stunned. What had just happened?

"I guess I got the bastard," Officer Crandall said from the doorway behind her. Feet spread, gun still pointed, he surveyed the scene.

Mary crawled to Camo John, then glared at Crandall. "You *killed* him!"

"Hey," Crandall said sharply. "That douchebag attacked my partner. I got here in time to hear her say she'd identified Whyte's killer, and I saw him go crazy." He glanced at Officer Ashton. "You okay?"

She staggered to her feet. "I'm okay."

Crandall strode to Camo John and pressed two fingers against his wrist. "Yeah, he's gone." He surveyed the three women. "None of you look fit for duty. Stay here. I'll go down and call it in." He disappeared again.

A wretched silence settled over the room. Chloe opened her mouth, but no words emerged.

Finally Mary said, "This man was a lieutenant in Vietnam, you know." She shrugged out of her coat and draped it over Camo John's head and shoulders. "He suffered from post-traumatic stress, but he still tried to watch over this mill." She crossed herself and began murmuring a prayer.

Chloe remembered the first time she'd seen the man, circling the perimeter. She felt sick.

"Did he kill Everett Whyte?" Officer Ashton asked.

"Amen," Mary whispered, before addressing the policewoman. "Whyte was abusing the girls here. Once John figured out what was going on, he tried to protect them. On Friday afternoon I came up here and found John…"

An actual coherent thought surfaced in Chloe's brain. "Wait. Whyte *was* killed up here? The coroner said—"

"John told me later that he'd found Whyte lying up here unconscious." Mary raised a hand to deflect objections. "I can't say I understand that."

I do, Chloe thought. Camo John had arrived shortly after Toby had decked Whyte.

"One of the girls collected rainwater in a big tub up here for her dog. When I walked into this room, I saw John holding Whyte's head in the water. And God help me, I just… froze. I might have been able to stop him, but I didn't even try."

Chloe tried to decide how she felt about that. *Nothing* condoned murder. And yet…

"When it was over, I thought the best thing we could do was hide Whyte's body. I started tugging at one of the trapdoors, but it was rusted shut. So John stuffed Whyte into the chute. But when the body got caught in the chute instead of sliding down into the bin…" Mary shuddered convulsively. "I just wanted to get out of here. So we left, and took the tub with us."

"What about Owen?" Chloe demanded. "What about *me*?"

A tear slid down Mary's cheek. "Everything is my fault. After John killed Whyte, I talked to him. I thought he understood that he must never do *anything* like that again. But when Owen got hurt, I knew that John must have damaged the machine. I think he saw Owen as part of the project that will ultimately displace the people who live here."

Chloe tried to find a more comfortable position for her throbbing wrist. "And I was guilty by association?"

"I guess so."

Chloe didn't know what to say. Would Whyte be dead if Toby hadn't punched the man, causing him to fall and hit his head on the gear wheel? She couldn't figure it out. Shock, some part of her observed. Besides, her wrist really, really hurt. When the EMTs got there, she would joyfully accept whatever drugs they offered. As if on cue, she heard a siren in the distance.

"I will take full responsibility for my role in this tragedy." Mary's voice trembled. "But I need to say something. Horrible things happen in this mill every single day. People die from exposure and hunger and venereal disease and tiny cuts that get infected. Our society doesn't have the will to stop homeless people from suffering. When you think of Camo John's actions, try to remember that he was mentally ill. Everett Whyte, the man Minneapolis is mourning, didn't have that excuse when he preyed on vulnerable young women."

The sirens were coming closer. Chloe didn't know what to think or how to feel.

"We have a decision to make," Officer Ashton said.

Chloe blinked. "We do?"

"Crandall believes that he shot the man who killed Everett Whyte." She looked at Mary. "He doesn't know that you were present when Whyte died."

"Are you saying that we shouldn't reveal my involvement?" Mary shook her head. "I can't accept that. My conscience—"

"What I'm *saying* is that your friend there is dead. You can't help him now. But there are still a whole lot of people in this mill who *do* need your help. How will your conscience feel about that when you're sitting in prison?"

Sister Mary Jude looked stricken.

"She's right," Chloe heard herself say. So much for not knowing what to think.

"In five minutes, a whole lot of men are going to charge in here and take over," Officer Ashton said. "Right now, it's just us three women. I don't know either of you very well, but I'm willing to gamble my career on your promise that what actually happened to Whyte is never spoken of again. I'll say John admitted his guilt right before Crandall arrived, and leave it at that. Are you in?"

The siren wailed from the street below, with a second coming close behind it. Shouts rang from the stairwell. "I'm in," Chloe said.

"I'm in too," Sister Mary Jude said huskily. "And I vow to rededicate my life to—"

A confusion of men burst in—Officer Crandall, several more cops, EMTs, Jay. Chloe yelped as one of the medical guys touched her left arm.

Mary crawled to Chloe and grasped her good hand. "You're going to be fine."

Chloe had one question left, one that seemed important. "When you were fourteen and needed help, was it a nun who helped you? Is that what led you to take vows?"

"It was a priest, actually." Mary managed a tiny smile. "A very kind old soul who devoted his life to helping others."

That tidbit was unexpected but enormously comforting. There *are* good men in the world, Chloe reminded herself.

And she'd found one. She still didn't know if she was ready or able to make a commitment to a police officer, but she would always care about him. Clutching Mary's hand, Chloe sent up her own prayer for Roelke McKenna's safety.

# FORTY-FOUR

WHEN THE LANE FORKED, Roelke studied the snow near the plowed pavement. There—fresh footprints heading north. I *knew* it, he thought. Earlier, when he'd tried to envision this confrontation, he'd identified the area where he'd hide if trying to kill someone approaching the chapel. An old abandoned garden shed had initially seemed ideal, but the angle was wrong. Nearby, though, was a big oak tree with a perfect line of sight to the portico about two hundred yards away. Evidently Rick's killer had the same idea.

Roelke eased his foot in the first footprint, hoping the rustle of wind through the trees cloaked the faint *crunch* of boot on snow. He carefully made his way among mossy gravestones and marble children and sculpted ten-foot angels. Among many meandering footprints, the tracks he followed veered only when necessary to skirt a monument. The gravestones and statuary cast fantastic shadows in the blue-gray light.

He paused to check his compass, shielded by the base of a memorial. Still good. He crept on, skin prickling. If he was wrong, if he wasn't stealthy enough, a bullet could find him any second.

But he was still unscathed when he spotted the two eight-foot evergreen bushes he'd chosen for himself earlier, about ten yards south of the oak tree. Okay, he thought. Last bit. He held his breath and inched one foot forward, then the other, on and on until he'd reached the shrubbery.

Once hidden he became aware of his rapid heartbeat, his sweat-damp shirt. God, this was *it*. *Rick, old buddy,* Roelke thought, *whatever happens here—I tried.*

He squinted through a gap in the greenery at the oak. He didn't see anything but tree. Damn, had he gotten everything wrong after all? Was someone creeping up behind *him*? Was—

Something twitched. Someone *was* pressed against the oak tree—focused intently on the old vine-covered chapel in the distance. Waiting for me to show, Roelke thought. He eased the hammer back on his .38 revolver.

Rick's killer inched to the right of the tree trunk. A rifle barrel appeared, black against the deep sky. Roelke frowned. Why risk aiming now? There was no one there—

Except there *was*. A figure appeared in the portico, clearly visible beneath yellow lights. Some innocent soul had just wandered into a kill zone.

Roelke side-stepped from his cover and took aim. "Drop your weapon! Get on the ground!"

The shadow whirled.

*"Drop your weapon!"* Roelke roared. *"Get on the ground!"*

No response. Roelke kept aim with his right hand and used his left to snatch the high-powered flashlight he'd positioned in his coat pocket. He thumbed the switch and aimed the beam. Lucia Bliss jerked when the light hit her eyes.

Although Roelke had known since Fritz Klinefelter matched Bliss to the prints on the handgun he'd found, seeing her face brought a new wave of rage. He walked forward, his .38 aimed at her heart. "You raise that rifle again and I'll drop you."

"Stop!" Bliss cringed against the glare. "McKenna, I swear to God—"

"God wants nothing to do with you." Roelke kept walking. "You shot Rick in the back of the head and left him to die in the street."

"I didn't mean to. It—it just happened—"

"Bullshit! You stole a gun from inventory!" Roelke stopped about five yards away.

"I just wanted to scare him!"

"Why, Bliss? *Why?*"

"My husband and I were going through a bad time, and an argument just—just got a little out of hand. He called 911 and pressed charges, but it was all so silly that the DA dropped the whole thing and cleared my record." She talked faster and faster. "But Rick found out somehow and told me I should quit the force. Quit the force! One little mistake, and I'm supposed to quit the force?"

Roelke could well imagine Rick's perspective, especially if Bliss's "little mistake" had popped up while he was trying to help Erin Litkowski dodge her maniac husband. "So you executed a friend?"

"Rick said that if I didn't resign, he'd go public with what had happened. He said I wasn't fit to respond to domestic violence calls. I waited for him by the park that night and tried to make him see reason, but he wouldn't listen—"

"Rick was a *good* cop."

"You don't understand. My marriage is in trouble, half the guys hate me, my dad is breathing down my neck… I've got nothing *left*! I've got nothing left but my job—"

"Oh, that's over, too."

She shook her head. "McKenna, look, you've got no proof that connects me to—to what happened to Rick at Kozy Park. I'll deny everything I just said."

"I *do* have proof. You wouldn't know this, because you were a class ahead of us, but Rick got chewed out during academy training after an instructor jumped out of a car trunk. Rick developed this ritual way of approaching a car from behind. He checked that the trunk was latched, but he also left prints in four different places, including just under the back bumper."

Bliss stared, evidently out of things to say.

"I figured you probably didn't use your own car the night you parked there on Lincoln Avenue, waiting for Rick. Somebody might have recognized it, identified it to the cops. But your husband has a nice red Thunderbird, right? Perfect for impressing clients? Rick wouldn't have known who was inside when he approached from behind, so he would have gone through his routine. You may have wiped his prints from the trunk and the fender, but I doubt that it occurred to you to reach beneath the bumper. One of Milwaukee's finest is dusting the Thunderbird right this minute."

That last bit was a lie. And since Roelke hadn't been able to get inside Bliss's garage, he had no idea if she'd cleaned beneath the bumper. But her shoulders slumped, and he knew he *had* her.

"You have no idea how hard it is for female officers," she said bitterly. "On my first day my FTO said, 'Let me give you some advice. You can be one of the guys, or you can be a cunt.' Well, I tried to be one of the guys. I tried so hard that I turned into somebody new. Or maybe … maybe being one of the guys just brought out a part of me that I didn't even know existed until—"

"Shut—*up*." Roelke's arms were getting tired, and he didn't give a damn about her sad story. "Drop your weapon and get on the ground."

She didn't move.

"Do it *now!*"

She still didn't move.

Roelke's world narrowed to the beam of light focused on Bliss. He sensed her mental debate, a decision being made. Her rifle began an upward swing. His finger moved.

But before he could squeeze the trigger, before she could aim, a shot exploded. Bliss stumbled backward. The rifle hit the ground. Roelke launched and landed on Bliss as she fell. She cried out in pain. He didn't care. Pressing her into the snow, he snatched his cuffs and shackled her wrists.

"Stay down," he warned. He quickly checked her over. He could feel the protective vest beneath her coat, and he didn't see any sign of blood. He scrambled to his feet, holstered his own gun, and grabbed the flashlight he'd dropped.

Roelke quivered with the desire to kick the woman. But a voice spoke in his head—his own or Rick's, Roelke wasn't sure—no, no, *no*. You're a better cop than that. You're a better human being than that.

Roelke hauled Bliss to her feet and dragged her to the nearby shed. He shoved her inside, slammed the door, and jammed his screwdriver through the metal loop intended for a padlock. Not quite as secure as the old holding cell he'd shown Justin at the museum, but it would do. Then he leaned over, hands on knees, panting and truly a bit dizzy this time.

Suddenly he remembered that he hadn't actually shot Bliss. So...who the hell had? He swung the beam in an arc. "Who's there?"

"Me," Fritz Klinefelter grunted. He lay on his belly, propped up on elbows, almost hidden behind a gravestone fifteen yards away. A Remington lay in the snow.

Roelke stumbled over and dropped to his knees. Jesus, Fritz must be half-frozen. "What are you *doing* here?"

"I'm not helpless." Fritz glared toward the shed. "That woman disgraced the entire Milwaukee Police Department. No way was I going to let you face her alone."

"But—"

"My wife dropped me off on the drive two hours ago. Believe me, I elbow-crawled a lot farther than this when I was in Korea." Fritz hitched and rolled to a sitting position, leaning against the gravestone. "I figured backup from an unexpected angle might come in handy."

Roelke almost said, I was about to shoot! I could have dropped her! I didn't need help!

"I know you had her," Fritz said. "But she might not have been wearing a vest. I didn't want you to have to carry that. You need this to be *over*."

Roelke swallowed hard. "Thank you."

# FORTY-FIVE

It was almost eleven when Roelke left the district station and made his way to Kozy Park. He walked around the statue again, leaned one forearm against the cold marble, bowed his head.

The past few hours felt surreal. Cops and EMTs had descended on the cemetery. Bliss went to the hospital. Fritz Klinefelter and Roelke had given statements at the station.

Sergeant Malloy had met Roelke in the hall. "Officer McKenna, I told you not to interfere with the official investigation."

"Yeah. I didn't listen."

The older man slowly saluted. "You're a good cop. A good friend. And I'm proud to know you."

When the formalities were done, Fritz and Roelke huddled in an empty interview room with Malloy and Dobry, piecing together Lucia's story. "Growing up with her dad can't have been easy," Sergeant Malloy allowed gruffly. "And I admit, life ain't always easy for women on the force. But to shoot a fellow officer in the back of the head? Unforgivable."

"Damn straight," Roelke muttered.

"I thought we were looking for a military man," Fritz said, "but I expect Chief Bliss gave his daughter firearms training that far exceeded that of the recruit academy. She had the skills of a sniper. Not quite the nerve, though. After killing Rick, she did a sloppy job of ditching the gun."

Roelke said, "I called her on Tuesday—asked if she'd thought of any reason a cop might have it in for Rick. That must have made her nervous. My truck is easy enough to tail, and I presented the perfect opportunity when I stopped by the statue. I lingered long enough to let her park back on Becher. It was simple enough to creep through the trees and find a dark spot with perfect line of sight, but I don't think she expected me to charge *at* her. She had the presence of mind to retreat in a straight line, but she must have had the handgun as backup. When she fell in the snow, she may not have even realized she'd lost the .38."

Fritz rubbed his chin. "She might have used the gun from Evidence on Rick because she didn't want any weapon she owned to be linked to the killing. Or maybe she just got the idea, grabbed it, and went after him. But we still don't know how she got into Evidence in the first place."

"Um … I have an idea," Dobry said. "She was having an affair with Captain Heikinen."

"Bleeding Christ on the cross," Sergeant Malloy muttered. "You know that for a fact?"

"I saw them in his office one night." Dobry's face was so pale that every freckle stood in sharp relief.

Roelke glared. "You tell the world you think you saw Rick drinking at the Rusty Nail, but you keep quiet about Bliss boffing the captain?"

"But—it never occurred to me—I had no way of knowing that—"

"Are you even sure Rick was drinking alcohol that night?" Roelke demanded. "Is it possible he was drinking soda while trying to chat up a truly bad guy?"

"Knock it off," Malloy barked, sergeant-style. "It's done. All the secrets will come out. Maybe Bliss thought she was in love with the captain. Maybe she was trying to get ahead. Either way, an affair could have given her the opportunity to pinch Heikinen's keys."

Fritz looked at Roelke. "Maybe she didn't have to pinch them."

Roelke nodded. If Bliss had told Heikinen that she was worried that Rick might have reported something that might get linked back to her, the captain could have pulled the Field Investigation cards. The captain might have been able to claim ignorance of the gun being taken from Evidence, but if he'd been the one to pull the FI cards, it would come out. Roelke remembered how the captain's wedding ring had glowed red and blue in the squad car's lights. The next few days were going to be very difficult for Captain Heikinen.

And he remembered the look on Lucia Bliss's face when he'd told her that a cop had been charged with domestic abuse. She'd looked sick. Now he understood that she was sick with fear, not disgust at his revelation. The coming days were going to be very difficult for Chief Bliss, too. Fortunately, Roelke had thought, not my problem.

Now, here by the statue, he breathed in the cold night air and focused on what *was* his problem. Namely, taking care of the people he cared about.

His best friend, for one. *Rick*, he said silently. *I DID it. I found your killer.*

Roelke had botched an investigation back in December, and some part of him now felt redeemed. Arresting Bliss hadn't provided any sense of that "closure" people yammered about, but his universe did hitch in a better direction. He was a good cop. And he'd proved that Rick was a good cop, too.

Roelke thought a moment before telling his friend, *I don't understand everything that happened with you and Erin, but I forgive you for keeping secrets.*

That felt good, and Roelke was glad he'd come to that place. He didn't want to carry anger or resentment around.

Just one more thing to say. *Rick, I am going to be okay. I will make sure that Jody is okay. I will do my best to take care of Chloe, and Libby and the kids. And I will always try to be the kind of man that you were.*

He thought he heard a whisper—*Well, of COURSE you will, dumbass!*—although it may have just been wind rattling through the trees. He swiped his eyes, blew his nose, and got back into his truck. Time to go.

He'd cracked the windows by the time he hit Eagle, using frigid air to help stay alert. As he drove Highway 59 toward Palmyra, he spotted a county sheriff's car by the side of the road, flashers throbbing in the dark. Deputy Marge Bandacck was dragging a board to the shoulder. It looked like some numbnut had lost a load of lumber and kept right on driving. Roelke pulled over and got out.

"Hey, McKenna," Marge said. "No need to stop. I got this."

"I know you do." Roelke grabbed a plank, wondering just how hard it had been for Marge to find a place in the sheriff's department. "But I'd like to give you a hand."

---

"You have company," Ariel announced. Owen and Jay followed her into the living room.

"We came to sign your cast," Owen said.

Jay presented Chloe a bouquet of roses. "Actually, we came to give you these."

Ariel intercepted them. "I'll find a vase."

"I'll help," Owen said, with bogus nonchalance.

Chloe and Jay exchanged a glance. "I think that's a good thing, there," Jay murmured, as the sound of a hushed conversation drifted from the kitchen.

"Me, too. Owen's recovered, I take it?"

"It would take more than a knock in the head to slow Owen down. He's already got the roller stand belt repaired, ready to demonstrate at the reception tonight." Jay gave her a piercing look. "How are you?"

"One broken wrist, a few pulled muscles, too many scrapes and bruises to count. I'll be fine."

"When I think about—"

"After going over what happened in microscopic detail with the police, I'm trying *not* to think about it. Listen, Jay... I've got a question. Did a woman ever get killed in the mill when it was functioning?"

"In an accident, you mean? Oh, no. Other than during World War II, men did all the heavy work. If a woman had died in the building, we'd certainly know about it." He gave her a quizzical look. "Why do you ask?"

"Just curious." She waved a hand: *It's of no matter.* But I know what I know, Chloe thought. She'd felt a female presence while she was trapped in the bin and freaking out. Just when she needed help, help came.

Owen and Ariel emerged from the kitchen. "Ariel let me try one of your *pączki*," Owen said. "Oh—my—*God*. The guests will love them."

"In honor of the Polish immigrants who worked at the mill," Chloe explained. "They're a nice complement to Gold Medal muffins and Pillsbury Bake-Off cake."

With the reception looming, the men couldn't stay long. After seeing them out, Ariel approached Chloe with a flat, square, tissue-wrapped package. "This is a peace offering, of sorts. And an apology. I'm sorry I didn't tell you everything right from the beginning."

"I am too," Chloe said. "But you didn't have to give me a gift." When she tore the paper away, her eyes went wide. She held a glorious example of *wycinanki*. The circular border contained two intricate roosters and a profusion of flowers. "Is this the piece your grandmother gave you? I can't accept this!"

"I want you to have it," Ariel insisted. "My grandmother went to Milwaukee once to see the Polish Basilica, and she got it at a shop near there."

Chloe squinted at the artist's signature. "It says… Lidia. No last name."

"I'm sorry I don't have provenance information."

"It doesn't matter," Chloe said. "I love it." She placed her gift on the coffee table beside the *wycinanka* found in No Man's Land. Both were amazing examples of folk art, but the strutting roosters brought Officer Crandall to mind. Eternally cock-sure of himself, she thought. Just like Everett Whyte must have been. She couldn't help thinking that if *she'd* been the Polish woman snipping away, she'd have skipped the rooster motif.

# FORTY-SIX

HELEN CUT THROUGH THE alley and let herself into the back door of Rose Cottage. "Grandma?" she called. "I'm home."

No answer. Helen walked through the kitchen and looked out the window. Yep, there was Grandma, bending over a dormant rosebush in her teensy yard. It didn't matter that the forecast called for snow. The old woman checked her gardens every day, murmuring to the plants, encouraging them to hang on until spring.

Helen hung up her coat and put the teakettle on. Gardens outside, she thought, and gardens inside. She regarded the framed *wycinanki* gracing the walls. No one did more delicate paper cuttings than her grandma.

Not that *she* was a slouch with the scissors, either. Helen's earliest memories of this house centered on the old Polish folk art. There had been more women coming and going in those days, long before Eve's House and other social groups emerged to provide refuge for battered women. As a child, Helen had watched the women creep inside, often in the middle of the night. "You're safe here," Grandma told them, but the women had nothing but fear to fill time while Grandma and a few trusted friends figured out how to spirit them out of Milwaukee.

So Grandma set them to paper cutting. Although she made traditional motifs to sell in a shop near the basilica, she set new rules for the women starting new lives. "No roosters," she'd say, and their tradition of cutting hens and flowers had begun. The design had become Grandma's secret calling card. Her trusted allies carried small cards made by the women in hiding, and if they managed to convince a threatened woman to flee, they gave her one to present upon arrival at Rose Cottage.

Years later, after Helen had become director at Eve's House, they'd modernized by having the cards printed. Now, most of the women she counseled sought help through restraining orders, housing assistance, job-training programs, subsidized childcare. But when that wasn't enough … Helen took one of the cards, wrote her name and the desperate woman's name on the back, and sent her to Rose Cottage. The few allies Helen trusted to help with their feminine underground railroad did the same …

The back door opened. "Oh, Linka!" Grandma said. "I didn't know you were home."

Helen kissed the old woman on the cheek. To the outside world she was Helen. In Rose Cottage, she was Halinka—Linka for short. "I saw you in the garden."

"I'm going to plant a rose for Officer Almirez, as soon as spring comes."

Helen nodded. "That's a lovely idea." Officer Almirez had stopped by their house shortly before the shooting. She and Grandma would always be haunted with the knowledge that he had died helping them.

She searched for something more uplifting to say. "I was just admiring your art."

Grandma flapped a dismissive hand. "No, no. You should have seen my Grandmother Magdalena's fine paper cuttings."

"Grandma Lidia," Helen said firmly, "you do fine work yourself. In many ways." Even in the old days, after Helen's mother died young, Grandma had managed to teach at the Settlement House, raise her granddaughter, and help the women who had nowhere else to turn.

The kettle whistled, and they sat down at the table. "I got a letter from Erin today," Grandma said.

"You did?" Helen's eyebrows rose. Communicating by postal mail was against the rules.

"She said she asked someone getting on a plane to mail it." Grandma squeezed her teabag against the spoon. "She wanted us to know that she'd left the state safely. And she included a letter for Officer McKenna."

"Really?" Helen leaned over the table. "Grandma, I don't think it would be wise to pass that on. We made an exception when Officer Almirez wanted to help our network, even let him come to the house once, and ... he ended up dead."

"I *know*," Grandma said sharply. "But this is an unusual situation. I hated lying to Officer McKenna that day he came looking for Erin. The least I can do is pass along her letter. After losing his best friend, Officer McKenna deserves whatever peace of mind he can find."

# FORTY-SEVEN

ARIEL HAD LEFT FOR work, and Chloe was dozing on the sofa that afternoon, when the doorbell rang. She opened the door and saw Roelke McKenna on the front step.

"I looked up the address." He shoved his hands in his pockets. "Hope you don't mind."

"Did you find Rick's killer?"

"I did. Last night." He noticed the cast on her wrist. "Wait. What the hell happened? Are you okay?"

"You better come in. We have a lot to talk about." She led the way into the living room and settled into a chair.

By the time Roelke had heard a condensed version of Chloe's week, he'd gone from sitting rigid with knee bouncing to pacing furiously with fists clenched. "So I'm going to be fine," Chloe concluded.

He turned on her. "I can't *believe* you didn't tell me what was going on up here!"

"It's not like you gave me much chance. You had all you could handle after Rick died."

"I don't care. Holy toboggans, Chloe! I don't think it's too much to ask that you tell me if you get mixed up in a murder investigation!"

Chloe wasn't in the mood for a lecture. "Would you sit down? I can't stand you looming over me." She waited until he dropped onto the sofa. "Besides, you're really not in the best position to accuse *me* of keeping secrets right now."

He scrubbed his face with his palms. "Yeah. I called Libby early this morning. She said she'd told you about Patrick. And that you're pretty angry."

"I am. How could you keep a secret like, you know, having a *brother*?"

"It's complicated."

"I don't care! Couples don't keep secrets like that."

"I never meant to deceive you," Roelke said. "I don't like to think about Patrick. So he just sort of ... never came up."

"Still—"

"Can you look me in the eye and swear that I know everything there is to know about you? That you've never not mentioned something important to me?"

Chloe opened her mouth. Then she shut it again. How could she argue? She had promised not to reveal Mary's complicity in Whyte's murder. Chloe had also promised Ariel that she wouldn't reveal Toby's role in Whyte's death.

Roelke's eyes narrowed, and he flipped from defensive to suspicious. "What?"

"I'm looking at the situation from both sides," Chloe hedged. "I *was* really angry at you. But ... I do get that there are times when it may be really hard, or even impossible, to talk about something."

Roelke leaned his head back. After a long moment he said, "I got really pissed at Rick because he'd kept secrets from me. Then I ended up not telling Dobry some stuff. I was trying to protect him."

Like Ariel was trying to protect her brother, Chloe thought. She looked at Roelke, trying to figure out what should come next. He is profoundly exhausted, she thought. Roelke's best friend had been shot less than a week ago, and he'd nailed the killer late last night. Nonetheless, he'd hit the highway *very* early this morning. As soon as he could, he'd come to find her.

"We need to talk about Patrick," she said, "but not today." She hesitated, then left the chair and snuggled on the sofa beside him.

She hadn't yet heard the details of Roelke's week. She still needed to sort out her own feelings about the promises she'd made, the secrets she had to keep, and what that meant for her and Roelke. Maybe it meant bad things. Maybe when they did talk, she'd realize that much as she cared for Roelke McKenna, she wasn't up for cop life. But right this moment, she was just too tired to figure it out.

———

A week later, the funeral for Rick Almirez took place with all the love and honor his family, friends, and the law enforcement community could provide. Chief Bliss did not attend. To Roelke's enormous relief, Captain Heikinen also did not attend. Heikinen had admitted to an affair with Lucia Bliss. He'd admitted that after Rick was killed, she'd threatened to expose the relationship if he didn't give her a chance to pull Rick's FI cards, just in case—she claimed—he'd mentioned talking to someone about her own arrest for domestic abuse. Heikinen swore that he hadn't given Bliss the key to Evidence and hadn't had a clue that she had stolen the gun she used to kill Rick. Heikinen had not yet resigned, but Roelke figured it was inevitable.

Some of Rick's friends shared memories during the memorial service. Roelke wasn't up for that, but he did read a quotation from the Bible: "*I consecrate this house you have built, I place my name here forever; My eyes and my heart will be here for all time.* That's from the First Book of Kings. The Polish people in Rick's old beat chose that verse for the Basilica of St. Josaphat. I like that last part especially."

Ten days later, a much smaller group gathered at Jody's apartment to watch the final episode of *M\*A\*S\*H*. "I hope Jody doesn't regret holding what she and Rick had planned as a fun party," Chloe murmured before they went in inside. But as they watched B. J. Hunnicutt struggle to say good-bye to Hawkeye Pierce after so many shared experiences, Roelke decided that the gathering was perfect. The friends who had shared so much with Rick Almirez laughed a little and cried a lot, and somehow they all felt better.

"That was good, don't you think?" Chloe asked, when she and Roelke settled into his truck afterwards.

"Yeah," Roelke said. He started the engine but didn't put the truck in gear. He knew Chloe had been giving him time, but there were unspoken things hanging between them. For some reason, this seemed like the time to confront them.

Chloe gave him a sideways look. "It seemed like you and Dobry were avoiding each other tonight. Are you two okay?"

"No," he admitted. "Dobry was too quick to believe that Rick was careless. And if he hadn't kept Bliss's affair with Heikinen secret from me, maybe I would have figured stuff out quicker. It's hard to just go back to the way things were."

Chloe sighed. "Yeah. I'm sorry that's the case."

"Me and Dobry will patch things up. Compared to Bliss…" Roelke let that trail away. He didn't want to think about Bliss, so he changed the subject. "I got a letter from Erin Litkowski today."

"You *did*? Where is she?"

"I don't know. Somewhere safe. She wanted me to know that she'd tried to get in touch with me, but when she learned I'd left the city force, she got hooked up with Rick instead. She asked him to keep an eye on her husband. I'm not clear on the details of Rick's involvement—how he got connected with Lobo, for example."

"You may never know," Chloe said.

"Yeah." Not with Rick dead and Erin gone again. The loose ends bugged him. He *suspected* that Rick had quietly gotten involved in the good work being done at Eve's House—probably on his own time, above and beyond what duty required from a beat cop. Roelke wanted to step into that role, to try to help in whatever way Rick had been trying to help. That Helen woman, director at the shelter, had given him exactly zero encouragement about coming back. Roelke figured he'd give it some time and then try again. *I'll wear her down,* he thought. Surely a cop could help somehow.

"Did you learn anything else from the letter?"

Chloe's question brought Roelke back to the moment. "She said that Rick got her the job at Kip's. One night she happened to hear a woman talking to a friend. The woman is a secretary at the DA's office, and she was real upset about domestic assault charges against a cop named Lucia Bliss being dropped. Erin told Rick. And Rick—"

"—wasn't willing to look the other way, even for an old friend."

"Right. After Rick got killed, Erin was terrified that any other cop she confided in might end up dead. She made Kip swear that he wouldn't admit she'd been there." Roelke stared blindly through the windshield. Erin and Kip and Rick had tried to protect him by keeping secrets. All it had done was piss him off. And yet… "I guess sometimes people have what they think are good reasons for keeping quiet." He realized how she might interpret that. "I don't mean me not telling you about Patrick. I do get why you were angry with me about that."

"Okay," she said cautiously.

This was *so* damn hard. "It's not just that I'm ashamed of him. It's also that…" His voice trailed away.

"You're not like Patrick. And it's not your fault he did what he did."

"Maybe. But I should have been able to protect my mom. When you're a little kid, you think your dad will protect everybody, you know? And then when he fell apart, Patrick said to me, 'Don't get into it with Dad. I'll take care of you and Mom.' And he did try for a while. But in the end, it was up to me. Mom moved out to the farm, and Dad died, but Patrick—I saw what was happening. I should have been able to stop him."

"You couldn't have saved Patrick, Roelke. You and Patrick grew up in the same house, with the same parents. He made his own choices. You've made different choices."

He shrugged. It wasn't that simple.

"Rick knew what kind of person you are. And you guys were best friends. That means something."

"Maybe." Roelke studied his gloves in the dashboard's faint glow. "You know… the week we were apart, I really thought I'd lost you, too. I want to be with you, Chloe, but I'll understand if you say it's all more than you bargained for. Me, my family, my job… all of it."

"Jody told me that it's really hard to be in a relationship with a cop."

"I know it is."

"Why did you get so cranky after the wedding?"

340

He tried to figure that out. It seemed so long ago. "We were there with my friends, and I could tell that you weren't really having a good time. It bummed me out, I guess."

"Well, I can't say I had a *great* time. It was overwhelming at moments. But I did enjoy hearing you play, and meeting your friends. And seeing you so happy."

Well, hunh, he thought. "Oh."

"Jody also said that Rick wouldn't talk to her about a lot of stuff."

Roelke sighed. *Now* they were getting to it. "He—I—yeah. I'm not surprised she said that."

"I know you did what you needed to do after Rick got shot," Chloe said. "But it hurt to discover that you'd shut me out like that."

"I know that wasn't good. But honestly, it was the best I could do right then." He became aware of a growing ache in his chest. This is it, he thought. She's about to break up with me.

"If our relationship is going to have any chance at all, you have to try to let me in during the bad times."

Try, Roelke thought. She just said *try*. "I will try to do better," he promised.

"Good."

"That has to go both ways, you know. You didn't tell me what was going on in Minneapolis, either."

"I wasn't given much opportunity," she reminded him. "But you're right. It has to go both ways."

He waited, hoping she would tell him whatever it was about her time in Minnesota that she'd left out. There was something there, he knew it. But seconds passed, and he realized that even now, in the middle of this very conversation, she wasn't going to share. That didn't feel so good. But after the way he'd acted when Rick got shot, he figured he'd better let it go.

"The thing is," Chloe said, "I need to know what kind of couple we're going to be, Roelke. Are we the kind who has fun and enjoys each other as long as nothing goes wrong? Or are we going to try for something more?"

"I want more."

"Part of me does, too. But I've also been trying to figure out if I'm strong enough to cope with the reality of your job. Knowing that every time you go to work, I could get the kind of phone call that Jody got."

Roelke knew Chloe was strong enough. She was one of the strongest people he'd ever met. But the answer had to come from her.

"I can't live in fear all the time," she added.

The ache below Roelke's ribs grew stronger. He watched a city truck drive by, spraying salt on the road because more snow was forecast. "I'm a cop," he said. "I don't want to do anything else."

"I wouldn't ask you to. It's who you are. The whole fear thing is my problem. Something I have to try to set aside, if I can." She looked at him. "I'm proud of who you are, Roelke. Even though it's really hard sometimes, you're the one I want to be with."

Roelke felt a lump rise in his throat. "I'm not sure why."

"Because you're a good man. Because you'd die for the people you care about. Because you drove to Minneapolis as soon as it was humanly possible, not even knowing I'd had a horrid week, just because." Chloe took a deep breath. "Because I love you."

Roelke kissed her—the kind of long, slow kiss they hadn't shared since Rick's death. Something eased inside, indefinable but good.

"I love you too," he said, when he finally let her up for air. "Let's go home."

*The author standing on a hatch in the floor beside the*
*turn-head distributor, Mill City Museum. (Photo by Scott Meeker)*

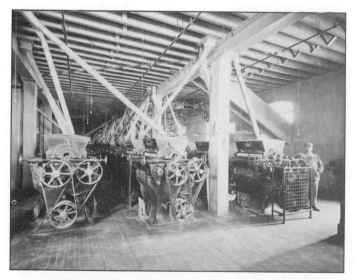

*Worker operating roller mills, Pillsbury-Washburn Mill,*
*Minneapolis, 1897. (Minnesota Historical Society)*

*Bohemian Flats below Washington Avenue Bridge, Minneapolis.*
*(Photo by F. M. Laraway. Minnesota Historical Society)*

*Early South Side residents ice skating in Kosciuszko Park, with the*
*Basilica of St. Josaphat in the background. (Photo by Roman Kwasnieweski.*
*Archives Department, University of Milwaukee-Wisconsin Libraries)*

*This example of* wycinanki *by an unknown artist reflects the Lowicz region of Poland. (Wisconsin Historical Society)*

# ACKNOWLEDGMENTS

I extend thanks to all of the Minnesota Historical Society staff who provided assistance while this project developed. Librarians and historic preservation staff at the Minnesota History Center helped identify resources and patiently dug out boxes of old files. Many organizations and individuals were involved in redeveloping and interpreting not only the Washburn Mill complex, but the riverfront area. The plans and proposals compiled over the years gave me a glimpse of the enormous and complicated effort to preserve and interpret the St. Anthony Falls Historic District.

The interpreters at the Mill City Museum did an amazing job of bringing the old ruin to life, and the shop staff always extended a warm welcome. Special thanks to Laura Salveson, Director, and David Stevens, Public Programs Specialist, for their thoughtful assistance. David's special exhibit *From Mill To Museum: The Hidden History of the Washburn Complex 1965–2003* provided great insight about the abandoned mill. I'm particularly indebted to Joby Lynn Sassily James, who once lived in the mill, for sharing her memories and photographs within the exhibit.

Thanks also to the Milwaukee artists and historians who helped me glimpse life in the Old Polish South Side: Kasia Drake-Hames, my talented *wycinanki* instructor; the staff at the Polish Heritage Center, Franklin; Principal Investigator Jill Florence Lackey and Executive Director Rick Petrie of the Old South Side Settlement Museum; and the helpful staff at the Basilica of St. Josaphat and Forest Home Cemetery, who have done so much to preserve and share the history of those special places.

I am grateful to the law enforcement professionals who offered suggestions and answered endless questions: Lieutenant Kevin

Porter, Lannan Police Department; Corrections Officer Gale Borger, Walworth County; and the officers at the Eagle Police Department, especially Sergeant Gwen Bruckner and Chief Russ Ehlers. Any errors regarding police procedure are, of course, my own.

Warm thanks to Agent Fiona Kenshole, to everyone at Transatlantic Literary, and to Terri Bischoff and the Midnight Ink team.

I appreciate the friendship and support I've received from editorial assistant Laurie Rosengren; photographer Kay Klubertanz; and baker Alisha Rapp and the crew at the Prairie Café.

I am indebted to the Council for Wisconsin Writers and the Shake Rag Alley Center For the Arts for providing a residency in Mineral Point, Wisconsin; and to Katie Mead and Robert Alexander, and to Liz Rog and Daniel Rotto of Fern Hollow Cabin, for providing writing space when I needed it.

I wouldn't be able to do the work I love without encouragement from my extended family; from Scott Meeker, my husband and partner; and from my wonderful readers. Thank you all.

If you are interested in learning more about flour milling and the St. Anthony Falls area, I recommend *Mill City: A Visual History of the Minneapolis Mill District*, by Shannon Pennefeather (Minnesota Historical Society Press, 2003.) To learn more about Milwaukee's Old South Side neighborhood, see *Milwaukee's Old South Side*, by Jill Florence Mackey and Rick Petrie (Images of America, Arcadia Publishing, 2013).

Geri Gerold © Kathleen Ernst

## ABOUT THE AUTHOR

Kathleen Ernst is an award-winning author, educator, and social historian. She has published twenty-nine novels and one nonfiction book. Her books for young readers include the Caroline Abbott series for *American Girl*. Honors for her children's mysteries include Edgar and Agatha Award nominations. Kathleen worked as an Interpreter and Curator of Interpretation and Collections at Old World Wisconsin, and her time at the historic site served as inspiration for the Chloe Ellefson mysteries. *The Heirloom Murders* won the Anne Powers Fiction Book Award from the Council for Wisconsin Writers, and *The Light Keeper's Legacy* won the Lovey Award for Best Traditional Mystery from Love Is Murder. Ernst served as project director/scriptwriter for several instructional television series, one of which earned her an Emmy Award. She lives in Middleton, Wisconsin. For more information, visit her online at http://www.kathleenernst.com.